THE HAUNTING OF BRANDEN BAY

KELLY MASON

LITTLE ORCHARD PRESS

Editor: Alison Knight

Cover Design by www.getcovers.com

This book was written in the UK and edited in British English, where some spelling, grammar and word usage will be different to US English.

Created with Vellum

For the family and friends, who have been supporting this journey :)

CHAPTER 1

"Where do you want it, love?" asked the delivery driver.

I was taking ownership of a rather-swanky, super-shiny, commercial coffee machine. I thumbed behind me at the glass doors of my sea-front café which were wide open. "Take it through there. It's going against the back wall."

"Right you are," he said as he helped his co-worker heave it out the back of the van. I leaned my jeans-clad legs against the low wall in front of my property, filling my lungs with sea air. I smiled as I looked across the grand Victorian prom. The sky was pure blue with only a few wisps of cloud. When the sun shone, Branden Bay was the most beautiful place on earth. The yellow horseshoe of sand was already being enjoyed by dog walkers and joggers passing each other up and down the beach, which rippled with gentle waves.

As far as life as a café owner was concerned, I'd really stepped it up a gear and was giving myself a huge pat on the back. I didn't have any family around to do it for me. Mum and Dad were in Borneo taking the trip of a life-time, volunteering at an orangutang rescue centre. And poor Grandma had died a year ago. Indeed, I'd opened my café at the front of the house she'd left me in her will. I'd had no intention of moving to Branden Bay from London, but after months of the house being on the market, with prospective buyers who kept pulling out at the last minute, I'd decided to move to the small resort myself. I had nothing to keep me in London since I'd broken up with my then boyfriend, Marcus. I gave a small smile. *If only he could see me now,* I thought. I'll be honest, I'd become a bit of a mouse over the three years I'd been with him. He was older than me, the one with the big career and I'd had a job on reception at the same company he worked at. That's how we'd met. I took a deep breath. *Yes*, I really had turned my life around.

I awoke from my daydream to the sound of a loud meow.

"Morning, Constance," I said as my cat peered at me from the wall with her green eyes. I'd taken her in as a stray. Picking her up, I had to be careful of the surgical collar placed around her neck to stop her licking a healing wound on her belly. She'd recently been attacked. "Don't worry, the cone will be coming off in a couple of days," I said, as I stroked her fluffy ginger head. "Let's go inside and check out our new coffee maker."

An hour later, when the coffee machine had been installed, the smile on my face was impossible to shift. I ran my hands over its smooth exterior as I saw my grin reflected in it.

Leaving the café area, I walked into the private section of my house and called up the stairs. "Dannie."

Dannie was the latest stray I'd taken in. Except Dannie was not a cat – she was twenty and seemed to have an issue shaking off her teens.

"Dannie," I called again, this time much louder.

"I'm not deaf," she said as she rounded the bend of the ornate wooden staircase. Her long blonde hair was bedraggled. She'd been out with a friend the night before and I'd agreed that she could have a lie in, on the understanding that she was fresh for the training session on the coffee machine at mid-day. It was nearly one o'clock.

She followed me to the front of the house and once inside the café, we heard a rap on the French doors. My friend Annie waved at us through the glass. I approached the door and opened it. She smiled as her gold-tipped brown afro blew in the sea breeze.

"Hi," I said, giving her a kiss on the cheek. "This is my new coffee machine. I'm just about to try it out."

Annie pointed at it. "That's what I'm here for. Staff training."

I laughed. "You're a friend, not staff. And you've already got a job." She'd recently been promoted to manager at the pier.

"I like helping you. That's what friends do. And it's getting really tense at work. Katherine only let me have the afternoon off because she wants me to ask you a favour."

"What can I do for her?"

"I'll tell you once we've made our drinks."

After an hour of grappling with the machine, and a few hits and misses, we finally got the hang of it. When I say 'we', I mean Annie and myself – Dannie was having issues. Big issues, which made an awful lot of mess. I wiped splattered milk from the machine after her final accident as she sloped out, no doubt heading for her bedroom.

Annie pulled out a chair and sat at one of the café tables. "I sense it's not plain sailing with your new housemate?" She blew on her frothy cappuccino. "You took on a lot there."

"What could I do? She's fallen out with her family and lost her job."

"She's not your responsibility though, and now you're stuck with a non-paying lodger."

"It's not free rent. She's helping me in the café."

Annie shook her head. "From what I've seen, she's not exactly taking to it."

"Hmm," I said. "Dannie's not great at waitressing, or in the kitchen. She keeps telling me it's not her skillset." I sighed. "I feel more like her mother than her boss and I'm only six years older than she is." I took a sip of my latte, which was absolutely delicious. "I guess I wanted to save her like I saved Constance."

"I bet she costs a lot more to feed than the cat."

"Not really." I laughed. "Remember, Constance only eats salmon and nothing out of a can."

As if she'd heard her name, my cat wandered into the room meowing.

"I was talking about you, not to you." I pushed my chair away from the table, so Constance could jump onto my lap.

"So," I said to Annie. "What's this big favour your boss wants?"

Annie shifted in her seat. "It's got worse at the pier." Annie's promotion had come about because staff were leaving. "There've been more accidents and two recent resignations."

"Do you think someone's wrecking the place on purpose?"

"Katherine thinks it might be –"

"A saboteur?" I asked.

"A poltergeist," she replied.

Constance hissed.

I sighed. "Oh, no. I'm not doing that sort of favour!"

As well as inheriting Grandma's house, red hair and green eyes, I'd also inherited her so-called gift for seeing the dead – ghosts, spirits or whatever you want to call them. "I can't help. You'll have to ask Lynn." Lynn was our friend who ran a spiritualist church in an old scout hut, which backed onto my garden. "I only get involved if the spirit contacts me first." I shuddered. Why did my friends not get it? I was scared of ghosts. "Do you think there's a poltergeist then?" I asked.

"No. I need you to put Katherine's mind at rest. I'd like you to come over, check the place out and confirm it's not a poltergeist."

I groaned as I stroked Constance.

"Please, Becky. It would really help me out. She's constantly bugging me about it."

"You're quite sure there's nothing there?"

Constance dug her claws into my lap and I scratched underneath her surgical collar.

"Absolutely," Annie said as she lowered her eyes and scratched her nose.

"I'll think about it," I said. Although my real answer was a big fat no.

ONCE ANNIE HAD LEFT, I cleaned and spruced up the café in preparation for the reopening. Dannie helped half-heartedly. Her face looked as if I'd asked her to clean out Constance's litter tray, rather than wipe down a few tables.

"Urgh." She muttered a few inappropriate words under her breath as she knocked over a carton of milk, which splashed on the table and dripped onto the floor. "Sorry."

Constance sniffed at the white liquid pooling on the floorboards but did not lick it. Even if she could have managed it with the cone around her neck, she only ever drank or ate off Grandma's china.

"I'll mop it up, Dannie. Take the carton out to the kitchen."

Her bottom lip quivered. "I'm no good at this. I was rubbish at being a daughter back home, rubbish at Uni, rubbish at dancing, rubbish at my receptionist job. I'm more of a hindrance than a help to you, Becky." She put her hands to her face and her shoulders shuddered.

In the few weeks I'd known her, I'd not seen her show this level of emotion. She'd appeared positively hard. And now she was literally crying over spilt milk. "I feel useless."

"Hey. Take a minute out," I said placing my hand on her shoulder.

Dannie slumped to one of the tables. I up-righted the carton from its side to stop the endless drip-drip of milk to the floor. Constance rubbed herself up against Dannie's legs.

After mopping up the milk with paper towel, I quickly rinsed and dried my hands and sat opposite her. "There's no pressure for you to be good at anything here. It's only short term. I'm sure you'll get your big break soon."

"I shouldn't have dropped out of university. I'd have been graduating next year." Her shoulders shuddered. "I've ruined my life."

"Who knows what opportunity will come your way?" I handed her a paper napkin.

She wiped her eyes. "You've been so good to me and I can't even do this for you without messing up." She shook her head. "I'm not good with people like you are. You take their orders and they look at you as if they love you, chatting away so easily." She sniffed. "People hate me, I've heard them calling me a grump. I don't do it on purpose. This is just me."

"Of course they don't hate you."

"They treat the cat better than they treat me."

Constance meowed and sashayed around the table.

"Interpersonal skills come with age," I said. "And remember, I studied performing arts at uni. A lot of the time I'm slapping on a smile and playing a part. I'm far from perfect." I laughed. Although, to be honest, my first impression of Dannie was that she was sulky and rude. But I wasn't going to confess to that. I could see that, whatever was on the outside, there was a heart on the inside.

She picked up Constance and held her close. "All I'm good at, and have ever been good at, is numbers."

Constance purred loudly.

I remembered the pile of paperwork I'd been putting off. Numbers were not my strong point, and some of the letters in my pile were unopened. "You can have a look at my bookkeeping if you like?"

Dannie blinked. "What? For the café?"

I nodded. "And I took money for the paranormal investigation I did recently."

I led her to the kitchen as she carried Constance in her arms. Heat rushed up my neck towards my head, which I guess had been buried in the sand. I'd only recorded details of income and outgoings for the first week of trading, when I'd applied for a loan. I opened the kitchen drawer into which I'd been stuffing my papers. "Here it is."

Dannie placed Constance on the tiled floor and pulled a few sheets out. "You seem to have your café invoices and investigating receipts all mixed together."

"Yeah," I said rubbing the front of my neck with my palm. "I've been meaning to set up an improved system." Not that I had any system.

"And these brown letters haven't been opened."

"Oh yeah. Probably junk mail."

Constance began a long meow which sounded like a groan.

"This one says, 'do not ignore' on the outside," Dannie said.

"I know. Marketing tactics, eh?" I gave a short laugh as I felt butterflies in my stomach. I should have at least had a look at the papers before I let Dannie get stuck in. But I knew myself too well, I would have gone on ignoring it for as long as I could. I felt a sense of relief as Dannie emptied the kitchen drawer.

Once I'd given Dannie the password to access my laptop computer, she left the kitchen with the bundle of papers in her arms. I pulled a salmon steak out of the fridge and made Constance's tea. I was planning on an early night – I wanted to be bright for the reopening of the café the following day. It was going to be the best day ever.

CHAPTER 2

I stood inside the café, looking through the glass doors. I was excited to see it was a beautiful morning. Before me was the patio area with two circular iron tables, each with matching chairs. The sunny scene before me had 'relaunch day' written all over it. Just outside, a new A-frame blackboard displayed the introductory drinks menu with all the usual favourites to enjoy in or take away.

Dannie had left a note on the kitchen table saying she'd gone to bed at five a.m., and needed to have an 'important chat', but not to wake her too early. *Fair enough,* I thought. She'd earned a lie in. Maybe she had ideas for increasing my profits. I'd never seen such a change in a person. When I'd said goodnight, she'd seemed positively animated ... by spreadsheets. I smiled to myself thinking the girl had definite problems.

I opened the doors as I saw Annie approaching the café with our friend Izzy.

Izzy, a local news reporter, breezed in. Tall and an ex-model, she was as graceful as a swan. "Can't wait to taste your cappuccino, darling. I'll take some pics for the paper in readiness for your next paranormal case." She looked around the room pushing a stray hair from her blonde bob behind her ear. "Have there been any takers for your gifts recently?"

Annie, who had followed her in, mouthed "no" to me, clearly not wanting the troubles at the pier to become common knowledge.

Constance stretched out, she'd been sleeping in her bed positioned in the corner of the café and greeted my friends with a meow.

Lynn from the spiritualist church entered the café from the rear of my house. She often let herself in via the kitchen door, as she could access my back garden via a gate in the wall between our properties. Her silver and blonde hair bushed out over her shoulders. With her purple velvet kaftan, and flowing blue chiffon scarf, she looked every bit the psychic she was.

Lynn looked around the room. "No H then?"

H was short for Henry – a name only his close family used.

"He's running late," Izzy said, holding up her phone to indicate she'd received a text from him. "He says he'll be here in five. So show me this machine, sweetie."

I led Izzy over while Annie had a low-voiced chat with Lynn, probably about the suspected poltergeist situation on the pier.

After a few minutes, H turned up. He nearly filled the whole door frame as he walked in. He towered over me, as I'm only five foot two and a half and he's well over six foot. He was usually clad in tight-fitting black which showed off his muscles and this occasion was no exception. He smiled at me with his dark eyes. I felt myself blush as his gaze rested upon me. For some unknown reason everyone seemed to think that H and me had some sort of magnetic attraction. But I was certain that was rubbish. He was forever telling me off, clearly unable to leave his job as a detective sergeant at work. Apart from that, he was so not my type. I'd always gone for suited city men like Marcus, clean cut and smart. Love was definitely not in the air for me with H. He'd even arrested me a couple of times – hardly the actions of a future beau.

"So, you're moving into the big time, Becky?" he said, flashing me a smile.

"Sure am." I passed him and pushed the glass doors wide open.

H bent down to stroke Constance and she gave a loud purr. "How long does she have to keep this thing on her neck?"

"It's coming off the day after tomorrow." I hooked the French doors to the wall so they didn't bang shut in the wind, which was prone to gusts when the tide turned. I re-entered the café. "I have a surprise for the first customer." I picked up a necklace of fake flowers from a nearby table. "I'll be adorning them with this garland and providing a free morning drink." I turned around just as a man wearing a suit approached the open doorway. "Welcome, sir. You're our first customer since our new coffee machine has been installed." I lifted the garland.

He tried to duck out of my way but he had a brief-case in one hand and a large brown envelope in the other, so there was not much he could do to avoid it.

"No need to be shy." I smiled. "Gotcha," I said as I managed to hook the garland over his head, which was covered with a dusting of grey hair. "It's like a game of hoopla," I turned around and the others were grinning, apart from H that was, who gave a slow shake of his head. I spun back to my customer. "So, sir, I'm pleased to award you a free coffee every morning, for a week."

I clapped and so did Annie, Izzy and Lynn.

Constance sniffed at the customer's trouser leg. A few people formed a short queue behind the garland-adorned man.

He coughed. "Is there somewhere we can speak in private?"

Oh no, not another one after a paranormal investigation, I thought. I'd got used to those. *Can you contact my dead aunt? Can you find out if my dog is haunting me?* I had a never-ending stream of people who I constantly turned down. "First we need to get you a coffee and drinks for these waiting customers." I pointed to the queue behind him, then at the A-frame. "We have cappuccino, latte or maybe an Americano?"

"No, thank you."

"We have syrup shots and also hot chocolate." I smiled. "With marshmallows and a squirt of cream."

"I take it you're the sole proprietor of this establishment?"

"Absolutely. I inherited the building from my grandmother. I came here every school holiday as a child." I felt it was nice to have someone take an interest. "I opened the café and named it Connie's Café after my grandmother. Connie is short for Constance, you see. And also the name of my cat, that's why there's a picture of her on the sign." I grinned, pointing to Constance who stared up at the man as if she was guarding me.

"What a lovely story," said a woman who was second in the queue.

There followed some tittering and chatter. My heart swelled with pride that the locals appreciated me so much and were willing to queue to taste my new coffee.

"Welcome to Connie's café." I waved him inside. "Now," I said turning to smile at him. "You look like a flat white type of guy, am I right?"

"I'm from Branden District Council."

"Excellent, I'm hoping to attract many of your colleagues on their way to work. I have a small poster here if you don't mind pinning it up at the office?" I reached for a flyer I'd printed off. "I'll be opening up early in future, to pick up the commuters." I held out the leaflet, then realised he didn't have a free hand so slipped it in-between his thumb and the envelope he carried. "Be sure to spread the word ..." I looked at the lanyard around his neck, "... Brian." I grinned.

He put the envelope under his arm and my flyer fluttered to the ground. He made no effort to pick it up.

Rude, I thought, as I bent down to retrieve it. "These things aren't cheap to run off," I muttered.

He lifted the I.D. card on his lanyard which was somewhat tangled with the garland. "I don't think you understand Miss, er ... ?"

"The name's James. Becky James. Our cappuccinos are frothed, not stirred." I heard a few titters and a long groan from H behind me.

"I'm here in my capacity as the trading inspector. Brian Elks."

I swallowed. "Really? You inspect?" I didn't realise the Council did that. But the place was extra clean. I'd been at it for hours the day before – so I knew I had nothing to worry about.

"I understand you've opened a catering establishment without permission."

"Oh? Was I supposed to ask?"

"There are procedures to go through, Miss James."

"I held an event for charity and everyone said I

should open up as a café. Mrs Jessup from next door told me it used to be a café when she was a little girl."

"Yes it was," called someone from the queue.

"I assumed planning permission wasn't required. Considering it was a café years ago. There are other shops along here including the ice cream parlour a few doors down. What's the problem?"

"The problem is, that you are unable to prepare and sell food without first receiving a license from the Council."

"No-one told me that." I put my hands on my hips.

"Ignorance is no defence, Miss James."

Charming, I thought as my legs trembled and my face flushed hot.

"It's an offence to run an unapproved food premises and you can be prosecuted for doing so."

My bottom lip quivered as the tittering in the queue changed to a low hubbub.

He waved his brown envelope. "I'm serving you a cessation notice. You must close with immediate effect. Any request to open a catering establishment has to be made to the Council twenty-eight days before the first proposed day of trading."

Constance hissed.

I looked behind him at the growing queue of customers. "But there are people waiting for drinks."

"I don't make the rules, Miss James. Please see our website for the correct and full procedures."

Tears pooled in my eyes as I felt Lynn's arm around my shoulder.

Mr Elks addressed the queue. "This establishment is now closed." He took a notice out of the brown envelope he'd been holding and taped it to my café window. As he closed the café doors, there were protests from those waiting outside and one of my regulars called him an unpleasant name. H, looking more like a bouncer than a policeman, went outside to disperse the crowd as Brian Elks marched away, still wearing my garland.

Back inside with my friends, Constance rubbed around my legs. I looked at the shiny new coffee machine and all the extra milk I'd bought, which would certainly not last twenty-eight days, and the freezer was already full with sponges I'd made up in case we were busy.

"I'll start a petition in the paper, darling," Izzy said as she whipped her notebook out of her shoulder bag.

"You need to follow the rules," said H as he walked back inside and closed the door behind him.

"I'm so stupid. I should have looked into it." I wiped a tear away from my eye with a paper napkin.

Constance meowed and I picked her up, holding her close.

"You've been so successful. Don't beat yourself up," Annie said.

"One of us should have had the foresight to check

that you'd okayed it with the Council," Lynn added. "To be honest I didn't know it was a thing either."

Dannie entered the café from the hallway, bleary eyed. "What's with all the noise? You lot woke me up." She frowned. "I thought you were opening at nine?"

"I've been shut down," I said, hearing my voice crack as tears tumbled down my cheeks. "I didn't follow the correct procedures."

"Hmm, I opened your mail. There were a few letters from the Council I wanted to speak to you about."

"They said I'll be shut for at least twenty-eight days." I hiccupped. "The application details are on their website."

"Okay, I'm awake now. Leave it with me," Dannie said as she turned and left the room.

"How things can change," I said, placing Constance on the floor and slumping down at a table. "Yesterday I thought Dannie was a liability and now I'm the wrong' un."

"Just learn from it and move on," said H. "And you have my cooking tonight to cheer you up." He smiled at me but I looked away, feeling such a fool in front of him – yet again.

"H, can you give me a lift to work?" Izzy said, then turned to me. "Good luck, darling. We can drown your sorrows this evening. See it as a minor setback – it's not the end."

"I agree," said Annie. "Your cakes are amazing. It's bound to work out."

When the three had left, I sat with Lynn in my kitchen.

"You've been doing a marvellous job, lovey. I feel it in my bones, you'll be baking again."

I sucked in a sob that threatened to take over. Standing up, I reached for the kettle. This was definitely a tea moment. I eyed the cakes I'd spent so long perfecting. There was chocolate fudge cake, my ever-popular Victoria sponge and zingy lemon drizzle muffins.

We sipped our hot drinks and were soon joined by Dannie.

"Don't worry, Becky. I'm transferring the procedures required to reopen the café onto a spreadsheet. I'll lead you through it later. And I wanted to say thank you."

"For what?"

"You've made me realise what I really need to do with my life. I love doing your books. I'm going to look for a course up at the college."

I opened my mouth but was too choked up to speak. Constance meowed and I sat back in my chair, so she could jump onto my lap.

"Hey, don't look so sad," Lynn said. "You'll be back up and running in a month or so."

A month or so of the summer meant I would miss out on thousands of day trippers.

Constance, now on my lap, nuzzled my hand. As I stroked her, I wondered how the three of us were going to survive with no money coming in.

CHAPTER 3

Annie, Izzy and H had been friends since they were sixteen and for years had been meeting at their respective homes, once a month for dinner. Since I'd befriended them they'd included me. I'd been to Annie's, they'd all been to my place and now it was H's turn.

As I walked up the hill to his place, music floated down on the breeze. There was a small one-day music festival being held up at Branden Bay Castle, which was perched high above the town, beside the woods. Tickets for the event had sold out well in advance. Indeed, well before I'd moved to town. I decided that, if I was still in Branden Bay next year, I'd get myself a ticket early. Grandma used to love music festivals and I'd had a great time with her at Glastonbury. Although, Branden Bay's music festival was tiny in comparison, with only a few hundred tickets available.

I reached H's home. He lived in a garden flat, which was at the bottom half of a converted Victorian house made from red and grey stone. I stood tall on the doorstep. I'm not one to wallow in self-pity and after giving myself a good talking to, I'd decided to hold my head up high. As Izzy had said earlier, the café closure was a setback – not the end. I rang the bell.

The door swung open and Annie grinned at me with a cocktail in her hand. "Hi, come on in."

I crossed the threshold. "I can smell burning."

She laughed. "There's always something burning when H is cooking. But at least he's outside at the barbecue this time, so the smoke alarms aren't bleeping like crazy."

We walked through the house to the garden. H had a decking area and a small lawn surrounded by green, low-maintenance bushes.

"Hi Becky," he said flashing his tall-dark-and-handsome smile as he approached us. "I thought we'd sit outside and listen to the festival." He nodded in the direction of the music which drifted down to us from the castle.

Izzy stood up. "I'll pour you a drink, sweetie."

"Not brought your cat?" H asked.

I'd left Constance at home, eating salmon. "I've kept her indoors since her injury. I don't want her wandering around, getting caught in bushes with that collar on her neck."

"Shame," H said.

That's nice, I thought. He clearly liked my cat.

"It would have been handy if I'd run out of meat."

"That's not even slightly funny," I said. "Even if eating cat was a thing, my Constance wouldn't feed many since most of her size is down to her massively fluffy coat."

H laughed. "True." He put a friendly arm around me. "How are you feeling now?"

"Positive." A tingle ran down my back. "We have an action plan. Turns out my new lodger is a whizz at accounts and paperwork."

"What? Dannie? A.K.A Nadine the stripper?" H asked.

I took a step back and put my hands on my hips. "She was not a stripper, she was dancing and that was only a couple of times. As you well know – she left that place of employment."

"Okay," H said slowly as if he didn't quite believe me. "Ma's heard about the café closing."

The Branden Bay grapevine was clearly in full swing if it had reached his mother, Carol.

"And she's invited you to supper in the week. You pick the day and I'll collect you when I finish work."

"Unless you're still sick with food poisoning after today," Izzy said as she passed me a cocktail glass containing a red coloured drink, with a paper umbrella staked in a slice of orange.

I laughed loudly.

"So the jokes are funny if they're at my expense? Rather than your cat," H said raising his eyebrows.

"There's something burning – again," Annie called pointing to the smoking barbecue.

We sat at a wooden table, as H prodded portions of meat in various shades of brown, before plonking them on paper plates. Each with a squirt of ketchup and American mustard, a finger roll and a bap. "Help yourselves to salad," he said pointing to a bowl of leaves, which looked as if they'd spent a lot of time in a plastic bag.

"This looks lovely," Annie said.

"Definitely better than usual." Izzy nibbled on a burger having first picked off the black bits. "Are you making an effort for our Becky here?" She winked at me.

I blushed.

"So how's work, Annie?" H asked, ignoring Izzy.

"Yeah, fine. Erm ... great. Yeah, cool," she said, her warm eyes open wide like she was in an interrogation room, looking from side to side like a meerkat.

I sucked my lips in, to stop myself laughing. Annie was an awful liar.

H placed a filled roll on his plate and leaned forward. "You're hiding something. What's going on?"

"No point in lying to a detective," I laughed.

"Okay," Annie said. "Katherine, my boss is worried there's negative paranormal activity on the pier."

Izzy stared across the table. "Why haven't I heard

about this?" Her beautiful face scrunched as she placed her food back on the plate and wiped her hands on a square of kitchen paper. "I'm the local paranormal reporter."

"Exactly," Annie said. "Katherine insisted that we didn't tell the police or the press."

"We?" H said, raising his eyebrows at me.

I shrugged my shoulders. I knew H hated it when I got involved with this type of thing. To give him his due – I had nearly got myself killed twice and ended up treading on the toes of a police investigation.

He crossed his arms and stared at me. "Please tell me you're not mixed up in this."

"I'm doing my utmost to avoid getting involved but someone," I stared at Izzy, "has painted me in the newspaper as the greatest paranormal detective since Lorraine Warren."

Izzy nodded. "The papers fly out when you're on the front-page, darling."

I looked back at H. "Knowing that I'm friends with Annie, Katherine is obviously on her case to get me involved."

He sighed. "So what's going on over there?"

Annie held her hands together as if in prayer. "Electrical equipment turns itself on and off. Things are moving and getting smashed. It's causing a bit of damage."

"She needs to call the police," H said. "It sounds like vandalism."

Annie shook her head. "Katherine doesn't want it to affect her business. Word's already getting round. If it's in the papers or the police show up, people won't brush it aside as gossip."

"And what do you think?" H said to Annie.

She shrugged her shoulders. "I don't know. After what we've seen happen with Becky over the past couple of months – I'm more open-minded than I used to be."

"I can go over in plain clothes at the weekend. Play the slots with Becky here?" he said smiling at me. "Have an ice cream and see what's afoot."

I blushed. Undercover work was something, as a trained actress, I was rather fond of – but not with H. I ignored his comment, sipped my cocktail and prayed for a change of subject.

AT GONE MIDNIGHT, I handed over the fare to the taxi driver. While it wasn't a long walk, H had insisted I took a cab. I staggered out of the car feeling a little motion sickness, which I put down to the drive. I'd succeeded in drowning my sorrows and felt rather numb. Leaning against the wall in front of my property, I looked up at my café sign, which was illuminated by the street lamp. Pins and needles filled my hands, and static shot up my back. I dismissed it, assuming I'd had too much drink. I jumped as I heard a voice.

Turning around, I swayed a little, feeling slightly

nauseous. Before me was an elderly man sitting at one of the tables on my front patio. My stomach lurched. I hoped I wasn't about to pass out.

"Can you see spirits?" he asked.

I groaned. "No." I swayed a little to steady myself.

"Yes, you can." He appeared to swim before my eyes.

I defo shouldn't have had those vodka chasers, I thought. "You'll have to contact someone else." I went on to recommend Lynn and her spiritualist church. Slurring out a lengthy five-star review.

As I opened my front door, Constance shot out and hissed. She was clearly angry at me, for keeping her at home.

The man pulled out a packet of tobacco from the pocket of the red puffer jacket he wore. It was more of a winter coat, than something you'd wear in summer. "It's you I need to see."

"It's the early hours. And I need sleep."

"I'll wait," he said rolling up a cigarette but not moving from my table and chairs.

I didn't have the energy to argue with him. Picking up Constance, I went inside. I stumbled up the stairs and climbed into bed, still fully clothed with my cat by my side.

I WOKE TO A RINGING SOUND. My head thumped like mad. I felt ill and didn't want to open my eyes. I couldn't remember the last time I'd had a hangover – certainly not since I'd been in Branden Bay. I heard my bedroom door open.

"Are you going to answer that or what?" Dannie said grabbing the handbag I'd left on the chaise lounge, positioned in the bay window of my bedroom.

I groaned and rolled over.

"Becky's phone. Dannie here," she said answering it for me. "Hi, Annie. She's got a steaming hangover by the looks of it. She's still wearing yesterday's clothes. The room stinks of booze and she's cuddling the cat. I'd call back later if I was you." She paused. "Oh no, I'm sorry."

I opened one eye to a slit and regretted it. The light seemed to pierce the inside of my head. "Is something wrong?" I asked in a hoarse voice.

Dannie ended the call. "You're going to have to sort yourself out. Someone's dead on the pier."

I felt a rush of adrenaline course through my body and sat up. "Who?"

"The caretaker called Benjamin. He was covering the night shift for the security guard."

Standing outside the closed café doors, I drank water from a bottle to rehydrate myself. The dark sunglasses were essential support for the pain killers which were doing their best to dampen my headache. *Never again,* I thought. I'd had a pile of sliced toast with lashings of strawberry jam, which had chased the nausea away. Charcoal clouds were heading in from the Atlantic as I waited for Jeff to pick me up. He was the local trainee paranormal investigator and we'd teamed up during my last two cases.

As I glanced at the pier in the distance, two police cars were parked on the prom, with their lights flashing blue, blocking the entrance. None of the usual swarms of families were walking up and down the boards. The pier spanned two hundred yards from the shore to the main building, which sat proudly above the sea. Beyond that was a short jetty where small foot ferries landed from Bristol and Wales.

I heard a meow at my feet and glanced down at Constance. "What are you doing? You can't come with me. Not with that cone on your neck. How did you even get out?" I guessed she'd slipped through the door behind me. She'd been desperate to escape the confines of the house. I retrieved my keys from my bag to return her inside but saw the van approach with its *Paranormal Jeff* sign slapped on the side panel. Jeff's mother was not keen on his spooky hobby, so he'd bought a magnetic sign, which he put on the side of his van when he was out of her sight. He was approaching twenty-one but was still very much under his matriarch's rule. "Oh, go on then," I said to my cat as I picked her up. I opened the van door and jumped onto the passenger seat.

As Jeff drove us the short distance, I removed

Constance's cone-shaped collar. It was only twelve hours until I was allowed to remove it anyway. I rubbed her neck where the collar had been, and she purred loudly.

"No licking that scar," I said to her as I inspected the healing wound visible on a shaved patch of her belly.

"It's great to see her looking well," Jeff said. He had the window down which created a breeze, blowing his unruly sandy hair across his face. It matched the colour of his scrappy thin beard.

Constance meowed and pawed at my lap making herself comfortable. I was glad I had my tote bag with me. Constance liked to follow me everywhere and although I'd purchased a pet bag with a window in it, specifically for transporting her, she always preferred one of the designer tote bags I'd inherited from Grandma. It would be handy to have my cat there because it turned out she could see ghosts too.

"What's happening at the pier then?" Jeff asked.

"There have been accidents when parts of the building have dropped. Machinery is affected with surges of electricity and faults. It's been frightening the staff. A good few have resigned. A couple of them have made accident claims against the owner. Annie asked me yesterday to confirm it's not a poltergeist, then last night the old caretaker died."

"That's insane. Was he killed by paranormal activity?"

"Hopefully it was just an accident. I don't know the full details. Annie asked me to come over, and to bring you with me."

"Sounds like they think it's a ghost then."

I shuddered as chills shot up my spine. I cuddled Constance close to me. "I hope not."

CHAPTER 4

As we reached the pier, I remembered the times I'd visited with Grandma. Carefree days, walking up and down the boards to the main building, eating a soft whipped ice cream in a wafer cone. Playing in the arcades and gazing wide-eyed at the jars full of traditional sweets in the shop. Cola cubes, strawberry bonbons and liquorice. And on special occasions, eating a knickerbocker glory in the ice cream parlour. They were such happy memories.

Constance nuzzled my hand. I smiled. I had the same comforting feeling when I stroked her that I used to get when Grandma was around.

As we approached the entrance, Annie waved at us. She spoke to a policeman who reversed his car, so that we could get by. Jeff drove through the wide entrance and stopped for Annie. When she opened the passenger door, I shifted into the middle seat so she could climb in next to me.

"Thanks so much for coming." She glanced at my lap. "And Constance. The complete paranormal team. She looks like her usual self without that surgical collar. I really appreciate your support." A tear escaped her eye. "Ben was such a sweet man. I can't imagine anyone wanting to kill him. It must have been an accident."

We parked up behind two other vehicles and Jeff jumped out of the van, clutching his EMF meter.

"Keep it turned off," I said. "Until we discover exactly what happened here."

"Okay, boss." He saluted me. At times, Jeff got carried away with his gadgets, and this was no game.

"Follow me," Annie said, leading the way.

We walked along the wooden boards. I held my tote bag containing Constance, tightly in my arms. I wished I'd worn a top with a hood because the wind chilled my ears.

"A storm's coming in," Annie said.

We reached the pier's main building. It was grand, with a tower at each side and ornate carvings of gargoyles. Although they creeped me out, Grandma had explained they were there to ward off evil. *Clearly, they've not been doing their job properly,* I thought. *If a poltergeist has indeed taken up residence.*

As we entered, I was hit with the familiar aroma, a mixture of candy floss and seaweed. My stomach churned, I didn't know if it was the hangover or the dread of finding something creepy. Inside was an array of arcade machines, plus the dodgems and a haunted house. Not that I'd ever been in the haunted house. I was always too scared.

As we turned a corner around the penny slots, Jeff nearly bumped into a young woman with brown curly hair wearing a fluffy pink jumper. She looked as if she was still in her teens and her face was flushed.

"Watch where you're going." She glared at Jeff.

"Oh ... sorry," he said, then rubbed his scrappy beard.

"Olivia," Annie said. "This is Becky and Jeff." She turned to me. "Olivia is Katherine's daughter." She turned back to the girl. "They're here to investigate the accidents."

Olivia raised her eyebrows. "The ghostbusters?"

"Becky has cracked two cases this year," Jeff said. "She has a strong gift and I'm her tech support."

"Hopefully there's no paranormal activity," I added. "We're just here to put your mum's mind at rest."

"I can't believe she called you in. Mother must be going out of her mind if she thinks it's a ghost." She eyed Jeff's EMF meter. "Is this for real?"

Jeff mumbled. "It detects changes in the electromagnetic field."

We heard a woman's voice echoing close by.

"I've already told you, Andrew. My position has not changed and never will. It's a family business. I'm not selling. So stop asking the same question, time and time again."

"That's Katherine," said Annie.

Olivia crossed her arms and huffed. "I keep telling Mother to get rid of this place."

A man's voice bellowed. "You're cutting off your nose to spite your face, woman. It's a merger, not a takeover. It would be mutually beneficial."

"Do you think I was born yesterday?" Katherine shouted.

"You're in danger, with all the accidents going on here. If you don't watch out, someone else could get killed. And that someone might be you," Andrew said.

"Oh. So that's what you're resorting to, is it? You're threatening me?"

"Mother's losing it," Olivia said, shaking her head. "Totally losing it."

The man's voice softened. "Don't be ridiculous. I'm thinking of you – of your position. I'm trying to help."

"You've been after this place for years. Now get out."

Constance poked her head out of my bag and I pushed it down again.

We heard footsteps approaching and stepped aside as a tall, blond man, who I placed at about forty years old, stormed by, bumping his shoulder against Jeff's as he went.

"Who's that?" I asked in a low voice.

"Andrew Farr. He owns the fairground," Annie said.

"If it was me," Olivia said. "I'd be taking him up on his offer. Mother's obsessed with this place, she always has been. Now the entire place is falling apart. It's her fault for sacking Clive."

"Who's Clive?" I asked.

"The manager," Annie said. "I took his job after the guy who replaced him left."

Olivia huffed. "No offence, Annie, but Clive had been here for fifteen years. He held the place together. He'll never forgive her for what she did to him. He's been a real support to me. Unlike her." She nodded in the direction of her mother.

"Katherine's working long hours," Annie said.

Olivia nodded. "I told her earlier, she has no life. No wonder she's gone crazy, thinking there's a killer ghost here."

Constance scrabbled out of the tote bag and onto the floor.

"Get back in," I said.

"Pets aren't allowed on the pier." Olivia turned her nose up.

"This one sees ghosts, though," I said.

Olivia gave a short laugh. "I'm sure you and Mother will get on just great." She turned and flounced off as Jeff grabbed Constance and put her back into my bag as I held it open.

She meowed in protest.

I held the bag close to me, wishing I'd kept my

mouth shut – after all, not everyone believes ghosts are a thing.

"Come this way," Annie said, her voice less bright than usual. Olivia's words about her not being as good as the previous manager must have stung.

"I think you're doing a great job," I said to her.

Annie laughed. "Clive was better. As much as I appreciate the promotion, a part of me wishes he was still here. He knew every inch of this place." She walked the few feet to the ice cream parlour door, which was open. "The murder happened in Katherine's office so the police forensic team are in there." She glanced over her shoulder at me. "And H."

"Does he know we're here?" I asked.

Annie nodded and spoke in a hushed voice. "He said not to allow you access, but Katherine insisted on it. He gave in but told me to pass on that he doesn't want us encouraging the ghost idea. To tell Katherine, 'It's not a ghost and clear off'. They were his exact words."

"As charming as ever," I sighed.

When we entered the ice cream parlour, a security guard dressed in a black uniform stood just inside.

"We're closed," he said in a gruff voice. He looked to be in his early thirties, was tall and had dark, closely-shaven hair, cut in a military style. He had bags underneath his eyes, which were bloodshot.

Annie stepped forward. "We know that, Nathan,

but Katherine asked them to come in. I'm showing them around."

"Oh. The medium." He glanced over his shoulder to the far end of the room, where a woman sat at a table, then shook his head. "Mad, the lot of you."

He walked away. I noticed he had a few patches of fluff on his uniform in the same shade as Olivia's jumper.

We entered the rectangle shaped room which had floor to ceiling windows to the front and each side. Outside were railings, with the sea beyond. It gave the illusion of being at sea.

"Take a seat." Katherine gestured as we approached her. She had wavy brown shoulder-length hair and was slim. I guessed she was approaching forty. Wearing a suit, she had an air about her that said she was used to bossing people around and getting her own way. *She was good at it, too,* I thought, considering she'd convinced H to let us in.

"Thanks so much for coming," she said once the three of us were seated.

"Pleased to meet you," I said. "And I hope you don't mind but I brought my cat."

She smiled. "Is this the famous cat, the one that was attacked by a mad knife-woman?"

Constance jumped on the table and sashayed towards Katherine.

"I'm so sorry. She's been cooped up for a couple of weeks and is a bit hyper. And yes, the wound is healing nicely. She's already spent at least two of her nine lives."

Annie laughed. "She sure has, she's better than a guard dog."

Katherine's frown smoothed away as she stroked Constance.

"I'm sorry for your loss," I said.

Katherine sighed. "I shouldn't have let Ben cover for Nathan. But he insisted."

"Can you go over exactly what happened?" I asked, taking my smartphone out of my bag to make notes.

"Ben was the caretaker who used to do odd jobs around the place. He was found dead in my office, slumped over the table."

"An accident?" I suggested.

"We don't know. There was a hammer on the floor, which they think hit Ben on the head. It's being checked over by forensics and Ben of course will have a post-mortem." She paused to take a breath. "This place is cold at night, even in the summer, and I have an old oil heater in the office. I use the hammer to hit the knob into the on position. It's kept on a shelf, beside the desk."

"I get it," Jeff said. "If there was a burst of spirit energy, you think the hammer might have fallen on Ben's head?"

"Those are my thoughts precisely," Katherine said. "The police are treating it as suspicious. They looked at me like I was a fool when I mentioned paranormal activity." She blinked. "I'm so pleased you're here. Many accidents have happened. It's got to be a ghost and from what I've learned from on-line research, specifically a poltergeist."

Jeff rubbed his scrappy beard. "It could be, I've seen examples of objects moving."

Annie pointed towards Katherine's office. "H has been giving Katherine a hard time about not calling them in earlier."

Katherine sighed. "Everyone's having a go at me today. Nathan's not happy with me allowing Ben to take his place. It's really shaken him. I'd called an agency to cover last night's shift. But it was difficult, with the music festival on. There was limited availability, as the event needed security. It's true, I shouldn't have put Ben at risk. Nathan was so upset. I guess he feels he should have been here, that it's his job to protect the pier." She let out a long breath. "Olivia has been telling me to sell this place as she thinks I can't cope. But the Sheringhams have owned the pier for over one hundred years. It needs to stay in the family. I just hope Olivia will come to her senses one day when she's older and realise this place is her birth right."

Part of me felt sorry for Olivia. I too had inherited something I didn't want – the gift for seeing the dead.

"She says all I care about is the pier and that I love it more than her. That's just not true."

Annie stood up and put a hand on Katherine's

shoulder. "People say things they don't mean when they're upset."

"She said it was my fault Ben died." Katherine dabbed her eyes with a handkerchief. "He was like a father to me and a grandfather to her. I can't believe he's gone. Olivia's heart-broken. I don't blame her for hitting out at me. It's all my fault. What was I thinking? He was so frail. He insisted and I thought he would have been offended if I'd said no."

"Where was Nathan?" I asked.

"Up at the castle. What's he doing, going to music festivals in his thirties? Isn't that a kid thing? Olivia and her friends were there. It's not for grown adults."

I thought back to Grandma. She was seventy when we went to Glastonbury. But I made no comment.

Katherine grabbed my hand. "It was the poltergeist I'm sure of it," she whispered, looking around as if it was lurking in the shadows.

I shivered, although noted that I'd not experienced the usual static that filled my body when a ghost was in the vicinity. I focussed on that fact to calm my nerves.

The pier creaked in the wind and the day darkened, even though it was still morning. Through the windows, I could see thick black rain clouds closing in.

"Do you think the state of the building may have caused the hammer to fall off the shelf?" I asked as the structure creaked again.

H entered the room before Katherine could answer.

"Mrs Sheringham, I'll take you to the station now, so you can make a full statement."

"I'll come with you," Annie said.

Katherine let go of my hand. "Stay here and see if you can find any paranormal activity."

"We'll do our best," Jeff said. "We're the best paranormal investigators in Branden Bay."

Hmm, I thought. We were the only paranormal investigators in the area, ever since Dave, Jeff's mentor, retired. I shuddered. "I'm not sure the police will allow us to remain on site."

"That's right," H said appearing behind me. "We want everyone off the pier while forensics do their job. We'll let you know when you can regain access, Mrs Sheringham."

"Please, Becky, come back and get rid of the poltergeist," Katherine said as she stood up. "It's evil. It's killed."

CHAPTER 5

The following day I worked on my application for a hygiene certificate with Dannie. It wasn't the most exciting of jobs but I appreciated being able to focus on the café, rather than ghosts. The call came in late afternoon from Katherine to say that Jeff and I were permitted to access the pier. Jeff was working his shift at the D.I.Y store, so we arranged to meet after supper.

As Jeff drove us down the length of the pier, Constance sat on the dash, looking out of the front window. The wet weather had passed but had left a ferocious wind in its wake. The gothic beauty of the historic building had a haunted castle appearance in the dark. The full moon shone with wispy clouds covering it, like scarves billowing in the wind. I swallowed hard and picked up my fluffy companion, holding her close to my chest. The wind shook the van as Jeff slowed to a stop. We jumped out and he disappeared around the back to unload his gear. I was pleased that I'd wrapped up warm in jeans and a hooded sweatshirt.

Nathan, the security guard approached. I clutched Constance, I didn't want her to blow away. He spoke in a loud voice to be heard over the weather. "You'd better not be here all night. The police don't need amateurs getting in the way."

"I'm not trying to do the job of the police," I said as the wind whipped my hair across my face. "Katherine asked us to look for paranormal activity. Not to investigate Ben's death." I shivered. "It's to put her mind at rest. That's all."

"You're ripping her off with your fake service." He pointed at the sign on Jeff's van.

Constance wriggled in my arms.

Jeff finished pulling his bags from the van and slammed the door shut.

"It's not safe here," Nathan said. "I don't want anyone else getting hurt." He paused as the wind blew another strong gust.

I leaned against the van, wishing I could put Constance in my tote bag, but it was full of Grandma's old Tupperware, which held enough snacks to get us through the evening.

Nathan gestured for us to follow him. He turned and led us to the building. He certainly didn't make me feel any better about this stake-out. Maybe deep down he felt responsible. Still, as far as I was concerned, it didn't excuse his aggressive stance towards us. He opened the door and held it against the wind as Jeff carried his equipment in. I jumped as the door slammed shut behind us.

"I'm sorry, I know all of this appears weird," I said to Nathan. "In my defence, I don't want to be here. Katherine practically begged me to come. We just need to get the job done and we'll be out of your way as quickly as possible."

Nathan rubbed a hand over his cropped hair. "I don't want anything else going wrong."

"Whereabouts are we going to set up?" asked Jeff.

I turned to Nathan. "Is there any place the poltergeist usually strikes?"

"There's no poltergeist." Nathan shook his head. "But the accidents have happened all over the pier. You can't go in the office, it's taped off."

"What do you think caused the accidents?" I asked.

"The age of the building. This place is falling apart. Katherine can't cope any more. It's not fair on Olivia either. It's probably best for both their sakes, if she sells up."

"Someone might be targeting her. If that's the case, it's not Katherine's fault," I said, getting a misogynist vibe from Nathan.

"Why don't you stop interrogating me and focus on what you're here to do, then go home."

"We'll get right on it," Jeff said.

"If anything happens, I'll be doing my rounds." Nathan looked up to the ceiling and sighed, as if to say, *you bunch of nutters.* His footsteps echoed as he walked towards the door, which he opened. Once he'd passed through, it banged shut again with the force of the wind. The sound reverberated around us and I shivered.

With the machines switched off and limited lighting, the pier building was one spooky place. Clown faces stared at me from the grab machines, motionless, as if the pause button had been pressed on a horror movie. All we could hear were our own footsteps and the wind whistling through gaps in the walls. *Nathan was right,* I thought, *this place definitely needs a refurb.*

I turned to Jeff. "Shall we set up in the ice cream parlour? It's the biggest space." I wanted to get away from the creepy clowns.

Jeff nodded and we made our way through the eerie arcade with Constance sashaying ahead of us.

"Ghosts don't really wield hammers, do they?" I asked.

"No, but items can fly across a room. You see it all the time."

I shuddered. I certainly didn't see that all the time, or want to. I scanned the room, checking out the various large items of equipment. Slot machines, video games, *an awful lot of metal,* I thought. "I guess this isn't the ideal location for a poltergeist, is it?"

We passed the dodgems, the haunted house, the

mirror maze and sweetshop. As I opened the doors to the parlour, I felt a breeze across my face, hoping it was a sign there was a window open and not an icy chill caused by a spirit passing by. The room smelled of ice cream and detergent. I walked to the far end and gazed out at the rough sea, which had white crests highlighted by the moonlight. Spray doused the windows as a huge wave thrashed the pier. I stepped back, feeling a little off balance.

Turning around, I watched Constance jump onto a table and clean herself as if she intended to have a sleep. I wished I could feel as relaxed as her. "Let's get this done," I said with a shiver.

"I'll stack a few tables and make space in the middle," Jeff said.

Having made room for us and the equipment, Jeff switched on the EMF meter. "At the moment, I think it's only picking up our energy. And Constance always gives off a lot. Much more than cats usually do."

Constance purred as I scratched her head. "You're one special cat."

Jeff studied his large SLS camera, which was fixed on a tripod. "I can only see you two through here." He fished his mobile phone out of his pocket. "You can use this. I've got a new app." He lifted the phone up and scanned the room. "It works the same way as the camera. I'm trialling it. It's much easier to carry around, rather than lugging the full set up. Although the camera is great for recording overnight."

I took the phone and pointed it at Jeff, his energy was mapped out on the screen as a neon green stick man. Other than Jeff, the only energy I could see was coming from Constance. I breathed a sigh of relief. Hopeful that there was nothing there. We sat at a table and waited.

After a good half an hour of no activity, I broke the silence that had fallen between us. "I'm getting nothing – not even the slightest tingle."

"Let's crack open the snacks," Jeff said. He seemed nearly as excited about the food I'd brought, as he was at the prospect of finding a poltergeist.

I opened the plastic containers of cakes and sandwiches. I'd cut thick slices of bread and filled them with ham and fresh tomatoes. With a generous dollop of mayonnaise and a crack of black pepper, it was one of my favourite combinations. Jeff nodded at me in appreciation as he bit into it. I took the cellophane wrap off a china dish I'd filled with steamed salmon and placed it on the floor for Constance.

Having finished his sandwich, Jeff reached for a banana muffin. "Just in case there's something in here which we're not picking up, shall we try the Ouija board?"

I scanned the still room. "We don't want to wake anything that's lying dormant. The point of the exercise is to look for something that's very much here, causing accidents."

"Can't you meditate and try to connect?"

I gulped. "What? Connect to a poltergeist, mentally and emotionally? No thanks. Our sole purpose for being here is to put Katherine's mind at rest regarding anything currently active, not to call up sleeping spirits." I closed the plastic tubs.

"But she wants us to find the poltergeist. The negative energy might be hiding."

I scanned the room as the walls creaked in the wind. "This place needs an overhaul. Like Nathan said, that's probably the cause of the accidents. Ben was an older man. Maybe if the hammer had fallen on a younger head, that person would have survived. And they don't know for sure how he died. They need to wait for a post-mortem to determine the reason for his death. Katherine said Ben was frail. I think we should leave it to the police."

"Where's your sense of adventure? I thought you loved a mystery."

"Maybe I do, but I don't like ghost hunting. That's your hobby. I'm not staying here all night." My voice echoed around the room and had a hint of my mother about it.

Jeff's shoulders drooped.

I sighed. "Okay. Let's cover the rest of the place with the EMF meter and your phone app to make sure. And then we'll call it a night."

Seemingly happy with the compromise, Jeff grabbed the meter and his phone.

I lifted Constance and placed her in my tote bag.

. . .

I JUMPED at every bleep of the EMF meter as we meandered around the slot machines. Constance had scrabbled out of my bag and trotted ahead of us. We were halfway around when I stopped. I glanced at Jeff, the equipment was showing no significant change, but I could hear something.

"Can you hear that?" I whispered to Jeff. I was sure I heard a voice crying, *sorry*.

"A wailing sound?" he said.

The noise had stopped. "I don't like this." I shuddered.

Constance looked up at me. She certainly wasn't sensing anything paranormal.

Jeff studied the screen of his phone as he pivoted. "No, nothing. It's a windy night. Let's have a look in here," he said, pointing at the entrance of the haunted house, which was accessed through the open mouth of a huge clown face.

"I don't think that's necessary, is it?" I said.

"Either we're scouting the whole place or we're not," he said. "You don't want Katherine to ask us back, do you?"

Constance trotted towards the opening.

"Okay," I said. "I'll leave the bag here." I followed my cat through the entrance.

"I'm right behind you," Jeff said.

Inside, there were glow in the dark pictures of

ghosts on the wall. *It's for kids don't be silly,* I told myself as my heartbeat quickened. I squinted in the dull light. Ahead of us was another door with an equally creepy clown face painted on it. I shuddered. "Do you think this is safe?"

"Just listen for any activity on the meter." Jeff pushed me in the small of the back towards the inner door. Once the other side, it was pitch black.

"I don't like this, one bit." I switched the torch app on my phone. I lifted it up. Illuminated in front of my eyes was a skeleton with red balls for eyes. I screamed.

Constance jumped up my leg, piercing her claws through my jeans into the skin of my thigh.

I screamed again. "Ouch!"

Jeff laughed but stopped abruptly as a voice in the distance called out. "Becky? Becky!" Followed by the thumping of feet.

"Who's that?" asked Jeff.

I groaned, recognising the owner of the voice. "It's H."

"Right, you two, out of there." He shone a torch in my face. "What do you think you're doing? You shouldn't be messing around when someone's been killed?"

"We were told to search the entire place by Katherine," Jeff said.

"So why are you screaming?" H asked me.

I turned and pointed to the skeleton, then

attempted to peel Constance off my thigh. "How did you know we were here?"

"I saw the Mystery Machine parked up," he said, presumably an attempt at humour. If I wasn't in pain, I may even have laughed. H continued. "And your bag is at the entrance. I want you off the pier. Now."

Constance withdrew her claws from my thigh and jumped to the floor, sashaying over to H before rubbing herself up against his leg as I rubbed mine.

We followed H out of the haunted house and Jeff sighed. "I have to agree with you Becky. There's no poltergeist here." The disappointment in his voice was apparent.

"Glad to hear it," H said.

I breathed out slowly. "I'll pop over and see Katherine tomorrow and confirm that the pier is poltergeist free. Let's collect your gear and go."

H followed us to the parlour.

"It's definitely a job for the police and not us," I said to Jeff, but loud enough for H to hear.

Jeff sighed. "A real shame."

"A shame there isn't a hammer wielding poltergeist on the loose?" I asked.

"So you want to leave the investigation to your boyfriend then?"

H coughed away a laugh from behind us.

I opened the door to the parlour. "He's not my boyfriend."

We packed away the equipment and Nathan

turned up, creeping around H, telling him he agreed that Katherine was mad to have let us on the property at night. The guy certainly got my back up, but that feeling was trumped by a sense of relief that we'd found nothing paranormal.

I YAWNED as I stepped down from the van outside my house and Constance jumped to the pavement. I watched as Jeff drove away in the quiet of the early hours. Feeling static snake up my arms, I frowned. That was often a sign there was a spirit close by. As if to alert me further, Constance hissed. I jumped as I saw someone on the patio.

"Oh, it's you," I said, relieved. It wasn't a shadowy ghoul or a deteriorating zombie, it was just the elderly man I'd seen before. He still wore the red puffer jacket and was sitting at the iron table and chairs at the front of the café. Pins and needles raced down my arm. I frowned and glanced up at my bedroom window, hoping there wasn't something lurking inside.

The man stared at me. He seemed to glow under the Victorian street lamps.

"What are you doing here?" I asked.

He opened his mouth but all I could hear was a distant whisper.

I crossed my arms. "Look. It's gone midnight and I'm off to bed. I suggest you get back to your own home and do the same."

"I can't." His voice came out like a crackle and a shot of static buzzed up my back.

The guy was seriously creeping me out.

I shook my head and took the door keys out of my tote bag. "Like I said before, if you have issues with the spirit world you can use Lynn at the Castle Road spiritualist church."

I opened my door and walked in, closing it behind me. As I neared the stairs, I shrugged off a pang of guilt. Then jumped as I heard his crackly voice again.

"I need help."

I swung around. The elderly man was now inside my house and standing before me.

I let out an uncontrollable scream. I could see straight through him.

CHAPTER 6

Trembling in my hallway, I stared at the ghost, then rubbed my eyes. Opening them again, I was disappointed to see he was still there. I heard footsteps thundering across the landing.

Dannie soon stood on the bottom flight of the stairs, in her Victoria Secret PJ's, with a can of hair-spray in her hand – poised as if it was pepper spray. "Is there an intruder?"

Constance stared up at the see-through man, her coat bushing out as if she'd been plugged into a socket. Unlike Constance and myself, Dannie clearly did not have the third eye, to see this ghost.

"What are you screaming for?" she asked.

I didn't want to say I could see a dead person. It would freak her out. "A spider." Another spike of electricity nipped at my neck and I casually rubbed it away.

Dannie dropped her arm to her side. "Are you serious? You scream the house down because of a spider?"

"Sorry," I said.

"Where is it?"

I pointed randomly at the wall. "It must have got away."

Dannie passed me and walked straight through the ghost to the front door. She squinted. "What, that?" She pointed to the tiniest dot of a spider climbing up the frame.

"I have a phobia."

"Well get over it." She walked towards the stairs. "You need your sleep. You've got that meeting at the council tomorrow about your licence."

How could I forget? I waited until I heard her bedroom door close then turned to the ghost. "I take it you're Ben?" I whispered rubbing the static off my arms.

He nodded.

"As you're contacting me. I'm assuming you were murdered."

"Help me." His voice sounded like it was blowing on a wind, as fear seeped into my chest. Not my fear. His.

He flickered on and off. "The coat," he said touching his red puffer jacket. He faded out and I was left with silence.

Constance's coat flattened, like a deflating balloon.

As much as I disliked Lynn's calls for me to let her

help me with my gift. I needed her. I hated that I couldn't control it. I pulled out my mobile and texted her.

Are you still at the hut? Can I come over? I need help.

She replied immediately.

No, but I'm awake. I'll meet you there in fifteen minutes.

A quarter of an hour later, I wrapped my coat tightly around me as I opened the back door. Lynn had opened the gate in the stone wall between our properties before I reached it.

"You look like you need a cuppa," she said.

"A brandy would be better." I followed her into the hut.

Lynn put an arm around my shoulders and led me inside with Constance trotting after us.

I took a seat at a table and puffed out.

"So what's wrong lovey?"

"I've just seen the man that was killed on the pier." I hugged myself feeling the aftershocks I usually experienced after a ghostly connection.

"What? The ghost of Benjamin Goldfield?" she asked.

I nodded.

"So, it's likely he was murdered. Did he speak?"

"Briefly."

"Will you now let me help develop your gift?"

I put my elbows on the table and held my head in my hands. "I just want it to go away. I'm scared that if I delve inside further, it'll encourage contact."

"I'm afraid they'll be coming anyway lovey." She stroked my hand.

I looked up. "I can't cope with it. It's like I can feel what they're feeling inside."

"What was Ben feeling?"

Constance jumped on my lap.

"A sense of urgency," I said. "Fear, and that something has to be done." I sighed. "It's enough for a person to feel their own emotions, without taking on other peoples'."

"I don't have the gift to fuse with spirits like you do. I feel the emotions of the living and transmit them to the spirit world in the hope of a response. But I still need to distance myself from the pain of other living people. I can give you exercises to help distance yourself."

"I'll think about it," I said, wary of getting in too deep.

"Did Ben give you a message?"

"The coat."

"What coat?"

I stroked Constance's head. "He was wearing a red puffer jacket and pointed to it." I sighed. "I feel he was killed by flesh and blood. Did you know much about him?"

"I know his sister, she told me he was terminally ill. He was given two months to live and that was three months ago."

"So he was living on borrowed time? Who would

dislike him enough to kill him? Who would benefit from him dying?" I asked.

"I guess that's what you need to figure out lovey. So he can rest in peace."

Constance meowed, as if in agreement.

Like it or not, I had a new case on my hands.

"WAKE UP," Dannie said with an air of authority.

I lifted my head from one of the café tables, I hadn't made it to bed the night before. I'd sat in the cafe, making notes about possible suspects on my note taking app, well into the early hours. I peeled my mobile phone off my face and wiped drool from my mouth. Constance was asleep next to me. I groaned at the memory of the ghostly visitor. Scanning the room, there was no sign of Ben. But to be honest, Dannie seemed scarier. How the tables had turned – only last week it had been me shouting her awake every morning.

"I can't believe you slept in the café!"

Constance stood up and arched her back in a stretch.

"We need to leave in an hour. We've got to go through everything we spoke about yesterday in case Elks interrogates you."

After a shower, I felt a lot more human as I sat in the kitchen, sipping a hot coffee, devouring the bacon buttie Dannie had made for me. "I'm not looking forward to this meeting."

"You can handle the likes of Elks," Dannie assured me.

I bit down on the soft bread and savoured its salty contents before replying. "You're right – the time for being passive and reactionary is over. I need to nail this."

THE WORDS *NAIL this* repeated in my head as I sat in the council offices. My name was called and I left Dannie sitting in the reception.

"Take a seat," Brian Elks said in the meeting room.

I handed over the paperwork. Dannie and I had prepared a list of equipment and work I'd carried out, which would count towards the license and hygiene requirements. It seemed I'd completed most of the necessary points anyway. "The few missing items will be in place within the next twenty-eight days," I said. "And I have requested an inspection."

"We still have to consider whether to issue a fine."

"I'm so sorry. I was providing a service for local people, following popular demand."

"So it would seem. I've had contact from a few of your customers and a call from the Gazette."

I swallowed as my palms sweat. "I can't apologise enough," I said, reminding myself to be neither rude nor sarcastic and certainly not confrontational.

He opened his mouth as if to say more when shouting blasted through the wall from the neighbouring office.

"This backward council needs to be brought down."

I recognised the voice and frowned trying to picture the face that went with it.

"I've told you, Mr Farr," a male voice said. "It was a collective decision."

Ah, it's Andrew Farr from the fairground, I thought.

Brian Elks cleared his throat. "It will help your case if you update us on any developments and ..."

"Over a year it's taken me to get to this stage," Andrew Farr shouted. "And now you say no? After I've paid out thousands to the surveyor and architect. Spent hours of my time obtaining contractor quotes. Why didn't you refuse it to begin with, rather than going through this whole rigmarole and costs? Some of us are out there trying to earn money for the town, not pen-pushing behind a desk, wasting everyone's taxes."

Brian frowned. "Our jobs do not make us popular."

The council officer in the neighbouring room continued. "I've already explained the reasons in full. The records are public if you want to view them online. This was a complex case, we had to consult English Heritage and the fairground is not to be modernised. But there are grants available to help with restoration."

"So, the fairground is stuck in the nineteenth

century, but you expect my business to survive in the twenty first?"

Brian Elks pushed my papers back together. "Until your application has been processed, your facilities must not be used for any commercial business whatsoever." He stood up.

"Is that it?" I said, feeling relief ebb through my body.

"Yes," he replied, walking towards the door. "We'll be in touch."

Dannie looked surprised to see me out so soon. "How did it go?"

"Short and sweet. Elks said to keep him updated on our progress. And not to use the kitchen for business while they consider my license."

Dannie rose from her seat. "So he's not going to fine you?"

"I have to wait to find out." We walked towards the exit.

"I've got a meeting up at the college about an accounting course I want to do, so I'll see you back home later." Dannie hugged me. I was taken aback. This was so out of character. It seemed that, out of my stress, Dannie was becoming a much happier person.

As I walked onto the pavement, Andrew Farr stormed past, red-faced, with his unruly blonde hair looking as if he had been trying to pull it out in chunks.

Bit of a temper, I thought and decided to go straight

to the pier to quiz Katherine. I needed to find out, what was the significance of Ben's coat. And who on earth would want to kill a dying man?

CHAPTER 7

The walk along the prom to the pier was a pleasant one. The bad weather had cleared, and the meteorologists were reporting that summer had officially arrived. The tide was high and the sun glistened upon it. Seagulls flew around looking for a late breakfast and I was sure that, come lunchtime, they would be swooping down to feast on leftover fish and chips.

As I reached the pier building, it had a different atmosphere to the eeriness of the night before. With the amusements in action, clashing tunes mingled with the laughter of children, it was a totally different vibe. Even the clowns looked friendly, and that was coming from someone who has a teensy clown phobia.

Entering the ice cream parlour, I found it half full. I had a sideways view of Katherine, seated at a table at the far end, with a tall guy standing opposite her. I stopped in my tracks and took a double take. At first, I thought it was Jeff. He had the same lanky look, faded jeans, cartoon emblazoned t-shirt and unkempt hair. Although, I soon realised, it wasn't my side-kick. This guy's hair was a different shade. A mousy brown, not the sandy colour of Jeff's. As I got closer, I heard them talking and sat at a nearby table to wait, turning with my ear in their direction, and eavesdropped.

"For goodness sake, sit down," Katherine said to the man.

"No. Tell me what you want and I'll be gone."

"Would you like a coffee? I've got bourbon biscuits in."

"Get to the point, Katherine."

I wondered who this guy was.

Katherine paused before she spoke. "I'll be straight up with you. With Ben dying, I've been thinking about what really matters. Life's too short for fallings out. You and I, we had a close relationship. I'm so sad that's gone."

I raised my eyebrows. He didn't look like someone I imagined Katherine would have a romance with.

"So, you're short of staff, is that it?"

"Clive. You've worked here for so long."

Ah, I thought. It wasn't an ex-boyfriend, it was the ex-manager.

"I see you as family," Katherine said. "And families squabble."

"You've had weeks to get in touch. This is all about

the tribunal isn't it? I'm not stupid. And as for our history, you didn't care about that when you sacked me."

"I overreacted. I was under pressure, getting stress from all ways. I'm sorry, please come back. I've a higher managerial position, with a brilliant salary, created just for you."

"No, Katherine. This is all your doing. I don't need or want your money. My business has grown since I've been able to give extra time to it. The tribunal is going ahead."

I opened my mouth in amazement as he strode by. He even had the same scrappy beard as Jeff. But he was older, maybe thirty.

Katherine shuffled papers on the table she was using as a desk. She directed a stiff smile at an elderly couple on a nearby table who were gawping at her. I rose from my chair.

As I approached, Katherine let out a sigh. "Becky, you couldn't have come at a better time. I feel so much calmer when you're here. There's something about you that's therapeutic."

"Are you okay?" I asked.

"I have staffing issues. The joys of running your own business," she said shuffling paperwork to one side. "So, what happened last night?"

I pulled out a chair and sat opposite her. I spoke in a hushed tone. "We found nothing paranormal at all.

I'm sure it's a person doing this. Someone living murdered Ben, not a poltergeist."

"But who would be so cruel to kill him? The poor man was dying."

"I don't know, but I suggest you get your CCTV fixed."

Katherine shook her head. "Ever since the accidents began, the CCTV has played up. Even though we've had it fixed twice. That's one of the reasons I thought it was a poltergeist, interfering with the energy. I can't afford to have it replaced. I'm having to employ new people on higher wages and my takings are down. I've managed to lure a couple of the original staff back, but clearly Clive – the guy I was talking to just now – isn't interested." She sat up and sighed.

I didn't want to mention I'd seen Ben's ghost. I felt like a freak. But I did need to ask about the coat.

"I wondered if there was anything significant about the coat Ben was wearing?"

"The one he died in? It was mine. It's extremely warm and filled with duck down. I presume he'd put it on to keep himself warm. He wasn't much more than skin and bone."

I felt a burst of adrenaline, this was significant.

She continued. "Even on a warm night, it's freezing down here, what with the tidal wind. It cost me a few hundred pounds, but it was ruined. The hood was covered in blood from the blow to the head."

"So he had the hood of the coat up?"

"Yes."

"What did the police say about your coat?"

"I didn't mention that it was my coat. I didn't want it back. Under the circumstances."

I gave Katherine a concerned look. "If he had his hood up, maybe the killer thought ..."

She stared at me blinking and put a hand to her chest. "You think they meant to kill me?"

"It's a possibility that someone is out to harm you."

"How did you know about the coat?" she asked.

"A gut feeling."

"You really are psychic," she whispered, placing her fingertips on her temple. "I'm in trouble then." She paused. "I've been reading about your other cases." Katherine reached for a folded newspaper. It was a back issue of the Gazette. Splashed on the front cover was me in a swimsuit and an open towelling robe with green gunk on my face from a face pack.

I groaned inwardly.

She tapped the paper. "I see you incorporate standard detecting techniques. Interviewing suspects and going under cover." She sighed. "But I can understand you might not be able to give me the time as you're busy with your café."

I lowered my voice as the couple on the nearby table stood up. "I've been shut down and they won't let me reopen for at least a month." I took a deep breath. "So I can investigate this for you if you like?" My words echoed in my head as if a part of me was saying, *what on earth are you doing?*

"Would you? What are your rates?"

"One hundred a day, plus expenses." I didn't know if that was over the odds, but that amount would help with the utility bills and put food on the table for myself, Dannie and my fussy cat.

"Can you start right away?" She leaned forward and clutched my wrist. "And not a word to anyone about it, other than Annie. Certainly not Olivia."

I pulled my phone out of my bag. "I'll get started on motives right away." I poised my thumb over the screen. "Tell me about Andrew Farr."

"Andrew? I find it a little far-fetched that he would cause me harm."

I raised my eyebrows. I would have thought a killer-poltergeist was more unlikely. "I'll have to look into everyone you're in contact with. Looking at motives and alibis."

Katherine sighed. "Andrew is after this place and is piling on the pressure to the point I was thinking of reporting him to the police for harassment. But I'm sure he wouldn't physically harm me."

I tapped *harasser* next to his name on my phone.

"He wants a joint attraction." She brushed the hair from her forehead and cleared her throat. "His theory is that we'll make more money as one, rather than two. With visitors buying a ticket to access both the fairground and pier.

Sounds like a good idea, I thought. "So what's your issue with Andrew?"

"I don't trust him. You give him an inch and he takes a mile. If we joined up, I'd be side-lined. He's desperate. Both of our businesses are failing. His latest idea is for us to dress up as some sort of Victorian throwback. He wanted me and the staff to join in as market testing, he called it. He's been employing my staff. Literally pinching them." She opened a box file and pulled out a flyer. "I caught him handing this to a member of my team."

I took the leaflet from her. *Hiring now, join the fairground for our Victorian themed day. Acting skills desirable but not necessary.* It went on to list various jobs. "This is great. I'll apply and see what he's up to. He could quite easily be the person causing havoc around here, pinching your staff, causing issues to break you into accepting his business proposition."

"Exactly, but I don't think he'd murder me. That's a bit extreme."

She had a point. Maybe the accidents and the killer weren't linked. "Tell me more about the guy you were talking to when I arrived."

"Clive began his career here straight from school. He worked his way up. But I came in one morning to find the kitchen oven on, it was blazing at full temperature. He was responsible for checking the pier before closure the day before. I said I had to record the incident on his personnel file as a disciplinary. If it was a one-off situation, I'd have let it go. But I was trying to make a point because he'd been coming in late and tired in the mornings, which may have led to his carelessness. Someone told me he was running a side-line business. That's fine, I've not asked any staff to be exclusive – many work part-time. But his moonlighting was affecting his job here and I had an issue with that." She sighed. "He answered me back, saying I had a cheek and that I couldn't run the place without him." Katherine pushed her hair behind her ears. "To be honest I lost my rag and fired him on the spot. Today was the first time we've spoken to each other for weeks."

I tapped the details into my phone.

"Thing is," she continued, "I'm worried now, that it wasn't his fault the oven was left on at all. That it was the poltergeist, or whoever has been setting traps in this place." She shook her head. "I should never have let Clive go. I really need him, and now he wants to take me to the employment tribunal."

"Maybe I could pay him a visit? To try and put your message across when he's not so angry?" It would also be a chance for me to check him out.

"Would you? In fact, Ben's family have asked me to arrange a wake locally as soon as possible, as they'll be burying him at the family plot out of town. I'll let you have an invitation to pass on."

"Have the police asked you about Andrew and Clive?"

"No. I guess they're focussing on who would have wanted to kill Ben." She put her hand to her forehead. "This is such a shock. To think someone wants me dead." Her hand shook. "I never told them it was my coat that Ben was wearing. I didn't think it was relevant."

I planned to tell H this as soon as possible. Before I left, I advised Katherine to make sure she was not left alone until the killer was found. On the way out I bumped into Annie and said I'd call her later to fill her in on the conversation I'd had with her boss.

Once home, I called Carol who asked me over that evening and H messaged shortly afterwards to confirm the time he would pick me up. I called Branden Bay fairground and enquired about their vacant positions. I was directed to their website and followed the *applications* portal. I plugged in my details, including my qualification in performing arts, I felt confident I'd be offered a job. Excitement filled my body. I may not have been keen on the paranormal, but I did enjoy the challenge of a mystery.

It was six o'clock the same evening. I'd found a summery dress to wear and entered the kitchen as Dannie was searching through the cupboards.

"Are you okay with making your own meal?" I asked as she turned the oven on.

"Of course, I've found something in the freezer."

She leaned against the worktop. "You look nice, are you going on a date?"

"No," I said. "H is picking me up and we're going up to his Mum's to talk about catering."

"What sort of catering?"

"Cupcakes for a christening," I said.

"I'm not sure how that will work officially with the licence situation. It might be better to do that as a favour. After all, it's for your boyfriend's family."

"He's not my boyfriend."

"Oh. You're not official yet?" Dannie raised her eyebrows.

"It's not going to be an official thing." I put my hands on my hips.

"I see. It's just casual then?" She winked at me. "Can't say I blame you."

"I have a business meeting with his mother about the catering job. That's all. We are not – and never have been – an item."

"Oh. So he hasn't asked you out yet? He doesn't look shy. Maybe you need to make the first move."

"He's not my type."

Dannie put her head to one side and smirked at me. The doorbell rang. "That's him, I guess. Your non-boyfriend. Have a great evening over at his parents. And yeah, you might be confused about your relationship status, but it might be handy if Elks thinks you're in love, in case word gets out about the christening cakes."

"I'll see you later." I went to the door and opened it as H rang the bell for a second time.

He grinned at me. "Alright?"

"Yes – sorry, I was talking to Dannie about the business. We've got a few things to do to get this place reopened."

As I went out, Mrs Jessup from next door was outside. "Ah, there you are, dear. I'm missing my daily cuppa and your tasty cakes. You will be opening again, won't you?"

"I hope so." I smiled at her. It was nice to feel appreciated by others. I made a mental note to pop a cake over to Mrs Jessup the following day.

"Have a nice evening with your young man," she said, then put her key in her door.

H was laughing when I reached the car. I found Constance sitting on the passenger seat.

"How did she get there?" I asked.

"She slipped by and jumped in the window, while you were talking to your neighbour. It's okay. Ma loves her."

I scooped Constance up and sat down, placing her on my lap as she purred.

H started the engine. "I hope you haven't eaten much today. Ma said supper but you're in for a huge meal." He put the car into gear.

"I'm starving, actually," I said. I hadn't eaten since breakfast. "So, how's the case going?" I asked as we began the short journey to his parents' house.

"I can't discuss the details with you. Sorry about moving you off the pier last night but I got spooked after hearing you scream."

"We'd pretty much finished anyway and you'll be pleased to know, I told Katherine earlier that no poltergeist or any evidence of spirits was found." I left off the part about Ben having visited me. "So, what's your opinion on the death? Was it an accident from a flying hammer?"

"That's unlikely."

"So you think it was murder?" I said as I stroked the top of Constance's head.

"As I said, I'm not going to discuss it with you." He smiled at me. "Stop trying to draw me in."

As far as I was concerned, I had to get my information over to him, so he could solve the case. So I ignored his rebuff. After all, Katherine was in danger, and I'd be stuck with Ben's ghost if he could not rest in peace. "As Ben was wearing Katherine's coat. Do you think maybe she was the intended target?"

"What? Who said the coat wasn't Ben's? This is news to me." He killed the engine outside his parents' house. "Okay, let's have it. Your full theory. Then it's off limits."

I grinned. I knew he wouldn't be able to resist it. "I think the intended victim was Katherine. Ben was wearing her coat. It's a huge puffer jacket, if he had the hood up and someone came up behind him, then maybe the killer picked up the hammer, bashed him over the head with it, before realising it wasn't Katherine. After all who would want to kill Ben when he was dying anyway?"

H took in a long breath, then puffed out slowly as he frowned. "Thanks for letting me know about the coat. Now promise me you won't go anywhere near the pier or interfere with police business."

"I er ..." I didn't want to tell him I'd been hired by Katherine or that I had applied for a job at the fairground.

Constance let out a low meow.

H frowned. "You've got a name for yourself now – someone might want to silence you if they're after Katherine and think you're snooping around. You've already had two close shaves with death. Leave it to me." His voice softened. "I'd hate for something to happen to you."

I stared into his eyes. The pupils became large, covering the brown of his irises so they looked black.

Constance purred and jumped off my lap onto H's.

I felt hot, gulped and nodded my head as I unclipped the seatbelt. "Shall we go inside?" I said in a squeaky voice.

CHAPTER 8

The aroma of Italian food reached my nose as I stood before H's parents' front door. I was so looking forward to the meal.

The door swung open and Carol opened her arms. She had chin length, dark brown hair with a blonde streak in the fringe and the same dark eyes as her son.

Pulling me in for a huge embrace she gave me a motherly squeeze. "How on earth could they do that to you? Shutting your café down, when you're the best thing to happen to Branden Bay for years. A local heroine, and they cut off your income? The council should be strung up."

Constance passed us and sashayed right into the house.

"Ma, put the girl down," said H. "The council have procedures to follow. She's lucky they're giving her a chance to get her application in for consideration."

"Less of the know-it-all talk, my boy. You'll never get our Becky to marry you if you carry on that way."

I'd explained numerous times to Carol that H and I were not dating. But she either chose to ignore it, or the reality had been squashed by her desire for me to be her daughter-in-law.

"Come in both of you. It's already on the table."

The dining area was situated in a conservatory, with views of their colourful garden. In the middle of the table was a steaming pot filled with penne pasta covered in a Bolognese sauce. H's dad, Paul, who was tall and broad like his son, but had fair hair, scooped a large portion of meat covered pasta and placed it on my plate, before offering me a serving dish piled high with garlic bread.

"Thanks, Paul," I said as Carol returned to the room, she'd been in the kitchen sorting something for Constance to eat. I waited for the others to dish up their meals.

"This looks and smells amazing," I said as I dusted parmesan cheese over my pasta. "A real treat." It was lovely to be sitting at a family table, I missed my parents so much. Their monthly call was not for a couple of weeks and as much as I was looking forward to it, I dreaded telling them that the café had been closed. I hoped I'd have some positive news by then. It was going to be terrible to admit I'd messed up and frittered away the money Grandma had left me.

"How are you going to cope with the café closed?" asked Paul.

A wave of emotion washed over me. I opened my mouth to speak but there was a lump in my throat. I gulped, swallowing it away.

"Paul, let the girl eat." Carol gestured to her husband probably picking up on my discomfort. "Becky, Henry can take you off to Corelli's wine bar later, to cheer you up. Can't you, dear?"

"Sure," he said.

I didn't look at H, I bet there were a thousand things he'd rather do than take me out.

Constance strolled in licking her lips and made herself comfortable on the wicker conservatory sofa.

Later, after we'd had dessert – which was a very sweet and gorgeous Tiramisu – we planned the christening. Originally, I was only making the cakes, but Carol asked me to provide a full buffet. It was kind of her to help me out, the perishable ingredients I had could be put to use.

As H and I left the house, I carried Constance in my arms.

He turned to me. "Do you want to go to the wine bar or somewhere else?"

"It's a lovely evening. I quite fancy a walk – to clear my head."

"No worries. Let's take a walk down to the bay and watch the sun set."

I smiled. "Great idea."

We dropped Constance off at my house and I changed into flat sandals. We took a walk along the beach, rather than the prom, barefoot, paddling in the cool water. Now if it was a date, it would have been a lovely one. But it was 'just mates', of course.

Once we reached the end of the beach, I brushed sand from my feet and slipped my sandals back on. The steps at the bottom were rather steep.

"Here, let me help," said H as he offered me his hand. His palm enveloped my entire hand as he hoisted me up the stone steps. Although, he seemed to hold on a little longer than was necessary.

"Thanks," I said as I retrieved my hand. H had a habit of being a little overprotective.

We walked back to my house along the prom as the sun disappeared into the watery horizon. Strolling alongside other couples, illuminated by the soft light from the traditional street lamps, we exchanged childhood memories of the bay and wondered whether we'd ever crossed paths as kids. We'd certainly attended a couple of summer shows at the same time.

"Maybe we could do a future event together," he said as we crossed the road. Ahead of us, I saw a taxi stop and Olivia got out. She leaned in, as if kissing someone goodbye.

H continued. "I was wondering if you'd like to come with me to..."

I zoned out of what he was saying and stared in the taxi as it passed by, peering in the window to see who was inside. With it being dark, it was difficult to make out any features but their silhouette suggested a tall man. It was possibly Nathan. I needed to take a closer look at that relationship.

I felt H's eyes upon me. "So what do you think?"

"Well, it could have been Nathan, I guess, they might be having some sort of romance."

"At least someone is," muttered H. "I guess you're talking about Olivia," he said pointing at her back as she walked ahead of us.

"Yes, I was. Whoever was in that cab, is someone Olivia doesn't want her mum to see, otherwise why would she get the taxi to drop her off five minutes from where she lives?" I turned to H. "So, what were you saying?"

"It can wait." He stopped walking. "We've arrived at your house."

"Oh yes." I looked to the café window and Constance pressed her nose up against the inside of the French doors. I laughed. When I turned around to say goodbye. H was rather close and I couldn't take a step backwards to widen the space between us, as the wall was only inches away.

"Thanks for cheering me up," I said looking up to his face. "I feel so much better." I leaned forward to give him an air kiss. But he moved in even closer. I dodged to the side quickly, like a sparring boxer. *That was close,* I thought. I nearly ended up kissing his mouth. I blushed horribly, glad that we were outside in the dark. "Whoa. Sorry," I said giving a half laugh. "What on earth happened there?"

"Er ... yeah," he said, thrusting his hands into his pockets.

I mock-punched his arm. "See you around, pal." I turned as heat rose up my neck and sidestepped so I could open the gate. Embarrassment tingled all over my body. *What a numpty I am,* I said to myself. I watched H stride back up the prom into the darkness of the night. Static shot up my back, I turned and jumped. Ben was at the patio café table again, rolling a cigarette.

I felt the buzz of electricity up my arm and shivered. I didn't think I'd ever get used to seeing ghosts. I thought I'd try ignoring him. I opened the front door and Constance appeared, she rubbed against my legs and purred loudly. I bent down to pick her up but she sashayed over to Ben's ghost. Her coat bushing out as she went. I raised my eyes to look at him. I sighed, realising I'd have to collect whatever message he wanted to give me. I moved closer to him as the static intensified, like pins being dug into my palms.

"Quick, what is it?" I said rubbing my hands together.

He mouthed something I could not hear.

I inched closer. "Pardon?"

"What ... about ... Peter?" He flickered and was gone.

I grabbed Constance and went inside, double

locking the door. Okay so it wouldn't keep a ghost out but I needed to feel safe. I felt invaded.

"Had a nice evening?" Dannie asked, smirking as she leaned against the banister. "I watched you out of the bathroom window, dodging his kiss. You must be the only woman in the world that doesn't fancy that guy."

I couldn't smile. I was experiencing the aftershock spasms from seeing Ben.

"Hey, sorry I was only winding you up. Are you okay?" She looked concerned.

"I've agreed to investigate Ben's death for Katherine. I'm just a bit stressed out."

She shook her head. "You've got enough to worry about with the café closed. Why have you taken it on?"

I couldn't tell her about Ben, it wasn't fair on her. "I felt sorry for Katherine."

"You need to put yourself first, Becky."

"I'm fine, I'll make myself a drink and relax. You go on up to bed."

Once alone in the snug, I opened the note-taking app on my phone as I drank a hot chocolate. Looking at the small screen, I considered my number one suspect was Andrew Farr, because of the pressure he was piling on Katherine. Not forgetting his temper, having heard him kicking off at the council.

As awful as it seemed, I had to consider Olivia a suspect, as she was due to inherit the pier upon

Katherine's death. From what I'd witnessed, there was a lot of tension between mother and daughter.

Another possibility was Nathan. Maybe he wanted Katherine out of the way so Olivia could inherit the pier and then he would propose marriage? And then there was Clive the ex-manager, he was a very angry person. But to kill? Maybe the killer saw the hammer and went for it, in a moment of madness. I sighed. By the looks of it, Katherine had alienated many people and now I had another name to add to the list. I tapped in the name 'Peter', which Ben had given me. I'd need to ask Katherine about that. But first thing in the morning, I was off to see Clive.

CHAPTER 9

"What's the plan?" asked Jeff as I jumped into his van.

Constance popped her head out of my bag as I placed it on my lap.

I didn't want to mention to Jeff that I'd seen Ben, he would have pestered me into rigging up my whole house with his equipment. "Katherine has arranged for staff and friends to say farewell to Ben. His body hasn't been released yet, but the family are planning a private funeral out of town, so have donated money for a wake to be held here in Branden Bay. We're inviting Clive on Katherine's behalf." I lifted an envelope with Clive Dent and his address written on it. "She's prepared an invite."

"So where are we headed?"

"He lives on the same estate as you." I grinned to

myself. The similarities between Jeff and Clive were uncanny. "You might know it. Magnolia Drive?"

Jeff put the van into gear. "Not sure exactly where that is, I don't think it's on my side of the estate."

I tapped the postcode into the sat nav app on my phone. It was only a short journey and as we rattled up Clive's street, there was not one magnolia tree in sight.

"What's he like, this Clive?" asked Jeff as he slowed the van.

"Just wait and see. I think you two will get along great."

The sat nav app declared that we had reached our destination and the van shuddered to a halt.

"There's number twelve," I said pointing to a grey brick semi with a yellow front door with a ceramic pot on each side, filled with colourful posies.

Once we'd walked up the path, I rang the bell holding Constance in my arms.

A lady in her sixties answered. "Yes?" She reminded me of Jeff's mum but without the harsh face, full of accusation. In its place was a weak smile. "Sorry, I've not got the money to buy what you're selling," she said as she began to close the door.

"We're not selling anything," I said.

"Oh." She glanced at Constance. "No, that's not my cat, I've never seen it around here before. Take it to the vet to see if it's microchipped."

"This is my cat." I smiled. "I've come to deliver an invitation to Clive, for Ben's wake."

"Oh. I see. You two must have worked with him on the pier."

I smiled and didn't correct her.

She stood to one side. "You'd better come in then. It's nice for Clive to have visitors. He's only had two since he left the pier, including that lovely Olivia. She's nothing like her mother. Go through to the front room, I'll put the kettle on."

We walked into the hall and through the first door on the right, bringing us to a sitting room. It had a worn carpet, striped wallpaper and a border that ran just underneath the coving, depicting a repeated picture of a cherub playing a harp. The room was clean and neat but somewhat dated.

"I'll fetch Clive, he's in the garage. He converted into what I think they call a man cave these days. But to me, it's just like a playroom. Full of gadgets and his computer stuff."

We made ourselves comfortable on the sofa.

Jeff looked around nervously. "This place gives me the creeps," he whispered.

"Really?" I thought Jeff's comment odd considering the house reminded me of his own home. After a minute, the tall and gangly Clive entered the room. My eyes darted to Jeff for his reaction. But there was none.

Mrs Dent shuffled in behind Clive. "Sit down, boy. It's your friends from the pier. They've come about Ben's wake." She nodded at us.

"These people are not my friends. Who are you?"

"I'm Becky, this is Jeff and my cat's called Constance."

Constance gave a low meow.

Clive looked at me as if it was weird to take your cat into someone's house. "What are you really here for? Has Katherine put you up to this?"

"She asked us to come over and invite you to Ben's wake."

"I doubt Katherine cares whether I'm there or not. She wants me to drop the tribunal case. I'm not stupid."

"Not at all," I said, in a breezy voice.

Constance gave another low meow.

Clive and his mother slumped in side-by-side armchairs which faced the television. We were perched on a sofa to the side of them. My cat approached Mrs Dent.

"Constance," I called her back.

"That's okay, dear. She'll be fine," said Mrs Dent as Constance sniffed at her blue velvet slippers.

I turned to Clive with, what I hoped was, a sincere expression. "At the request of Ben's family, Katherine is arranging a wake for his friends at the Branden Arms."

"Why hasn't she come herself?" asked Mrs Dent. "That woman ruined my Clive's life. She's got an awful lot to answer for."

I looked Clive in the eye. "Katherine said Ben thought the world of you. It's only right for you to be there and she didn't want to antagonise you by saying the wrong thing."

We heard the click of the kettle from the next room and Mrs Dent groaned to standing and shuffled out. Constance returned to me and jumped on my lap.

Clive stroked his scrappy beard and squinted at me, Jeff and Constance in turn. "I'm sure I recognise you."

I shuffled in my seat. "I think Katherine misses you."

"More like she's scared of being sued. According to my lawyer, there should always be a double check of dangerous equipment. She shouldn't have blamed me for the oven being left on. It's down to the management to ensure the safety of staff."

"I thought you were the manager?"

"I wasn't ultimately responsible. It's the owner's job to set up risk assessment files and the related procedures." He leaned back in the chair with his hands on the arm rests. "Katherine's at fault and she expects me to show up to the wake and pretend everything's okay." He shook his head. "It's not okay."

"I think she wants to make peace. She told me herself how sorry she is that you two parted ways. She's genuinely upset."

"I heard there were accidents over there and that Katherine's gone mad. Thinking it's something paranormal. She should give up the pier and move on. It's gone downhill ever since Mr Sheringham died." He paused as he stared at us both. "Ah. I knew I recognised you. You're the medium and you're her assistant." He stared at us. "I've seen you in the Gazette."

I nudged Jeff. He'd been noticeably quiet.

"Yes, that's us," Jeff said. "We checked the pier for any sign of paranormal activity and found nothing."

"So, you're here checking me out, as part of your little amateur investigation. I've read all about you. This has nothing to do with the wake." He stood up from the chair. "Katherine's out of order."

Constance dug her claws into my lap and I gulped.

We were getting recognised, a lot. My face burned red.

Mrs Dent came in with a tray of slopping teas. "They're all milk with one sugar and there's no biscuits."

Clive pointed at us. "This pair of muppets aren't staying. Show them the door."

Constance hissed as Clive left the room.

"And don't tell them anything," he called over his shoulder.

Mrs Dent waited until we heard a door slam. "Have your tea first, my dears, seeing as I've made them." She offered the tray to us and we took our drinks. "You'll have to excuse my Clive. He's ever so sensitive when it comes to the pier. It's been his whole world and he feels really let down." She placed the tray on the table.

Constance jumped from my lap and returned to the arm of Mrs Dent's chair.

"He's also found it hard this year, ever since my Eric

died." She glanced at a framed photo on the sideboard. "All Clive ever does is sit in that garage with them computers and gadgets. Some nights he even sleeps in there." She reached for the photograph of her late husband and stroked the picture. "My Eric was such a good man." She returned the picture to the sideboard and gave us a watery smile. "It's never easy being a step-parent you know. Hark at me going on." She shuffled over to her armchair and sat down.

"What sort of business is it that Clive does in there?" I asked.

She looked in the direction of the garage then lowered her voice. "He said not to tell you anything." She sighed. "But he should be proud of himself. He makes computers from scratch – he was always into building things as a kid. He loved making stuff. Him and Eric used to spend hours making models and painting them. He's been doing great and says he's enough orders in, so I shouldn't need to worry about money for much longer. He's even buying a car." She whispered to the point where she was only mouthing the words. "He's got a tin stuffed with notes." She leaned back in her chair. "Such a good lad. Always has been. He wouldn't do no harm to anyone. Even that Katherine." Mrs Dent took a sip of her tea. "She's always been a nightmare that one, from when she was young. Carrying on around town with Darren like that."

"Who's Darren?" I asked.

"The one who got her pregnant. Olivia's father." She gave a low whistle. "Now that was a shot gun wedding. Her Dad had the pair of them down the aisle before the baby started showing. But you can't keep that sort of thing secret in Branden Bay. The marriage didn't last long, poor little Olivia." She sighed. "The product of a broken home."

Katherine hadn't mentioned her ex-husband. "Where is Olivia's dad now?"

"He upped and went abroad." She paused. "Now, listen to me being a right old gossip. My Clive knows me well," she said with a laugh. She put her hand out. "Leave that invitation with me and I'll see if I can get my boy to poor old Ben's wake." She took the envelope from me. "Word on the street says he was murdered, is that true?"

"The police are looking into it," I said as I rose from the sofa. I felt I'd exhausted the conversation and wanted to check out this Darren, Olivia's dad as well as the mysterious Peter. I seemed to have an ever-growing list of suspects.

"THAT GUY IS SAD," Jeff said as we got into the van having left the Dent's house.

I pulled on my seatbelt as Constance made herself comfortable on my lap. "Why do you say that?"

"Still living with his mum. And staying in his garage all day."

"I'll be honest, Jeff – he reminds me of you."

Constance meowed, as if in agreement.

"I'm nothing like him. And I'm still in education. I need to keep my outgoings down. I don't want to get left with a massive student debt."

I attached my seatbelt, being careful not to knock Constance onto the van floor. "You dress the same. He seems as obsessed with his computers, as you are with the paranormal."

Jeff tutted. His leg pushed down on the clutch with a thud. He'd clearly taken offence.

"If you don't move out of your mum's house, you'll end up just like him," I added.

Jeff huffed and crunched the van's gears before lurching forward.

I grabbed Constance, so she didn't hit the dash. As we reached the end of the road, I asked him to drop me at the pier. I needed to speak to Katherine.

Jeff mumbled a goodbye to me as Constance and I got out of the van. I watched as the van rattled down the seafront. I knew I'd hit a nerve and no way would he be so sensitive if there wasn't an element of truth in what I'd said.

I carried Constance down the pier. It wasn't so busy that day and the sea was out, leaving a large expanse of sand, where various species of birds pecked, looking for tasty seafood.

Katherine had moved back into her office and waved me in. "How did it go?"

"Clive wasn't that responsive, he asked us to leave."

She sighed. "So that backfired then."

"There was something his mother mentioned though which I need to discuss with you."

"Yes?"

I sat down opposite her. "It's about your ex-husband."

She sat back with a jolt. "Oh. He lives in the Balearic Islands. In Ibiza."

"When did you last see him?"

"I, er ... not for years." She rubbed her petite nose. "He left when Olivia was two years old. She has no relationship with him." She pushed a stray hair from her forehead. "When you say ex-husband, the truth is, I never filed for divorce. I guess I would have if I'd met someone new."

"You never mentioned him. What's his full name?"

"Darren Box. I never took his name when we married. It doesn't have the local history that Sheringham has. And he used to call me Kat."

"So, if you are still legally married, he could have a claim on your property. Did you have a prenup?"

She shook her head. "When we married my father was still alive. The pier wasn't mine and I never imagined I'd inherit it at such a young age. Mother wasn't interested in it, so when Dad died at fifty-eight, it came to me."

"I'll have to add Darren to my list of suspects. If you find any contact details for him. Let me know."

"Of course."

I hesitated. Choosing my words. "I've had a name come through."

"What, psychically?"

I nodded. "Peter?"

Katherine sat back. "I had an uncle called Peter. He was the original heir to the pier, not my father. When my grandfather died, instead of the pier going to Peter, the eldest son, who he'd had with his first wife, it went to Dad instead."

"Why was that? Did they fall out?"

"Peter, was in prison."

"For what?"

"Robbery. He was involved in a bank job and linked to various high-profile heists in London's Hatton Garden."

"Ah, where all the jewellery shops are."

"Yes. He used to be great at blowing things up." The papers called him Diamond Pete. Not that they found any on him. He was about forty when they put him inside. He must be in his sixties now."

"With good behaviour maybe he's out."

Katherine visibly swallowed. "You think he's been released and is out to get me?"

"If you die, do you think he would come forward as the rightful heir?"

"It's certainly possible that he could contest the will."

"If he's been released, he's definitely on my list of suspects"

Katherine shook her head. "I think we're getting carried away here. I'd have at least seen him about the pier, if he was causing accidents. And I'm sure the papers would have ran a story, if he'd been released. Although, he's not been mentioned for over two decades and has certainly gone off the radar."

"What prison is he in?"

"I've really no idea, the last time I heard his name was when Dad took the pier on. As you can imagine, my family soon pretended he'd never existed. He brought a huge amount of shame to the Sheringham name."

"I'll see what I can find out about him. You might want to mention him to the police."

She shook her head. "I'll wait to see what you come up with first. I have more faith in you."

I gulped. It was nice for her to think so well of me, but I couldn't help feeling like a fraud, fumbling around in the dark

Back home, I opened my front door, to find Constance waiting for me in the porch. Dannie called out, as she descended the stairs.

"You have an email from the fairground. Apparently, you've got a job offer?"

"Great. I applied as a casual worker." Things were really moving along.

"They want you to sell cookies. They'll provide the ingredients and clothes, just turn up at seven thirty tomorrow morning."

Constance rubbed against my legs.

"Shall I see if I can get a job too?" Asked Dannie. "The college course doesn't start until September."

"No, I'll be there snooping as part of the investigation. You focus on the bookkeeping and the licence application for the café, while I earn some money for our living expenses, until we reopen."

"Don't get yourself into trouble or draw negative attention. I'm sure that won't help."

"Let's have dinner I'm starving," I said changing the subject.

Later in the snug, while I listened to music, I added to the case notes held on my smartphone. The next day, I would be checking out Andrew Farr.

CHAPTER 10

There was a gentle morning breeze as I sauntered along a quiet prom on the way to the fairground. As I passed the pier entrance, I spotted Olivia chatting with Nathan who was presumably on his way home after the night shift. I wondered whether it was possible that they were having a romance. They seemed an unlikely couple. Him being so authoritarian, he'd be more like her dad than a boyfriend. *Maybe that's it?* I thought. *She wants a father figure*. With her own leaving when she was so young.

The fairground entrance was only a few yards away from the pier and I appreciated why Andrew would want to make them into one attraction. The traditional fairground had always been the same in my lifetime. There was the helter-skelter, a carousel and a rickety roller-coaster. *You wouldn't get me on that!* I thought. I loved the fairground, the coconut shies,

Punch and Judy. But fast rides were not my scene. I used to watch Grandma from the ground, as her bushy hair billowed in the wind as she was flung this way and that. She had an adventurous streak which I'd always admired and had made me love her even more. A lump formed in my throat. I took a deep breath of sea air and carried on walking until I reached the entrance.

Andrew Farr was just inside, dressed as a ring-master with a red velvet tailed jacket and a black and gold top hat. "I have to say what an absolute honour it is to have someone of your reputation working at the fairground. And from such a wonderful family."

I was quite taken aback. "Did you know my Grand-parents?"

"Absolutely. I remember your grandmother, her wavy red hair was quite mesmerising. There are pictures of her in Branden Bay Museum, from when she was a fortune teller on the pier. And of course, she was well known around here for her acting. Not forget-ting her stint as a Bond girl."

I was surprised that I didn't know she featured in the museum. Grandma had never taken me there. She'd been modest and rarely spoke of herself. It wasn't the first time that I felt sad, not knowing more about Grandma's life. Our time together had always revolved around me.

"And you too," he added. "Have studied performing arts?"

"Yes, sadly I wasn't successful in gaining exciting parts."

"I was so pleased you applied for the position." He gestured in the direction of my house. "I noticed you'd been shut down when I was passing. Branden Bay Council are a total shambles. You'd think they'd want the town to prosper, but no. All they do is put obstacles in the way of successful entrepreneurs like you and I." He smiled at me.

I quite liked the entrepreneur tag, especially when it was preceded with 'successful', but Andrew was laying it on a bit too thick. Maybe trying to put me off the scent.

"Before I start, I wonder if you could run me up a simple contract of employment, because the council are on my case. They may think I'm catering for you otherwise."

"Follow me. The offices are this way. My assistant may have already prepared it."

We passed the coconut shies and the 'hook a duck' stall and entered a stone building.

Once inside there was a small waiting area and various doors with notices on.

"Andrew opened the door with Administration Office written on it. "Oh, he's not there, let's wait in my office. Hopefully he won't be long."

I followed him in. There was an old-fashioned leather topped desk, a bookcase and a Chesterfield sofa.

"This room hasn't changed since my grandfather's days," Andrew said as he led me inside.

There was a huge plan for modernisation on the wall. It included the pier as well as the fairground.

"This looks interesting," I said. "It's a great fusion of the traditional and modern."

"Too modern for Branden Bay District Council, I'm afraid. They want to keep everything one hundred percent traditional. There's no point in me wasting any further energy on it. I've had a total rethink. I'm planning on turning the whole town into a Victorian experience, with everyone dressed up in traditional clothes of the era. When I say everyone, I mean all local businesses, like yourself, and any of the locals who want to get involved. The town would become one huge attraction, bringing hordes of visitors to the bay. I'm in talks with Somerset Railway to put on a steam train to bring visitors here from across the county."

"That's amazing," I said, feeling myself getting excited and thinking of all the traditional cakes I could bake.

"I've tried speaking to Katherine Sheringham about it. She's in the same boat as me, having to keep all the original features and spend a ridiculous amount on maintenance. But she thinks all I want to do is take over her business. Although, she's clearly shaken up after the recent death." He gave a large sigh. "Still, small steps. I've got the Gazette in doing a piece on today's Victorian theme and hopefully that will gain interest from the locals."

"You're really serious about this then?" I said.

"Absolutely. And I've a great outfit for you to wear today. It's not arrived yet, it's coming from a fancy dress supplier in Bristol."

This is so up my street, I thought. I was most chuffed that he'd ordered something in especially for me. I was so looking forward to trying on a traditional Victorian dress. Although, I had to remember, I was supposed to be here snooping on Andrew.

The door swung open and a flustered young guy leaned inside.

"There you are Jack," Andrew said. "I need you to run off a casual contract for Becky here. She's on the system, the full name is Rebecca James."

"Sure, but we've got a situation with the guy on stilts."

"He's not turned up drunk again, has he?"

"He's wobbling all over the place singing dirty songs. We need to sober him up before we open, or send him home. But he won't listen to me."

"Make him a strong coffee and I'll see whether it's salvageable." He turned to me. "Sorry about this. Wait here and I'll be right back with that contract."

I wandered over to the door and peeked outside into the reception area and watched Andrew and Jack disappear outside. There was no-one around, so I slowly shut the door, realising it might be my only opportunity. I looked around his desk. Apart from a phone, pen tray and calendar there was nothing to see. My heart thud hard as I opened the drawer. I wasn't quite sure what I was looking for, but I had to start somewhere. I glanced inside and lifted a few papers. At the bottom, was a ticket to the Summer Masked Ball. I shuffled around inside, but there was nothing else to see, apart from stationery items. I heard the door handle turn, so slammed the drawer and gave a fake sneeze.

It was Andrew.

That was close, I thought.

"Are you okay?"

"Yes," I smiled, feeling my cheeks burn.

"I'll take you to the cookie kiosk, Jack will bring your contract over when it's ready."

I breathed in a sugary aroma as we passed one of the kiosks where donuts were deep frying. Staff in various period costumes were preparing their stalls.

We reached my new location of work. It was a small shed, situated around the edge of a large, concreted area where I had previously seen pop up shows, including jugglers and magicians. The 'Punch and Judy' stand was also there.

The cookie kiosk was a grimy, wooden hut with peeling paint. As Andrew opened the door it creaked.

Really? I thought, wondering how my perfectly clean café had been shut down and this old shack was okay. *It doesn't seem fair.* I followed Andrew inside the musty smelling space. There was a tiny sink, a cupboard with a small worktop above and an oven containing baking trays.

"I'll drop the float down to you. And there's the dough." Andrew pointed to a bag of ready-made mix sitting in the corner.

I lifted it. It was heavy and rock solid. "You're joking. I can't use this. I'd assumed you'd be handing me flour, sugar, and butter."

"It cuts down on time and mess."

"But people might think they're mine."

"No they won't." He pointed to a sign that said *traditional fair recipe.*

He left me to it and marched away with his hat in his hand, very much the man in charge, his light blonde hair glinting in the morning sun. He was certainly charming when he was not angry, not really like someone I'd imagine to be a hammer-wielding murderer. But I had to remember, I'd heard him in a temper.

I got straight to work, managing to soften the dough enough to make cookie-shaped discs for the baking trays. Ten minutes later I pulled the first batch out of the small oven. I flapped a clean baking tray over the top of the cookies to cool them down. They were chocolate chip. I picked one up and bit into it. The chocolate was bitter and the high sugar content made the biscuit brittle. *I can't serve these,* I thought.

"Could I please try one of your cookies?"

I turned around at the recognisable voice. "Izzy?"

She took a step back. "Becky, darling, what on earth are you doing here?"

"With the café being closed, I need a job."

She raised one elegant eyebrow. "You can't pull the wool over my eyes, sweetie." She scanned the area to ensure no-one was listening. "You're undercover, aren't you?"

I blushed as Andrew Farr reappeared at the kiosk.

"Isobel, thank you for arriving so early. I'm pleased the Gazette is covering today's events." He smiled.

"Such a genius marketing idea of yours to get Becky to provide the cookies," Izzy said. "Everyone knows she's the best baker in town."

"Indeed," Andrew said running a hand through his unruly hair. "I'd better carry on with my rounds." He strode off to the neighbouring kiosk.

"I'm not providing the cookies,' I said to Izzy. "Don't put that in the paper. I'm here as an employee."

"Noted." She peered at me. "Is Andrew your prime suspect?"

"Shh," I said as a middle-aged woman approached. She was dressed as a chimney sweep, carrying a large bag on wheels. She handed me a money wallet. "Tie this around your waist. Inside are two fives, a ten and the rest is change. Don't remove it."

"Thank you," I said watching as she moved to the donut kiosk.

Izzy leaned into the hut and stretched her long

arm inside. She picked up a cookie between her forefinger and thumb with the rest of her fingers fanned out. Frowning at it, she took a small bite. Her face slowly changed from serine to scrunched-up in a nano-second. She pulled a tissue from her bag and wiped away the contents of her mouth. "What on earth are they?" she said fanning her face.

"Chocolate chip."

"My assessment would be synthetic, brown-coloured, muck. It's certainly not chocolate."

"I had to use ready mix."

"Ready mix what? Cement? I nearly lost a tooth!" She ran her tongue over her front teeth. "You can't sell these. It'll ruin your reputation, darling." She shook her head. "Remember, I'm a food critic. I couldn't possibly say I ate a tasty cookie at the fairground if it was actually revolting."

"I didn't think you were a critic anymore?"

"I'm doing a day in the life of a Victorian fair-ground. Having a traditional cookie is part of the experience."

Andrew reappeared. "Miss James you've got work to do." He winked at me but I guessed he was being serious. I needed to bake a day's worth of cookies before opening time.

"Izzy says I can't sell these and I have to agree. They're pretty revolting." I handed one to him.

He crunched on it, chewed then swallowed. "Okay,

so it's not going to win Branden Bay's bake-off, but the punters here will eat anything."

"Izzy has a point, though. What if my regulars come along and buy them?" I went hot and cold at the thought.

Andrew's fair eyebrows lowered into a frown. "We don't have the ingredients here and I don't have time to get to the wholesalers."

I turned the oven off and tipped the cookies into the bin. "I've loads of ingredients at home."

BACK AT THE HOUSE, I measured out a quantity of flour, when Dannie entered the kitchen. "What happened to the job? Did you get the sack already?"

"No, of course not. They had ready-made cookie dough and it was disgusting. I'm having to make them up here."

She tutted. "You can't use this kitchen for commercial purposes. Remember?"

I knew she was right. "I'm sure Elks won't find out, and I don't feel guilty, as this kitchen would pass an inspection with flying colours. The kiosk isn't big enough for my equipment. I can't make it all up by hand it would take forever. I need to use the mixer."

Dannie crossed her arms. "Don't blame me when you ruin your chances for a licence."

I carried on, with the money wallet still tied around

my waist. True, I was breaking the rules, but my reputation was on the line.

Two hours later, after mixing and baking batches in turn, I'd filled Grandma's old, wheeled basket trolley with boxed cookies. I opened my front door and looked up and down Beach Road, making sure there was no sign of anyone that looked as if they worked for the council. Confident I hadn't been spotted, I shut up and wheeled the basket down the path. It was extra heavy as Constance had decided she was coming with me and hitched a lift, perching herself on the basket rim. Andrew had allowed me to bake the cookies at home, on the understanding that I returned to the fairground by ten o'clock. It was ten minutes to the hour. I'd be bang on time. Although I needed to change clothes. Andrew had messaged me to say my costume was in the staff room.

At the fairground, I made my way to the stone building where Andrew's office was and opened the door with *staff room* written on it. Once inside there was a rail with only one costume bag. It had my name pinned to it. I left the basket of cookies and took the costume to the staff toilets with excitement, until I removed the outfit from the bag.

This isn't a Victorian lady's dress? I asked myself.

It was a purple blouse, a long black velvet skirt, a multicoloured paisley shawl with a matching headscarf. *He's joking surely?* I thought as I went into the cubicle and pulled on the outfit. By the sinks, I looked at myself in the full-length mirror. The skirt was far too long.

Constance meowed, circling me, as if excited.

The door opened and a young woman with long dark hair walked in. "Nice. The colour of that top suits you. I love it."

"I was expecting traditional, upmarket Victorian lady. I look like I'm ready for the fields."

She laughed. "You're the fortune teller. Didn't Andrew tell you?"

"No." I frowned. "He didn't."

"He's not going to pass up on the opportunity, when we have the Medium of Branden Bay working for us." She lifted a fake white beard. "Count yourself lucky, I'm Charles Darwin." She put her beard on a chair and took the paisley shawl and wrapped it around my waist, over the money bag. Then tied the smaller scarf around my head. "That's better, now you really look the part."

I exchanged a glance with my reflection. *Oh well, this is an undercover operation,* I thought. *It's not supposed to be fun.* "Come on Constance," I said. "We've got a job to do."

CHAPTER 11

I pulled the basket of cookies towards the area where the kiosk was situated. It seemed that most staff were at their posts, wearing an array of Victorian dress. I took a moment to look about me, it was like stepping back in time.

"Smile," Andrew said as he took a snap of me with his phone. "Nice touch bringing the cat." He took a snap of Constance who tilted her head as if posing. "It's for our social media site. We're posting throughout the day and asking people to share our page to win a season ticket to the fairground. Now get to your station. We open in five minutes." Andrew appeared decidedly cooler towards me than he'd been earlier in the day. I guessed he was in manager-mode. He gestured me to follow him. Constance trotted beside me. When we reached the wooden shed, there was the addition of a table and chairs with a blackboard A-frame beside it. Written upon it was 'The Medium of Branden Bay. Free cookie with every fortune told'.

Oh no, I thought. Dressing up as a fortune teller was bad enough.

Andrew pointed at the sign. "You can charge what you like and keep the profits, as you provided the ingredients."

"But I'm not a fortune teller."

He laughed. "You are today."

Constance jumped onto the table and arched her back with her nose in the air, looking around her, as if she was the prize-winner at a pet show.

"This isn't what I expected, Andrew. I'm selling cookies, not ripping people off."

"It's entertainment. If it was good enough for your grandmother when she was young, it's good enough for you. She was a real star in her day."

Constance gave a loud purr.

Andrew looked at his watch. "The doors are opening so hurry up." He strode off.

I parked the basket inside the shed and closed the A frame, leaning it against the side of the kiosk. There was no way I was going to be playing that game. I took time to arrange the cookies on the table and sat down as the first customers wandered over.

The cookies proved to be popular and I got a kick out of selling my bakes again.

Izzy waved at me. Bypassing the queue, she sidled up, picked a cookie and took a delicate bite. "Divine darling. Mmm." She moved to the side as I served a woman with short blonde hair.

"Uncle Henry. It's your girlfriend."

H and his twin nephews, Ollie and Freddy, were next in line, behind the lady I was serving.

"The one you arrested," the boy continued.

"Yeah, the one that was in prison," said the other. They were identical and I hadn't seen enough of them to be able to tell them apart.

Izzy laughed. "I'll leave you to it sweetie." She moved on.

"Four cookies please," the woman I was serving said, in a clipped voice.

"It wasn't prison," said H. "Just the police cells." He raised his eyebrows at me. "I hope she's behaving herself right now."

I focussed my gaze on the kids and slapped on what I thought was a pleasant grin and nodded. "That's me. Well, me that was in the cells, not me being Uncle Henry's erm ..."

The woman I was serving snatched the bag as I spoke. She thrust her hand out for the change, as if I intended to keep it.

"You look hot," H said as he reached the front of the queue.

I blushed.

"Oh, I don't mean hot as in ... I mean hot in temperature. With that outfit on. Not that you're not hot in another way."

"Urgh," Ollie and Freddy said in unison.

He leaned forward and spoke into my ear. "Please tell me you're not here snooping around."

I felt the warmth of his breath and gulped. "I'm selling cookies that's all." I filled a paper bag and passed it over.

"How much do I owe you?" he asked.

"Five pounds."

He gave me a twenty and I handed back the fifteen change.

"Nice try," he said as he thrust a ten-pound note back at me. "That went out of circulation in 2018. It's the second one I've seen in a week. A few have been doing the rounds."

"Oh! Sorry, I didn't notice." I took back the note.

He lowered his voice. "We've got someone on it. Tell Mr Farr he can exchange it for a new one at his bank."

"I'll have to give you some in coins, I'm afraid." I deposited the change into his open hand.

"That's fine, no doubt this pair will spend it on the rides."

He took a large bite out of a cookie. His eyes widened and he nodded his head. "It's perfect. Just like ..."

"Uncle Henry, can we go on the Waltzer?"

H gave me a small wave as his nephews dragged him towards the attractions.

"Wake up Becky," said Andrew as he appeared in front of me with the A frame I had hidden. He placed it in front of the table then lifted a megaphone to his mouth. "Roll up, roll up for Branden Bay's resident fortune teller."

My face flushed hot.

"Isn't that Becky from Connie's Café?" I heard someone say.

"Yeah. Desperate times. Desperate measures," said another.

"Get to work then," Andrew said as he swiped a cookie and strode away.

He's really taking the biscuit, I thought as a couple in their twenties who were next in line stepped up to the table.

"Can you tell my future?" asked the young woman. She had huge blue eyes and light brown hair which was dead straight to her shoulders.

"It's a con," said the guy she was with as he thrust his hands into his sweatpants' pockets.

I can't argue with that, I thought. "The cookies are five pounds for four."

He handed over the payment in coins.

After depositing them into the money wallet, I put four cookies from a box into a paper bag using tongs. "Here you are."

The young woman nodded as she took the cookies

then sat on the chair in front of the table. "What's my fortune then?"

I heard Andrew's voice in my head. *If it was good enough for your grandmother ...* Constance sat on my lap and meowed. A sense of adventure seeped through my veins.

"What's your name?" I asked

"Ellie," she replied.

I put my hand on Ellie's and shut my eyes.

Constance gave a long and low meow.

All I could think of was how Andrew was playing me for a fool. I thought a generic piece of advice would be safe.

"Never let a man take advantage of you."

"What?" her boyfriend said. "Are you having a laugh?"

"If a man treats you badly, you need to move on."

"Hey, I don't treat her bad."

I ignored him and opened my eyes. "That's it, I'm afraid. Nothing else is coming in."

"You're amazing," the girl said. "That makes a lot of sense to me."

I heard clapping. Behind Ellie, a much longer queue had formed. Her boyfriend was not happy and muttered something inappropriate about me.

I noticed Andrew was back, taking pictures.

"Can I go next?" asked an older lady with a blue headscarf. "I wanna know how much longer I've got left before I die." She thrust a five-pound note into my hand. "Forget the cookies I'm on a diet."

"Even if I could give you an accurate answer, it would be unethical. My advice to you is to live each day as if it counts, then you know you've covered all bases." I put my hand out to return her fiver, but she refused it.

"Tell me something else."

Constance dug her claws into my lap.

Come on Becky, I told myself. *You have a degree in performing arts, you can handle this.* I took a deep breath. I needed to go with the flow and if I wanted to get back to Andrew's office for a better look around, I had to at least appear as if I was doing the job. I took her hand. "Now let me see." I gave a little moan. Hearing the crowd gasp, a flutter of adrenaline hit my chest, reminding me of my time on stage, in my student days. I was in the zone.

Constance gave a low meow.

I took a deep breath. "You like gardening, you have a bench for two. I see a man wearing uniform gazing, as you weed your flower bed."

"That's my Bert! He must be watching over me."

I opened my eyes to see tears in her eyes and gulped, she seemed quite taken. I was hit with a huge pang of guilt.

"You're good. I will have a couple of those cookies after all," she said.

"I'm next," a girl with piercings said as she sat down.

I felt confident with Constance on my lap and gave the girl advice about getting her life in order. I suggested she signed up for a hairdressing course. She seemed happy with that as she walked off with a bag of cookies.

The queue became longer, rather than shorter. I was aware of Andrew in the background, taking yet more pictures. After about ten customers, I felt a teensy bit like a fraud. Although weirdly, they all seemed to say my words made perfect sense. Constance was with me the whole time and appeared to be enjoying it, her coat was so bushed out, she looked twice her size.

An elderly man flashed a fiver at me.

"I need a break I'm afraid, to restore my psychic energy." I lifted Constance into my arms and rose from the table to a collective groan of disappointment from the queue.

Andrew approached me. "While you're resting your powers, I'd like to take more shots." He pointed to his left. "This way."

Constance jumped to the floor. I decided to do a few more photos, then slip away to get a better look in his office. Andrew stopped me for a picture at the coconut shy. After a few shots of me sitting on a carousel horse and one of me with a toffee apple, he pointed to the Big Dipper roller coaster.

"Oh, no. I'm not going on that," I said.

Constance trotted towards the attraction.

Andrew laughed. "I only want a picture of you in the car. That's all, it won't go anywhere. But you're right – maybe you should get back to telling fortunes."

I glanced behind me, there was a growing queue at the cookie kiosk. "Okay, maybe a couple more photos."

We reached the monstrous ride, which was a mass of wooden rails. It had rattled to a stop. Andrew raised his arm and signalled to the operator that we needed a few minutes to take some shots.

I climbed into the car and smiled as Andrew took pictures, from various angles. A claxon sounded.

"Hey," I called, as the operator pushed a safety bar over my head, clicking it into place before it touched my knees.

"What's happening?" I said as the car jolted forward.

"Smile, Becky," Andrew said. "You're on video."

"This isn't funny, now let me out," I said.

Constance jumped into the car and onto my lap, against the money belt which was digging into my stomach.

"My cat could get hurt," I called as the car clicked into gear and shunted along. "She's still convalescing." I panted as my heart raced. I checked inside the car for an emergency stop button. There was none. But my main concern was for Constance. "Shut this thing off," I called. Pulling the shawl from my waist, I wrapped it around my cat, then tied it to my body like a baby sling, with her facing outwards so she could breathe. I could feel her purring close to my chest. I doubted that would continue once the ride got going.

The climb to the top seemed endless. Palpitations fluttered in my chest. The rickety old car jolted and creaked as I blinked away tears, feeling I was going to full-on sob, knowing the only way back – was down. As we reached the top, the car slowed. The wind whistled against my ears. For a moment, I was in awe of the view. I gazed at the blue sea and the crescent of yellow sand, with the windows of Millar's hotel glinting in the sun at the far end. Pretty stone houses lined the streets of the residential area, backed by lush green woods with the grand castle, overlooking the bay like a royal protector.

"Ahhhrrr," I screamed, shutting my eyes, clutching Constance to my chest as we hurtled towards the ground. My insides lurched as we pushed up the other side of the dip. But I continued to feel Constance's purr against my torso. Opening my eyes, I instantly regretted it. My stomach felt as if it had been turned inside out. Over the top we went, then back down, shunted to one side and then the other. Just before I felt I would be sick, we shuddered to a stop with a final jolt.

I took deep breaths to calm myself before opening my eyes. My vision blurred with moisture. The bar lifted, as I stood up my legs trembled. All I could hear was laughter, with one person's voice trumping all others. Andrew's.

He approached me and held out his phone. "I've some great footage. You look a bit green though."

I untied Constance who jumped to the floor and was instantly fussed over by the growing crowd. Some were taking their own pictures of her.

"I'm going home," I said, stopping myself from hurling abuse at Andrew. I turned towards the kiosk and bumped straight into H.

"Don't go via my office," Andrew called out to me. "I have CCTV in there."

My face instantly coloured up. I turned my back on H and faced Andrew.

He continued. "Tell Katherine if she wants to know what my plans are, to ask. She's welcome here any time. She doesn't need to send you over to spy on me and turf through my drawers."

"She ... I ..." I didn't know what to say. I felt Constance rub against my leg.

"You must think I'm stupid," Andrew said. "I saw you the other day, at the pier. I know you've been over there doing one of your investigations." He laughed. "But thanks for the publicity. No hard feelings, eh? Let's call it quits." He stuck his hand out to shake mine.

I folded my arms and left his hand hanging.

"Fair enough. Feel free to stay on and make some cash." He nodded at me and walked away laughing.

I turned around to find H glowering at me.

"Has she been bad again?" asked one of his nephews.

I side-stepped them and hurried away with Constance by my side.

"Becky, stop," H called.

I sped up but caught my foot on the length of the dress and fell, as if in slow motion, until I hit the ground. I lay there motionless, with my palms stinging, catching my breath, with my cheek to the floor, until I saw H's size elevens. *This is all I need,* I thought.

He pulled me to standing. "What have you been doing?"

"What do you mean?"

"Actually, you don't have to explain. It's clear from what Farr said — you've been trespassing. I've a good mind to take you in."

My temper rose. "I've been working."

Constance meowed, as if to back me up.

H came up close and growled in my ear. "You're clearly on one of your so-called private investigations. Stop. Get back home, stay in your kitchen where you belong and keep out of police business." He stepped back and grabbed his nephews' hands before moving off, as if leading them out of harm's way.

I grabbed my basket from the kiosk, ignoring the calls for more fortune telling. I dumped Constance inside it and stormed to the exit. I didn't stop until I reached home.

As I stood at my doorstep fumbling for my key,

cursing Andrew and H, my phone dinged with a text. I pulled it out of my bag, it was from Izzy.

She'd sent a picture of me, eyes scrunched closed, mouth wide open in a scream. In front was Constance, her bushy hair surrounding her kitty face like a lion's mane. I groaned. Underneath the picture she wrote:

You're a star and trending on social media.

#catcoaster.

CHAPTER 12

I ignored my calls for the rest of the day. Although my escapades must have got back to Katherine as she texted me to say Andrew had accused her of spying. I was pleased when Dannie said she was going out with a friend for dinner. She'd been giving me a wide birth and I guessed she could tell that I wanted to be left alone.

After the sun had disappeared, I wandered into the lifeless café with Constance at heel. I pulled the blinds. A buzz of electricity shot up my back, alerting me to Ben's presence. The static felt even more intense than usual, as it travelled to my hands. I spun around.

Ben flickered in the middle of the café, with a roll-up in his mouth. His white hair glowed like illuminated candyfloss.

I stared at him as I clenched my fists, attempting to

eliminate the static from my hands. "Before you start. I've had a bad day. I can't cope with this."

Constance gave a low wailing meow as her coat bushed out.

I felt a surge of emotional pain, a mixture of desperation and helplessness, emitting from Ben. I stepped back as he opened his mouth.

"Accept it." He stretched his hand out.

I moved back. Static nipped at my fingers and his emotions dragged through my chest.

"You are not alone." He disappeared as if that was all he could muster.

I slumped to the table and put my head in my hands, feeling the tears wet my palms, as my body fizzed with dissipating electricity. I attempted to shake off the negative emotion.

"They aren't my feelings," I whispered.

I was lucky. Unlike the ghosts I had seen over these past couple of months, I was alive. Indeed, since moving to Branden Bay, I'd felt more alive than ever. I guess the extreme bad times had resulted in extreme good times. And there was no point in running away. What would I do if I went back to London? I sighed and sat up to allow a meowing Constance to jump on my lap.

I assumed when Ben said 'accept it' he'd meant I had to accept the gift. Fighting it was probably making things worse. And I was charging around trying to do too much myself. Ben was right. I wasn't alone. I had a great bunch of people around me. But not H. *No*, I thought. *If he comes knocking on my door, he can forget it.*

The doorbell rang. I hoped that wasn't him.

I went to my private entrance. Before opening the door, I checked my reflection in the porch mirror. Mascara had smudged down my face like chocolate sauce oozing over an ice cream. If it was H, I would definitely not answer.

The letterbox lifted.

"Becky, hey. Are you in?" It was Annie.

I puffed out then opened the door. As soon as she came in, I threw my arms around her.

"I thought I'd pop by. Are you okay?" she asked.

"I presume H sent you?"

"I … er …"

I leaned back and studied her eyes. "Don't even try to lie."

"He's worried about you. And so am I, now I've seen you. You've clearly been crying."

I sighed. "I can't sit at home and hide in my kitchen, as H suggested. I've got to accept who I am." I lowered my voice and smiled at her. "But I do need a little help from my friends."

THE FOLLOWING EVENING, I kneaded dough with determination charging through my veins. Hankering for something savoury, I tried my hand at pizza dough. I'd worked on the case from home and texted the gang, inviting them over for dinner. Well, everyone except H. I was in no mood for his criticism and attitude. He had a blooming cheek telling me to stay at home in the kitchen. What kind of century was he living in? He seemed to forget that women had come a long way since Victorian times. He was the one who should be donning an antique costume and prancing around the fairground. A picture of H appeared in my mind, dressed as an old-fashioned policeman on the beat ... wielding a truncheon and blowing a whistle. I smiled to myself.

As six o'clock approached, I prodded at the pizzas I'd made. My tablet leaned against the kitchen tiles, with a dusting of flour on it. I'd watched a few internet videos on pizza making.

"Wow," Dannie said, as she entered the kitchen. "They smell yum."

"It's my first attempt."

"What are the toppings?"

"This is a plain and simple Margarita. I've used a mix of cheddar and mozzarella." I gestured. "This is chicken and sweetcorn. And I have a spicy one with peppers and chillies and, of course, your favourite – a Hawaiian." My stomach rumbled and I looked forward to tucking into them.

"What time are we eating?"

"The gang should be here soon and I've an apple pie in the oven," I said. "It's my grandma's recipe."

"I can't wait."

. . .

I WAS SOON EATING pizza with Dannie, Izzy, Lynn, Annie and Jeff, around a couple of tables in the café, that we'd pushed together. I don't like to blow my own trumpet, but the pizzas were divine. The bases crisped nicely, I wondered whether I should add pizza to the café menu – assuming I was allowed to reopen.

Once everyone had eaten, I stood in front of my coffee machine facing them. I put my hands together as if in prayer. "I've done some soul searching and realise – I need to accept that I'm here to receive messages from poor souls that need me."

Lynn put a hand to her chest. "Oh, love. I'm so proud of you, standing on your own two spiritual feet. I'm always here, if you need help."

I continued. "Try as I might, I can't shake the ghosts off."

"Excellent." Izzy nodded and pulled her notebook from her bag, then began to write.

"But I need help. And I've been seeing Ben's ghost since he died."

"You have?" Annie said. "Is he okay?" Tears pooled in her eyes.

Izzy looked around the room and whispered. "Is he here?"

Dannie frowned. "Am I living in a haunted house?"

Jeff opened his backpack and brought out his mobile phone.

"No, Jeff. We're not here for that." I knew he would be pulling up his new ghost hunting app.

He frowned but didn't protest as he returned his phone to his bag.

I smiled. "I can't see Ben right now. But I feel he won't rest until I find out who murdered him. I'm convinced the intended victim was Katherine and have a sense of urgency to wrap this up. That's why I called you here to help. I can't do this alone."

"I'll do anything I can," Annie said.

"For starters, I need to go through my list of suspects with you. To get my head around who they are and what motives, if any, they have."

Dannie crossed her arms. "I don't really think you should be providing a detective service. Yeah, you got away with it last time, but you probably need a licence for that too."

I smiled. "I've already checked. There's no requirement in the UK to have a registered detective agency. And anyway, we're paranormal investigators."

"We certainly are, sweetie," Izzy said, not looking up from her notes.

I pulled my smartphone out of my pocket. "I've recorded notes on my phone. As I believe the killer meant to kill Katherine, I'm looking for people who have a motive to kill her, rather than Ben."

Dannie huffed, stood up and left the room.

"What's up with her?" asked Annie.

"I don't think she approves," I commented. "I can't

blame her. She didn't come off well after my last investigation."

Dannie reappeared at the door with my laptop computer. "It'll take you ages tapping all that information into your phone. I'll set up a file for you on here."

"Thanks." I smiled at her. Dannie was a major asset.

"Sync the list you have so far to the cloud and I'll pick it up," she said.

"Eh?"

Dannie held out her hand and I passed her my phone.

"I've airdropped it," she said as she handed it back to me.

I took a deep breath, "So firstly, I have Andrew Farr. As you probably already know, he's the owner of Branden Bay fairground. He's been trying to get Kathrine to go into business with him for some time, to make the pier and fairground one attraction."

"I take it she's not up for that?" asked Lynn.

"No, she doesn't trust him and thinks he will take over and she'll lose control."

Annie nodded in agreement. "She's very proud of the fact that the pier has been in her family for years."

I sat down. "As you all know, for some weeks now, there have been accidents happening at the pier, which would appear to be the work of a saboteur. It's possible that it's Andrew trying to scare Katherine into accepting his help."

"When we were at the pier," Jeff added. "We overheard him saying to her, she could be next."

"Exactly, so for this reason he's top of my list of suspects. I snooped in his office yesterday but the only piece of information I found, was that he's going to the Summer Masked Ball up at the castle – which Katherine is also attending. With people wearing masks, this would be the ideal opportunity for the killer to strike."

"What's our plan?" Izzy asked.

Dannie frowned. "Maybe Katherine shouldn't go to the ball."

"She goes every year, without fail," Annie said. "There's no way she'll miss it."

"Darling," Izzy said. "Anyone who's anyone goes to the Summer Masked Ball. I'll be there for professional reasons, of course, covering the event for the Gazette." She widened her blue eyes. "I have two tickets. We can go together, Becky. You can be my undercover plus one and flush out the killer."

I remembered what going undercover with Izzy was like. Impossible. "I can't go under the radar with you. You stand out too much." Izzy was, after all, the 'It girl' of Branden Bay.

"Darling. It's fancy dress and everyone wears a mask."

"Becky needs more than a mask to cover her carrot top," Jeff said.

"Hey," I laughed, and so did everyone else. I loved the togetherness I experienced with my friends.

"Don't worry about that. I'll dress you up so no-one will recognise you," Izzy said. "We'll cover your hair or use a wig."

"I could go with Dannie," Jeff said looking over at her.

"I think Izzy and myself can cover it," I said, observing the expression of horror on Dannie's face.

Jeff cast his eyes downwards as Constance trotted over to him and rubbed around his legs.

"The tickets have already been allocated," Izzy said with her head to one side. "They sell out six months in advance. I only have one spare, I hadn't decided on my plus one."

Dannie let out a long slow breath and recommenced typing.

"So, is there anyone else you think that could have committed the murder?" asked Lynn.

"Unfortunately, yes," I said. "There are a few ..."

CHAPTER 13

I sensed my guests needed a mental break, so I brought out the apple pie and popped on the percolator. I would have made drinks from my new coffee machine, but I was mindful that if I had to sell it on, I would need to do so in pristine condition if I was to get anything like the price I paid for it.

As I reheated the custard on the hob, I remembered the times I'd eaten Grandma's pie made with apples straight from the tree.

Constance gave a loud meow from where she sat at my feet.

I stooped to stroke her. She always seemed to sense the exact moment that I needed affection. "What an intuitive cat you are," I said. Picking her up, I looked out of the kitchen window at the apple tree in the fading evening light. The apples would be ready in a month. I wondered whether the café would be open by then, so I could put pie with home grown apples on the café menu. I sighed as I placed Constance back on the floor. After checking the custard was warmed through, I poured it into a jug. I picked up the serving tray to deliver dessert.

As we ate, I wolfed down the apple pie. The pastry was crisp, the apples soft with a sharpness that complimented the sweetness of the added Demerara sugar and cinnamon. The vanilla custard was worth the effort to make and paired with the pie beautifully. After Lynn had cleared away the bowls for me, we sipped coffee. Constance repeatedly licked her lips, having lapped up a pool of custard from a china saucer.

"Let's get back to it then," I said from my seat. "Next we have a disgruntled employee. Clive. He'd been working at the pier for years before Katherine sacked him."

"I was there when she gave him the chop," said Annie. "Since then, everything's gone wrong. He really kept the place together."

"Katherine is trying to get him to take his job back," I said. "But he won't forgive her and is taking his case to the employment tribunal."

"Surely he wouldn't want her dead," said Izzy. "He'd never get a payout."

"It could be a smoke-screen," said Jeff.

"We have invited him to Ben's wake and assuming he turns up, Jeff is going to try and befriend him."

Jeff remained silent.

Annie sighed. "I do hope it isn't Clive."

Dannie tapped away at the keyboard.

I finished the last dregs of my coffee. "Next on my list are Nathan and Olivia. I suspect they're a couple."

"Isn't he a bit old for her?" Jeff asked. "She's more my age."

"She's younger than you," Annie said. "Nineteen. But I've seen them together a few times. Huddled away chatting."

"Interesting," Izzy said as she made notes. "So tell us about this Nathan."

"He's a bit of a jobsworth, who hates it when we're over at the pier."

"Why would he want to kill Katherine?" Lynn asked.

"Because if he marries Olivia, and she inherits the pier, she will likely sell it on and they'll be rich."

"Won't Olivia take on the pier?" Dannie asked.

"No," Annie replied. "She resents it. She says her Mum loves the pier more than her."

"I can't believe Olivia would kill her Mum," Lynn said.

"Jealous people do evil things," Jeff said.

"So is it possible that Olivia is the saboteur?" Izzy asked.

"Clive got sacked shortly after she got home from Uni," Annie said.

"This is messy." Dannie typed notes into my laptop. "And I thought my family had problems."

Constance pawed at Dannie's leg.

"Exactly," I said. "That's why I need everyone's help with this. My head is going around in circles. A few people have a motive, but none of them seem like killers."

"Annie, if you could keep an eye on Olivia and Nathan at the pier. When the opportunity arises, Jeff and me will follow them."

"So that's it then?" said Dannie. "Four suspects." She closed the lid of the laptop.

I sighed. "I'm afraid not. I have two outsiders."

"Katherine's not a popular woman, is she?" Izzy commented.

"If we list everyone she has annoyed we'd be here all night," Annie added.

"The next is Darren Box," I said.

"I've not heard that name for years," Lynn said. "He's her ex-husband, isn't he?"

"You've got the right person but he's not an ex. They're still married, Katherine never filed for divorce."

"Darren liked to drive flash cars and wanted a flash girl in the seat beside him," Lynn said. "He wooed Katherine when she was with Andrew."

"What, Andrew Farr?" Annie asked.

"Yes, they were childhood sweethearts," Lynn replied. "Gossip at the time was that after Katherine had Olivia, Darren couldn't deal with the responsibility of being a father. As I understand it, he said he was popping out to the shops for milk and disappeared. No one knew where, until his Mum received a postcard from Ibiza."

"If Katherine died, would he be able to make a claim on her estate, as her surviving spouse?" Izzy asked.

"That's what I wondered," I said. "I suggested to Katherine that she should check her position with her solicitor. All I know is that he's a DJ in Ibiza and is forty years old. I don't even have a picture of him."

"I'll see what I can find out," Lynn said. "One of my clients at the spiritualist church is friends with his mother. She moved to Bristol a few years back."

"I can help with that, too," Dannie said. "If he's a DJ he's bound to have a social media presence. I'll see if I can locate him. I've done the Ibiza circuit myself."

"What, as a dancer?" Jeff's eyes widened.

Dannie's face coloured up and she looked as if she was about to punch him. Constance jumped onto the table next to Dannie and meowed at her.

Dannie stroked the cat's head and took a deep breath then spoke through gritted teeth. "I went to Ibiza on a clubbing holiday with my friends."

I jumped in quick. "As with all suspects, we need to establish whether he has an alibi." I looked at my phone. "And that leaves my last suspect Peter Sheringham. Jewel thief."

Lynn gasped. "I forgot about him. Kathrine's uncle. Wow, that's a blast from the past. I was in my thirties when he was banged up," Lynn said. "My dad, God rest his soul, used to play darts with him. He was completely shocked when he discovered the secret life he'd been living."

"This is an amazing story, darling," Izzy said. "I'd love to do a spot of investigative journalism on this. How did I not know about Branden Bay's famous jewel thief?"

"Or not so famous," laughed Annie. "This is all news to me too and I work for Katherine."

"It made the BBC news at the time," Lynn said. "But it was years ago so you would have only been toddlers. Times move on and so do the memories."

"This is going to make my career." Izzy scribbled more notes.

"Do you want me to help you to connect to Ben again and ask him who did it?"

I shook my head. "If he knew that, he would have told me. The killer approached him from the back," I said.

"Okay," Jeff looked down at his hands.

I felt energised. "I've been so muddled with this, but feel we have a plan going forward. We need to keep each other informed of developments. If you could email me across any notes you make and any thoughts you might have about the suspects, or local gossip you hear."

"I'll add them to the spreadsheet as they come in, if you like?" Dannie said.

I smiled at her. Dannie really was an asset to me right now.

"The police asked Katherine to compile a list of the accidents at the pier with dates and times. I'll see if I can get a copy and email that over," Annie said. "It seems they're now coming around to the idea that Katherine was the target."

"Excellent." I smiled. "And also find out exactly who has keys to the pier. If there's a saboteur it's got to be someone with access, considering Ben was killed at a time when the pier was shut to the public. Thanks, guys."

Izzy, Annie and Lynn left and Dannie went up to her bedroom, leaving me with Jeff.

"Do you want a cuppa?" I asked. "I have cake. I put a batch in the freezer before I was shut down and took a few out earlier, in case someone didn't like apple pie."

He nodded silently and went through to the snug, followed by Constance.

I handed him his tea, placing the cakes which I had iced earlier that day, on the coffee table. There was a chocolate cake, filled with buttercream and a ginger cake with a thin layer of lemon icing. I sat beside Jeff on the sofa. "Are you alright?"

He nodded as he stroked my cat, who was now sitting on his lap. But he said nothing.

"Come on. Out with it."

"It's just that usually, it's me and you." He ruffled the fur on Constance's head. "Now the others are getting involved."

I laughed and dug my elbow into his ribs. "Don't be silly. You're my right-hand man. We're doing the difficult stuff. We need to put surveillance on the suspects."

"But I'm not going to the masked ball. I'm your gatekeeper. I need to be there to protect you from the killer."

Jeff had once overheard Lynn telling me that for every bridge medium – that's my type, apparently – there's a gatekeeper who is someone who feels compelled to protect them from harm. Jeff was convinced that was his job, although I doubted it. But I had to give him credit, he'd been there on a few occasions when I needed help.

"It's a shame there are limited tickets," I said.

"When is it?"

"Friday, next week."

"I'll be your transport and wait in the car park for you in case you need me."

"That's great." Even better, he could also give me a lift home if I'd had enough. Once Izzy started partying it was impossible to drag her away.

My cat meowed.

"You can guard Constance too. She can't afford to lose any more lives." I gestured at the plate. "Now come on you numpty – eat cake."

CHAPTER 14

I jumped out of bed with renewed energy. I glanced at my phone as it dinged with a text and groaned. It was from H.

Can we meet for a walk and an ice cream?

I ignored it. Whilst I felt happier, I wasn't going to allow him to trample all over my confidence. I guessed this was his way of saying sorry. But as far as I was concerned, I didn't need that sort of person in my life. I made breakfast for myself and Dannie, who seemed to be getting up a lot earlier these days.

Twenty minutes later my phone dinged with another text. It was from Annie.

Meeting Izzy and H for ice cream at the beach at one – do you want to come?

I realised H had put her up to it. I sighed. I knew I'd have to break the ice at some point. Especially as I had a catering job to do for his mother. Deciding there was safety in numbers, I texted back and confirmed.

WE HIRED a batch of deckchairs on the beach and were sitting down as Annie arrived with a cardboard holder containing our ice creams. All were 99 style, soft-whipped ice cream in a wafer cone, with a Cadbury's chocolate flake. I sat in my chair, the sun was warm and it was lovely to relax as I tasted the sweet creamy treat. But I was distracted by the sight of the fairground which dominated that end of the beach. It was difficult to erase the memory of the Big Dipper roller-coaster from my mind, when it was in my line of vision.

"Can you hold this for me?" I passed my ice cream to Annie and dragged my chair to the opposite side so I was facing the right of the bay, with Millar's hotel as the backdrop. I was now sitting next to H. But at least that meant I didn't have to look at him.

He turned and smiled. "As you've come within a foot of me – does this mean I'm forgiven?"

"What it means is that I'm blocking the view of the fairground and the memories I associate with it."

He shook his head. "Look, I overreacted, but it's only because I worry about you. Let's face it, you've got form."

"Forgive him, sweetie, and stop giving him such a hard time," Izzy said. She licked her ice cream and gave a thoughtful look and nodded.

Once a food critic, always a food critic, I thought.

"I agree with Izzy," Annie said. "I wish you two would do us both a favour and go on a proper date."

"But we're not remotely attracted to each other," I said gesturing my ice cream cone towards H.

Annie laughed.

Having finished his ice cream in quick time, H sat back and pulled his sunglasses from his pocket, put them on and leant back with his face to the sun. "I do need a plus-one for an event I have tickets for." I couldn't tell whether he was being sincere or not, with his eyes covered by his shades.

I gave a short laugh. "After the last time I was your plus one I didn't think you'd ask me again." I'd accompanied him to a police awards night and had embarrassed myself horribly.

"It's the Summer Masked Ball up at the castle," he said.

I needed to think of an excuse, there was no way I wanted H blowing my cover at the ball. And I was pretty sure he wouldn't play along with our plan to watch Katherine all night. "As long as it's not Friday, next week. I've already got something planned," I said then took another mouthful of ice cream from my cone.

H sat forward and shook his head. "That's a shame. It is." He turned to Izzy. "Have you got a date for the ball yet?"

"Sorry, darling. I've a new romantic interest."

"That's amazing, Izzy," Annie said. "You've been single for so long." Annie sounded so sincere, I wondered whether she'd forgotten that Izzy was going with me. "Are you very close?"

"At the moment, yes," Izzy said with a small smile.

"So, Annie, how about it then?" H asked.

Annie looked momentarily shocked. I could see her trying to come up with a reply. She leaned back. "Sorry, H, but I'll be no-one's third choice."

H sighed.

Annie giggled. "I'm only joking. But I'm still not going. You know it's not my scene. I couldn't bear it. The fish egg muck."

"Caviar, darling," Izzy said.

"Call it what you like, it's nasty. And sloppy salmon. Just because something is expensive doesn't make it tasty. Don't even get me started on truffle shavings covering everything." She mimicked retching.

I giggled. "You don't have to eat it."

"It's not my idea of a party at all." She shook her head as her hair blew in the wind. "I'm sure the music will be cheesy as well. Sorry, H, it's a no."

H pulled himself out of the low seat. "That's me out of it then." He looked down at us. "I'll see if I can give my tickets away to someone at work. See you later." He walked off with his hands in his shorts' pockets.

"Poor boy. That must have been why he dragged us all here. So he could casually ask Becky to the ball," Izzy said.

"We don't want him going to the ball when we'll be there undercover," I said.

Izzy peered at me over her sunglasses. "You'll have to make it up to him with a proper date soon, otherwise Prince Charming will lose interest and think you don't care about him."

I frowned. I didn't want to say I didn't care – of course I cared. H had pretty much saved my life. "As I have the attention of both of you at the moment, tell me – why does everyone think we're an item?"

Izzy smiled at me over her sunglasses and shook her head then gave a laugh.

Annie sat back, giggling. "You're so funny, Becky. But I agree with Izzy. H could quite easily go out with someone else. He's never short of offers."

"Everyone enjoys the chase, sweetie. But you'll have to stop teasing him at some point, before he runs out of energy."

"I've no interest in a date with H or anyone else." I stood up.

"Charming," Izzy said pouting.

"Okay, I'm looking forward to our date," I laughed. "So come on, while we walk back, tell me about this disguise you have planned for me."

Izzy was soon by my side as the three of us walked across the sand to the prom. "I have the most beautiful mask for you, darling, and I'll braid your hair and spray it silver."

Annie slipped her arm into mine. "You're going to look like an ice princess."

"Ice? For a summer ball?" I asked.

"It's nice to stand out, darling," added Izzy.

I wondered if Izzy would ever get the concept of 'undercover'. But if my hair colour was covered and I wore a mask – who would recognise me?

"And lose the London accent, darling. It's such a giveaway."

We sauntered up the beach in silence for a while, listening to the waves crashing and the distant laughter of children having fun in the sand.

As I neared my house, I saw a tall man exiting my property wearing a dark blue boilersuit and a cap. He walked away in the opposite direction. As I reached home, I found Dannie standing on the doorstep, holding on to Constance who struggled to get free.

"What's wrong with her?" I asked.

"She attacked the electrician I don't know what's got in to her. She bit his leg." She pointed to the electricity meter cupboard in the porch. "He fitted the new smart meter today."

I groaned. I'd had a couple of emails asking me to connect a smart meter. "That's all I need."

"What's wrong? I thought they were good for the environment."

I took Constance from her who growled at me to be let free. I held her tightly.

"Yes, I guess they are, but I've been receiving estimated bills since I moved in, based on what Grandma used to use. What with running the café for a couple of months, I'm bound to be stung with a massive bill. Just when I can't afford it."

"They might do a payment plan or something?" she said. "I'm sorry,"

"Hey, it's not your fault," I said. "I should have sent an accurate reading weeks ago."

"And there is more bad news I'm afraid."

"Go on?" I said.

"Seems someone snitched on you to the Council, telling them you prepared cookies for the fairground. There was an email from Elks saying he has no evidence, so will not prosecute but if he gets the slightest hint of you breaking the rules, you won't get a license to prepare food, ever."

"I'm sorry," I said to Dannie as she crossed her arms in an I-told-you-so pose.

For the rest of the afternoon, Dannie and I worked on the café. Completing yet more paperwork which had arrived from the council with queries on my application.

Annie had emailed over a list of dates and times relating to accidents on the pier. There was no pattern what-so-ever, all at varying times of the day. On every day of the week, apart from Sundays.

Maybe they go to Church? I thought.

Dannie was plugging the details into her spreadsheet, when I received a text from Izzy.

Had a development on Peter Sheringham. Can you be at mine for six?

IZZY LIVED IN A SWANKY PAD, so I left Constance at home with Dannie. I wasn't sure if pets were permitted. Surprisingly, I'd not been to her place before. It was in a contemporary block which backed onto the woods and every apartment had a long glass balcony with glorious views across the bay.

"Come up, darling," she said through the intercom as the door unlocked with a buzz.

As I exited the lift, Izzy's apartment door swung open. She ushered me in.

"Wow," I said. "It looks like a show home in here." It was open plan with a kitchen area which was spotless with white glossy units and a chandelier over a marble-topped island. Oak floors spanned the whole apartment and the lounge area had white leather sofas and floor to ceiling windows which provided an uninterrupted view of the bay. I glanced to the end of the lounge and glimpsed a four-poster bed in the adjoining room, again dressed with white.

"I've poured you a glass of wine, darling. Sit down."

I picked up the glass from the island and followed her to the sofa. I was glad to be drinking white and not red wine. I sunk into the white leather. "What information have you found out about Peter Sheringham?" I asked.

"Well." She crossed her long bare legs and leaned back. "He had a life sentence for armed robbery and spent most of it in Belmarsh Prison in London. But he was moved to an open prison in Somerset five years ago."

"Oh my goodness," I said. "So he could have slipped out and killed Ben, thinking he was Katherine?"

"That's what I thought, darling. But it turns out, open prisons aren't that open to allow out of town trips and, more importantly, he died two weeks ago."

I sat back in my chair. "Being dead is a rock-solid alibi."

"Maybe you and Jeff should contact him via your paranormal channels."

I shook my head. "As I've said many times, I have to wait for spirits to contact me first." I took a gulp of wine then licked my lips. "He might have had something to do with it, though. What about the stolen money and jewels?"

"They never recovered them. That's why he wasn't released from prison. I do have a contact at the prison, though."

"Who?"

"An old school friend works there. I convinced him to meet us so we can find out more. My boss is loving the investigative piece on Branden Bay's home-grown jewel thief. He gave me a budget so I can pay this guy for information. If the story goes national, I'll get a cut."

"When are you meeting this prison officer?"

"In about half an hour, sweetie. That's why I called you over."

"Izzy, you're amazing."

"Yes I am, aren't I?" She fluttered her eyelashes.

By the time we'd rustled up a few questions between us, the intercom went off and Izzy buzzed the prison guard up.

Opening the door, she gave him an air kiss. "Jason, you're nice and early. Long-time no see."

Jason's eyes were wide open, as if he was staring at a rock star. "Shall I take my shoes off?" he asked in a strong west country accent.

"If you don't mind, sweetie." Izzy gestured towards an oak shoe rack.

After he'd removed his footwear, she led him towards me. "This is Becky."

"Alright?" he said briefly, before switching his gaze back to Izzy.

"Would you like a glass of wine?" she asked him.

"I'm driving."

"Okay, I'll get you some water." She took a glass out of the glossy kitchen cupboard and a bottle of mineral water from the silver American-style fridge. I guessed tea and coffee are out of the question when you have white furnishings.

"So, Jason," I said from the sofa. "Izzy filled me in on the background. She's got all the general info on Peter – that he stole a bunch of jewels, diamonds and cash over five separate heists."

"I guess you want to know if he told me where he stashed it?"

"If you knew that, darling, you'd be halfway to the Bahamas," Izzy said, laughing as she returned the bottle of water to the fridge.

Jason shook his head. "I'd be happy enough with the reward. A lot less hassle."

"Do you have any clues at all as to where it could be?" I asked.

"All Pete ever said was that he'd stashed it where no one would ever find it – unless he told them."

"And did he have any visitors?" I asked, wondering whether Peter was in cahoots with someone on the outside.

"Well, not until the last few months of his life."

"Who visited?" asked Izzy, passing Jason the glass of water and gesturing for him to take a seat.

"They used to come at the weekend and I don't work Sundays – it's my day off. I'm in the Sunday football league. I play in goal." He smiled at Izzy with his palms outstretched. "I've got big hands." He sat down opposite me.

Izzy flared her petite nostrils and frowned as she sat beside me.

"So how do you know about the visitor?" I asked.

"My workmate told me. Oggy said Pete was always quiet after the visitor."

"So, was it a man or a woman? Were they old or young?" I asked, leaning forward.

"No idea. Oggy calls them 'Pete's visitor'. To be fair, I wasn't taking that much notice."

"Could you call this colleague of yours?" Izzy asked.

"He's on holiday, but I can ask him when he comes back next week."

"Surely you can get access to visitor books?" Izzy said.

"Security is high when it comes to prison records. To get to the office, I have to go through two locked doors and every door entry is registered. If they know I've been in there, when your article comes out, they're gonna know that it's me what spoke to the press. I don't want to lose my job. Oggy'll be alright though, he's sound. If I slip him a fifty, he won't mention anything." He held out his hand.

"I'll add fifty to your fee," Izzy said with a wave of her hand.

"Can you ring him?" I asked.

"No, he's not a mate like that. I only know him from work. I haven't got his number."

Izzy chatted away to Jason, asking for details of

Peter's day to day life. His likes and habits and whether he ever talked about Branden Bay, for her article.

Half an hour later she saw Jason out. "Be sure to call Becky as soon as you get any details on the visitor."

LATER, we ate a take-away meal. Izzy said it was too late for her to rustle anything up.

I chewed thoughtfully on my chicken chow mien. "It might be nothing, but I got the feeling that Peter Sheringham's visitor could be the key to the case. The only thing is, if he had a stash of jewels and cash, why on earth would he want the pier?"

"Because it's rightfully his?" suggested Izzy. "Sometimes it's not about the money. It's about what people think belongs to them. So what next sweetie?"

I stood up. "Jeff and I are planning to tail Olivia and Nathan in a few days to see if anything is going on with them. Annie said he collects her from work once a week, at three, which is the end of her shift. He starts his at seven. I'll be interested to see what they're up to."

"Good luck. I'm sure we'll crack this case, with us all working on it together."

"I do hope so. I'm worried for Katherine's safety."

CHAPTER 15

I felt weary as I unlocked my front door at nine. The porch light flickered as I turned it on. I scanned the area for Ben, I couldn't see him. Constance gave a low meow. I smelled something odd in the air. Constance growled.

"What's the matter?" I asked her. Something was definitely wrong, I felt it deep inside my stomach. "Dannie," I called out. I reached the foot of the stairs and called her again. "Dannie?" My heart thud.

I heard her bedroom door open and she leaned over the bannister above. "Is everything okay?"

"That's what I was going to ask you. Constance is acting weird."

Constance gave a low wailing meow and trotted back to the porch.

"I know," Dannie said. She's been sitting by the front door hissing. I thought she was missing you."

The lights flickered again.

Dannie ran down the stairs. "Tell me this isn't one of your hauntings?"

"No. And Ben is not here."

"What's that burning smell?" she asked.

Constance sped towards us as smoke snaked out of the electricity cupboard.

"It must be the new smart meter," I said.

I grabbed hold of Dannie and faced away from the porch as the electric cupboard door blew off, crashing onto the tiled porch floor. The lights went out. Sparks flew from the exposed consumer unit. I felt Constance at my feet.

"Are you okay?"

"I'm fine," said Dannie in a shaky voice.

I leaned down and picked up Constance, checking she was still in one piece. "Here, take the cat." I passed her to Dannie and fumbled in my bag for my phone. My hand shook as I called the emergency services, letting them know our address. Once I ended the call, I turned on the torch app. Shining it towards the porch, there were still sparks emitting from the consumer unit, which was surrounded by smoke.

"Let's get outside," said Dannie as the three of us made for the back door. As soon as I opened it we found Lynn on the step.

"Are you okay lovey? I sense danger."

"The electricity cupboard has exploded and blown

the electrics. We had a new smart meter fitted today, it must have been faulty."

We soon heard the rumble of the fire engine and blue lights flashed through the house.

"I'll let them in the café entrance," I said.

"We'll all go," added Lynn.

As the four of us moved through the house, we saw that the cupboard had ignited. Flames crackled from the porch. I rushed to the café doors and threw them open. "It's in the porch, access it this way because I can't get to the front door to open it."

The fireman ran past with an extinguisher,

The small fire was contained within seconds, but my electrics were shot to bits.

"Is there anywhere you can stay tonight?" the fire officer asked. "I'm afraid that it wasn't a faulty smart meter, it was an incendiary device."

"A what?" I asked.

"A bomb," Dannie said, her eyes wide open.

The fire officer looked grim. "I'll called the police."

DANNIE, myself and Constance climbed up the stairs to Annie's flat. She lived on the top floor of a three-story house conversion. We'd been at the police station giving statements about the smart meter installation. It soon became apparent that the man who visited the house was not from the electricity board. Dannie had not taken much notice of the electrician and knew nothing other than he wore tinted glasses, a cap and was tall. He'd also worn a surgical mask, saying he was allergic to cats. She had no idea about his age, hair colour or eye colour. He had a local accent, was all she could say.

"I've made up the spare room and the sofa bed," Annie said.

"You take the guest room Dannie," I said. My mind was racing, there was no way I was going to sleep.

Dannie yawned as she went to the bedroom, followed by Constance.

"I'll make us a pot of tea," Annie said.

We sat drinking tea and eating biscuits.

"So, who do you think left the bomb in your place?"

"It was a tall man. That's all we know. It could be any one of the male suspects. But whoever it is must think we're on to them. The only saving grace is that H wasn't on duty to give me a hard time."

"He's away on a course at Hendon, at the police training unit. I've already spoken to him," Annie said. "He'd have gone mad at us if he didn't find out until he got back. He wanted to come home, I told him you were fine. He'll be back in a couple of days."

I felt my eyelids droop.

"Well, I'll be off to bed now Becky."

I moved to the sofa bed and laid awake for a little longer. No doubt H was going to tell me to back off, but I was angry, the killer was not going to get away with it.

The saboteur at the pier, was likely to be the same person trying to wreck my house. Grandma's house. How dare they.

As PREDICTED, I received a text from H the following morning advising me to stay at home and not to open the door to anyone. As it happened, I wasn't permitted back to the house, until the forensics team had been in. And we didn't want to return there, without any electricity. I arranged for the electrics to be repaired, luckily the insurance company covered it. The porch was in a mess, but the physical damage was contained to the cupboard and the electrical equipment. Although the porch needed redecoration as the smell was hideous.

After two days, the electrics were back on and Dannie and I thanked Annie for her hospitality and moved back home. Despite the threat to my life, I was still determined to find Ben's killer. Indeed, I was even more determined. I wasn't going to just sit by and do nothing. H was back in town and had asked to see me, however I'd put him off as Jeff and I had arranged to tail Olivia and Nathan that afternoon. I didn't know when I'd be free, so I said I'd text him later to arrange a time.

At three o'clock Jeff and I, jogged along the prom at a snail's pace. We both wore caps, and I had my hair tied back in a ponytail, poking it under the cap. Jeff wore shorts revealing a very pale pair of legs, even paler than mine. His training shoes looked as if they were left over from his school days. We paused for a rest and leaned against the sea wall, looking back to beach road

"We're on," I said adjusting my cap to cover my face. We turned around to look out to sea as Olivia and Nathan passed us along the prom. Both were dressed for running. We waited until they had travelled a few yards then jogged along after them, although they continued to walk. We followed them for some way.

"Where are they off to?" asked Jeff. "They aren't running."

"They're carrying bags. It looks as if they're going to Millar's gym," I said as they walked towards the hotel.

"I'm not dressed for a five-star hotel," Jeff said.

He wasn't wrong.

They entered Millar's.

"Come on," I said. "We'll have to go in."

"What? No, way. I'm not going in there."

I glanced at his frayed Marvel t-shirt, realising he would stick out like a sore thumb. But I was not up for a gym session either. "Wait here. I'll pop in and see if I can overhear any snippets of conversation. I'll only be a couple of minutes. We can follow them once they're done."

I pulled the peak of my cap downwards as I entered the reception. There was a queue of people. I stood directly behind the pair, but they weren't in conversation.

I recognised the guy on reception, Mike, he was a friend of H's and I'd met him during my one and only trip to the gym.

"Those who've pre-paid the spinning class – go straight through," he called out.

Olivia and Nathan followed the stream of fit-looking people heading towards the gym door. I hesitated. I'd not been spinning before, but I'd heard of it and knew it was some sort of freakish bike workout. I turned around, heading for the exit.

"Hey, it's Becky isn't it? H's friend." Mike called from behind me.

I turned around and slapped a smile on my face. Clearly wearing a cap wasn't a good enough disguise. "Hi."

"I'd recognise your hair colour anywhere. It's so bright."

I groaned silently, touching my ponytail which was no longer under the cap.

"I've been waiting for you to come by. I thought we were going out for a drink?"

"I've been busy." I felt the heat rush to my face and took my cap off, using it to fan myself.

"Yeah, I've seen that, from the newspaper articles."

I gave a short laugh. I turned as I heard a voice.

"Mum put you up to this didn't she?" Olivia had her arms crossed.

"What? No – I'm here for ... spinning." I said and beamed at them.

Nathan narrowed his eyes at me. "I saw you following us with that kid you knock around with."

"We met for a pre-workout jog. I like to warm up."

"So where is he now?"

"He didn't feel up to it."

"Come on guys, the session is starting," called a woman. She was tall and fit with glossy chestnut hair tied back into a high ponytail.

Olivia raised her eyebrows. "Come on then, Becky."

"Yep, go through, we received your advance booking and payment." Mike winked at me, obviously lying, to save my embarrassment. "Go straight through."

I was happy for his help, but not so happy about having to join the spinning class. I followed Olivia and Nathan into the studio. I wasn't too concerned. After all, when I'd been to the gym, the bike was the least strenuous of exercise machinery. Inside the room, rows of racing bikes awaited us, they were not the chunky kind found in the main gym with the comfy wide seats.

"I'm Tara, pick a bike and let's get started," she said.

I retrieved my mobile phone from my pocket and jumped onto a bike but found my feet didn't quite reach the pedals.

Olivia smirked at me as she placed a large water bottle in a cradle on the front of her bike.

I jumped off and grappled with a lever under the seat.

"Here, let me help," a familiar voice said. I looked up. It was H, clearly back from his training.

Oh, no, I thought.

"I was pulling weights. Mike told me you were in here. I didn't think this was your scene." He glanced at Olivia, then back at me and gave a slow shake of his head. He was clearly on to me.

Olivia laughed. "I'm going to enjoy this."

"I'll be right behind you," H said to me.

I gulped, knowing he'd give me a hard time, once the session was over.

Tara called out in an excited voice. "Get ready to sweat your butts off. Pedal ... fast."

The room was dark. Music pumped and lights flashed as if we were in a nightclub. *This is going to be great,* I thought.

After ten minutes, I was totally beat.

"And now we've warmed up, let's take it up a gear. Come on, put the tension up." Tara nodded at me, so I switched up the tension of the bike with the gear lever. My legs burned. But I couldn't quit. I didn't want Olivia and Nathan to be proved right, that I was just there to spy on them. Neither did I want H to have the satisfaction of knowing I was a total weakling. Gone were the days when I worked out hard in my Uni dance classes.

Half an hour in, my head buzzed. Not in a ghost way, more in a 'I'm going to pass out' way. My vision blurred with swimming lights, until I slipped off the bike and everything went black.

I opened my eyes to find myself in reception, with Mike calling my name as he fanned my face with my cap. "Becky can you hear me? It's Mike. I'm the first aider."

I lay in the recovery position. Blinking, I eased myself up to sitting.

"Drink this," Mike said, handing me a filled paper cup.

I took the cool water and sipped it as he went to see to someone at the reception desk.

H's hand appeared before my face. "Come on."

I considered it typical for him to witness it. I tried to stand without his help but ended back down on my bottom.

"Take it," he said in a gruff voice. And proceeded to hoist me up. He leaned close to me and growled in my ear. "You were snooping again, weren't you? What part of keep away from danger don't you understand? You need to back off – someone tried to blow you up."

"Katherine was worried about Olivia," I whispered feeling tingles shooting up my neck.

"Olivia comes to this class with Nathan every week. I could have told you that."

"Well, maybe you should have." I pulled my hand away from his.

"From what I've seen, there isn't anything romantic going on between them. If that's what Katherine is so concerned about." He shook his head. "Is this what you've turned to? Next you'll be getting involved in divorce cases. That's bread and butter for your kind."

"My kind?"

"Yes, a so-called private investigator."

I opened my mouth to protest but was interrupted by Tara.

"How's my new spinner?" she called out, as the reception filled with post-spinning, sweat-clad bodies. "You looked quite the hero, H, lifting the poor limp thing from the room."

Oh even better, I thought, not realising H had carried me out. I blushed – hard.

Tara gave me the once up and down. "You should have said you were new to exercise. I would have suggested an alternative class."

Tara hardly had a sweat on and I didn't like the way she was looking at H. Not that it should bother me. We were, after all, just friends.

"You need to improve your fitness before you start spinning," she continued. "I run gentle aqua aerobics on a Tuesday for those who need to build up their strength." She cocked her head to one side. "Maybe you should start with that?"

Okay, so I wasn't as fit as I used to be when I was a student. And I'd put a few pounds on since I'd moved to Branden Bay. I was a baker, after all, I had to taste the cakes, it went with the job. I clenched my teeth together. I didn't want to say something rude to Tara who I sensed was being more than a tad patronising.

"Speak to Mike, he'll book you in." Tara gave me a tight smile which morphed into a grin as she turned to gaze at H.

Nathan passed with Olivia. "Serves you right."

"I'm off now," I said in a breezy voice to H and Tara who didn't seem to be listening.

Mike approached. "Hey, before you go," he said handing me my cap and mobile phone. "Would you like to go to the Summer Masked Ball with me? H gave me a couple of tickets. I'd love to take you."

"Sorry, I'm busy that night." I gave a short laugh. "See you all later." I about-turned and headed into the sunshine, taking in deep breaths of sea air. Jeff was nowhere to be seen and I guessed he'd given up waiting.

When I arrived home, I found Jeff in my kitchen. I presumed Dannie had let him in.

"How did it go?" he said, as he sat at the table eating a slice of chocolate cake.

"Don't ask," I replied, but still proceeded to tell him.

I sighed as I read a text from Katherine. She was not pleased as Olivia had challenged her about my surveillance trip to Millar's. The text summoned me to the pier. She wanted to meet me after they closed at six o'clock.

"Cheer up you two," Dannie said as she entered the room. "I've found some information on Darren Box. Do you want my report?"

"Great, I need something to justify the fees I'm receiving from Katherine," I said.

She sat opposite us and spun the laptop around so we could see the screen. "I located him on social media. He posted this picture a couple of weeks ago."

Darren had dark hair, a weathered tanned face and sat smiling, with a pint of beer in his hand. There was a boat in the background.

"Recognise that?" Dannie asked pointing to the vessel.

"Yeah. It's Bristol harbourside," Jeff said.

"So he's in the area?" I asked. This indeed was a development.

"I called Lynn," Dannie said. "And she's made a few enquiries. Darren Box has been staying with his mother in Bristol and has been spotted a few times in Branden Bay."

"I'M SO SORRY," I said as I entered Katherine's office. "I know I totally messed up earlier."

"Tell me you've made some progress. Or am I wasting my money here?"

I sat down and lowered my voice. “I have some disturbing news about your husband.”

Katherine pursed her lips but made no comment.

“He’s been spotted in Bristol and here in Branden Bay.”

Katherine sighed and I noticed that she didn’t look surprised. “He came to see me a few weeks ago.”

I sat back. “This is important. Why didn’t you mention it? The police will probably want to question him.”

“I didn’t want Olivia to find out. I don’t want her to have anything to do with him.” She put a hand to her forehead. “I’d assumed he’d gone straight back to Ibiza.”

“But why not mention it?”

She sighed. “I was going to, I nearly did when you brought him up, but I’ve always believed that if you have a secret the only way to keep it, is to tell no-one. Olivia must not know he’s been in contact.”

“We must report this to the police. If he was in the country at the time of Ben’s death, they need to know.”

“Please don’t tell them yet. Olivia is bound to find out that he’s here. She wasn’t good enough for him when she was a toddler so he’s not good enough for her now. He thinks he can just walk into her life after I’ve spent years taking on the role of mum and dad. He’s got a nerve and I told him, in simple language that he could understand, to get lost.”

"You have to deal with this, Katherine. Don't you think Olivia has a right to know he was here?"

"I guess you're right. But we have the wake tomorrow. And then the masked ball on Friday. It's the only great thing Olivia and I do together. It might be the last ball we attend before I lose her for good."

My gut feeling told me I should tell H immediately about Darren Box being in town, he'd go mad at me for withholding information. But Katherine was the client and had specifically told me to keep it to myself. I agreed to stay quiet until after the ball. Until then, it would be up to me and my team, to keep a close eye on Katherine, just in case Darren was out there trying to hurt her.

CHAPTER 16

It was the day of Ben's wake. Finding a parking space during the summer months along Beach Road was a nightmare, so Jeff parked his van at the spiritualist hut and walked into my kitchen through the back door with Lynn.

Dannie and I were ready and the four of us planned to walk to the wake together. There was a strictly 'no black' dress code as it was to be seen as a celebration. We wore an array of bright clothing. I was dressed in a pink soft top with a yellow skirt. Lynn wore a patterned purple and pink kaftan, Dannie had a light blue top on with white trousers and Jeff wore his usual clothes with a less washed-out t-shirt, which I presumed was new. As we left my house through the private front door, Constance wriggled her way out, before I could shut her in.

"Constance, no."

"Let her come lovey," Lynn said. "She always brightens the atmosphere."

Constance trotted to the pavement and we followed her towards the pub.

"Seems she knows where she's going." Lynn laughed.

Dannie linked arms with me. "How are you feeling about the café?"

"The wait for the license is killing me."

"I think you've got a great chance," Lynn said.

"The fact that they've not fined you is a good sign," Jeff added.

"I agree," said Dannie. "No news is good news."

I felt cheered by their support. Jeff opened the pub door and held it as we went inside, then followed us in. Around the walls were pictures of Ben pinned to a line of bunting. I smiled as I checked out the photographs of him as a lad and one with his wife Gloria, already in spirit, on their wedding day. As I moved along the stretch of photographs, I felt a buzz. Ben flickered, in the corner of the room and I rubbed the static from my arms.

I kept his presence to myself. "It's busy in here," I said turning to Annie as she approached us.

"It's because there's a free bar. That's why we had to issue invitations, otherwise half of Brandon Bay would be here."

"Where's Katherine?"

"She's with the landlord's wife." Annie lowered her voice. "She's had way too many drinks."

"We need to keep eyes on her and watch out for Darren." I still felt it was wrong of us not to tell the police he was in the area. I felt nervous as I scanned the room and decided that, no matter what Katherine said, I would contact H when I returned home to let him know Darren was in the country.

I glanced at a long table where hot buffet food was on offer and my tummy rumbled. There were fat, juicy sausages, onions, bread rolls and chips.

"The food smells lovely," Lynn said.

"It was Ben's favourite." Annie gestured at the table. "He always ordered sausage and chips when he came here."

"Help yourselves to food," shouted the landlord.

As the five of us dug in, I scanned the room. "Did Clive turn up?" I asked.

"No," Annie said. "I don't expect him to show."

"That's a shame, isn't it, Jeff?" I said.

Jeff huffed and stood up with his plate of food. "I'll be at the bar."

"What's wrong with him?" asked Dannie.

"I told him that he reminded me of Clive. He took offence."

"I see what you mean," Annie said. "Same sense of style and fashion. Clive could pass as Jeff's older brother."

"I sense you miss Clive," Lynn said to Annie.

Annie nodded. “It’s not the same at the pier without him.”

“Even though you took his job?” Dannie said.

Annie bit her lip. “I’d rather have had him there than the promotion. It’s been hard.”

I heard raised voices and noticed Katherine swaying at the bar. “So you turned up then?” She pointed at Olivia who stood just inside the door. “And surprise, surprise, you’re with Nathan,” she slurred. It looked as if it could get messy. I stood up and approached them.

“Hi Olivia, Nathan,” I said smiling. “Would you like me to get you both a drink?”

Olivia shook her head. “I’m quite capable of asking for my own. After all it’s a free bar.” She rolled her eyes. “Come on, Nathan,” she said as she took his arm.

“Why is she so rude?” Katherine slurred.

I approached her. “Maybe you should have a coffee?” I suggested.

“You youngsters are all the same,” she said to me. “You don't know how to have a proper drink.”

The landlady rushed from behind the bar and supported Katherine. “Come on, Kath. Let’s go back to the kitchen. I’ve a nice stodgy sticky toffee pud with custard waiting for you.” She smiled at me and led Katherine away.

Hopefully that pudding will soak up the booze, I thought. Katherine was becoming the most awkward client I’d had so far. Although, to be fair, I’d only had one other. Still, her keeping things from me and now misbehaving was making my job difficult.

I felt I should apologise on her behalf and approached Olivia. "Your mum's had too much to drink."

"You don't say." Olivia gave a slow blink and sighed.

"Katherine doesn't like it that Olivia and me are close," Nathan said.

"Are you just friends?" I asked.

"That's none of your business," Olivia said. "Or Mum's." She passed a pint of beer to Nathan and stared at me with a sparkling water in her hand. "I guess you won't be doing the spinning class again?"

I decided that was time for me to move on. As I turned, Katherine appeared behind the bar.

"Oh, look who it is." She'd clearly escaped the clutches of the landlady. She held onto the taps of the draft beer to steady herself.

I turned my head to see who she was staring at. It was Andrew Farr.

He raked a hand through his unruly blonde hair. "Don't start, Katherine. I just want to pay my respects like everyone else. Today is not about you."

"Be my guest," she said as she gestured her hand around the room.

"There you are," the landlady said as she ushered Katherine out the back.

I glanced at the corner where Ben stood. He flickered on and off. As I approached him, pins and needles shot up my body. I flinched. “I’m doing my best.”

Constance meowed as if to back me up.

I heard Olivia behind me. “Are you talking to yourself?”

I picked Constance up.

“Or are you wearing an earpiece and reporting my movements back to base?” She gave a sarcastic laugh.

I glanced behind me. Ben had disappeared. “I was talking to my cat.” I stroked Constance now in my arms.

Constance gave a low meow as if to corroborate with my lie.

Over Olivia’s shoulder, I saw the door open and in strolled Izzy, making an entrance with an over-the-top mourning outfit. I wasn’t sure whether she’d got the memo about the dress code, or simply chose to ignore it. She was in all black, with fifties style pointed shades and a veil net. She scanned the room and came towards me.

“Darling. Sorry I’m late.”

“Don't worry, there’s still food left,” I said.

She pulled her shades down and peered at the sausage, chips and congealing fried onions. “I’ll give it a miss, sweetie.” She gave a regal wave to Olivia. Nathan scowled at her, but Izzy did not register it, if she had noticed at all. Izzy waved at our friends sitting at the table, now tucking into bowls of pudding and custard.

"Have you had any updates from Jason?" I asked her.

"He says he'll get back to you after the weekend. He has your number."

I sighed as I glanced around the room. This case was proving to be the most complicated. My head spun as I stroked Constance, it seemed that Clive was definitely not turning up.

THE NEXT DAY was the Summer Masked Ball. I'd emailed H the night before, from an anonymous account, warning him that Darren Box was in town. I felt much better, even though I'd told Katherine I would keep it to myself – because her safety was my primary concern.

I arrived at Izzy's with a suit bag, containing the dress she'd sent over to my place. As I reached her apartment door, it was open. I entered to find Izzy sitting at a mobile dressing table in her lounge with a hairdresser and make-up artist doing their work. I noticed there was a dustsheet down, no doubt to keep the place spotless.

"Becky, darling, pour yourself a glass of fizz and help yourself to nibbles."

"It looks like it's your wedding day," I said with a grin as I lifted the bottle.

Izzy gave me a royal wave. "It's all about keeping up appearances, darling. Meet Trina and Beth."

"Hi," I said as they smiled back at me. I noticed that Izzy's hair was a lot longer than usual.

"Becky's next," Izzy said.

"Me?" I frowned at her. "I thought you said you were doing my makeup and hair."

Izzy laughed. "I said I would sort it. Not do it myself. Goodness, no."

"I feel I should contribute."

"Nonsense, darling. I'm calling in favours," she said but I saw her winking at the women as they carried on with their work. "You're going to love this evening. It's the best night in Branden Bay if you ask me. They've been holding the Summer Masked Ball up at the old castle for years. They used to do New Year's Eve parties there too, but one year some poor guy was murdered on the dance floor so it was cancelled as a mark of respect."

"Is it run by Millar's Hotel?" I asked.

"Yes. They hire it out. The hotel is full in the summer season, so it's easier for them to hold the ball at the castle. They have a shuttle bus for their guests to ferry them up. People come from all over you know and some minor celebrities."

I wondered whether Izzy saw herself as a minor celebrity.

"Perfect," she said when Trina and Beth had finished their work. The extensions added to her hair were amazing. She looked like a Greek goddess with a crown of white Ivy.

"Izzy, you look lush," I said.

"And so shall you, Cinders," she laughed and gracefully stood up.

Goodness knows what I'm going to look like next to her, I thought.

"Sit down, sweetie." She lifted a small piece of white lace. "This is your mask. It goes over the eyes but allows for false eyelashes."

"Wouldn't it have been easier if I wore a full-face mask?"

"Darling, take it from me, they make you sweat and you can't see what's going on through the eye holes. It would be useless for surveillance." She waved the mask. "This is the better option. Now, sit still so Trina and Beth can do their magic and turn you into someone new."

Trina braided my hair, adding extra strands of white to create two thick, lengthy braids. I covered my face with my hands while she sprayed my locks silver. When Trina had finished, I opened my eyes and could not see any evidence of my red hair at all.

"Wow," I said. "I already don't look like me."

"Just wait until Beth does your make-up," Izzy said.

By the time Beth had finished, and I looked in the mirror, I was astounded. She'd used shading and colours I would never use. She even changed the shape of my nose with her expert contouring. I had different eyebrows and jawline and then, when Izzy added the small white lace eye mask, the look was complete. “That’s amazing,” I said.

“This,” Izzy said, “is a proper undercover look.”

Izzy saw Trina and Beth out of the apartment and turned to me. “Let’s get our dresses on, sweetie, and finish off that fizz.”

We gazed in the mirror, side by side. Izzy with her tall figure in a long flowing white dress peppered with rhinestones and me – not so tall, in a sparkly short dress with a tutu underneath to give the skirt fullness. It was covered in sequins and I wore silver stockings and soft ballet-style shoes.

“You’re a winter mythological queen and I’m some sort of snowflake,” I laughed.

“You look amazing, sweetie. Definitely an ice princess. Now, have you decided on your accent?”

“I’m going sophisticated – Queen’s English,” I said, as I adjusted my voice to drawling posh mode. “So pleased to make your acquaintance. I’m Penelope.”

Izzy laughed. “Come on, Penelope my darling, let’s spy.”

CHAPTER 17

We drew up at the castle in a limo. Izzy had balked at the suggestion of Jeff giving us a lift in the van. The driver opened the door first for Izzy, then came around to my side of the car.

"Thank you," I said as I took his hand.

Jeff's van was stationed in the far corner of the carpark with Constance sitting on the dash. He flashed his headlights at me and I gave him a small wave. I felt better knowing he was there, looking after Constance.

Izzy put her arm out for me to hold and she gracefully led me up the stone steps to the castle. There were flame torches flickering in the breeze but not yet lighting up the sky, which was still tinged yellow and pink.

"Remind me of the plan?" she whispered as we climbed the steps.

"We know that Andrew and Olivia will be here as

well as Katherine. I want to keep an eye on anyone who gets close to her or is acting suspiciously."

As we reached the door, a guard in uniform opened it for us. "Tickets?"

We passed them over.

"Thank you, ladies. Enjoy your evening," he said waving us on with a smile.

I needed to find Katherine and I glanced around the room. There were maybe two hundred masked revellers. *This is going to be tough,* I thought. Katherine had told me in a rather apologetic text, following her drunk behaviour at the wake, that she would be dressed as Marie Antionette and wearing a blue and gold dress, so at least I would know who she was. She also mentioned she would be on the soft drinks. Annie and I had near carried her home after the wake.

"Isabelle, my beauty, you look totally ravishing," said a man dressed as the Scarlett Pimpernel. He lifted his mask so Izzy could see his face. She held out her hand and he kissed it. "And who is your little friend?" he asked.

Little? Blooming cheek, I thought.

"She's my dear friend from Kensington. Penelope Flemington-Hyde."

"So pleased to meet you," I said in the poshest voice I could muster, wishing I had thought of a surname rather than having to use one Izzy had made up on the spot. After all, I hadn't considered that people would be exchanging full names at a masked ball. I'd assumed it was all about anonymity.

The Scarlet Pimpernel nodded at me briefly before turning his full attention back to Izzy. "Can I get you a glass of Champagne?"

"Oh, Jonny, you're such a darling," Izzy said.

"I have a table with space for both of you, if you'd like to join us?"

We followed Jonny to a table where another man was sitting, leaning back in his chair dressed as a highwayman. He eyed me up and down.

"This is Kirk, he's big in tech," Jonny said. "And I'm sure you'll recognise the famous and stunning Isabelle."

"Indeed, no mask could disguise your beauty," Kirk said to her.

Oh, do me a favour, I thought.

"And this is her friend, Pamela," Jonny said as he picked up the bottle of champagne in an ice bucket and poured us both a glass.

"Penelope," I corrected him. "Flemington Hythe."

"I thought Isabelle said Hyde?" he frowned. "I know the Hyde's of Kensington. I assumed you were related?" He handed me a flute of fizz.

Izzy tapped my shoulder. "Poor Penelope has a lisp. Don't you dear."

"Yeth," I laughed nervously, hoping they would not realise you don't lisp on a 'd'. There was no way I would remember a lisp all evening. It was challenging enough keeping up the posh voice. "Oh, I've theen thomeone I know," I said. "Tootle pip."

I made my escape. I needed to concentrate on the case, not make idle and awkward chit chat. As I looked over my shoulder, I saw both men cooing over Izzy. I tutted.

A low balcony ran around the edge of the ballroom. It wouldn't have been part of the original castle, five hundred years ago. A buffet table was situated at the opposite side to the entrance and there was a constant queue for food. The acoustics of the castle were not ideal, with the music from the live band reverberating around the room, but no-one seemed to mind. It was difficult to tell with the masks, but I imagined the room was wall to wall smiles. Not spotting Katherine, I scanned the area for a sign of Andrew. His hair was distinctive, blonde and unruly. I wondered why he wasn't married. Maybe if he had a wife she'd get him a proper haircut. Whilst hunting for him, I noticed that most men had dressed as highwaymen with black hats and masks.

I recognised a few of those present. There was Eleanor Corelli from the wine bar, recognisable because of her gorgeous dark locks, and Mrs Simons, President of the Ladies society with her husband whose walking stick gave their identity away. And in the corner was a guy I recognised from a reality TV show, he was dressed as Bond, and not wearing a mask.

I passed a mirror and jumped at my reflection – I

didn't even recognise myself. After finishing the flute of fizz, I bought a soft drink from the bar and sipped it. As I gazed into the sea of partygoers, I took a sharp intake of breath. Striding towards the bar was a very muscly, tall, dark haired phantom of the opera in black tight trousers, a white silk shirt, and a tight-fitting black waistcoat with a long black cape. Even though he was wearing a white half mask, I'd recognise him anywhere. It was H.

I thought he'd given his tickets away to Reception Mike? I thought.

He headed straight for the section of the bar where I stood. I realised it was not just looks and accent I had to deal with. If I recognised H's gait, maybe he would recognise mine. *Channel your inner Izzy,* I told myself. She always glided along as if on the catwalk. I may not have the height of a runway model, but I could strut that way. As H approached, I sashayed away from the bar, passing him. When I reached the balcony of the dance floor, I leaned up against the barrier. I glanced at him over my shoulder and he was at the bar ordering drinks. It was lucky that he didn't recognise me. My heart thud in my chest. I needed to focus on the reason I was there.

After finishing the last dregs of my drink, I left the empty glass on a table as I walked onto the dance floor. I glanced casually around for any sign of Katherine, Andrew and Olivia. I was soon at the opposite side of the room and took the short flight of steps back up to the balcony. I spotted H walking around the periphery with two drinks. *I wonder who he brought?* I thought following him with my eyes until he stopped next to a woman in a tight fitting long red dress, which had a split all the way up to her thigh. She had a black satin mask and glossy chestnut hair. *Tara the spinning queen,* I thought. They probably overheard Reception Mike talking about the Summer Masked Ball. H must have taken the tickets back and invited Tara. I frowned and looked away and it was then that I spotted Katherine in her Marie Antionette outfit with a large blonde wig. She was with a highwayman. They were dancing very close up indeed. I wanted to get nearer to them but not dance on my own. I needed Izzy.

Travelling along the balcony I spotted H on the dancefloor with Tara. I frowned as they moved to the music. Her calves looked strong above her red stilettos. He held her hand and she twirled around laughing, then he tipped her back, balancing her torso on his arm.

Show off, I thought but I had to admit, they were a striking couple. Both tall and attractive. I felt juvenile in my outfit. *Don't put yourself down,* I told myself. Sticking my nose in the air, I flicked one of my silver coated pigtails over my shoulder and went to find Izzy.

She was still at the table, laughing with the men and looked up as I approached. "Darling Beck ... Penelope. There you are. Seen anything interesting?"

"Yes," I said.

"Maybe you should show me. I need to stretch my legs." She stood up to the protests of her admirers. "I'll be back."

"And then can I have a dance?" Jonny asked.

"Later," she said.

I shook my head as we walked away.

"Have you spotted Katherine?" Izzy asked.

"Yes, she's on the dance floor and H is here. We need to avoid him."

"I thought he was giving his tickets away. Is he alone?"

"No, he's entangled with some woman."

Izzy laughed. "You sound jealous, sweetie."

"Rubbish. I just don't want him to spot me here."

"He'll never recognise you. Don't speak if we bump into him."

As if on cue I heard H's voice. "Izzy."

The hairs stood up on the back of my neck.

"H darling," Izzy said as he approached us with Tara on his arm. "You look positively dashing." She gave him an air kiss. "And this is?" she said looking at his date.

"Tara," he said.

"Ah, let me guess. You met at the gym?" Izzy asked.

H was well known for his gym girlfriends. He frowned. "Tara is my spinning instructor."

"I do a lot more than that," Tara said. "I've spent years as a personal trainer across the country. I've noticed you at the gym, Isabelle." She smiled. "I didn't realise you were friends with H. I've come to Branden Bay on a short-term contract, but I love it here. There's a lot about this town to admire." She placed a hand on H's chest.

"And this must be the new girlfriend you were telling us about?" H nodded at me.

"Indeed. it's Penelope Fitzgerald Heath," Izzy said.

I wish Izzy would keep to the same name, I thought keeping my lips pursed, not wanting to speak.

"That's a mouthful. I'm just plain H," he said to me as he put out his hand.

I didn't want to touch it, so gave him a short wave.

"Well don't let us stop you." H pointed to the dance floor.

My heart thud. "That was awful," I whispered to Izzy as we walked away.

"I told you no-one would recognise you. Just relax."

As we danced, Izzy bent down and spoke in my ear. "I see him."

"Who?"

"Farr. There." She pointed.

He ran his hand through his unruly hair then put his hat back on. He was also dressed as a highwayman and was being led onto the dance floor by a woman dressed as Marie Antoinette.

"That's Katherine he's with," I said. "We need to get closer." My heart thudded ... as I wondered whether she realised it's Andrew she was dancing with?

As we moved close to them, I strained to hear their voices over the music.

"Can we stop pretending?" Andrew said.

"Hey," Jonny tapped me on the shoulder. "Can I cut in? It's my turn to dance with the local celebrity." And with that he whisked Izzy away, leaving me standing there like a lemon.

"All alone? Penelope?"

I spun around, it was H.

Oh, no, I thought.

He held out his hand. "Where's your date?" he asked.

I pointed to Izzy dancing with Jonny.

"Seems we're both at a loose end." He pointed to Tara who was dancing with a superhero clad in blue and gold. H grabbed my hand. "Let's dance."

He spun me around and I near fell over.

"Sorry." He brought me in tight. "I'll make sure you don't come to harm," he said. "What was your full name again?"

"Penelope Fitzpatrick ..." I wracked my brain. "Hythe."

H laughed. "Wrong. Try Becky James." He held me tight and whispered in my ear. "I clocked you as soon as I walked past you. You should have worn a different perfume."

"Ever the clever Detective Blake."

"What are you up to you, little frosty fairy?"

"I'm not a fairy. I'm an ice princess."

He laughed and spun me around again.

I looked up and saw Tara, her arms crossed as she watched us.

“I think maybe you need to get back to your girlfriend.”

H chuckled. “I asked you here first, remember? Don’t be jealous.”

“I’m not jealous,” I shouted. The couple next to us stared. I wasn’t sure why it came out so loud.

“I know you’re up to something. What are you doing?”

“I’m keeping an eye on Katherine, she insisted on coming so I decided to go under cover. I didn’t mean to turn you down as your plus one, but we’d already arranged to come. And I didn’t want to have to explain myself to you.”

Izzy danced over.

“Lover’s tiff?”

H stepped back and kissed my hand before leaving the dance floor.

“He knew it was me straight away.” I crossed my arms.

“Well, it was a tall order, sweetie. With the sizzling attraction between the two of you. Where’s Katherine and Andrew?” she asked looking around.

They were gone.

CHAPTER 18

We crossed the dance floor and took the steps up to the balcony, passing H who was in deep conversation with his date.

Izzy tapped me on the shoulder. "I've been telling you for ages to snap him up. You've only yourself to blame."

"I'm not bothered," I said through gritted teeth.

Izzy and I scanned the room for Andrew and Katherine.

"I can't see them anywhere," I said.

"It's impossible," Izzy said. "Most men show up as highwaymen. I guess it's a more macho look than some of the other options."

"Although there's only one Marie Antionette to look for, so let's focus on finding Katherine," I said.

I glanced around the room at the women when I spotted Olivia, wearing a long blue dress with her brown hair in ringlets. She was with a highwayman and whether or not she'd started in a mask, she was not wearing one anymore. I assumed the tall man she was with was Nathan.

The music had slowed to a ballad and Jonny approached, whisking Izzy back down the steps. I watched as Izzy moved gracefully around the floor, laughing as if she didn't have a care in the world. At that point, my life was more like the dance I'd had with H, the sort that could easily trip you up. Still, I was determined to get this case solved. I could feel it inside – I was getting close. In to view came H, dancing with Tara, her arms languishing around his shoulders, as they gazed into each other's eyes. I didn't know why it wound me up so much, but I certainly knew I no longer wanted to watch. I turned around and bang – I bumped straight into Katherine.

"Ouch," she said.

"I'm so sorry," I bit my lip. "It's me, Becky."

Her mask was attached to a stick, held up to her face. She pulled it to one side. "That's an impressive costume."

A highwayman grabbed her hand. Katherine giggled and waved at me as she was swept down to the dance floor. Clearly there was a lot about Andrew that Katherine was keeping from me. I shook my head. How was I supposed to protect Katherine when she kept so much information from me? Andrew was hardly the killer, if they were having a secret romance.

I'd wasted hours and embarrassed myself investigating him. As I kept my eyes on Katherine, I noticed her demeanour change. She didn't look quite so happy. As the man bent his head, I saw no sign of unruly blonde hair underneath his hat. *That's not Andrew,* I thought. They didn't stop to dance, and the highwayman gruffly led her off the dance floor and up the stairs to the opposite balcony. He pulled her along and she dropped her mask on the floor.

"Stop," I shouted. I ran around the periphery rather than across the dance floor. As I passed the bar, I bumped into Andrew who was scanning the room with his hat and mask off.

"Andrew, it's me, Becky. I think Katherine's in danger."

He frowned at me. "Becky James?"

"Yes. Katherine was dragged away by a highwayman. I think she thought he was you."

"I told her she should have come with me to the bar."

I could tell instinctively that this man did not want Katherine dead. "Quick," I said. "I sense she's in danger."

"That woman is a pain in the – "

"Follow me," I said interrupting him, as I ran towards the area of the balcony where they'd disappeared.

As we reached it, there was a door with 'no entry' written on it.

"Where does that go?" I asked Andrew who was puffing behind me.

"Up to the turrets."

I pushed open the door which revealed a stone spiral flight of stairs. "Look," I said. There was a glittering stilettoed shoe at the bottom.

Andrew ran forward and picked it up, like he was prince charming. He called out as he climbed the steps with the shoe in his hand. "Katherine! Katherine!" He sounded like a crazy man – not as in crazy killer – but as in crazy scared.

I followed him up. The steps opened out into a circular room. Katherine cowered on the other side. "No," she shouted as a figure in black lurched for Andrew knocking him to the hard floor, before turning to me, his eyes barely visible through the small slits of his mask. He thrust me against the wall and my head thud against the stone. Then he was gone, his cape billowing behind him.

I stood leaning against the wall, to catch my breath, my eyes smarting with the pain searing through my head.

Andrew moaned as Katherine crawled across the room and leaned over him.

I rubbed the back of my head and looked at my hand. There was no blood on my hands, just silver hairspray.

"Andrew, are you okay?" Katherine's voice was hoarse.

"Who was it?" I asked her.

She rasped. "I don't know. But he had his hands around my neck." She raised her head and I noticed red marks on her skin. "Thanks so much for finding me."

"I watched him drag you off the dance floor," I said.

Andrew moaned. "Sorry Kathy, I should have taken him out."

"If you hadn't come in, I might have been killed," Katherine said.

"Did you recognise the man's voice?" I asked.

"He never said a word. He pushed me up the stairs, I thought he might have a knife, I went into a panic and could hardly breathe." The tears brimmed in her eyes. "I thought he was going to throw me off the top of the turret. I feel hot." She pulled out a couple of pins and pushed off her wig revealing her dark hair, which had been tied into a bun.

I took her hand. "You're safe now, Katherine."

"On and on, he squeezed my neck. Then I heard Andrew calling me."

Andrew sat up. "We need to find him."

I placed a hand on his shoulder. "Now take it slow. Don't stand up yet, I'll go and get help."

We heard someone climbing the steps and H rushed in. "There you are. I saw you running off. I've been up and down multiple flights of steps, searching for you. I've knocked my head on three doorways." He rubbed his forehead.

"Someone dragged Katherine up here," I said. "Her attacker was tall and dressed as a highwayman, which I know doesn't help, most of the guys in here seem to be dressed that way. He tried to strangle Katherine to death, knocked Andrew to the ground and pushed me up against the wall, then fled."

"We had a tip off yesterday about a person of interest. Can you call an ambulance? I'll contact the station." He reached for his pocket pulling out his mobile phone and left the room.

I guessed the tip off, he'd referred to, was the one from me to say Darren Box was in the neighbourhood.

We heard another set of footsteps. "Mummy," Olivia appeared at the door and ran over to Katherine, giving her a hug.

I moved away to give them space.

"I need to get attacked more often," Katherine said with a weak laugh.

"The police are onto it already," I informed Olivia. "Detective sergeant Blake is here and I've let him know what happened."

"What did he do to you?" Olivia asked her mother.

"He roughed me up, but I'm fine." She rubbed her neck. "Becky and Andrew scared him off."

I lifted my phone. "I'll call the paramedics now." I had no service. "I'll go up to the turret to get a signal." The thick walls were probably the issue.

I took another flight of stone steps until I reached the top. The wind blew my pigtails and I felt chilly in the dark night looking down at the twinkling lights of the town. I called Jeff.

He answered immediately. "Are you alright Boss?"

"Yes, but Katherine has been attacked. She's fine – just shaken."

"What happened?" he asked.

"I can't chat now, but if you see a lone, or suspicious highwayman leaving the scene – follow him with caution. Do not approach. He's dangerous." My hand shook as I ended the call. The realisation that I'd been so close to the killer struck me. I took a moment, before calling the emergency services.

Having requested the paramedics, I made my way back inside.

Katherine, Andrew and Olivia were huddled together on the floor. They looked like a proper family. I felt a pang of sadness. I missed my parents desperately.

"Are you going to listen now, Mum? It doesn't have to be like this. The pier is ruining our lives," Olivia said.

"I'm sorry," Katherine said. "It's in my blood, I can't leave it."

"You don't have to," Andrew added. "Why aren't we together anyway? We come here once a year and pretend we don't know who the other person is and dance together all night. It's madness." He took her hand. "I look forward to this evening all year. It's when you're Kathy again – the girl I fell in love with years ago. But the rest of the time you're so cold."

"I ..." She looked up and noticed me watching. "We'll discuss this later."

"But will you? Outside of these walls?" Andrew asked. "Will you discuss us?"

Katherine put a hand on his arm. "I promise."

Olivia stood up. "Let's get out of this place." She put her hand out to help her mother to standing. Then we all heaved Andrew up, who appeared wobbly on his feet. I guessed he was concussed.

"I've called the paramedics," I said. "Let's go downstairs to meet them, as this crime scene has been contaminated enough."

It was a slow journey down the stairs. By the time we reached the function room, Katherine had her wig back in place, although it was slightly skewwhiff. Andrew's hair was sticking out in all directions and Olivia had mascara running down her face from where she'd been crying. The music had stopped and the lights were on.

"It looks like they've caught him," said Andrew.

My stomach burned inside as I saw H restraining a masked highwayman on the dance floor who shouted. "Let me go."

As I got closer, H removed the man's mask, like the big reveal in a movie. I was waiting for the guy to point at me and say, 'And I would have got away with it if it wasn't for her...' A few people stepped back as if in shock. I squinted at him. It was a face I'd seen before, but not someone I'd met.

A woman nearby gasped. "Oh my goodness, it's only Darren Box."

I felt a sigh of relief. It wasn't some random person, it was someone on my suspect list. Someone with a motive. And he'd been caught. I turned to Katherine and Olivia. Both had their eyes and mouths wide open.

Katherine marched up to Darren with her hand to her throat. "How could you? After all the pain you caused me? And now you want me dead?"

Andrew called out. "Come on Kathy, he's not worth any more of your energy."

Katherine turned back and approached Olivia. "Darling. It might be better if you go home." I saw fear in her eyes as if she waited for her daughter's explosive reaction.

"You've got the wrong person," Olivia said pointing at Darren. "Dad's not a murderer."

Katherine blinked rapidly. "You know who he is?"

"Yes, and he's innocent. He must be."

"You knew he was in town?" I asked Olivia.

"He contacted me, and we've seen each other a few times."

"Why didn't you tell me?" asked Katherine.

"He said he'd asked your permission and you said no. But he couldn't leave without meeting me. I've got a brother and two sisters in Ibiza." Tears pooled in her eyes. "But I didn't want to upset you. I've been so stressed and ratty about it." She looked at her father being pinned down by H. "I invited him here tonight."

He was the guy Olivia was with, I thought. I'd assumed it was Nathan.

Olivia appealed to H. "You've got to believe me. Dad can't have hurt Mum."

I felt sorry for Olivia. She'd only just been reunited with her father and here he was being arrested for the attempted murder of her mother.

The uniformed police arrived.

"This is Darren Box," H said. "Arrest him on suspicion of the murder of Benjamin Goldfield and for the assault of Katherine Sheringham."

"No." Olivia put her hands to her face.

Darren shouted as a police officer handcuffed him. "It's not me."

The paramedics arrived and H pointed out Katherine and Andrew. "Are you okay?" He asked, as he reached my side. "Do you need to be checked over?"

"No. I'm fine," I said. "So, you caught him then?"

"Katherine was lucky, you spooked him. He's been in the country long before Ben's murder. Thanks for the anonymous tip off."

"What are you talking about?" I smiled. "I'd better collect Izzy and get going."

"I'll be off too. I have to leave it to uniform." H said

goodbye and made a bee-line for Tara. They strolled off hand-in-hand towards the exit.

"Oh, sweetie, cheer up. It might be a quick fling," Izzy said as she appeared by my side.

"What?" I asked.

"H and his gorgeous date."

"Good luck to him. He deserves a nice girlfriend," I said.

"I'm staying to interview a few people for the story. I've messaged the driver to get here in half an hour."

"I'll be getting off," I stifled a yawn. "Jeff will give me a lift." I bade her farewell. As I stepped outside, I felt a huge sigh of relief. The killer had been caught and I wasn't down as being the one who'd apprehended him. A case solved, without the media hype, without the embarrassing pictures in the press and hopefully Ben would be able to rest in peace and I'd have a ghost-free home.

Outside, I called Jeff because his van was no longer in the corner. He said he'd be with me in five minutes. I presumed he'd been to the fish-and-chip shop.

Jeff drew up to the drop-off point. I climbed in.

"Sorry, boss. We lost him."

"We? And lost who?" I asked.

"The highwayman you called about. He was running out and your cat bolted after him through the open van window like a bullet."

"You let her go? I thought you were keeping an eye

on her." I stroked my cat as she stared out of the front window.

"I followed her straight away. I got to the bottom of the drive and she was sniffing around in the bushes. The guy had disappeared. I drove around looking for him, but he was gone."

I shook my head. "You were following the wrong man. But no worries, more than half of the men in there were dressed as highwaymen."

He sat back in his seat. "Who was it?"

"Darren Box," I said as I saw him being led down the path by the police. "They're taking him in." I pointed to the unmasked highwayman.

"He looks mean," said Jeff as he put the van into gear.

"He's certainly angry." I shuddered. "Let's get home, I really need to relax."

Constance hissed from the middle seat as Jeff drove us away.

I picked her up, ruffling the hair on her head. "Calm down Connie. Are you hungry is that it?"

"I can't believe it," Jeff said. "It's insane to think Katherine's DJ husband is the killer."

Constance gave a low wail.

"He's denying it, of course," I said, as I watched the convoy of police cars behind us, in the van's wing mirror.

"Congratulations then," Jeff said as he drove us

down to Beach Road. "I wish I'd been there to see it. I expect you'll soon be on the front page of the Gazette."

"It wasn't me that caught Darren – it was H. Although he did thank me for sending him an anonymous tip off."

Constance meowed and growled all the way home.

CHAPTER 19

It was gone eleven when we rolled to a stop outside my home, I invited Jeff in.

"I'm popping upstairs to take these plaits out," I said pointing to my pigtails. "Can you make us a drink? I'd love a cup of tea."

I stared at my reflection in the bathroom mirror. My head ached from the tightness of the braids. As I unravelled them, the extra white strands appeared welded to my own locks. With the braids undone, it was if I had silver branches sticking out of my head. *What a total mess,* I thought and decided to have a tea with Jeff before tackling it further.

As I descended the stairs, I heard a rapping noise. *Who's that this time of night?* I thought as I hurried to the front door and opened it. I found H standing before me, still dressed as the phantom of the opera, sans the white half mask.

He burst out laughing. "Hello Medusa."

"Is something wrong?" I asked. "Aren't you supposed to be at the police station?"

"I can't process the suspect, I've been drinking. We must wait until we're both sober. He'll be sleeping his beer off in the cells." He looked over my shoulder. "Are you going to leave me out here?"

I opened the door wide to let him in. The wind blew his cape as he entered.

"It still smells of smoke in here," he said.

"I need to give it a new lick of paint," I said. "Your date didn't invite you back to her place then?"

"She lives in Bristol and took a cab back."

"So you didn't offer her a bed for the night?"

He laughed. "On a first date?"

My stomach churned at his mention of first date, no doubt there would be more to come. I wasn't jealous, I just didn't like the girl. Would she be joining our gang? Would she be at the monthly meals? My heart thud. I'd never felt so enraged about another woman. *Stop being ridiculous,* I told myself.

"Is that how the girls do it back in London?" he asked. "A sleepover on the first date?"

I ignored his comment as I led him to the kitchen. "You seemed to be getting on well."

"Tara's great company. Easy to be with," he said as we walked through the hall. "Not hard work like some people." He spun me around as we reached the open kitchen door. "You look angry. What is it? Are you sore because you won't get credit for catching Branden Bay's latest criminal?" He grinned.

I knew he was only teasing, that's what mates do. And we were just mates. So why was I so livid?

Jeff rose from his seat at the kitchen table. "I think I'll go. I'm not working tomorrow, so let me know if you need any help." Jeff knew I'd planned to spend the following day, baking for the christening.

"Thanks for the offer, I'll let you know," I said, watching him leave.

H folded his arms and leaned on the kitchen counter. "I came by, to make sure you got home safely and for a chat."

I flicked the kettle on again, to make him a coffee, I had some granules at the back of the cupboard. I felt he needed sobering up. He seemed way more relaxed and friendly than usual.

"So, come on then," H said. "Why don't we have a proper date? We've been out on things that felt like a date. At least, they did from my point of view. Dinner in Corelli's, walks along the most romantic prom in England. You've even been back to meet my folks. Let's bite the bullet, put everything else aside and go for it with an official date."

I gulped, feeling heat rise up my neck and was glad for the thick foundation Beth had put on my face.

"Everyone says we should go out," He lowered his voice. "I'm curious. Aren't you?"

I can't deal with this right now, I thought. I was tired

and confused. And while a killer had been apprehended, I didn't feel anything like the closure I had in my previous two cases. I presumed it was because H grabbed Darren and not me. The kettle clicked as the water reached boiling and the silence became increasingly awkward the longer it lasted.

"Tara's keen, really keen. She wants us to be exclusive," H said.

"She seems nice," I lied through gritted teeth.

"She's great. But if there's any chance of us ...?"

He stared into my eyes. I didn't know what to say. Was he asking me to be his girlfriend?

"Did you feel something tonight? When we danced?" He took a step towards me.

"I ... er ... "

The front door opened and a clattering sound followed as I heard the umbrella stand fall to the floor, accompanied by giggles.

"Hello?" I called out to the hall. "Is that you, Dannie?"

H sighed. "See you around, Medusa." He saluted me and left, letting himself out of the front door.

Dannie entered the kitchen with a spiky blue-haired girl. "Did you have a tiff with your non-boyfriend?" She nodded in the direction of the front door as it closed.

"No," I said.

She put a hand on her friend's shoulder. "This is Blue, my mate from Bristol."

"Hi, Blue." I forced a smile.

"Your hair is sick." Blue nodded at me whilst giving a victory sign.

"It's certainly different," Dannie said. "But somehow it's really you."

I scratched my head. "I'll probably be in the shower for an hour trying to get this out." I sighed. "There's hot water in the kettle and cake in the usual place. Help yourselves, I'm going up."

Using heavy duty remover at my dressing table, I scrubbed the make-up from my face. After wiping away the last of the eye liner, I opened my eyes and jumped, as static coursed through my body. I spun around. Ben was sitting on the end of my bed.

"Have you come to say goodbye?" I asked, relieved. I looked around the room for a glimmer of light that he would be walking into, now that the killer, Darren, was in custody.

He opened his mouth but all that came out was a crackling sound, like a radio stuck in-between stations. I felt immense fear. Electricity fuzzed up my arm as I watched him flicker on and off. He disappeared.

That's it then, I thought. It was odd, I didn't have the usual feeling of love when a spirit passed on, and he hadn't moved into a beam of light. Maybe he'd gone elsewhere? I shuddered, there was so much about the spirit world I didn't understand. And I wasn't sure that I wanted to be educated on the subject either. *Poor Ben,*

I said in my head. I hoped he was going to be reunited with his loved ones.

It was the morning of the christening and I had Lynn's help in the kitchen. I was decorating the cupcakes. The previous day had passed in a whirl of cake baking, with the help of Jeff, Lynn and Dannie. I gave the buttercream swirls on top of the cupcakes a light spray of catering glitter. I would add the little letter flags to spell out 'Victoria' and 'christening' once we were at the venue.

"They look amazing," Lynn said as she pulled a batch of sausage rolls out of the oven. "I'm so pleased to be back in here, love. I've not known what to do with myself with the café closed."

"If I reopen, I can give you a proper paid job if you like?"

She laughed. "Oh nonsense, I don't need paying."

Dannie joined us, buttering bread. We needed eighty slices. I felt butterflies in my stomach every time I thought of the christening. I'd not heard from H since our awkward chat, when he'd clearly had too much to drink. No doubt he was busy interviewing Darren Box and celebrating cracking the case.

Jeff offered to transport the food. He'd left the van at the spiritualist hut. I didn't want the likes of Brian Elks noticing I was doing a catering job – even though I could explain it as a favour for a friend.

"Here's the chicken," I said as I handed a bowl to Dannie. I'd roasted it the day before. "Mix the curry powder into the mayo, combine it with the chicken and add a handful of sultanas." My mouth watered – I love coronation chicken sandwiches.

Lynn opened the back door and let Jeff in. Constance wandered in behind him. She'd been sitting on her favourite bench underneath the apple tree in my garden.

AT TWO P.M. I entered the church hall with the cupcake boxes in my arms. I'd worn a simple lilac shift dress that used to be Grandma's, and my hair was tied up in a bun. We arranged tables for the buffet in front of the raised stage and the food was soon set out.

"Well done, lovey. It looks marvellous." Lynn rubbed me on the back. "I'm really proud of you."

The door swung open, and the christening guests streamed in, led by Carol and Rachel. Her husband followed, holding his baby daughter in his arms, who wore a long white embroidered christening gown. The twins burst in, running around the room.

"Becky, my love, it looks gorgeous," Carol said gazing at the buffet. She gave me a hug. "Henry should be here soon. He said he was dropping his car off."

It was great to watch people enjoying my food again. Paul chatted to me for a short while, telling me how well the christening went. Once the guests had filled their plates, myself, Lynn and Jeff loaded up with food and sat at a spare table. I'd made the sausage rolls with buttery flaky pastry and sausage meat from the butcher. There was a wide selection of sandwiches which I'd cut into fingers. I'd cooked mini vegetable quiches and also savoury scones onto which I'd added a generous swipe of butter.

Carol approached me. "I want you to meet someone."

I wiped my mouth and hands with a paper napkin and rose from the table. She guided me to a rotund woman in a royal blue suit and a large yellow handbag. "This is Sonia Elks," Carol said, widening her eyes as if I should know the woman. I'd never seen her before.

"Hi," I said. "Pleased to meet you."

"Becky has provided all of the food today."

"So I heard. It's gorgeous," Sonia said, pointing to her empty plate. "I'm going to have seconds."

"I'm glad you enjoyed it," I said.

"Becky owns the café on the seafront. Connie's Café."

"Oh yes, I know it."

"It's been closed down. By the Council." Carol crossed her arms and raised her eyebrows at Sally.

Sally frowned. As she stared at me, her surname echoed in my head. *Oh surely not,* I thought. *Not the wife of Brian Elks?*

CHAPTER 20

My palms sweat as I smiled at Sonia Elks. "I've provided the food as a friend of the family, I'm not trading." I wrung my hands together.

"You're more than a friend. You're family," Carol said. "She's dating my Henry."

For once I decided not to correct Carol. It seemed totally feasible for me to provide food for a family party, if I was her son's girlfriend.

I heard the twins shout in unison. "Uncle Henry, Uncle Henry. Your girlfriend's here. The one from the cells."

I gave a short laugh. *Great timing,* I thought as I turned around to search out H but found him already by my side.

Sonia looked at me then to H and raised her eyebrows as if surprised.

Maybe she doesn't believe me, I thought. After all, we didn't look like a couple with me at five foot two and a half and him at least six four. I slipped my arm into his, looking up, smiling at him with what I hoped was an adoring look.

H's eyes widened so I could see the full soft brown of his irises and the whites surrounding them. I wished he'd donned a more relaxed and happy expression.

Then I heard Tara's voice. "Lovely to meet you, Mrs Blake. Dating H is amazing. I get to go to the loveliest events. Sorry we're late, H passed me on the way and invited me. I was a bit sweaty from a body pump class." She giggled. "And my shower took a little longer than planned."

At that moment I didn't dislike Tara, I loathed her with a passion. I peered around H's chest to find that Tara, also had her arm in his.

H continued to stare at me, as I slowly pulled my arm out of his, like I was playing a game of Jenga. I gave a short laugh as my face burned with a humungous blush.

Carol narrowed her eyes in the direction of Tara, before guiding Sonia away.

"H, what's going on?" Tara asked.

I slipped away, hearing him say, "We're just friends. The kids and my mother got the wrong idea."

I puffed out a long breath as Lynn and Jeff approached.

"Awkward," Jeff said.

"I hope you're not too upset, lovey. I didn't realise you two had split up."

I shook my head. I thought Lynn was supposed to be psychic? She'd got that one very wrong. "We weren't going out, and I'm not upset."

"If you say so, lovey."

I gestured in the direction of Sonia. "I'm worried. That woman with Carol is the wife of Brian Elks, the trading inspector. Carol told her I was doing the catering because I was H's girlfriend. Then his real girlfriend showed up. It looks like I was lying." I gulped. "Which I was."

"She doesn't look pleased," Jeff said. "The girlfriend that is, not Mrs Elks."

"Upsetting Tara is the least of my problems. If this gets back to the Council, I'm ruined, I'll never reopen." I swallowed away the lump forming in my throat.

"Nonsense, dear. I feel you will definitely be reopening," said Lynn. But I attributed this not to any fortune telling ability she may or may not have. It was more akin to a mother saying 'Don't worry everything will be fine,' when things were really bad.

Lynn waved over my shoulder. "There's my friend, Dawn. I was going to tell you about her. She's been in contact with Clive, who used to work on the pier. He's building her a computer. He's great with gadgets, she says he can make absolutely anything if he puts his mind to it."

"That's interesting," I said, but didn't really mean it.

I'd had enough of the now-closed case, enough of my troubles with getting a license for the café and enough of H.

I heard H's voice. "Great job you've done today."

I swung around to find him smiling down at me. To the right a few feet away, Tara scowled. It was comforting to know she was able to look slightly ugly.

He lowered his voice. "Tara invited herself. She flagged me down as I passed her in the street. I wouldn't have brought her. I haven't even told Ma about her yet. In case you wondered."

I opened my mouth to say it was none of my business who he went out with but was interrupted by Carol's voice.

She stood at the front of the stage. "Can I have a moment of your time, please?"

The noise fell.

"I'd like to thank everyone for coming and please give a hushed applause to my christened granddaughter, Victoria Caroline Moss."

A succession of soft claps followed, accompanied by oohs and ahhs as Tori slept in her mother's arms.

"I'd also like to say thank you to Becky James for the buffet. I love her as my own daughter." I was sure I saw Carol's bottom lip tremble.

I smiled as another soft applause was received and many of the guests nodded at me in appreciation.

"Please help yourselves to this beautiful christening cupcake display that Becky has baked."

An orderly queue formed at the table and my chest filled with pride, as the guests bit down on my cupcakes and nodded their heads in enjoyment. This was what made me happy and was what I wanted to do, not chase criminals or see ghosts. I sighed and then caught Tara scowling at me. She walked towards myself and H, so I turned away, straight into the path of Lynn.

She smiled. "Look, love, if you want to get off, Jeff and me can tidy away when they've finished."

I REACHED the house and wearily opened the front door. All I wanted to do was find my cat, curl up in the snug and watch an old film. But the voices coming from inside told me I had a visitor. As I reached the small sitting room, Izzy looked up from the sofa. Dannie was at the laptop.

"Darling, I was just about to come to the church hall to see you."

Dannie glanced up from her typing. "Izzy's had a development on the Peter Sheringham story."

"Are you still following that up?" I asked.

"Of course. My boss is expecting an article on the town's local jewel thief. And I paid Jason and his co-worker Oggy for information. Can you help me with it?"

I could hardly refuse Izzy, after the times she'd helped me out over the past couple months. "Okay, let me call Constance in." I opened the French windows and Constance jumped from the bench underneath the apple tree and bounded down the garden. I picked her up and fussed her in my arms before joining Izzy on the sofa.

Dannie frowned at me. "You look well shattered."

She was right. "Can it wait until tomorrow?"

"Sweetie no, it can't," Izzy said. "Jason tried calling you, but your phone was off. So called me instead."

I frowned, my phone had been on all day. More like Jason preferred to speak to the model rather than her less beautiful friend. "Who was Peter's mystery visitor then?"

"His son."

"He had a son?" I sat up.

Constance meowed.

"I don't remember anything about a son?" I scratched my head. "So that would be Katherine's cousin. She never mentioned a cousin."

"Are you surprised?" asked Dannie. "She didn't mention that she was having a secret annual fling with Andrew Farr. Or that her ex-husband was in town. If she had, then you would have got to him before the police did."

"True," I said.

Izzy continued. "Apparently, Sheringham was shocked after the first visit. Jason said that Oggy reckoned it was the first time Peter found out he even had a son."

I felt a rush of adrenaline and the tiredness dissipated. "What's his name? How old would the son be?"

"No idea on the name. But age wise, anything from twenty upwards. Considering Peter went inside early 2001."

I put my hand to my mouth. A few things started to fall into place. Peter Sheringham had been the explosives expert on the diamond heists. He may have passed on bomb making tips. He'd stashed cash that had never been discovered. His son would consider himself the rightful heir to the pier. Maybe a son that had access to the pier and knew every inch of it? And then there were the mysterious expired ten-pound notes appearing around town. Could it be that H had the wrong man in the cells?

I CHANGED into jeans and called Jeff, asking him to pick me up immediately. Dannie rushed up to the church hall to help Lynn. Izzy stayed at mine, waiting for any update.

Constance crouched on the front dash, looking ahead as Jeff drove the van up Clive's road. My heart thumped as he killed the engine a couple of doors down from the Dent household. Jeff reached for a muffin with a T flag on top, which he'd clearly brought from the christening.

"There's no time for snacking," I scolded.

"Stake-outs require food," he said.

"You'll have to save that for later. This isn't a stake-out. We're going in." I opened the door. "Come on."

Constance followed. I hesitated, being overprotective, but didn't want to leave her in the van on her own. "Keep an eye on Constance at all times." I said to Jeff.

Outside the van, Jeff scanned the street. "What are we looking for?"

"Money. Specifically, the cash his Mum told us was stuffed inside a tin. And I want to have a look at the photograph of Eric Dent."

We reached the door and knocked. There was no reply, so I rapped louder. Everything appeared quiet. "There's no one at home. But we need to get inside."

"We can't break in. Call your boyf ... I mean H. Ask him to get a warrant."

"It'll take too long, and he won't take me seriously. Not only will he tell me to keep out of it, he thinks Ben's murderer has been apprehended. The papers have reported it and Darren's behind bars. But I feel in here." I thumped my chest. "The killer is still at large." I walked to the garage door and turned the handle. "It's locked." I pointed to the side of the property. "Let's go around the back and see if we can get inside."

I tried the side gate. It was unlocked. Jeff and Constance followed, as I sneaked alongside the house. The garden was a square lawn with border plants. A pear tree created a central feature with a sun lounger positioned underneath. I reached for the back door of the house and turned the handle. "Bingo. It's open," I said.

"What on earth do you think you're doing?" came the stern voice of Mrs Dent.

I swung around. She was heaving herself to standing, from the sun lounger. I didn't realise there was someone laying on it.

"Sorry. We knocked a couple of times," Jeff said.

"So you get no answer and just waltz in? You people have got some nerve."

"It's Clive we want to see," I said.

"He's out."

"Where did he go?"

"I've no idea."

I realised I was being forthright in my determination. My heart pounded. I softened my voice. "Clive has been assisting Jeff and me on an important case," I lied. "We are actually private investigators."

Mrs Dent raised her eyebrows. "Really?"

"Yes, it's a secret, so he wouldn't have mentioned it to you. But we're at a crucial part of our investigation. Clive may have a vital piece of evidence." That part was true!

"I see, well ..." she hesitated.

Constance meowed and approached Mrs Dent, rubbing herself against her shins.

I held my breath hoping she'd let us gain access.

"I'll phone Clive, to make sure he's okay with it."

My heart pounded as she ambled past and picked up the house phone.

"Shall we scarper?" Jeff whispered in my ear.

Constance darted inside.

"Grab the photo of Eric Dent," I whispered back to Jeff. "It's in the front room." I followed my cat.

"What's the cat doing in here?" Mrs Dent shouted.

Constance ran straight to an internal door on the far wall of the house. She scratched on it until it swung open and revealed Clive's man cave.

"I'll just get her," I said as I ran into the room. It was dark with no windows. I switched on the light, which flickered a couple of times before a bright florescent bulb lit the space. It was full of plastic and metal gadgets with wires poking out and pizza takeaway boxes. It was like a mad inventor's workshop. I scanned the room for a container.

Mrs Dent followed me in. "I'm sorry but you're going to have to leave. Clive's not answering his phone. He's always told me never to let anyone in here. I don't even come in myself."

Constance jumped on the desk and scratched at a red tin, in the shape of a London bus. I picked it up.

"Hey, what are you doing?" Mrs Dent asked.

I opened it up to find it stuffed with notes. I pulled one out. It was an old ten-pound note, the one which went out of circulation in 2018.

I spun around. "Mrs Dent, this is really important. I need to know where Clive is."

"Honestly, I don't know. He said he'd had enough of people taking advantage of him and side-lining him. He said he was going to finish it once and for all and stormed out. He's probably sat in his car somewhere taking time out to cool off."

Constance arched her back and hissed as her coat bushed out.

I felt a surge of electricity, so intense it caused my arms to cramp. "Ouch," I cried out.

Then Ben appeared, flickering, between me and Mrs Dent. "The pier," he said so faintly, it sounded as if the words were carried on a wind. He fizzled away.

"It's time for you and your weird cat to leave," Mrs Dent pointed at the front door, which was closer than the back.

I stepped out of the man cave with a bushy Constance in tow, rubbing my arms to eliminate the aftereffects of the spiritual connection. Having seen Ben, I knew for sure the killer was still at large.

I found Jeff in the porch. He nodded at me.

Back in the van he pulled the photo frame from beneath his T shirt. "Here you are boss."

I stared into the smiling face of Eric Dent and was one hundred percent sure, who the killer was.

CHAPTER 21

We arrived at the pier. With it being open to the public, we couldn't drive down the boards so parked on Beach Road. I hesitated before I got out of the van, staring at my phone. Should I call H? What if I was wrong? I decided against it.

I opened the van door with Constance in my arms. Jeff and I ran along the boards. As we neared the building, we heard screams as families spilled out.

"What's going on?" I asked a woman carrying her small child. Fire alarms peeled from inside.

"There's a bomb."

"Evacuate, Evacuate," I heard someone shouting.

"Oh no," I said and hesitated, looking at Constance and Jeff. I felt responsible for them both. There was no way I could take them in there. Just as I reached for the phone in my pocket, Constance wriggled to the floor and bounded off, meandering between the sea of legs like she was doing a downhill slalom. Jeff ran after her.

"Stop," I shouted at him but he took no notice.

A woman passed me, as she spoke on her phone, I could hear her calling the fire brigade, police and ambulance.

I followed Jeff, his scrappy hair just in sight. My heart pulsated in my chest. My breath was short as I cursed both Jeff and Constance. I bumped shoulders with escaping visitors, and hopped to the left, to avoid a man in a wheelchair.

Once I'd fought my way to the pier building, I found it free of anyone. The fire alarm ceased. But the machines continued to kick out their clashing tunes and the clowns laughed at me as I searched for Constance and Jeff. As I passed a grab machine full of fluffy purple dinosaurs, Jeff stepped out.

I jumped and held my chest. "You scared the life out of me." I put my hands on my hips. "What are you doing running off like that? There's a bomb in here. Are you mad?"

"I was following your cat."

"Where is she?" I looked about me.

Jeff pointed.

Constance repeatedly scraped at the closed door to the ice-cream parlour with her paw.

I heard muffled voices from inside. I knew I should collect Constance and drag Jeff out of there – but what if a bomb was about to explode and people were inside?

"We can't let him blow the place up," I whispered. "You stay here and call H," I passed Jeff the phone.

As I reached the door, I grabbed Constance and lifted my head to peer into a ship-style porthole. Clive had his back to me as he screamed.

Oh no, I thought. *That's all we need, Clive losing it.*

To the front of him, standing before the windows were Katherine, Olivia, Andrew, Nathan and Annie.

"OMG Annie's in there," I whispered. Tears stung my eyes.

The door creaked as I leaned on it and Clive swung around with a large metal pole in his hands.

"In here. Now," he screamed at me. His eyes were open wide, darting from side to side as he pointed the bar at me.

"You stay here with Constance," I whispered to Jeff. But as I opened the door, Constance overtook me, and Jeff followed.

"I'm your gatekeeper," he mumbled from behind me. "I'm not leaving you, ever."

I sighed, wishing Lynn had never mentioned the gatekeeper theory.

Andrew stepped forward. "Clive, you need to calm down, man. We must evacuate." He pointed. "There's a bomb for pity's sake."

I glanced to where he was pointing. Against the window was a small metal and plastic device, with wires coming out of it. I was aware that it could go off at any second. I had to convince Clive, who'd appeared to have totally lost it, to let us go. Surely, as a group, they could overpower him, I guessed they were waiting for the right moment.

Clive gestured at me with the length of metal. "Stand with the rest of them."

I decided to do as he said and stood next to Annie, with Jeff the other side. Constance remained at the door watching.

"At last I have everyone's attention," he said.

"Clive, it's dangerous in here." I stared at the bomb. "You're angry I get it but you'll regret it if we do get blown up. In this room are people you care about. Like Olivia and Katherine. They could be maimed for life. How would that make you feel?"

Constance sashayed over to Clive and rubbed herself against his legs. I saw his chest rise and fall. *Is she calming him down?* I wondered.

"None of you care about me," Clive said. "You all think I'm stupid. A pushover."

Constance gave a wailing meow and stared up at him.

Clive pointed his pole at Katherine. "I thought we were family. The pier family."

Katherine broke into a sob. "I've apologised. I asked you to come back. What else can I do?"

Andrew put his hands up. "Clive, man, we need to

get out of here else we could all die. Now please let us pass."

I stared at the end of the room where a push bar door was situated, with the ferry jetty visible through the glass. Clive could not take us all down. I realised that one person would have to sacrifice themselves in order to save the rest. I worried Jeff would take it upon himself to be that person. I glanced sideways at Jeff, then Annie and over at Constance. I'd not known them for long, but the bond between us was so strong, it brought a lump to my throat. I took a deep breath but just as I was about to launch forward, Andrew beat me to it.

As Andrew catapulted across the room, Clive lurched at him with the pole in both hands, thrusting Andrew to the ground.

"Andrew," shouted Katherine.

Andrew groaned in pain. He clearly hadn't got over his previous encounter. Clive's reaction had been so quick, no-one managed to pass.

Clive screamed, waving the bar around him. He'd seriously lost it. Constance jumped onto a table, meowing loudly at him. I was worried he might take a swipe at her too.

I glanced at the bomb, wondering how it would detonate. Was it on a timer? Was there a trigger button somewhere? To be honest, bombs weren't my area of expertise.

"For goodness sake – we've all got history here,"

Andrew called from the floor. He pushed himself up to sitting. "Clive. We've all had dark days when we feel like ending it all, but you don't really want to die. And what about Olivia here? She's only nineteen!" Andrew's voice became louder.

Clive stepped back, out of Andrew's reach as the older man pulled himself to standing.

"You're scaring me Clive," Olivia said, her voice shaking. "Mum's been so sad since you left. Honestly, she means it when she says she's sorry. Please let us go." She looked across at the bomb.

"Let's all stay calm," Annie said as she glanced at me, her eyes filled with tears.

Clive pointed at Olivia. "You hate the pier. You don't even deserve it. You want to sell the place. It should go to someone who loves it. Someone who has the pier in their blood."

Nathan, had been quiet. He appeared calm. He was clearly off duty, wearing a t-shirt and Khaki shorts. "Come on, Clive," he said in a cool steady voice. "I understand you've had history with the Sheringhams and Farr. But there's no need to tie me up in it."

Clive swung the pole at him "You? You're the reason I'm here. You little parasite. You owe me five hundred pounds. You made a right idiot of me."

"It was a misunderstanding," Nathan said as he put his hands up and walked towards Clive.

Police sirens cut through the air. "Now give me the

metal bar and we can sort this out before the police get here."

Clive bent his head, his shoulders drooped and shuddered. Nathan was breaking him down.

I stepped forward. "Don't give it to him," I said thrusting out my hand.

Clive jolted upright, looking from me to Nathan.

Nathan narrowed his eyes at me. "Stop interfering."

"Let Nathan take the bar," Andrew said.

"Yes, Becky," Annie said shaking her head in disbelief.

"I'm keeping it," Clive said.

"Well done you fool," Nathan said to me.

"Back off," Jeff said. "She's only doing her job."

I crossed my arms and turned to Clive. "What was it that Nathan did to upset you?" I asked, knowing exactly what it was.

"He paid me for a bespoke computer with dodgy tenners." He stared at him. "I took the cash with me to pay for a car."

"They weren't fake," I said. "They were ten-pound notes which had gone out of circulation." I turned to face Nathan. "Where did you get them from?"

Nathan ignored me. "Clive. There's a bomb about to go off. This isn't the time to talk. Give me the bar, so we can get out of here," he said in a steady voice. "I'm the security guard. The police will be looking to me when they arrive to let them know what's going on. If you hand it to me now, we can pretend it never happened. Hey, mate, everyone loses their temper now and again."

"Don't give it to him." I pointed at Nathan. "He's the one that made the bomb."

Nathan's eyes darted around the room. "Shut up you idiot. You don't know anything." He lurched forward and grabbed the pole from Clive then shoved it at him. Clive fell to the floor. "Right, Dent, join the rest of them over there."

Clive stayed where he was and broke down in tears.

"Is this a joke?" Andrew said. "You're the guy Katherine promoted to look after the place?"

Annie put her arm around Olivia who burst into tears.

"Can someone please explain what's going on?" Katherine asked.

Constance stood in front of me hissing at Nathan.

"Nathan is your Uncle Peter's son," I said.

Nathan narrowed his eyes at me. But said nothing.

"Peter never had a son," Katherine said.

"It would appear he did and he was just as surprised as you are, when Nathan visited him in prison for the first time a few weeks before his death."

Olivia pointed at Nathan. "You kept saying, pretend we're family, I want you to treat me, like I'm your cousin." She wiped away her tears with the back of her hand.

"This is my pier. It belongs to me, I'm the rightful heir," Nathan said. "It should have gone to my father, the eldest Sheringham and now he's died. It's mine. Mum told me on her death bed, she'd managed to keep it a secret from my dad – or should I say, the man I thought was my father. She'd had an affair with Peter when Dad was still in the army, before he became an electrician. She convinced everyone I'd been born early."

"I can't take this in," Katherine said as she slumped down to a chair. "So why now?"

"My mum was desperate for me to know the truth, before she died. How is it right that the pier should end up with that brat?" he said pointing to Olivia.

"And you planned to kill Katherine and dispute her will when the pier was left to Olivia," I said.

"Oh, here we go, the amateur detective," Nathan said. "I only wanted to scare Katherine off and buy the pier from her, once I'd sold the jewels and laundered the cash. Yeah, my mistake." He pointed at Clive. "I didn't realise they were old ten-pound notes. But even without the cash, I'd have better means than that fool." He pointed at Andrew.

"So your father told you where his secret stash of stolen money and diamonds was. Did he?" I asked.

Nathan smirked at me.

"And he clearly told you how to make a bomb."

He gave me clues about the location of the diamonds. I had to use this." He tapped his head. "I found out how to make the incendiary devices on-line."

"Weren't the diamonds enough?" Katherine asked.

"You could have been long gone by now," added Andrew. "No-one would have known about it."

Nathan didn't reply so I continued. "You didn't mean to kill Ben though, did you?" I remembered the wailing and crying Jeff and I had heard on our pier stake-out.

Jeff squeezed my arm as if to say, 'keep quiet,' but I wanted to keep Nathan talking, to give the police time to arrive. I kept my eye on the bomb, hoping they'd get there before the explosion. The sirens still sounded some distance away.

Nathan pointed at Katherine. "Ben's blood is on your hands. You killed him, not me." He took a step towards her. "I'd never have hurt him. You shouldn't have left him here. I didn't hit him all that hard. I'm not a murderer. But after he died, I realised your death would be the easiest option. I got inside that masked ball, pretending to be security, knowing all about Farr going there every year as a highwayman. Dear little Olivia told me all of her problems, including a lot about you." He pointed at Katherine. "And your pathetic life."

"You pig," Olivia said.

"You're as bad as your father," Katherine added. "A real chip off the old block."

"Sorry, to disappoint you cousin dear," Nathan laughed.

Andrew put his hand on Katherine's shoulder.

Clive began to laugh hysterically, rolling around, on the floor. Constance sat observing.

"We're related," Olivia said to Nathan. "We're your flesh and blood. I felt a connection to you, Nathan. Honestly, I did. Didn't you to me?"

"I ..." he faltered.

"And now you're going to kill us? Over this dump of a pier?" she added.

"Shut up," Nathan screamed.

All went quiet, even Clive became silent.

The bomb bleeped.

Nathan dropped the pole and leapt away. Jeff and I ran to Clive and lifted him up, I had Constance under my arm as we all dove out of the way on mass. Screaming for our lives as we went.

Boom.

The sound of splintering glass, splitting wood and tables and chairs skidding across the floor added to the loud blast. Dust and debris rained down and I kept my eyes closed. After what seemed like forever, but was probably mere seconds, I lifted my head as the wind blew particles in my face. My ears rang, as I felt the fluff of Constance moving against me. She stood up, with her coat filled with bits of glass.

Annie brushed herself down. Jeff stood up rubbing debris from his scrappy beard. Andrew leaned over Katherine. Blood dripped from her forehead.

"Mum," Olivia cried.

"I'm fine, it's just a cut," replied her mother.

Clive sat with his head in his hands sobbing. "I'm sorry."

I eased myself to sitting, looking for Nathan.

Jeff scooted over. "Becky, here let me help you."

I grabbed his hand and he hoisted me up as I kept my eyes trained on Nathan who stood up, then leaned on a table as if catching his breath. He clocked me, then scarpered, dodging tables, chairs and shards of glass, making his way towards the shattered side of the ice cream parlour.

I grabbed both of Jeff's hands. "Leave him. He can't go anywhere."

But I couldn't stop Constance chasing Nathan. She caught up with him and let out a low meow, before launching herself at his bare calf.

Nathan shook his leg. "Off."

Constance hung on for dear life, before sinking her teeth into his flesh.

Nathan screamed and leaned down wrenching Constance off his leg with another yelp. He held her in front of his face, and she hissed. My heart stopped as he threw her outside. She floated through the air like a soft toy. I made my way across the room, dodging the mess, breathing a sigh of relief as Constance landed on her feet in true feline fashion, a foot from the barrier.

Nathan had jumped through the space where the window used to be and had turned towards the jetty at the end of the pier.

"Constance, leave him," I called out as she followed.

Behind me I heard the door swing open.

"Armed police, armed police."

I checked behind me, H burst into the room with his colleagues holding large black guns, sweeping the room with their eyes, before disappearing into the post blast fog. Turning back, Constance and Nathan were gone.

I scanned the pier wildly my heart banging in my chest, until I spotted Constance, sitting on the right-hand side of the pier. I rushed over and as I picked her up, a bag was thrown next to her. Nathan heaved himself up, reaching for the holdall, but I grabbed it first.

"Becky, leave it," H bellowed from behind me.

No chance, I thought.

Nathan grabbed the handle. But I wasn't letting go. He started dragging me and the bag down the jetty, but I could tell by the vibrations of the wooden boards below me, that H was getting closer.

Nathan swore at me then let go, leaving me clutching the holdall.

I lifted my head, watching him run. H passed me in pursuit.

Nathan reached the very end of the pier jetty, took one last look behind him and jumped.

CHAPTER 22

After having been examined at the hospital by the doctor, she advised me to put my feet up. I spent two full days lazing on my bed, wearing loungewear, curled up with Constance, in front of the TV as I ate unhealthy snacks, none of which I'd baked myself. I could relax. The killer was now in the hands of the police and Ben had moved into the light. I'd watched his wife, Gloria, collect him the previous evening.

On the third morning of my recuperation and relaxation, the sun beamed through the windows and Dannie came rushing up the stairs with a brown letter.

"Open it," she said. "It's from the council."

"It can't be the license, it's not twenty-eight days yet," I said. "It's more likely to be a fine, or worse, a refusal."

"Just open it."

I tore the envelope and removed the letter and read it aloud. "Your application for a licence has been approved." I sat up. "How?"

"I already knew. They emailed your business account yesterday. But I wanted to keep it as a surprise and you really needed to rest."

"I wonder why it was approved early?"

"I bumped into Carol at the grocers. She was moaning to Sonia Elks about the closure, suggesting she put pressure on her husband. And what with you being a local hero, catching a murderer and solving the mystery of Branden Bay's stashed jewels, I doubt the council want you telling a sob story about them closing a profitable business when Izzy's article goes live. Especially if the nationals run it."

I laughed. "It's always who you know."

"You open in two days."

"I jumped off the bed. I've supplies to buy and baking to do."

THE DAY WENT from good to excellent. Nathan had caved in for a favourable sentence and told the police exactly where the remaining money and jewels were stashed. They'd been hidden underneath the pier, some of which required cutting machinery to free. No wonder Peter Sheringham was keen for his son to claim the pier.

Nathan was in hospital. Jumping off the end of the

pier can be a great escape route if you're a good swimmer, but not when the tide is out. He had multiple broken bones and was in traction. And the reward which Jason told us about? That was earmarked for me following the diamond filled holdall I'd recovered. I decided it was only fair to split it between the whole gang, plus Jason and Oggy. I would have been rich if I'd kept the whole lot, but I'd never have worked out that Nathan was the killer without a little help from my friends.

Having showered, I descended the stairs. There was a knock at the front door and upon opening it I found Katherine and Olivia stood there holding a pot with a cerise flowering plant in it.

"Hi Becky," Katherine said handing it over. The wound on her forehead had a plaster on it.

"We wanted to say thank you for what you did," Olivia said.

"This plant is beautiful. Go through to the café area, I'm reopening in two days. I'm so excited."

I fired up the coffee machine, there was no need to keep it mothballed any longer.

We were soon sipping delicious lattes.

"So how are you doing at the pier?" I asked.

"I've decided to go into business with Andrew after all," Katherine said. "We've come to an understanding."

"Mum proposed," Olivia laughed.

"Congratulations," I said.

"It's the only way of making sure everything is equal," Katherine said.

"Mum's not that great at expressing her emotions. She's mad about him."

Katherine flicked her hair over her shoulder.

"And your father?" I asked Olivia.

"He's back in Ibiza. He said he's never stepping foot on British soil again. I'm going over there for a week, before I start back at Uni."

"You can take the divorce papers with you," Katherine laughed.

Olivia and I joined in.

"And Nathan?" I asked, wiping my eyes.

"We've visited him. Understandably, he's concerned about the future."

Olivia put a hand on top of her mother's. "But we told him we're family and we'll write and visit."

"Obviously, he intended to hurt me," Katherine said. "Ben's post-mortem finally came back. The hammer blow brought on a heart attack. It isn't a great start. But I don't want to carry the feeling of hatred around with me. It'll help me move on if I can find it in my heart to forgive Nathan."

Katherine and Olivia left and said they would visit when the café reopened.

I was cleaning the coffee machine, when there was a rap at the café glass door. Annie grinned at me and Izzy waved the Gazette.

Oh no. Here we go again, I thought. I wasn't

expecting the article to come out for a couple of days. Izzy pressed the paper against the window so I could read it.

Medium of Branden Bay solves mystery of stolen jewels.

I opened the door.

“It’s going live tomorrow,” said Annie. “Izzy’s done an amazing job on the story.”

Wait for the phone to ring darling. The nationals are going to be on your case,” Izzy said.

“And the local TV channels are bound to pick it up,” added Annie.

I let them in, wondering what on earth my old friends in the City of London were going to think, if they read it. Especially my ex, Marcus.

As they came in, H walked up the path. He’d been keeping his distance. I didn’t know why. Was it because he thought I’d got one over on him? Was he angry with me? Was he busy finding stolen jewels and collecting statements?

“Hi, Becky,” he said smiling.

I looked across the prom to see the answer. Tara leaned against the sea wall in a pair of shorts showing off her long, tanned legs.

H handed me a bottle of fizz with an orange bow around the neck. “Congratulations.” He lowered his voice. “I know I give you a hard time. But I think you’re great. Well done. Don’t ever change.”

I took the bottle from him, a little stunned.

He bent down and kissed my cheek. He about

turned and strode away. Constance followed him to the gate and then jumped on the wall. I watched as he crossed the road. When he reached the prom, Tara leaned up and gave him a kiss, full on the lips. They walked away hand in hand. The sea breeze blew Tara's tied up hair, which looked like a prized race-horse's tail as it storms over the finish line. I closed the door feeling a pang of something, I found hard to ignore.

Lynn joined myself, Annie and Izzy as we ate the last of the cake from the freezer and drank the fizz H had given me. We looked through Grandma's recipe book, to find new bakes for me to try.

After my guests had left, I busied myself with the washing up at the kitchen sink. I had an hour to wait until the call I'd scheduled with my parents. I'd toyed with the idea of telling them about the whole pier escapade, but decided not to worry them, when they were so far away. I'd have a big catch up with them when they returned at Christmas.

The back door swung open. I jumped, not instantly recognising the tall young guy who'd entered my kitchen.

I put a hand to my mouth leaving washing up suds on my face. *No way,* I thought. I clocked that it was a clean-shaven Jeff. "Wow," I said, looking him up and down. His hair was brushed, and he wore a plain polo shirt with crisp jeans and new trainers. "What's with the new look?"

"You were right," he said as he came in. "If I don't leave home, I'll end up like Clive."

I laughed. "That was before he held us hostage with an iron bar and had a full-on meltdown. No, you were right – you're nothing like him." I wiped my hands on a tea towel.

"I've left home."

I gave him a proud smile. "Good on you for taking this important step." I returned the tea towel to its hook.

"Mum also found out that I was with you when the pier blew up. She said to keep away from you, or I'd have to move."

"Right. She kicked you out then?" I laughed. "So where have you found to live?"

Constance meowed from outside. I stepped to the side and looked around Jeff. My cat was sitting on top of a pile of boxes next to a huge case on wheels.

"It's just for a couple of nights," Jeff said with a sheepish grin. "Until I get sorted."

AS I MADE up a second guest room, I realised I'd taken in yet another stray – one who probably wouldn't be leaving any time soon.

A NOTE FROM KELLY.

Thank you very much for reading The Haunting of Branden Bay. Why not try the next book 'The Ghost of Branden Bay', where Becky has accepted that she's going to be contacted by needy spirits. Nothing she can do will change that. However, she considers it a step too far when a ghost shows up in her bathtub. And she is haunted by a nightly replay of his murder.

Becky enlists the help of her friends to discover who killed the unfortunate soul, so she can set his spirit free. But with her being well known around this small town, the killer is aware she is on the case and is coming for her.

Can she unveil the murderer before it's too late?

Find out on The Ghost of Branden Bay

Reviews are really helpful to an author so please leave one if you have a few moments.

If you would like to join my mailing list and receive a free digital copy of my novella about Becky's grandma Constance, then please visit www.kellymason-books.com

ACKNOWLEDGMENTS

I'd like to thank my creative writing tutor Rosemary Dun who encouraged me to pursue novel writing. Thanks also goes to my mentors Jenny Kane and Alison Knight of Imagine Creative Writing.

I'd also like to thank my best writing friends – Callie Hill, Claire O'Conner and Jenny Taylor, for their support and for sharing the journey with me. And also the friends I met at the Romantic Novelists' Association.

Thanks to my ARC team. And to my Beta readers Cinnomen Matthews McGuigan and Michelle Armitage.

Thanks to my friend Tracey Hadfield who always has a ghost hunting experience to scare me with.

Thanks to my sassy cats, even though they boss me about on a daily basis.

And finally, thanks to my husband Gary who puts up with me tapping away at the keyboard 24/7.

Printed in Dunstable, United Kingdom

66951863R00143

THE VALUE OF SEO

100 ILLUSTRATED ESSAYS AND STORIES TO HELP ANYONE TO BETTER EXPLAIN THE IMPORTANCE OF SEO.

Andrew Holland

THE VALUE OF SEO

ISBN: 978-1-3999-1842-8

First published in Great Britain
in 2022 through Amazon
self-publishing service

Produced by samanthahoughton.co.uk

Zoogly Media

Contents

SEO is Not What You Think

When I first started in the SEO industry, I didn't know I was in the SEO industry.

I was a police officer working as a Detective in the Covert policing world, and my role was to generate intelligence for the police using informants. Then place that intelligence onto a police internal search engine.

And that's how I learned SEO, without knowing it. None of us knew that what we were doing was SEO. We were just cops, doing our job, using the tools we were given.

This strange entry into the world of SEO provided me with the skills to understand networks and search engines. Also, in a strange way, it naturally gravitated me toward creating websites and content. Pushing me to enter the strange world of Search Engine Optimisation as a side hobby.

What I learned over the next few years was that the same basic principles work across all search engines.

And among the most important of principles is this.

Search engines are built to help people.

The police intelligence search engine helped officers to protect the public and to catch criminals.

Google is designed to help its users find the information they need.

But you know this already. In fact, you head to Google because it does its job...very well.

Convincing people to use search engines isn't a problem, almost all of us use them. The real problem lies in getting businesses to invest in wanting to be found via search.

Over the years, police officers were expected to contribute information to search engines. And if something went wrong, and they hadn't added relevant intelligence, they would soon find themselves in hot water.

For businesses, there isn't that pressure. You have to want to be found by search and be part of the world of online content creation.

You'd think it would be an easy sell.

There are over 2.5 trillion searches made on Google every year. But the truth is...the art of SEO has a bad reputation.

Often seen as a shady service, an up-sell, a long term process that generates little to no real-world return on investment.

Yes, SEO is a service that few people think they need or indeed want.

But what if they're wrong?

What if they are wrong because they are looking at SEO from the wrong angle?

That's what I believe and that's what this book is about.

Over the following pages, you will read 100 essays, stories and options for thinking about SEO differently. Each accompanied with an illustration to make my point clear.

By the end of this book, I have one goal. For you to see the overwhelming value of SEO and to be able to understand it and also explain it with more clarity.

Because if you can explain the value of SEO to business owners, more will invest.

I passionately believe SEO has the power to change businesses, add more jobs to the economy and change lives.

But this book is much more than that. It's also about you, the SEO.

You don't operate in a shady industry.

You don't sell a service that takes years to deliver results.

You provide a service of incredible value to customers.

And yet, that service is often undersold and indeed undervalued.

So if I do my job, by the end of this book you will look upon the subject of search engine optimisation with new eyes and perhaps new passion.

And so, I have one last thing to add.

If you want to follow my adventures in the wonderland that is search, head over to my website **www.zoogly.co.uk** and sign up for my newsletter.

But enough with the self-promotion. Pour yourself a drink of your favourite tipple, mine will be a large glass of Merlot.

Relax, and let's dive deep into the Matrix that is SEO.

Turn Your Website Into Your Best Salesperson

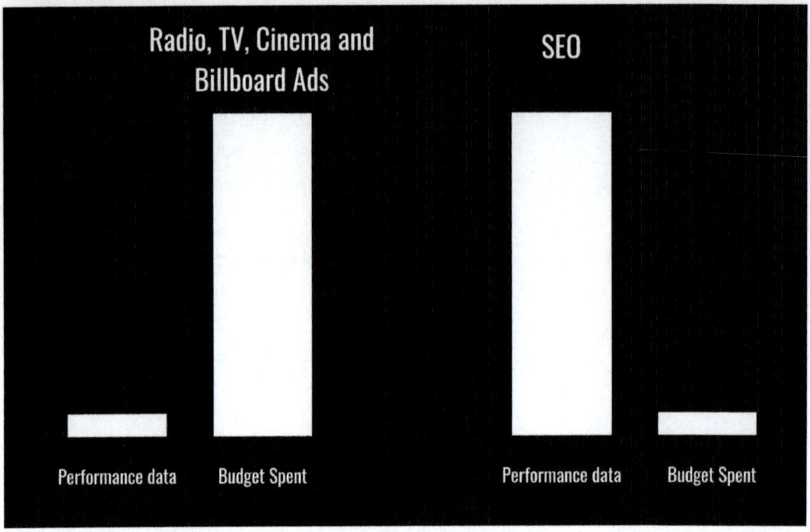

£23 billion was spent on ads in the UK in 2020 and that figure is expected to grow by 15% this year.

And yet, marketing master Dave Trott famously wrote that 89% of advertising is not noticed or remembered.

There are well over 4000 billboards in the UK and it's rare to see one without an ad.

£614 million was spent on radio advertising in the UK in 2020.

In 2020, cinema advertising spending amounted to £54.7 million which was a huge drop due to Covid19.

In 2021, cinema ad spend is forecast to see a growth of 266.8 per cent.

The fact is, businesses will spend billions on advertising routes that are likely to be ignored, cost a fortune and have little to zero analytical data of any use.

And then there is SEO.

A method of brand marketing that is both packed with performance data, supports every other type of marketing activity and places your site in front of your target audience...when they are searching for expertise or answers to questions that a traditional salesperson would normally answer.

Shifting your marketing budget into content and SEO isn't a sensible thing to do.

It's a logical thing to do.

Large businesses with big budgets ignore SEO and content marketing all the time.

And yet, we know of its power.

Despite this, most SEO costs less than hiring a full-time member of staff.

Why? Because no one ever got fired for putting a billboard campaign up.

The boss will love it that her business is being displayed so openly and prominently.

The boss wouldn't ask what sales came from the billboard, or how many of their ideal prospects saw it and read it.

The thing is.

SEO success and performance are both over analysed and criminally underfunded.

Especially when compared with other advertising methods.

The sad thing is that performance data is what hurts SEO campaigns because they focus on short term results and ranking gains.

The obsession with acquiring links and page 1 rankings forces many SEO agencies to create content that doesn't help the target customers and indeed engage in tactics that could risk your site.

If you reframe SEO from being about rankings to instead being about building the most useful website in your industry for your target customers.

SEO becomes a long term game.

And long term games make sense.

Long term games require proper investment.

I appreciate this mindset is a tough pill to swallow for Marketing Managers and business owners who live in a results-driven, high ROI world.

But it's logical.

And if it helps, don't look at this as being an investment in SEO.

Look at this as creating the best website for your customers.

One that educates, inspires and answers their questions.

SEO turns your website into your best salesperson.

Billboards and other ads will never do that in the same way.

Invest in SEO and build a website that can't be ignored.

Content Promotion is Dead and Buried; Do This Instead

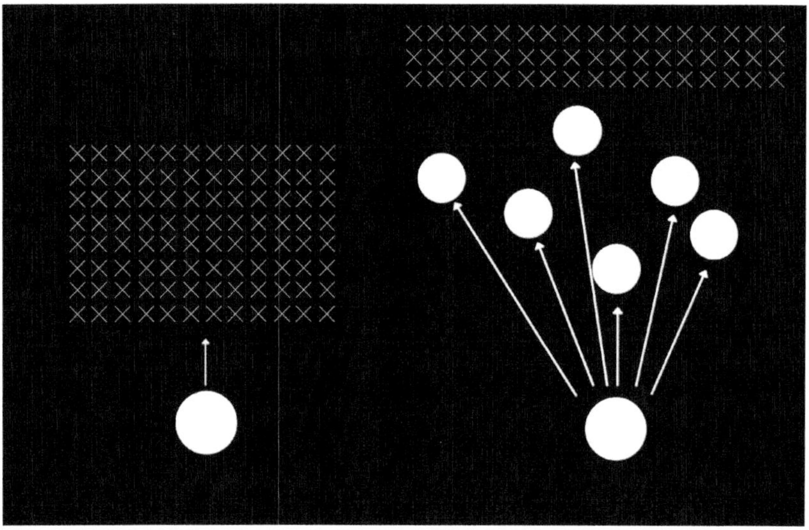

The idea is old.

Create content and promote it.

One problem.

No one cares about your content or wants to read it.

And let's face it.

To create one article and promote it, you need to be in the Goldilocks zone of promotion.

You need to have a great email subject line, a great email, your content needs to be amazing, loved by the reader and somehow, compel them to either share or link to it.

If that's your approach, good luck.

And then there are the communities.

The Facebook groups which have now all decided to ban self-promotion.

The gatekeepers of Reddit and the forums are just as bad.

The message is simple. If you want to use these communities you need to engage in them.

And maybe, just maybe, your post won't get deleted.

Oh and don't forget the shotgun outreach.

Find a list of people who shared something similar to what you've created and email them with a template and hope they share or link to you.

No reply? Follow up four times.

This approach is over.

Now I know in the past I have said to write once and promote it 20 times.

And I still mean that.

You should promote your content. But do so effortlessly.

Promote on social media, and in groups and forums.

If it gets deleted or flagged as spam, so be it.

But your promotion should not be exhausting or time-consuming.

It should be easy for you.

And easy for them to ignore it if they choose to.

But here's what you should do.

Focus on building a body of work and share that with those that matter.

YouTube videos might go viral, but it's the channel that people subscribe to.

I discovered Casey Neistat from his 'Make it Count' video.

I've since devoured almost all of his content.

I found Seth Godin on Amazon, I've since read hundreds of his posts, bought his other books and his courses.

Your website, YouTube, newsletters and for some, even their tweets are a body of work.

A collection.

The old adage is to spend 20% of your time creating content and 80% of your time promoting it.

Not any longer.

Today, spend 80% of your time creating something and spend 20% of your time sharing your progress with those that will enjoy it.

I'm building up a body of content and SEO case studies right now, but a few studies aren't worth hard promotion.

A collection of 1000 case studies is.

Do you think promotion is easier when you tell people you created 1000 content marketing case studies or one?

Sure, during your sharing of your progress, you might get a hit.

You might get shared, go viral and indeed generate thousands of subscribers.

And I hope this happens.

But it's rare.

Your aim shouldn't be to create a single piece of content that changes your business.

The aim is to create something that can't be ignored.

Something that wows people.

That's the goal.

Aim to build something that makes a dent in the universe.

The rules are simple.

Create often, promote progress often and build something incredible.

Don't Chase Traffic, Chase Relevance

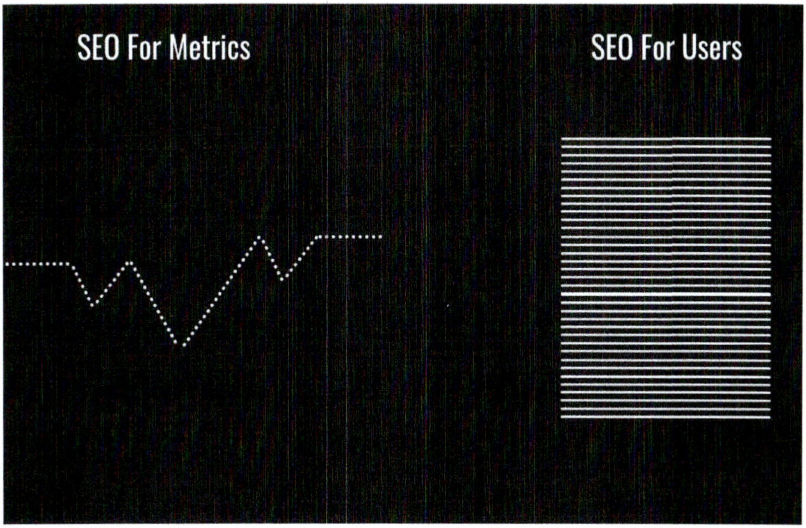

If you want truly exceptional SEO results, do SEO blind and don't look at a single metric for a year.

I did this once on a site I own, and the results were incredible.

The problem is this.

Because SEO delivers such great metrics, business owners are irrationally obsessed with them.

And so it's a difficult sell for any agency.

This is because business owners are still comparing SEO with direct advertising.

It's not.

If you enter SEO with a goal to win traffic that will earn you money, you'll lose.

You are competing against high budgets and algorithms.

And it makes no sense.

As SEO is a brand marketing tactic, you compare it against things such as billboards and radio ads.

And let's face it.

You don't obsess over how many people saw your billboard, do you?

Or your advertorial in the glossy magazine.

The metrics in SEO were never designed to rule the show.

The key with SEO is not to go after traffic and revenue (albeit I know that's what customers want and indeed judge SEO results on).

The key is to make the most useful website on the internet for users.

That's the battle.

And it's what should dictate keyword research.

What is useful vs what generates the most traffic.

The sad thing is, I rarely see business owners look at the problem like this.

"How can we be useful to those we seek to serve?"

This is user-focused SEO.

Sure, we hear about user experience (UX) but user-focused SEO (UFS) is not talked about much.

And that's what the visitor really wants to know.

"What does this site do for us?"

The trouble is, to take this approach requires a Marketing Manager to sell it to the powers up above.

And for most business owners and managers, all they want to measure is traffic and revenue.

In a dream world, the best SEO is focused on the user.

Sure, keyword research is part of that.

But spending a year with a focus to turn a website into the most useful content experience for the target audience on the web is a better plan.

And then, once the site is built for the users, you start to look at the metrics.

Of course, this is not what most businesses want.

It's far easier to promise rankings and traffic.

But what does the user actually want?

What is likely to drive revenue and sales for your business?

A focus on traffic or a focus on customer acquisition through highly targeted and relevant SEO and content?

Blind SEO is not completely blind.

It's impairing yourself by not chasing traffic, but chasing relevance.

You Must Invest in Marketing if You Want to Last

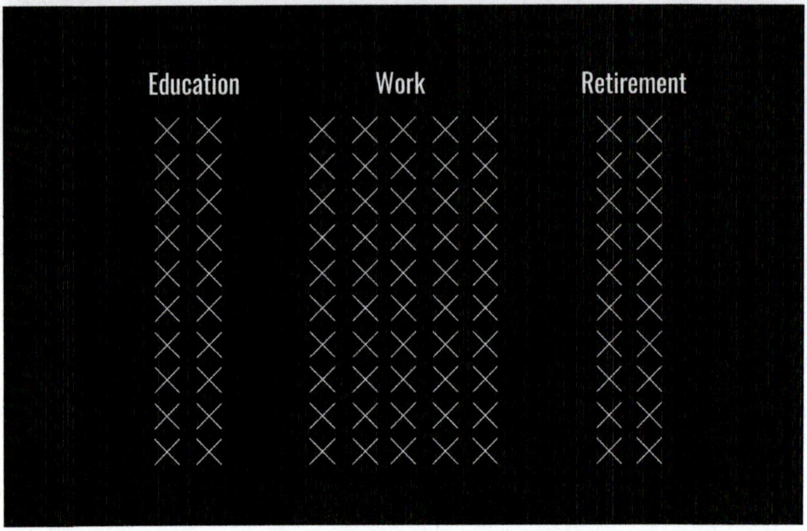

Your life and business, visually broken down into years.

When you look at just how long you spend at work, you can see why 'jobs for life' were always so high in demand.

Leave school, get a job, retire.

The problem today is, most businesses don't make it to 18 years of life.

But we all know this.

The carcasses of dead businesses can be seen all around us with empty office buildings and shops.

And it doesn't surprise me.

Most businesses fail to invest properly in marketing.

And many fail to invest in the right activities.

I speak to Marketing Managers almost daily.

They tell me their struggles to get upper management to invest in marketing.

They see it as an expense.

Yet marketing is one of the few areas of business where if you spend money, you should earn more as a result.

And if you aren't your marketing is failing.

It's that simple.

Marketing is designed to make change happen.

If the change you seek to happen is to double your annual turnover within three years, you'll need marketing to make this happen.

You'll have to build marketing assets and processes that fuel this growth.

And yes, this will cost money.

Budget management is an area of marketing that most businesses fail in spectacular fashion.

I see huge money spent on vanity marketing that only a few people see or even utilise.

Why? Because many Marketing Managers are forced in this direction by bosses that truly fail to understand where the future lies.

'Blockbuster thinking' is still alive and well.

Today, if you aren't investing in the growth of your own website, you are being negligent in marketing.

Too often I see people scraping to grow their social media presence and neglecting their own digital assets.

The old promotion methods are dying.

We are seeing the death of cookies.

Today, the primary marketing tactic used by most businesses should be to become searched for and found by search.

That's it.

It's not to grow your social media presence. That is a by-product of becoming searched for.

It's about building your own digital and physical marketing assets and marketing universe that is totally immersive for the customer.

This can include building a website that serves as a go-to destination for industry knowledge.

Building an app for your customers to occupy real estate on their devices.

Creating your own video content that is hosted only on your website.

Building a newsletter, maybe even a physical one that gets printed each month.

Writing books, both physical and digital.

Clothing ranges.

Meetups.

And much more.

The truth is, over recent years. Many businesses have become lazy with marketing.

The digital age meant that many activities were free.

But that is now changing.

We are in a pay-to-play and pay-to-access online world.

If companies want to be around for years to come.

If you want your business to be around in 25 years and thriving.

You MUST INVEST IN MARKETING.

The Recipe for a Great Blog Article

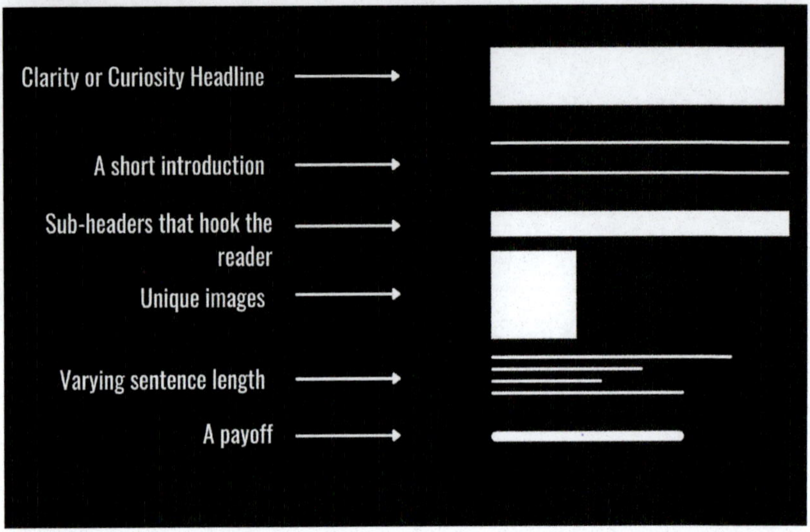

1. A clarity or curiosity headline.

If I want to read a post to get some ideas for my daughters Christmas presents, I want a headline that has words similar to 'Christmas gift ideas for 8-year-old girls.'

This is expected content.

But a post with the headline 'New problems, old problems' doesn't tell me much about what I am going to find in the article.

I wonder what it's about, what I'll learn and what I'll miss out on knowing if I don't click.

Stick with clarity or curiosity and you'll get more clicks.

2. A short introduction.

Writing a good introduction is an art in itself and most of us are terrible at it.

As such there are a few options.

The first is to not bury the lead. In essence, just get to the point. Brian Dean's APP formula is good to avoid this.

Agree - preview - promise.

Get the reader to agree to a point of view, preview what you'll cover in the post and promise they will learn something.

3. Hookable sub-headers.

Most people don't read, they scan.

They scroll down the article to see if it's worth their time to read. As such your sub-headers have to follow the same rules as your headline.

4. Unique images.

Not every blog post needs images, but most are better with them.

They break up the text and help to explain the key points of the blog post in different ways.

5. Varying sentence length.

People hate reading walls of text online. You aren't writing books, so vary the length of the sentences and paragraphs you use.

This isn't a style thing, it's a utility thing. Make it easy and indeed interesting to read.

6. A payoff.

The payoff from an article is one of the weakest areas for most writers.

It's the key takeaway that you want the reader to understand, that action you want them to take or the emotion you want the reader to feel.

Seth Godin is a master of this.

Here are some options for you.

Give the reader something to do.

Challenge them to take action.

Fire them up like a coach.

Clarify the key learning points.
Writing content online is tough.

Getting people to read your content is difficult.

Ensuring they come back is even harder.

Hopefully, this book might help to make that task a little easier.

With SEO, Experience Makes All the Difference

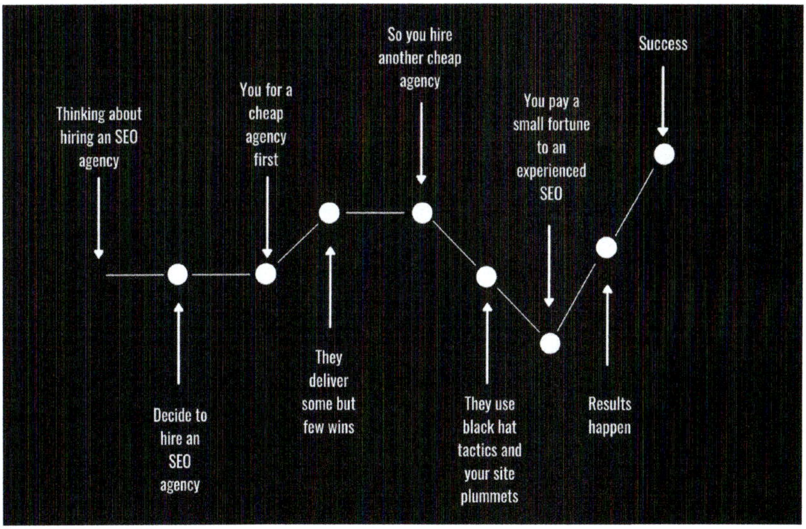

I have delivered SEO for a lot of websites...and the pattern is almost always the same.

The business thinks about doing SEO and gets some prices.

They go for a cheaper option first.

It's less risky.

Unhappy with results, they change agencies but not their investment.

The next agency promises the world but uses black hat or other dangerous SEO techniques.

The site nosedives.

So they reach out to a specialist.

It's expensive.

But they turn the ship around.

And finally you get the results you want.

The lesson in my experience is simple.

Good SEO specialists charge a lot.

They generally charge for strategy first.

They generally want you to pay upfront.

But that is because they have specialist knowledge.

Each site a good SEO works on is a learning curve.

It adds to the network effect of their SEO brain.

Building a skills database that allows them to see patterns.

It's these patterns they see when they examine your site.

It allows them to know whether you really need to spend a fortune on technical SEO.

It allows them to know whether you have enough back-links or you need more.

It allows them to know what content will work for your site.

When it comes to SEO, experience really does make a difference.

Seek it out.

Content is Marketing

One blog post each week looks like nothing.

But at the end of the year, you have a lot of content.

This is how content compounds.

The problem is, what to write?

There are three types of content.

1. Content for content's sake.

2. Expected content.

3. Unexpected content.

The first type is what we mostly see online.

It's content put out because someone thinks it matters, but it doesn't matter enough to take it seriously.

It's a blog post by the employee who hates to write.

It's the '5 things you never knew about' type of post.

It's the filler that most companies put out because essentially it's free.

It's better than nothing, but it won't do much for the business.

The second type of content is expected content.

This is great for a business.

It's an article by a phone dealer that compares the latest iPhone against a Samsung.

It's the complete guide to HR.

You might rank on Google with these with some SEO support, but it matters not. This type of content is what your visitors want to read.

The problem, most businesses won't invest in this type of content unless the SEO company prescribes it (and most won't as they are lazy and just want your cash for the least amount of work).

The third type of content is unexpected content.

It's the content people didn't know they needed or wanted to read.

It's the surprise.

It's the article you share with your boss, your friends or your loved ones.

It's content that changes you when you read it.

It makes your brain work and feel different.

Again, very few businesses invest in this type of marketing.

It's hard, it's creative and it's not cheap.

It's not cheap because so few people are good at it.

The businesses that invest in expected and unexpected content will win over time.

They will generate more leads and more sales.

I know this because the data tells us this.

I know this because there is an abundance of examples online.

But why aren't you investing in good content?

It's probably because you are holding onto an outdated model of thinking around marketing.

The reality is this.

Content is marketing.

SEO Success: Perception vs Reality

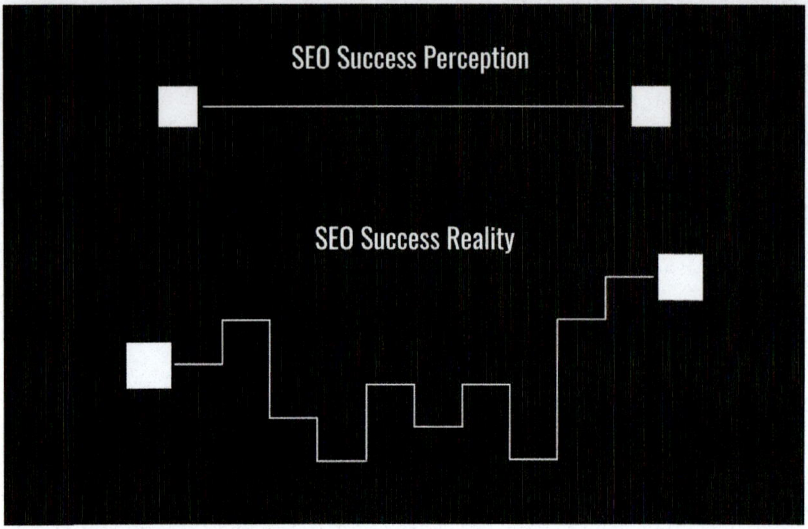

People believe that SEO is easy.

You pay an SEO agency or specialist X amount of money and they deliver Y results in a certain amount of time.

In reality, SEO is like the Royal Rumble.

One where Google sends in new opponents every few minutes to try and throw your site over to the page below.

Even if you manage to contend with the harsh rules of search engines and their ever-changing algorithms.

You then have to deal with the thousands of competing pages from other websites. Many of which are older and enjoy higher funding and more domain authority.

Yes, achieving SEO success is a battle.

Take today. I want a link for a client on a certain web page.

The reality is that if I email the webmaster, I'll get nowhere.

So instead, I'll be phoning the organisation (it's a huge one).

I know I'll be passed from pillar to post for a while.

Eventually, I'll probably find the person I need to speak to.

And maybe, just maybe, I'll get the link.

The client won't know how I've got the back-link.

They won't likely care.

And they won't know if I don't get the link.

But that's part of the battle of SEO.

You write content that fails.

You write content that doesn't rank.

And then you write content that does.

And then an algorithm change happens and you get kicked off the first page.

And then a few weeks later, they reverse the change and you're back on track.

So, if it's so hard...why bother?

Well, that's kind of the point.

If it was easy, everyone would be doing it.

If it was easy, no one would use Google, because terrible businesses and content would rank on the first page and you wouldn't get the answers you need.

For any marketing to be powerful it needs to contain an element of difficulty, cost, absurdity, inefficiency, extravagance, scarcity and a lack of logic.

SEO is all of them.

It makes absolutely no sense to try and rank yourself on the first page of Google.

It's expensive, prone to failure, out of your direct control and puts you in a never-ending competition against thousands of other websites, each trying to get on that first page.

But we all know this.

The people searching Google, who have never even heard of SEO and have no idea how a website gets ranked on there.

They know it can't be easy.

And that's precisely why people rarely go past page one of Google for anything.

Because the businesses and websites that are on that first page cared enough to put the effort into being there.

And that's why people go to search.

Because that's where they find the businesses that care the most about getting the customers to come to them.

They show up when the customers need them.

Yes, SEO is hard.

But if it wasn't, it wouldn't be such a powerful marketing method.

SEO Strategy - SEO Implementation - SEO Success

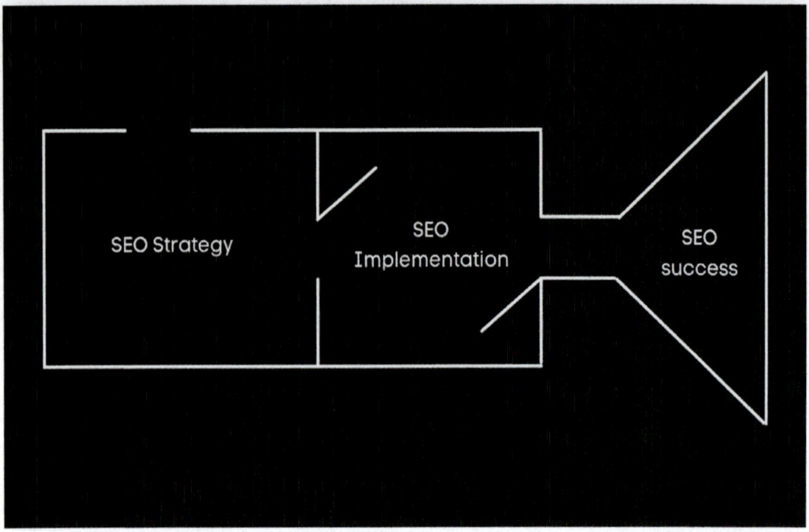

The proven path to generating results online.

I see it too often; SEO implementation without any strategy.

This is commodity-based SEO.

And when dealing with commodity-based SEO, the provider must reduce each service element to its cheapest possible deliverable to maximise profit.

It is the McDonald's of SEO service.

"Do you want blogs with your order?"

McDonald's has over 39,000 locations in its business.

But I wouldn't go there to order a steak.

Or pasta.

I'm not going to ensure I get low-fat food.

I'm going for fast, tasty food.

I'm going because it's simple.

I'm going because the kids like it.

I know what I get.

The problem with McDonald's style-SEO is that the customer doesn't know what they're getting when they order.

They order the blogs, they order the links, they order the on-page updates.

And they pay for SEO.

The order is in the system and it must be sent to the assembly line.

"Order 56 is ready".

The customer gets their SEO.

It's what they ordered.

But their business isn't getting full, no matter how much they eat.

The problem.

They wanted SEO success.

They wanted business success.

That's what they thought they were ordering.

The reason that commodity-based SEO fails is that it is done to maximise profits and not results.

There is no strategy.

It is sold as a package.

A deliverable only.

Commodity-based SEO works on the basis that all sites need exactly the same to grow.

And if that were the case, the only difference between SEO success and failure would be doing SEO or not doing SEO.

We all know this isn't true.

Strategy happens first, then implementation.

Each unlocks the door to the next stage.

And this is how success happens.

If the strategy isn't right, the door to success doesn't open.

Implementation can be commoditised.

But only if it is based on a solid strategy first.

That's the recipe to follow.

The plan the builders work to.

I tell all my customers that the first stage of working with me is strategy.

After this, they are free to either use my services to implement some or all of the strategy.

Or they can get another agency, create a team or use their own team.

That's the great thing.

After a strategy is developed you can create a conveyor belt process to generate the results.

And that's how you reduce wasting marketing budgets.

What kind of SEO are you buying?

Strategy first?

Or production first?

You need to know the answer because that's where failure often lies.

The Architecture of Belief

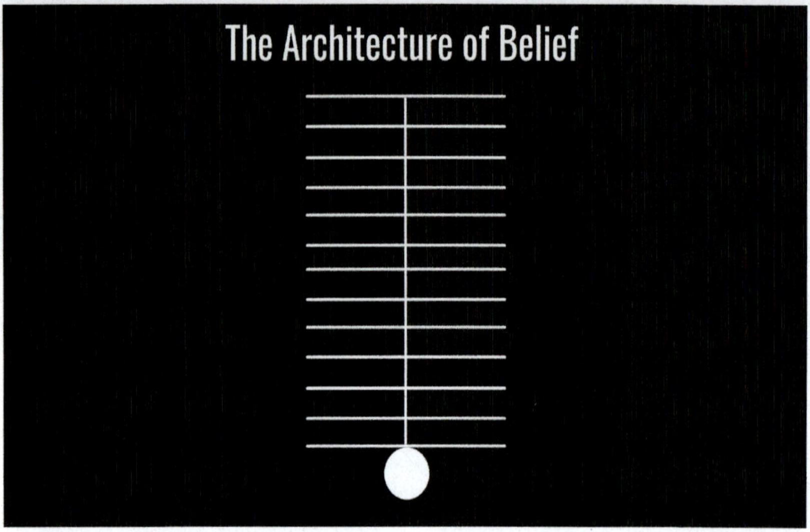

Copywriting legend Eugene M. Schwartz first wrote about the architecture of belief in his book 'Breakthrough Advertising.'

And while his commentary was for a different era and medium.

It applies to content marketing and SEO today.

Your content has two separate sources of strength.

1. The content itself.

2. The preparation you have made for that content.

Or in other words, what came before.

Schwartz was of course referring to the content within an ad itself.

However, the lessons can be applied to modern-day content writing and SEO.

Much of what is written online today is designed for the short click.

Media blogs that pump out article after article, hundreds a day, all so you will click and get served an ad.

They aren't in the game of taking you anywhere other than to an ad.

It's a sad sport.

For businesses to succeed online their content must be both of interest to the reader and believable.

But that belief doesn't have to be sold in a single post.

In fact, it most likely won't be.

Each post builds upon another until the reader feels that they can achieve the goal that your product or service helps them to achieve.

If you are an e-commerce store that sells luxury bathrooms, you aren't selling bathrooms, you are selling experiences.

You are selling the luxury boutique hotel bathroom experience.

The glass of wine in the candlelit bathroom after a long week at work.

But ads won't just be able to sell this very easily.

The reader is thinking "I can't afford a bathroom like that".

"I don't know how to measure my bathroom."

"What are the best tiles?"

"How do I find a good bathroom fitter?"

And hundreds of other questions that make them believe that they can NEVER have that luxury bathroom experience.

You can swap bathrooms for any niche, product or service.

B2B or B2C, it matters not.

Your prospect must believe that they can achieve their goal with your help or they won't buy.

And that's tough to do with a single Google click or Facebook ad.

Each piece of content you create must build upon another.

Until your site is filled with content that helps the user believe that their goal is truly possible.

That might take minutes, hours, days, months or years.

But when they are ready, you want them to buy from you.

This is why it's essential to invest in the content you create for your website.

It is your digital home.

You need to make it strong and able to withstand market pressure, downturns and indeed, even global pandemics.

Invest in your business.

Invest in content.

Reinforce the digital walls of your business.

Be Obsessed With The Long Click

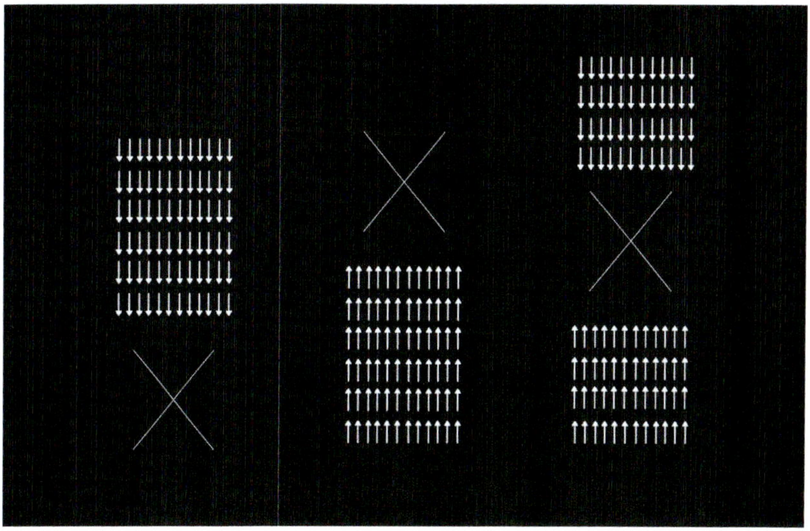

Don't aim to be found via search.

Don't aim to be searched for.

To win in today's SEO game, you need to be both searched for AND found by search.

I see it all too often.

The PR agency says 'use PR.'

The PPC agency says 'use PPC.'

The SEO agency says 'use SEO.'

The reality is that they are all right and yet each is missing something critical.

Being found is just the first step.

It's never been more expensive to acquire customers digitally.

You know this.

And yet, people spend more on acquiring traffic than they do on creating a digital asset that the people you want to serve will love.

As marketers and businesses, we treat our prospects with an obsession with the short click.

"How can we get them to click this?"

Instead, we need to think about building greater online structures in the digital landscape.

We need to be asking;

"How can we get them to come back of their own accord?

What do we need to build for them?"

This is an obsession with the long click.

It's not about just writing for search engines and humans.

It's about building a digital asset for search engines and humans.

It's about wowing the prospect and showing them that you are prepared to go the extra mile for them.

It's about the customer telling their friend "I found this awesome website, I'll send you the link".

It's about the customer landing on your site and finding the best resource on the web.

Something so good that they stay.

Something so good that they come back, without you paying for the pleasure.

This is where budgets should be shifting.

To aggressively scale the size and experience of websites.

Do this and you win.

Wait until a few years and someone will have beat you to the punch and catching up will be too expensive.

Ad costs are rising, SEO costs are rising.

Now is the time to act.

Get building digitally.

And build your business an online palace.

Marketing With a Big Budget vs Marketing With Persistence

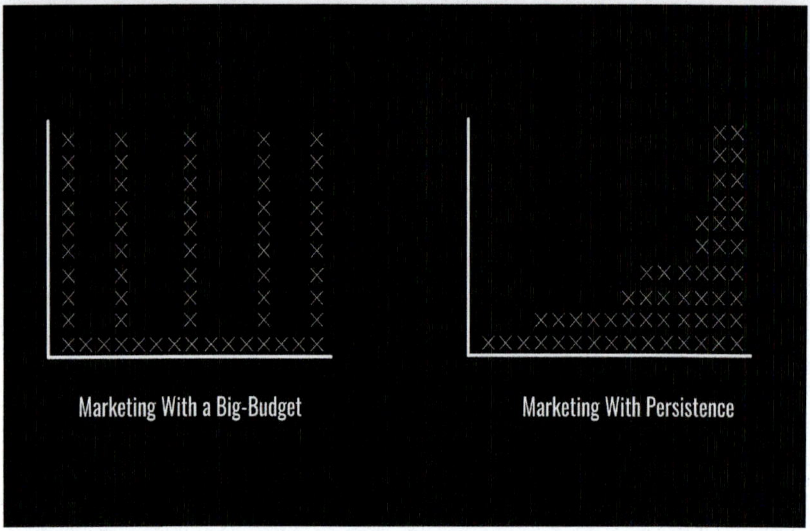

People think that big budgets will change the game.

In reality, they rarely do.

Big budgets tend to produce some of the most average and lazy marketing.

There is a good reason for this.

For many big companies, they simply need to be seen to alter behaviour.

We reach for a brand in the supermarket without thinking or knowing that it's because we saw their ads 30 times over the past five days.

The thing is, most marketing rhetoric is based on tactics that simply won't work for 99% of businesses.

Most people aren't selling food to people in supermarkets.

Most people sell products and services that are more complicated.

The solution for most businesses is persistence.

By showing up as often as possible when your target customers need you.

And when they do find you, go BIG.

Not in budget but experience.

Give them a digital experience that will cost you peanuts when compared to advertising.

Your email newsletter costs you nothing to produce.

Your blog content is one of the most cost-effective marketing tools you will ever use.

Your social feeds reach out with creative content on a daily basis.

You show up.

If you do this correctly, creatively, honestly and generously, you'll win.

You'll earn the permission of those you seek to serve over a longer period of time.

The thing with big advertising budgets, mostly you'll interrupt people.

You'll show up when they don't need you.

You'll show up and annoy people.

Sure, you'll get reach.

But you won't gain connection.

And that's what you want.

To connect with your audience.

Big budgets are rarely the answer.

Marketing with persistence often is.

Stop treating your audience as if they are buying breakfast cereal.

They aren't.

Market to them the way you like to be marketed to.

Don't Be The Best, Be The Only

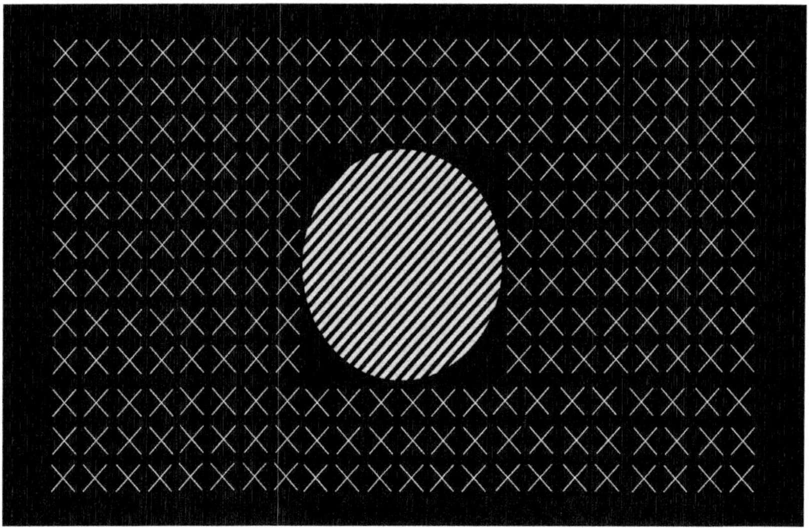

"Don't be the best, be the only" - Kevin Kelly.

Old SEO is over.

The idea that you can game search engines and ride the wave of free traffic is gone.

SEO is going to cost you.

Either in time or expert application.

And the price is going up.

As well as the competition.

Right now, if I want to buy a site on Empire Flippers that brings in just $866 a month in profit.

I'd have to pay $37,251.

And that's a cheap site.

If I want a site that generates $12,000 a month in profit, I'd have to pay half a million.

That's the reality of the web now.

People realise that it is a great place to invest money.

But how do you make SEO and all of your other marketing reward your business?

Evolved SEO.

This is creating a website that rewards visitors with the depth of experience that no other site can bring.

Be that the best articles, content that you never knew you wanted, a community.

There are many ways to stand out.

But you give the people who arrive at your site a huge reason to come back.

Because you are NOT like the other sites.

You are the only site that does (insert your unique approach).

Be different enough to become bookmarked.

Heck, be so different that they don't even need to bookmark you, they remember your site because of how unique you are.

This is the aim.

To be searched for and not just found by search.

Don't just invest in SEO.

Don't just do SEO.

Become a destination for those you seek to serve.

That's evolved SEO.

If You Want to Grow Online, You Must Become a Creator

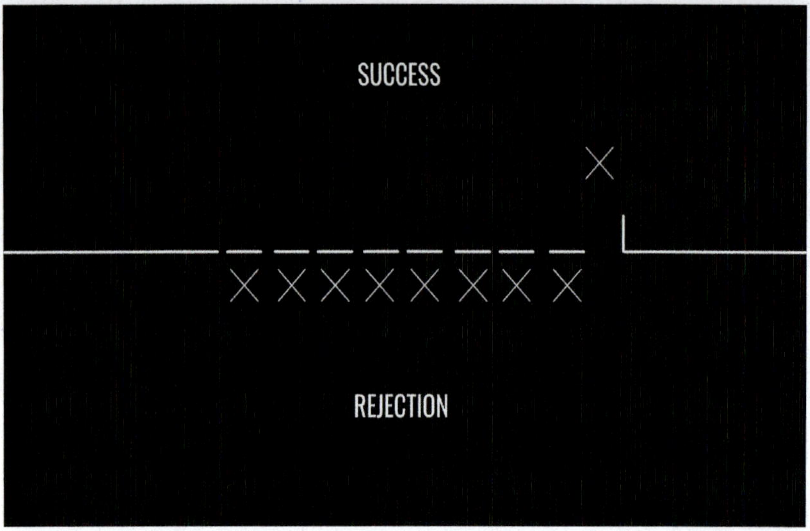

Squid Game, the smash-hit Netflix show, was originally created by Hwang Dong-hyuk in 2009.

But studios rejected the concept for 10 years.

This shouldn't be a shock.

There are stories of people who struggled for success all around us.

One of the most famous is Harry Potter writer J.K. Rowling.

Not only did her Harry Potter book face 12 rejections, but when she decided to write under the pen name of Robert Galbraith, one rejection letter advised her to get writing lessons or to join a writing group.

So what does this have to do with marketing?

It turns out...everything.

The odds of achieving success in today's world are dramatically against you.

The gatekeepers are too powerful.

The solution?

Persistence.

To make a dent in today's online world, you have to keep creating. You have to keep publishing.

Hwang Dong-hyuk didn't just write and direct the Squid Game once he came up with the idea.

He made multiple films before Squid Game was accepted, many of which were successful.

He got better at his craft each time until eventually, he created the biggest show on Netflix.

If you want to grow online in any niche, you must become a creator.

All businesses and individuals have to become media creators to stand out from the crowd.

What did you create and put out into the world today?

What did you create this week?

If the answer is nothing, perhaps you need to up your creation quota.

Grow Your Website or Get Left Behind

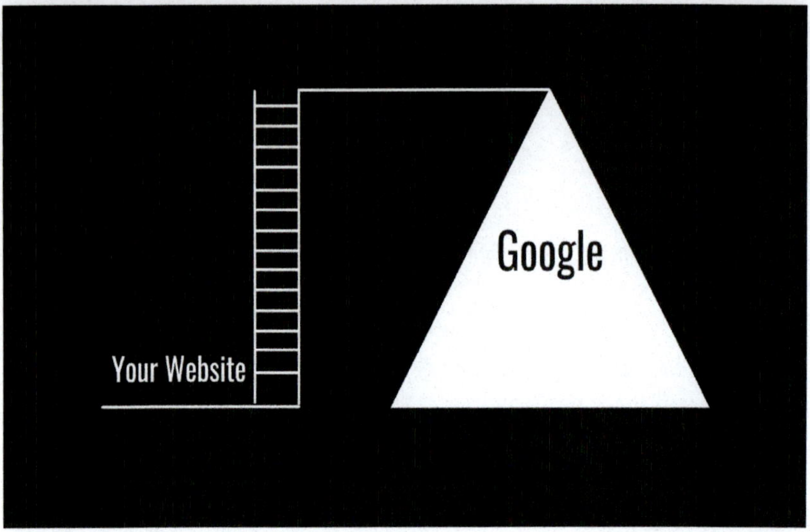

If you want to reach the top of Google and have your business seen by those you seek to serve.

You're going to have to build your platform to get you there.

This is what 90% of businesses get wrong.

They don't see their sites as something that they need to grow or build.

They see them as leaflets.

Flat, boring and static creations that are designed as just a place to hang your business hat in a digital landscape.

The times have changed.

Your website is your shop within a digital world that we occupy about a third of the day (if not longer).

And if you want it to be visible, you need to be found by the people you seek to serve.

Because they are looking for answers.

They are looking for knowledge.

They are looking for their life to be made easier.

And if you don't show up for them, someone else will.

You must choose to build an effective web presence in today's world.

Because it doesn't happen by accident, it happens on purpose.

Get building before your competition are so far ahead that you can't catch up.

We are in the digital information race and every day you leave it, you get further behind.

Write For Your Target Audience to Keep Them Coming Back For More

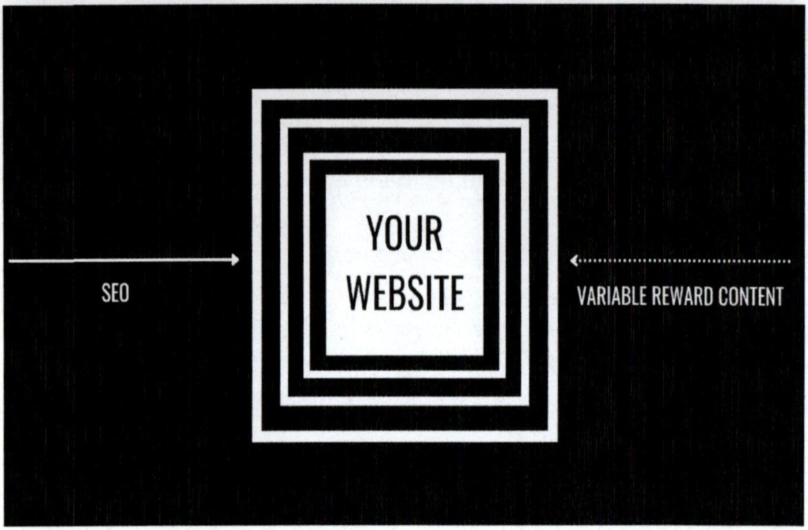

SEO gets people to your website.

But how do you get them to come back?

Sure, more SEO can work.

If I search for 'best bikes for girls under 10' and I find your site, what happens if I don't buy?

I might come back if you also rank for 'best bikes for girls.'

Or 'girls bikes.'

But other than that, you need to spend on re-targeting ads.

But there is another way.

It's called variable reward content.

And the internet is cluttered with great examples.

From YouTube, Instagram, Tik Tok and indeed, email newsletters.

It's content that the searcher didn't know they needed.

Why? Because they don't know what they don't know.

In this example, the company that offers me a free guide might win my email address:

"Everything a parent needs to know about choosing a bike for their child".

How could a parent turn that down?

And then you've earned their permission to offer them variable reward content.

And here's where most people go wrong.

Sure, you can send them sales emails.

But what if you offered them more content as well, content that you as the expert knows that they'll enjoy.

How about an article such as "27 Fun Bike Activities For Your Child To Do on Christmas Morning".

Or "The Chain Just Came Off; a Parent's Guide to Solving This and Every Bike Problem".

The list is endless.

But here's the thing. Writing for search engines is great, and you should do this.

This is writing for humans to read but for search engines to rank.

But YOU MUST write for people.

Not just any people, but your target audience.

You must give them the content that they didn't know they needed or wanted.

But why do this?

Simple, you are taking yourself out of the game of comparisons and taking them off the search engines.

Google wants people on Google.

They want to show your customers the ads of your competition.

This is how they earn money.

You, however, are not in that game.

You are in the business of being you and making the competition obsolete.

And you do that by 'hooking' your target market into coming directly to your site for answers.

You train them into knowing that they come to you first.

You train them into opening your emails because they are always packed with value.

You train them to come to your website and read your content.

Invest in both content for search and content that surprises.

And become searched for and not just found by search.

Who is Doing Your SEO?

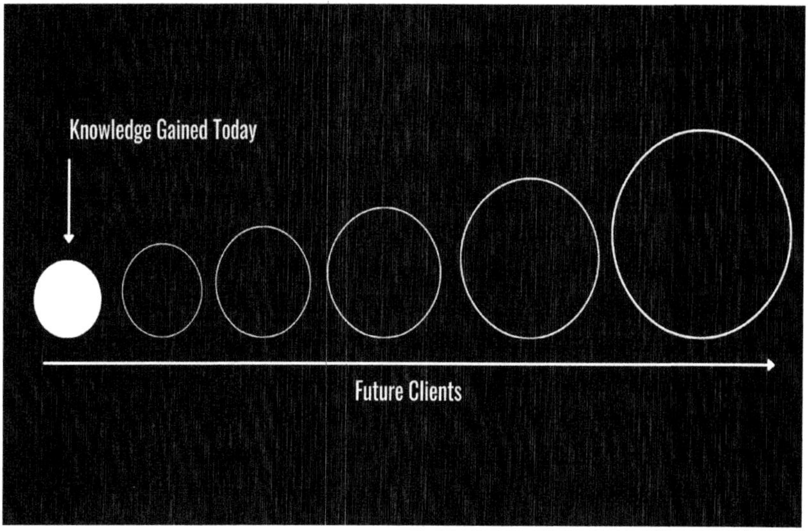

When you do real SEO for people, the knowledge you gain each and every day compounds in value for each and every future client.

This means that your work is more powerful and more impactful for businesses.

It's how SEO expertise is earned.

You just can't do that with commodity-based SEO.

If an agency runs their SEO through junior account managers and outsources it to others to fulfil, it doesn't matter how long they spend in SEO and with the title of SEO Manager.

They are managing SEO and not doing SEO.

The thing is, you can't effectively manage SEO until you have done SEO.

This is where the chain breaks down for agencies and often why results in SEO are so poor.

It's a disconnect in the chain.

No one is learning this way.

No one is gaining expertise.

It's fast food SEO.

Yes, it's possible to do SEO this way and many experts do.

But that's the difference.

It's OK for an experienced SEO to outsource things.

Because they've done those things hundreds of times already.

They understand them, they know when the job is done correctly and when it isn't.

For clients, you need to know what you are paying for when you buy SEO.

Is it expertise or management?

Or is it expert management?

Ultimately you need to know WHO is watching this for you.

Who in the agency is the person with the skill that oversees it all?

And what is their experience?

It's the big question.

WHO is doing your SEO?

It's your money. It's a fair question to ask.

So get asking.

Understand the Value of Your Experience

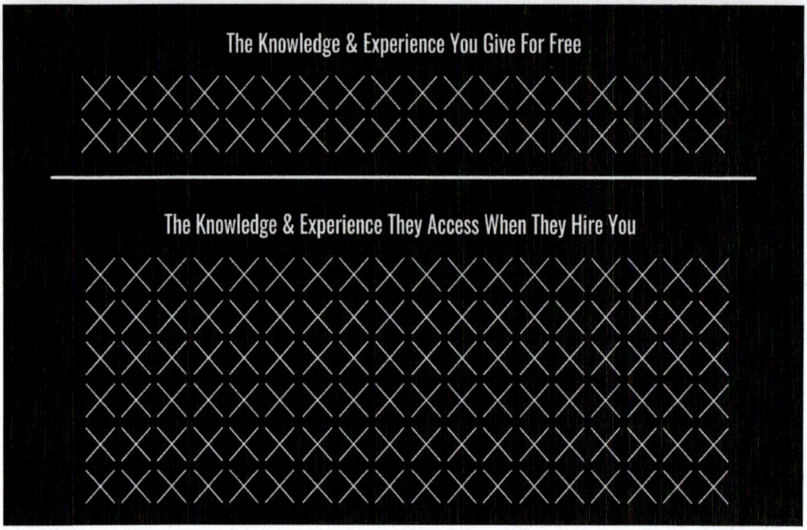

The greatest power that agencies, freelance marketers or consultants have is how they share their knowledge, expertise and experience.

In reality, this is simple. You give as much as you want to for free

Yes, you should be answering the questions your prospects ask.

But that's not where your advantage is.

Your advantage is knowing the questions that your leads don't know exist.

The questions they can't ask because they haven't understood the topic enough yet.

They don't know what they need to ask, because they just don't know.

You do.

You know what their next 30 questions will be.

You know what their questions will be at each stage of their journey.

Because it's a journey that you have made many times.

Reading a map and knowing the territory are two different things.

There are plenty of map readers out there but few experienced guides.

Choose wisely, be wary and seek those who charge early.

For those are the people that understand the value of their experience.

Strategy is the Brain Work That Leads to SEO Success

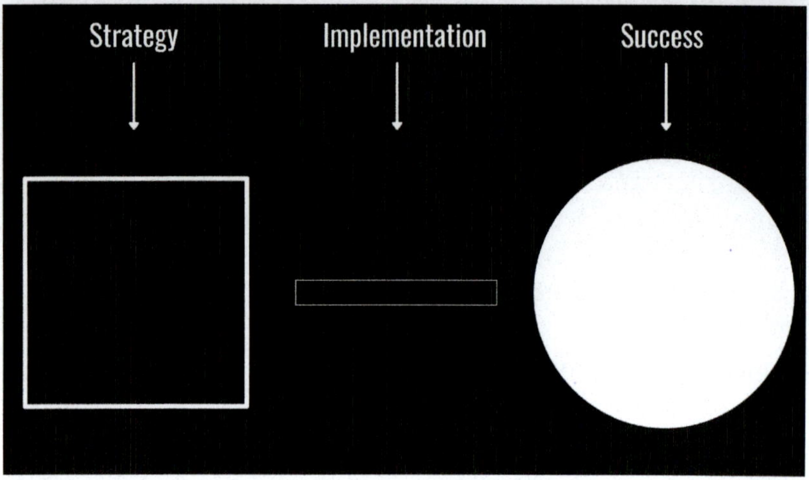

Not implementation. But what are you paying for?

There are thousands of implementation based SEO and digital agencies on the planet.

And some are very good.

And some are useless.

Generally when a client comes to me, they have spent around £24,000 on SEO and got nowhere.

And this is almost always because they have been paying for implementation agencies to produce a commodity-based form of SEO.

The thing is, as an agency owner, if all you do is offer implementation as a commodity, you must do this at the minimum cost and maximum profit.

That's business. And it's certainly the business of commodity-based SEO work.

You pay £2000 and get five articles and five back-links a month on the 'bronze' SEO package.

The unspoken truth of this type of package is that the agency is selling you what you asked for.

You wanted SEO and they are giving you SEO.

Neatly packaged with a bow on top.

And you know what, sometimes these services work. They just hit the right keywords and you get rankings and leads.

But generally, they fail to deliver anything because it's shooting in the SEO darkness.

People choose this approach for its simplicity.

And with us all spinning so many plates, simplicity is seductive.

The truth is, to generate SEO results for your business, STRATEGY must come FIRST.

And yes, strategy should be expensive.

And yes, you won't like paying for it.

But it's a pill you must swallow to avoid wasting your precious budget.

Strategy is how you avoid shooting your budget into the SEO darkness hoping you hit something.

SEO is a brand marketing activity.

It's how you tell the story of your business to others and become discovered by your target audience.

And yes, you should be strategic about this.

Because it's your business and your money.

If you're reading this and paying for SEO, you need to ask yourself 'what's our strategy?'

And if you don't know. Ask your agency.

SEO strategy should be documented.

SEO strategy should be targeted, deliberate and open.

In truth, the implementation is often the easy part of SEO.

The strategy works out what you need to do.

The implementation is the doing.

Underpaying for strategy and overpaying for implementation is the road to failure in SEO.

Make sure you aren't on this path.

Start Marketing Today

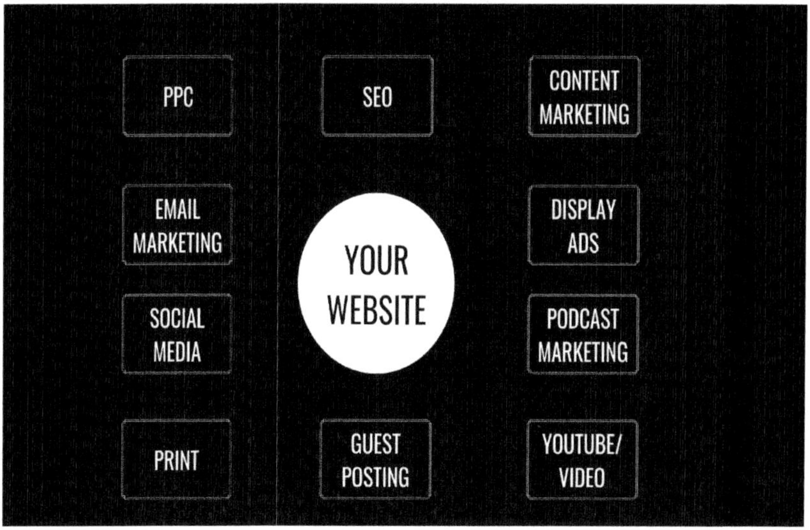

If you want your business to become resilient, you need to surround it with STRONG marketing.

It's not complicated.

Never in history has there been more ways to market your business.

And some channels are going to be more powerful than others.

But it still staggers me how many businesses do next to no marketing.

"We're too good for marketing, people come to us".

"If we market people will think we are struggling for business".

"We did OK for the last 30 years without much marketing, we have one manager and that's all the staff we need".

This is what I call 'Blockbuster' attitude.

I could easily call it 'Toys R Us' attitude as well.

No hotel chain saw Airbnb coming.

No taxi company saw Uber coming.

Disruption can occur in any industry.

It's only by strengthening your brand through marketing can you withstand these tremors.

But I get it.

It's tough to suddenly start a mass digital marketing campaign.

So start small. Pick one method and focus on that for a while.

Prove that it works.

Explain it to the stakeholders.

Watch them become surprised.

And generate more budget as a result.

It's tough asking for money.

Especially if those in control of the purse strings have a rigid mindset.

But it is doable.

However, it all starts with strategy. That's what comes first.

You must have a strategy for growth.

Don't leave your business vulnerable.

It's your business, you built it.

People depend on you.

Market today as if future times are going to be tough.

They might not be, and if you start marketing today they aren't likely to be. But don't take that chance.

Start marketing.

SEO Knowledge vs SEO Experience

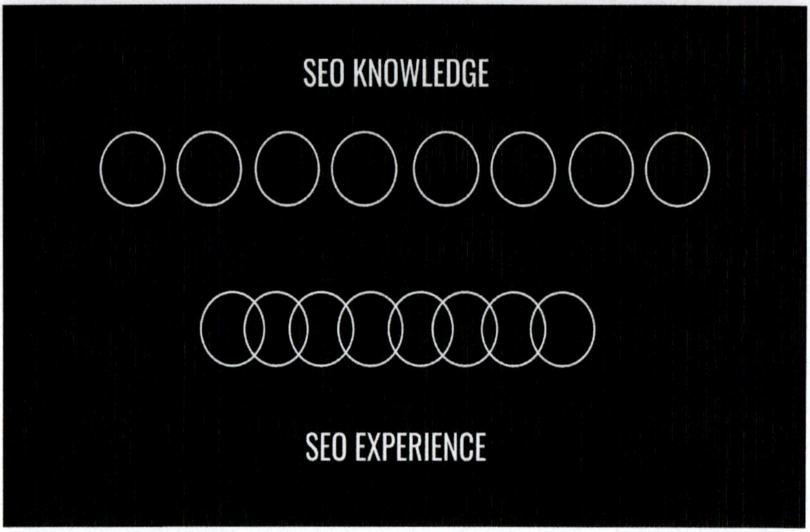

You can read 100 blog posts about SEO and content marketing.

You can understand page titles, links and anchor text.

But that's not doing SEO.

When you do SEO for long enough, you start to see patterns within websites.

It's these patterns that compound in the mind of the serious SEO specialist.

And it's these patterns that allow a great SEO to look at a site and be able to work out what to do to grow the organic traffic.

This is the difference between real SEO and selling SEO as a commodity.

Because SEO is part science and part art.

Experience matters in SEO.

And the more experience you have in SEO, the better equipped you are to give advice and help others.

You can't learn SEO by reading.

You have to learn SEO by actually doing SEO.

Content Compounds

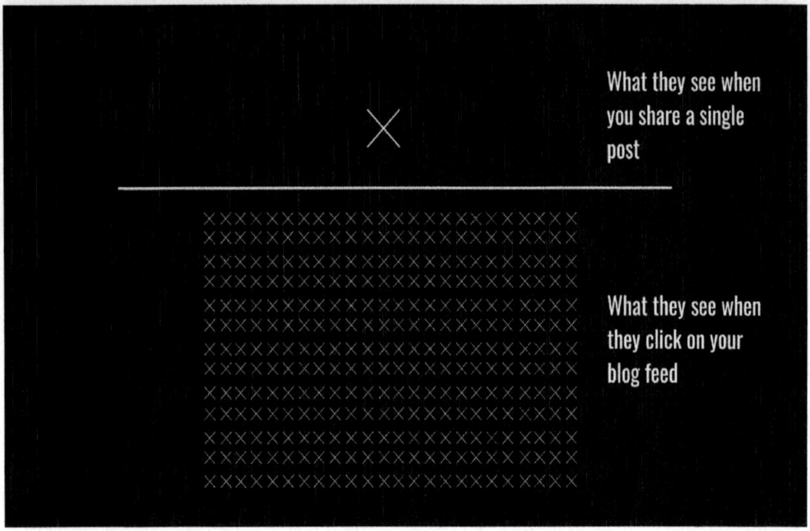

Old tactics - aim to create a blog article that goes viral, generates thousands of followers, back-links and email subscribers.

Evolved tactics - aim to create a website that is packed full to the brim of awesome content that people devour.

Sure, you might create the odd unicorn post that changes your life.

But today, the odds are against you.

Content feeds are rammed with average content from the big players in every industry.

Sure, you might get lucky and an influencer shares your work.

But the reality is simple.

You might create the most incredible article of all time...yet the algorithms prevent it from being seen.

The influencers are too busy to read it.

So you become deflated.

The answer is not to create a world-beating post.

The answer is to create a world-beating site.

This is at the heart of reason-based SEO (you can read about it on my site).

Reason-based SEO is about creating a site experience that people search for, that people talk about and that people love.

The aim isn't just to have a great product or service.

The aim is to create a great website.

Does your website match your product or service?

If it doesn't, then do something about it.

And yes, this takes time. Yes, this takes budget.

But aiming to be the best blog in your industry is doable...over time.

That's the goal.

To create something that stands out. You don't have to create world-beating content each week.

Great and even just good content compounds to create an amazing website.

Amazing content is exactly that. Amazing.

It's rare, it's hard to create, sometimes people do it by accident and sometimes on purpose.

This is why, when it happens we all love it.

The thing is, if you focus on creating good and great content on a regular basis.

You'll create amazing content once in a while.

But you'll be building an amazing website, one post at a time.

They might only see a good post when they click on your link.

But when they click on your blog feed, they'll discover an amazing website.

Don't Miss Out, Create a Sales Process

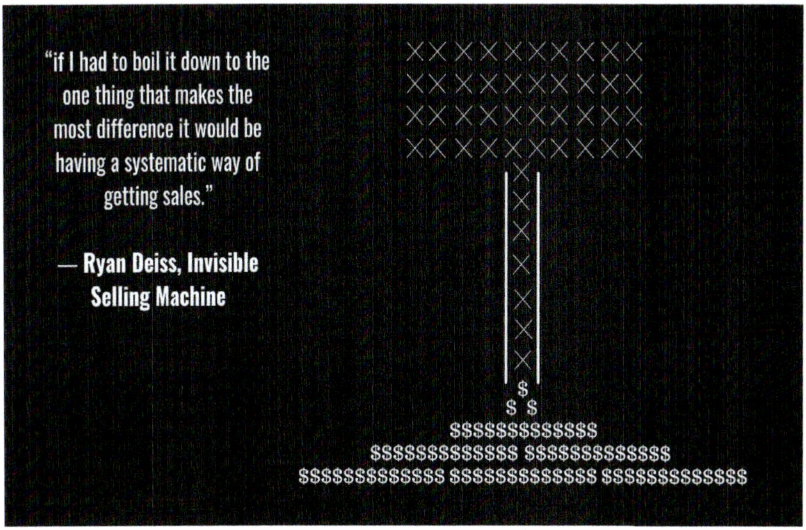

"If I had to boil it down to the one thing that makes the most difference, it would be having a systematic way of getting sales."
— Ryan Deiss, Invisible Selling Machine

If you don't create a sales process for your business, you're missing out on opportunities.

And only having a 'contact us' page on your website is about as uninspiring as it gets.

How to Become Great at Marketing

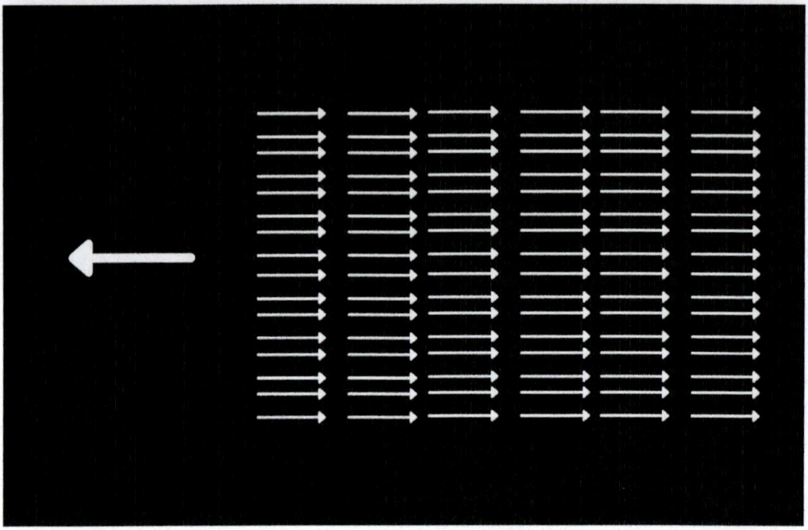

Look at how everyone in your industry is doing marketing.

Then, do the exact opposite.

Aim to Influence the Smallest Viable Audience, Often

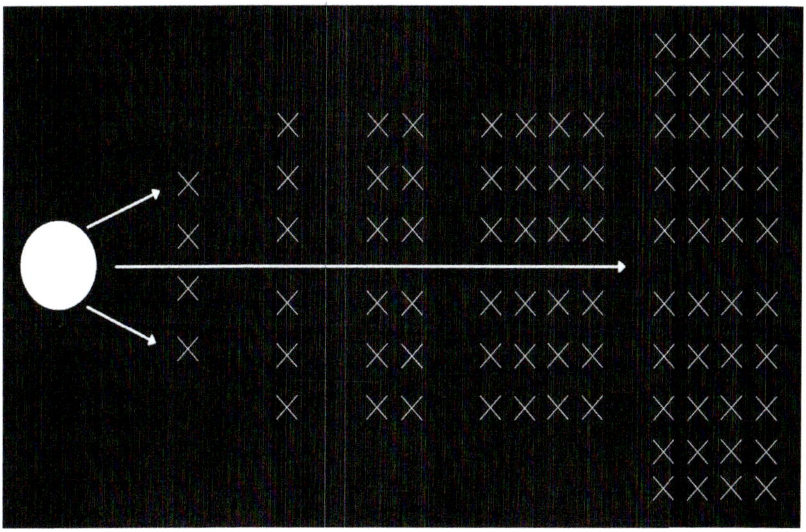

The actual recipe for online success, fame, fortune, building an audience and living your dreams.

I've made people go viral and had millions of video views online.

It's not all it's cracked up to be.

And to be honest, it doesn't actually do as much for your business as you might think it would.

That's because there is a difference between virality and valuable virality.

And that's the tough part.

Engineering growth online that leads to value, and not simply voyeurs.

Sure, people can make money being watched. The rise of Instagram and Only Fans have proven that people can earn from being seen and watched.

But for most, this simply isn't achievable.

So what can we do? What can businesses, freelancers and anyone wanting to make an impact do?

The answer is surprisingly simple.

Try and influence a very small group of people.

And try to influence them often.

Daily if you can.

You do this by sharing your ideas, your content, your experience, your world-view, your work, your knowledge.

Every once in a while, you'll create something that resonates, so people share it with others.

And so, your ideas will spread.

Rapid success comes when people with greater influence than most, resonate with your work and share it with others.

Sometimes we refer to these types of people as influencers.

And yes, it's often possible to skip the line, go straight to the influencer and ask them to view and share your work.

And depending on the work, some will either do this or they won't.

Some will want payment, and some won't.

But for the 99% of us that can't influence the influencer, you need to concentrate on this simple idea.

Aim to influence the smallest viable audience.

And do it often.

That's all you need to do.

You don't know who is reading your work.

You don't know who is watching your videos.

You don't know what might happen.

But send your ideas into the world.

Do so with generosity.

And that approach is the core of great marketing.

So stop judging marketing success by reach.

And start judging it by depth.

Why Strategy Must Come First in SEO

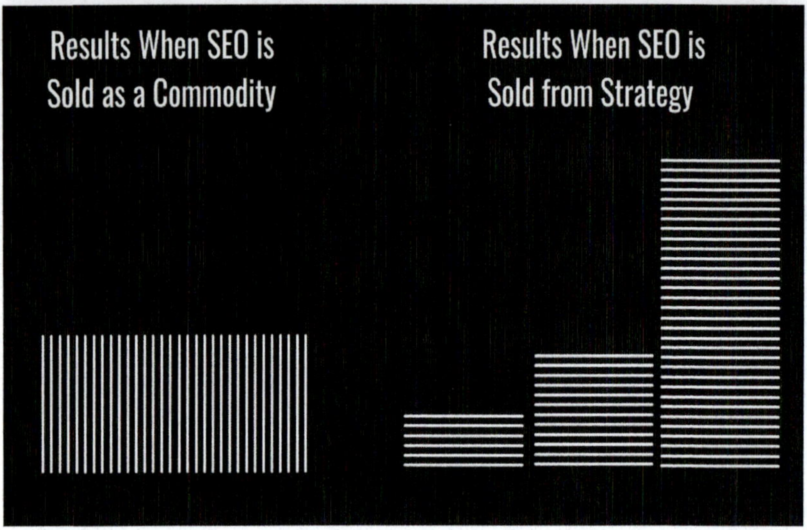

When a client comes to me, I almost always advise them to undertake a strategy.

Rarely will I work without one.

There is a good reason for this and it comes down to the type of SEO that you want to do.

There are generally two types of SEO.

Commodity-based SEO:

This is the type of search engine optimisation that happens usually as an up-sell after another service.

For example, you tend to find this with web design and full-service agencies that offer SEO as an up-sell.

To make this type of SEO profitable for the agency, it must be clearly defined.

As such you end up gaining a service based on deliverables such as 'five articles a month and 10 back-links.'

Trust me, if this is a service you are buying, stop now. It just won't generate results.

Strategy Lead SEO:

The secondary core type of SEO is strategy lead.

This is where the agency completes its SEO to some kind of strategy.

Each website is different and has different needs, and as such it needs to be assessed by the SEO to create a plan for growth.

It is at this stage that the SEO can understand what it is likely to cost to generate the desired results for the client.

This is why when I get asked how much it costs for SEO, I need to examine the site, the industry, the keywords and the competition before I can give an answer.

And that's what good strategy does.

It tells you what you need to do to achieve success and then you can give clients a price.

SEO is highly creative work.

It requires skill, experience and a look into the future.

This is why strategy is so important.

Don't buy SEO that is done on a conveyor belt.

Don't Build a Following, Build an Audience

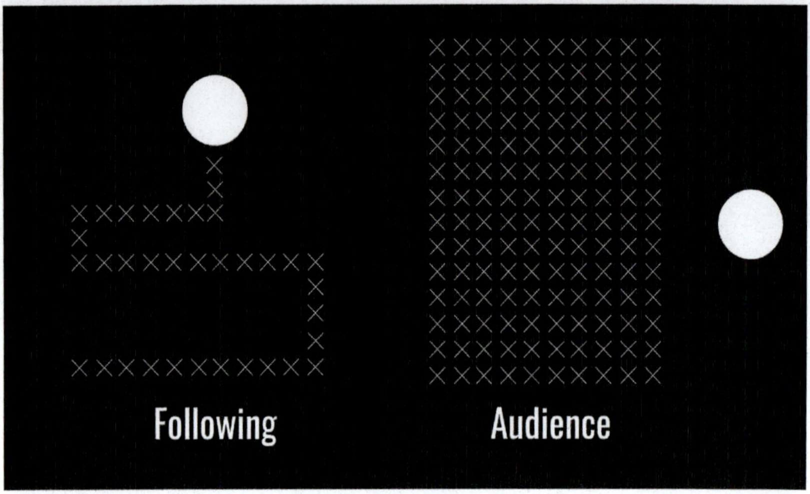

There are a lot of people with 'followings.'

Every social media platform is full of them.

They get a lot of likes for their posts, their selfies always look amazing, they might post toxic content that generates a huge following of like minded people, or they could be the voice of positivity that people watch every day.

For every Tik Toker and Instagrammer, there are a thousand more just like them on every platform.

And sure, you might make some money having a following.

But the odds are against you.

A follower is a supporter or admirer.

And we all have them.

The 'like' on our post feeds our ego, the follower count makes us feel more 'special.'

An audience on the other hand, is an assembly of spectators or listeners.

They didn't see you because they clicked your like button or an algorithm served you up.

No, they came to watch you.

They came to listen to you.

They came to read your thoughts and ideas.

It's a deeper connection.

Is there a real difference between an audience and followers?

Of course there is.

One of the first signs you have followers and not an audience, is that they won't come with you across platforms.

I saw this recently with a person with 29,000 LinkedIn followers and yet, their YouTube Channel had less than 700 subscribers.

They wouldn't cross the chasm into another platform for him.

It was too much effort. They followed him once, they won't follow him further.

The thing is, people are addicted to building followers, when they should be thinking about building audiences.

And especially if you're a business, the approach should be around building an audience.

Sure, you will find opportunities by building a following.

You'll likely make some money too.

But it will be 'platform' dependent.

So, how do you build an audience and not a following?

Firstly, you show up where the people you hope to interact with hang out.

The obvious places are forums, Amazon, real and digital groups, Google and yes, social media.

You give generously with your content, your ideas, your knowledge, your experience, your world views.

And you offer them a way to join you off the platforms.

This is the key part.

And yes, that is likely to involve an email list.

But it could be a free course or even a phone call.

Because once they come 'off platform' you can build a deeper and closer relationship with your audience.

My friend has an email list of just 6000 people and generates eight figures in revenue.

I know another marketer who made £40,000 this year from just over 5000 email subscribers.

My email lists are notoriously tiny.

My biggest of several thousand has made me the least money.

Yet my email list of just 350 subscribers has allowed me to work with 7 and 8 figure companies on a regular basis.

Audience quality will always tend to beat follower quantity.

If You Aren't Investing in SEO, You'll Regret It

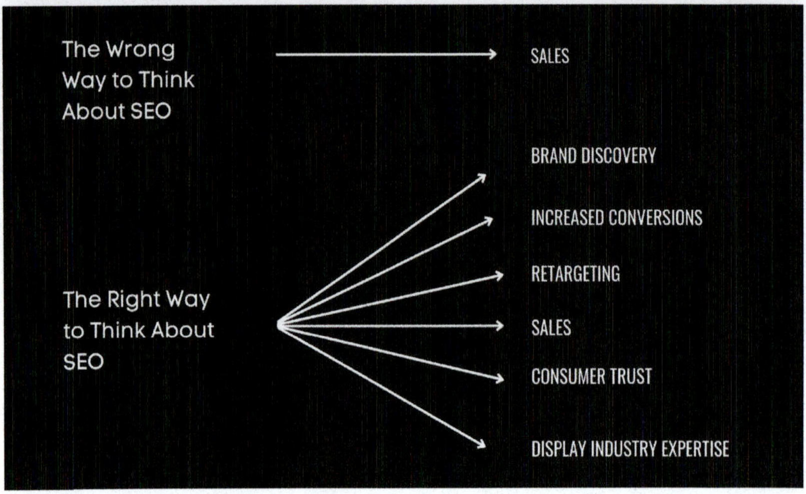

Somewhere there lies a graveyard of abandoned SEO campaigns because the results were measured incorrectly.

Here's the thing...if you are using SEO to make sales directly, you are going to be sorely disappointed.

It's too slow, too vague and too indirect for SEO to be a powerful sales mechanism.

If you want sales directly, run direct ads.

But when it comes to brand marketing, very few things out there can even scratch the power of SEO.

Showing up in search results leads to increased brand discovery, re-targeting options, increased conversions, be that for an email list, sales call or request for brochures, improved consumer trust and of course you get to display your industry expertise and knowledge.

And yes, you'll make some sales. But that's not why you start using SEO.

You do so because it is the most effective brand marketing method on the planet.

You do so because your ideal audience uses search engines when they have a problem and not the yellow pages or encyclopedias.

The problem with SMEs is that their marketing tends to be mean.

"If I pay this, what do I get in return today?"

SEO and indeed modern marketing has truly burned this idea and thought process to the ground.

Gone are the days where SEO is a 'pay £400 a month and get four blogs and a few links' gig.

Modern, evolved SEO is about the decision to show up where your ideal customers are when they need you and to showcase your knowledge and expertise.

It is generous marketing.

It is brand marketing.

Yes, you should run ads.

You must run ads.

But what works best? Ads to a single page with no other content linked to it?

Or ads to a website that has a superb user experience and a wealth of information that signals to the consumer that you are the ONLY choice for them.

If you aren't investing in SEO, you'll regret it.

Sure, build that following on Instagram, Tik Tok, Facebook and LinkedIn.

But you don't own that resource.

In 12 months time, you can have an incredible website that drives organic traffic.

Or you'll stay the same and the competition will have that website that your customers want and need.

This is the choice businesses face right now.

It's not IF you need to invest in search, it's WHEN.

And the longer you put it off, the harder it will be to catch up.

Become a Digital Creator

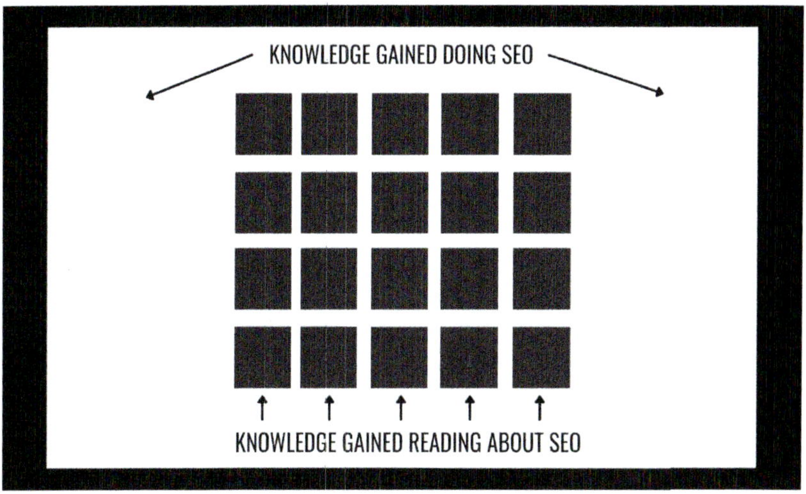

You can't learn SEO without doing SEO.

Reading about SEO and doing SEO are two different worlds.

Blogs might give you the map, but that's not the territory.

Blog articles and YouTube videos give you an understanding, an overview, an abstract look at SEO.

Doing SEO is far different.

Each niche, industry and model of growth is different.

Every website has its own challenges, and only by solving those challenges and figuring out how to grow a site and seeing traffic and rankings increase will you truly understand SEO.

Sadly, there are an abundance of SEO specialists, writers, and even agencies that do not do what they sell.

They don't have skin in the game.

They never have.

There must be someone, at least one person, who has done SEO and not just read about it in an agency.

And when I say done SEO, I mean taken a site from idea to ranking.

The thing is, setting up a website costs peanuts.

And if you want to learn SEO, it truly is one of the best learning experiences you can have.

Nothing beats it.

I write about the value of SEO and content marketing every day.

Because I have seen that value.

My entire business is built from that value.

Build a website, write content, build back-links, rank online.

It sounds simple. And it is.

But there is much more going on behind the scenes.

The things you can't see.

And that is why experience matters in SEO.

The great thing. You don't need anyone's permission to start learning about SEO.

You can start today.

SEO is digital building.

SEO is digital architecture.

SEO is digital creation.

Become a digital creator...that's the only way to truly learn SEO.

SEO Knowledge vs SEO Knowledge That Generates Results

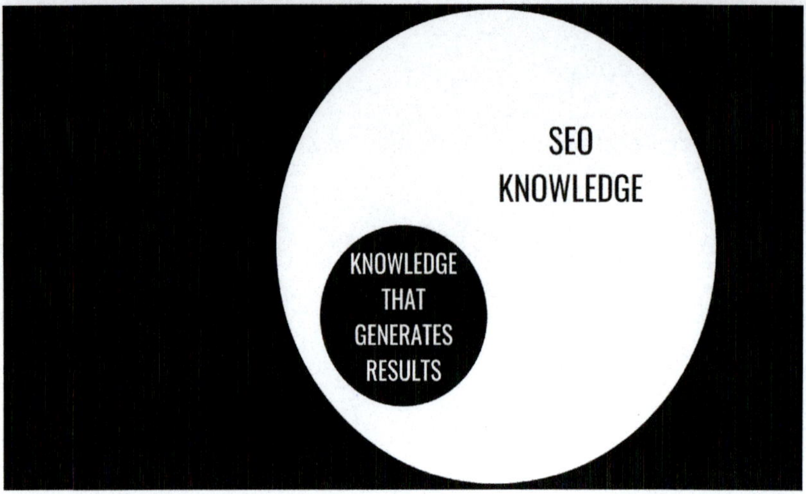

The biggest failure in SEO today is that many agencies have turned SEO into a conveyor belt of industrial output.

And when that happens, you must always look to apply the cheapest labour.

Here's how it works for those that don't know.

Agencies offer SEO either as a full service or up-sell.

They hire a junior account manager.

The agency then outsources the SEO to one of the huge SEO factories.

You get four blog posts per month and five back-links.

Your website is filled with '5 things you never knew about' type posts that never get read, attract visitors or are of any use.

The links are pointless and also of no value.

The junior account manager on £10 an hour can manage 30 clients like this.

Agency charges £1000 a month.

£1000 x 30 = £30,000 a month.

And so the machine grows.

Sales people and ads bring in the leads, high margins and low costs keep the game going.

This is what gives SEO a bad name.

It's what leads to people not trusting SEO agencies in the future because they never got results.

The thing is.

There is an abundance of superficial SEO knowledge out there.

Create content, have a keyword-focused page title, good meta description, get back-links from websites.

This superficial knowledge has allowed agencies to industrialise SEO.

To turn SEO from being a creative activity borne from experience and tailored to an individual company and website.

Into a factory activity.

SEO is not a 'one size fits all' approach.

It can't be, it's a brand marketing activity.

SEO is the difficult task of reaching your target audience in ways that they will be truly grateful for.

SEO is about introducing your brand to the people that need it, right when they need it.

SEO is a generous marketing activity.

You spend hoping you'll get a return on investment, but knowing that SEO is a great way to tell the story of your brand and business to others.

SEO is storytelling.

It's positioning your business as the guide that your clients need to help them reach their desired outcome.

Yes, you'll make money from SEO.

And yes, there are metrics that need to be monitored and reported on.

But the aim is to show up. To say 'here we are, we can help you.'

And this takes thought, expertise and strategy to do this.

There is a lot of SEO knowledge out there.

Look for the SEO knowledge that will generate you results.

That is a lot harder to find.

Make Your Website A Digital Palace

Your website is the digital home for your business.

SEO makes the home bigger, stronger, more visible and worth more.

When people think of ROI when it comes to SEO, they try to compare it to PPC.

It's not direct advertising.

It's brand marketing.

The best way to think about SEO is that you are building an asset for your business.

Your website isn't a website.

It is the digital base, home and central focus of your business.

Do you want a shed or a palace?

Do you want a house made of sticks or bricks?

It's not a complicated process to wrap your head around when you look at it that way.

The problem?

You've been educated to think that ads were the answer to all of your problems.

But let's face it, I never went to an advert when I had a problem.

I went to the internet and searched for information.

The thing is, you know this. You use the web every day like this.

Yes, you'll make money through SEO.

But that's not the objective, the objective is to market your brand.

To show why you're different.

To show you care.

To show up when your perfect customers search for information that you can give them.

This is the power of SEO.

Build your digital home, make it more powerful.

Invest in SEO.

The Difference Between SEO Knowledge and SEO Experience

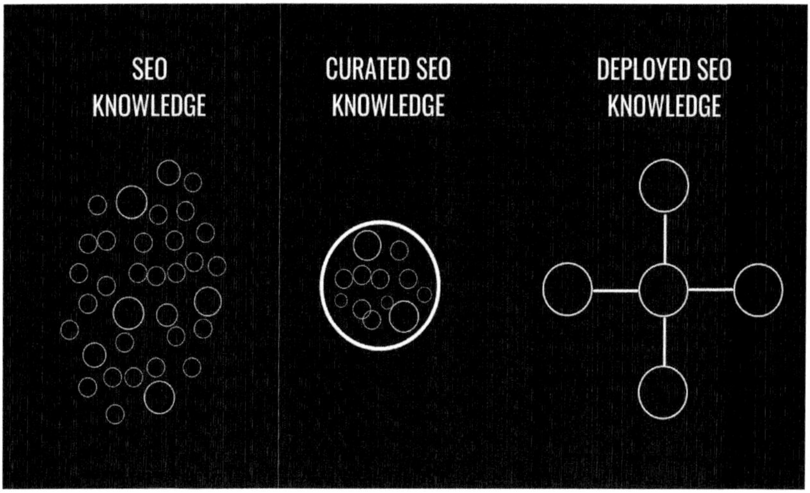

The web is full of SEO knowledge. The abundance of it is incredible.

And as people become better at SEO, they curate the best knowledge in their minds.

Through trial and research, they know what works and what doesn't work.

And that's when you find an SEO who looks at a website and investigates what needs to be done to grow a site.

This is when they deploy their knowledge to provide clients with results.

It's not about knowing the best SEO practices. It's about having a large amount of knowledge and experience to be able to generate results without waste.

Waste on unnecessary link building.

Waste on content that will never rank.

Waste on outreach that is spammy and inefficient.

The definition of the word deploy is:

Bring into effective action.

And that's what a good SEO and content marketer does.

They bring their years of knowledge into effective action.

It's also why as SEOs become older and have worked on more sites, their knowledge becomes even more incredible.

Because they don't only know what to do, they know what not to do.

That's one of the major reasons that these days I am hired to create SEO and digital marketing strategies for businesses.

It's to reduce waste.

It's to know what is likely to work.

I charge between £4,000 to £12,000 for strategies.

Which is far less than the average SEO contract.

And still, I meet so many people who have paid £24,000 over the course of two years and got nowhere.

This is often because the agency is deploying the wrong SEO knowledge.

SEO isn't about doing everything, it's about knowing what to do to give the greatest chances of success.

And it's about knowing what not to do.

That's why experience in SEO matters.

And why good SEOs charge more.

Hire wisely.

And as the saying goes.

If you think it's expensive to hire a professional to do the job, wait until you hire an amateur.

SEO Expectation vs Reality

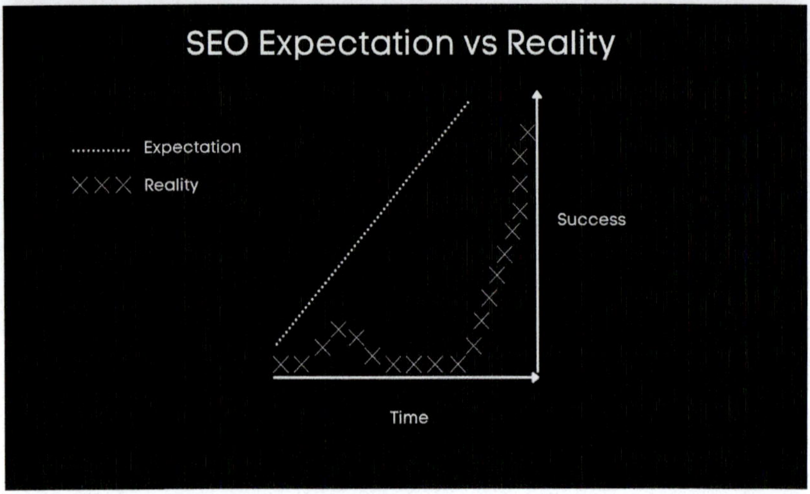

There is a graveyard of wasted SEO budget.

It lies in the land of poor understanding of how search engines work.

And it's known as the place where 'results were not seen.'

One of my most successful SEO campaigns, the client cancelled at month five of a six month contract.

Well, the truth is that I let them out of a contract because they were continually voicing their unhappiness at not seeing results.

Within the next eight weeks, the pages we had created based on a strategy I developed ranked and now generate 180,000 visits a year and is worth a PPC spend of $65,433 a year.

The thing is, I knew the pages would rank.

It wasn't if, it was when.

I know this because I've been involved in SEO for the best part of 18 years now.

And doing it professionally for six.

I've been running sites for over a decade and seen what each and every type of SEO strategy can do.

I've done it all.

Links from Fiverr, shotgun outreach, Skyscraper, PBN's, buying links, guest blogging, power pages, Digital PR, HARO, Journo outreach, viral content.

I've run countless large, small and even micro SEO and content tests to see what works and fails. I'm running five this week alone.

This experience allows me to be in a relatively unique position to know what works, what doesn't, and the probable time scales and costs.

The problem with SEO is that for clients it's a tough pill to swallow.

They have to have HUGE amounts of faith that even after a six month SEO campaign, you might not see results until months eight, 10 or even 12.

It all depends on the site, the strategy and the process you use to get success.

But if the SEO is done in a structured, targeted and logical way.

RESULTS WILL COME.

However, what if they don't?

Have you wasted your SEO budget and time?

It's possible, but unlikely.

Instead, another SEO might be able to come in and see what was done and move the project to the point you can see the results.

To build upon what was done before.

This is because SEO is like building a house that is never finished.

You are building a structure over time.

And that time is the lifespan of your business.

This is why SEO never ends.

And really, you should never cancel or stop doing SEO.

Stop doing SEO when the business doesn't exist.

That's the reality.

Of course, we all know of the shady practitioners out there that don't generate any results...ever.

Yes, they are around.

So choose your SEO agency, consultant or specialist with care.

And hopefully the results are just around the corner for you.

The Content Success Framework

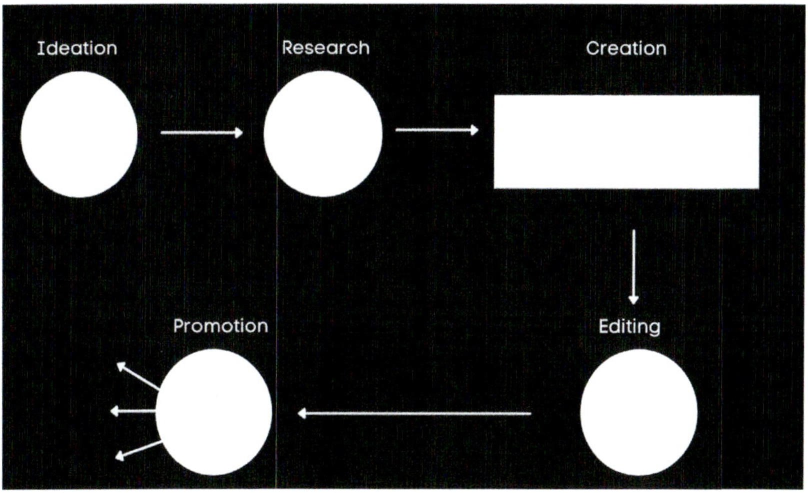

Step 1. Ideation

Here you come up with content ideas and research topics to see what you should be writing about.

Step 2. Research

What do you need to make your idea a success? Research first and assemble your ingredients.

Step 3. Creation

Be kind to yourself, write in drafts, write when motivated, write when you have the time, energy and focus.

Step 4. Editing

All content needs editing. Again, be kind to yourself, it's simply content.

The great thing about the internet is that content can always evolve.

Step 5. Promotion

The place where we almost always fall down as marketers. As great as you are, other people are busy. So you need to write once and promote 20 times.

That's the great thing about content. I often share content written from years ago. That's why evergreen content is so important.

Your writing process matters.

Create one.

(P.S. I have a lot of different processes depending on the type of content I am creating).

What You Think You're Getting With Most Digital PR vs What You Actually End Up With

A few years ago, digital PR wasn't a thing.

In fact, no SEO specialist really cared about it.

Move on a few years and today, digital PR is an 8-figure business with campaigns thrown out daily.

But does it really work?

Well, first we need to examine what digital PR is.

Here goes.

PR is changing the way the public relates to your brand or business.

Publicity is getting the media to talk about you for free.
Digital PR is the art of getting media websites to talk about you for free.
And that's it.

At its core, digital PR is all about mentions and links.

You get mentioned and hopefully, you get a back-link.

So why do we care?

Well, it's supposed to boost rankings.

But does it really?

In my personal experience...no.

It's very hard to quantify any long term SEO benefits from digital PR link building.

Why? Because most sites doing this are also doing a large number of other things.

They are creating content, running other marketing campaigns, being interviewed, making technical changes to their websites and more.

In addition, a site of any decent size generally attracts links naturally.

And that's the reality of digital PR.

You think you'll get a huge amount of links.

But sadly, mostly these are links from low to zero traffic pages buried so deep in a media website that no one will ever find it, let alone read it.

So, what does work when it comes to digital PR?

In my experience, two things.

Firstly, being quoted or interviewed on your subject knowledge on a regular basis.

The sheer body of back-links starts to add up and make a difference, and people really start to link your brand or business with a specific industry.

This is all about frequency, not flashy campaigns.

The second thing that works when you use digital PR correctly is when you have a good story to tell.

Good stories actually change the way the public sees a business. And this is the backbone of good PR.

Donating 1000 laptops to a local school is a good story.

A CEO that spends the night sleeping on the streets to raise money for charity and to better understand the world is a good story.

Growing your business from 7 to 47 staff in a year is a good story.

The reality of digital PR is that getting links buried on zero traffic web pages that no one will find, let alone read, is awful PR.

Creating a story that makes people think differently about your business is good PR.

Being talked about as an industry expert is good PR.

Digital PR should be done with business and brand purpose.

And not just used to gain links.

Because if that's the goal, I assure you, there are far cheaper, more consistent and more effective ways to build back-links and keep them.

You should be using PR for your business. But make sure you use the right approach.

Don't Focus on Building a Following, Focus on Building an Email List

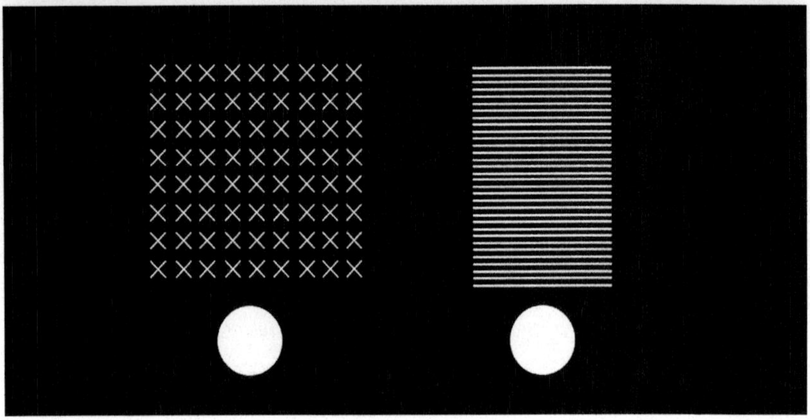

If last night taught anyone anything (Facebook's services went down).

It's the power of having an email list.

Facebook can go down, Google can change its results and take your traffic away.

You own your email list.

So ask yourself:

"What are we doing to grow our email list?"

Because people don't just sign up for email lists anymore.

You must have a big reason that makes them want to sign up.

And this is the same reason why they are going to bookmark your site and keep coming back to your site...without you paying for it.

If You Want to Get Ahead of Your Competition, Sometimes You Have to Go in a Different Direction

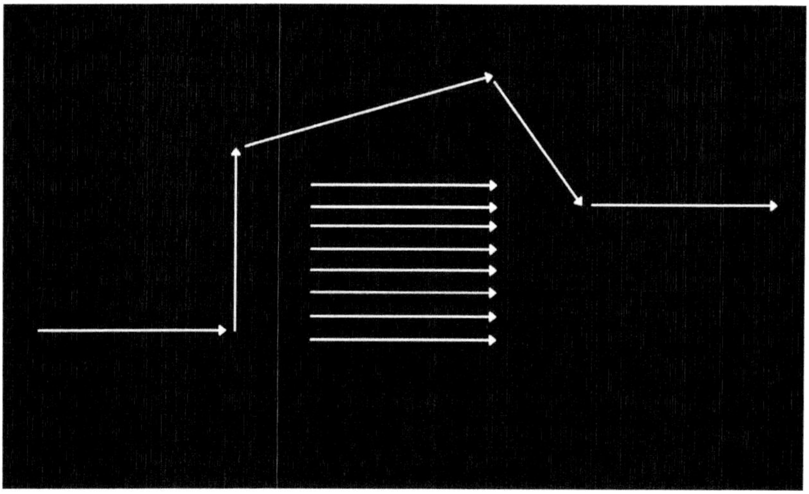

When I advise a business online, I almost always ask to analyse their competitors.

Why?

Because they have likely gained some kind of result in online marketing you can learn from.

It's a trail of breadcrumbs we can follow.

And this tells us what is working and what isn't.

The real benefit of this is that we don't need to spend years figuring this stuff out and blowing a load of budget in the process.

And we can use the best approaches of the combined competition to deploy across your site.

This allows for rapid scaling and growth.

But that's only one part of it.

We also need to look at what they aren't doing.

What is the gap?

What can you do that they haven't considered?

In other words, how can you be in a league of your own?

This is where REAL growth happens.

When people seek you out, and not find you through a query.

There are two learning points here.

The first is that every business needs to devour what their competition is doing so you can learn from them and, where the data suggests, deploy the same content and SEO model.

The second is that you'll probably need to change direction.

Yes, you'll get copied eventually, but by then you have a first-mover advantage.

And the final tip is this.

If you need to move in a new direction and aren't sure what to do.

Smash your site with another big player in any niche or industry.

And use your imagination to see what comes out.

What happens if you smash together YouTube with a travel website?

You get Travel Vision: daily original travel content from top influencers that will inspire you to see the world.

What happens if you smash a car leasing website with Buzzfeed?

You get Car Throttle (that's a real-life example there).

I think you get the point.

Getting ahead of the competition is all about taking their best tactics and using them to compete on search.

And then stepping in a new direction to become searched for.

Do this and win big.

Always think about your next pivot.

Always think of reinvention.

Running water never grows stale.

You Won't Find Success Online Until You Stand Out

If you Google almost anything these days, you'll find the first four pages of results are almost all the same.

Content designed to rank and answer a question.

The only difference tends to be the depth of that answer.

And sure, that makes sense, because that's what search engines are for.

To find answers.

And so, SEO is largely about answering questions in the hope that both more and better answers will win people over the brand.

And yes, that works.

But it's simply not enough any longer.

You need to STAND OUT from the crowd.

You need to give them a reason to bookmark your site, to come back for more, to seek you out.

There are ways to do this.

You might simply be the biggest online resource in your industry.

You might produce new content that shows your expertise as a business each week.

You might run a weekly online quiz for your industry to challenge people's knowledge.

You might have a podcast.

You could have the best examples and tips in your industry and produce them in a list that you email to people every week.

There are thousands of ways to stand out online.

And that is the future of content marketing and SEO.

STANDING OUT from the crowd.

And offering something different.

SEO and PPC will get people to your site.

But only by being different from everything else out there will you start to generate traffic without effort.

The great thing about content is that you can test approaches easily and cheaply.

And if it resonates with those you seek to serve, you can add more budget and go bigger, until you decide to go ALL IN for a period of time.

A Website With Little to No Content vs One With A Lot

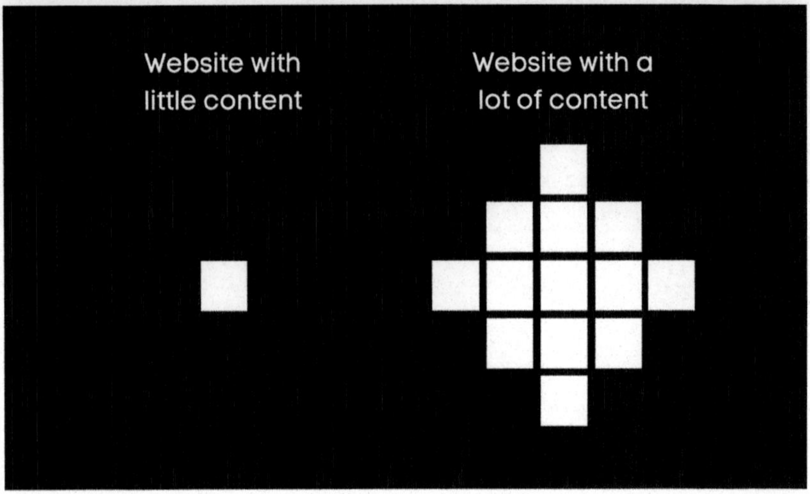

One is boring, one is interesting.

We over-complicate marketing with desires such as 100,000 visitors a month.

Month-on-month search growth.

Immediate ROI.

Sometimes the simplest way is the best.

"Is my site interesting for my audience?"

"Is there enough to read for my audience?"

"Is it any good?"

The number of businesses that I see who have boring websites with thin content that they paid the cheapest writer they could find to throw together is astounding.

You want your visitors to care enough about you to buy from you.

So invest in educating them.

There really are no excuses anymore.

And your audience knows it.

Why Do Most Businesses Fail Online?

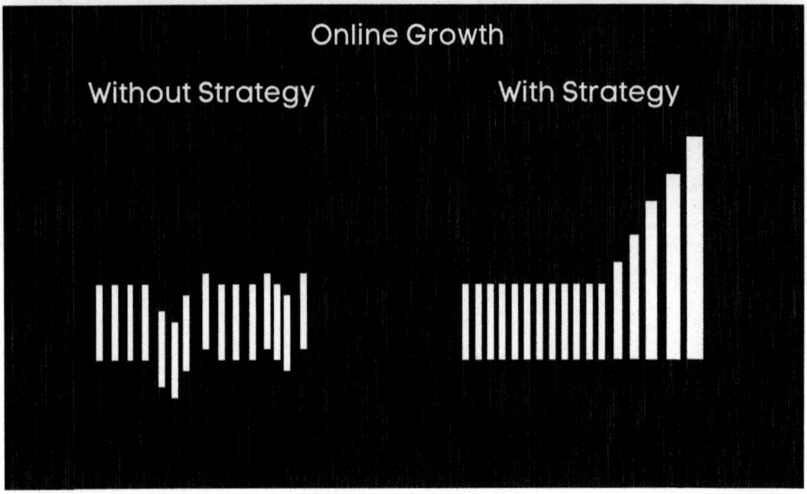

Answer: They don't have a plan.

I have advised a lot of businesses over the last five years.

From small ones to clients that, if I dropped their names, would bring me a flood of leads, praise and get me even more work.

(I don't drop their names because that's not how I work).

People come to me because they tend to have a few issues.

The first is often an inexperienced digital team.

This isn't anyone's fault, just a product of the fact that digital marketing is both young and rapidly evolving.

And the second reason is that a companies marketing team just has their wealth of experience in areas other than digital.

As a result, many companies want an outsider's view on both where they are at and how to move forward online.

Bringing in outside consultants to create digital and/or SEO strategies for your business is perhaps the smartest decision you will ever make.

Why?

Because you are so close to your business that it is almost impossible to see the wood for the trees.

Growth Leads to Popularity

Do you want to know what the true secret to online success is?

It's that growth leads to popularity.

And popularity then leads to further growth.

The one hit wonders are rare.

And I've rarely seen a single web page lead to mass internet success.

The uncomfortable truth is that any website or online business never grows through a single marketing act.

Six months of SEO won't cut it.

Neither will a few social media posts that are identical to everyone else's.

Nor will a few blog posts.

And it certainly won't come by spamming people for back-links.

No.

The true route to online success comes from growth.

You post once, then twice, then more and you promote.

People either stay or they go.

They return if they like what you do and don't if it's not for them.

As your website or social presence grows, Google looks at you.

You start to naturally build a few back-links.

First by the web 2.0s, then some directories, then some forums start to talk about you and finally people link to your content.

Your pages link to each other and rankings start to increase as you build your own online network.

And then as your growth increases, so does your popularity.

People talk, they link and they engage with you.

It's the long game.

That's the marketing game you SHOULD be playing.

Sadly too many businesses are playing short term games of spam outreach, email scraping, annoyance and intellectually lazy content.

You can do better.

Use All of the Tools in Your Marketing Chest

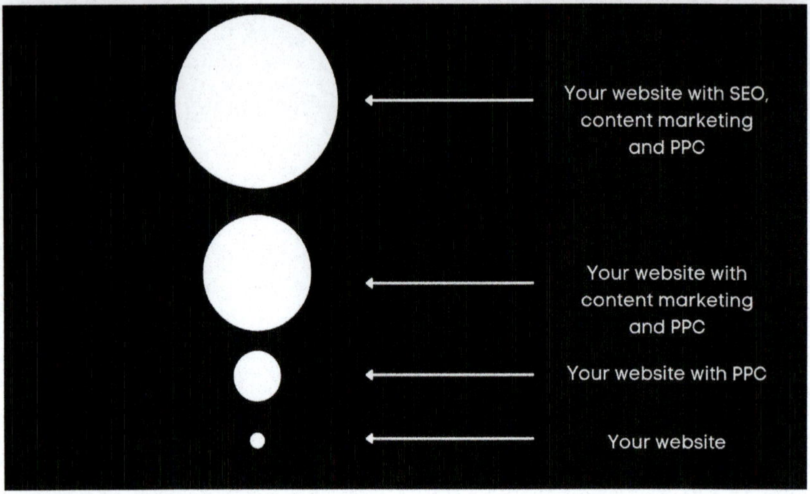

"I'm getting no leads"

"What are you doing to get them?"

If you build it, they won't just come.

If you create it, they won't just buy it.

And if you try and force them to buy, they'll resist.

Marketing is about making change happen.

And we use it every day.

Charities market, schools market themselves to parents.

Businesses market to people.

Yet often, we don't utilise ALL of the possible marketing tools in our chest.

Why?

Budget.

I often get calls asking for SEO services so they can reduce their PPC spend.

And that's fine, albeit I often ask "why not try to make better ads?"

SEO might reduce PPC spend, but it's a clunky way to do it.

What it does do is expose your brand to more people at scale.

And it does this more effectively than PPC.

PPC, SEO and content marketing are all parts of the marketing tool chest.

As can be other activities.

But it's rarely one activity that wins the race for a business.

You need to engage in other channels.

And yes, one will start to gain traction and you'll invest more in it.

That doesn't mean the others don't, won't or can't work for you either.

Perhaps it's the approach, the strategy, the budget or even the skills of the practitioner or agency.

Marketing works.

Investing in your website is possibly a business's greatest investment, after its staff.

So look at your marketing and ask yourself "are we doing all we can do, or are we being lazy?"

Being lazy is fine.

Until you look around and see the competition outgrowing you.

Invest in digital marketing and you'll soon see results.

The Compound Effect of Content on Your Website

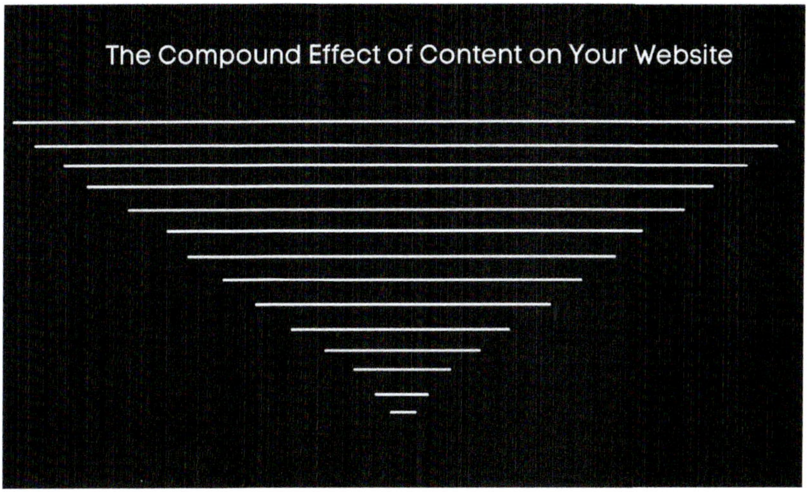

You start with one article about your subject.

Then add another.

The traffic is zero or your mum reads it.

And then you add another.

Repeat this 10 times and now you have some great posts.

When read, someone leaves your site feeling educated and more knowledgeable.

You made a change in their life.

You add another 20 articles.

Each sharing your views and your expertise.

Soon you have 100 articles.

Many of them are being picked up by Google and generating traffic.

Others are being shared online.

Before long, you have 150 added to your site.

It's now a database of industry content, views and opinions.

People stick around for longer.

You aren't a 'quick read and leave' kind of site, you're now a 'stick around and devour the content' kind of site.

You add a twist, each week you will put out content that your audience will love.

They look forward to it, they check their inboxes and Google your site to see where it is.

You have them hooked.

And more people become hooked on your website and your business.

You provide the answers they need.

And the content that keeps them informed.

People tell others about you.

Word of mouth spreads.

"You need to check out..." is what they say about you to others.

People choose you because you are the only choice.

You are positioned everywhere they look.

This is how content compounds when you invest.

Realise that every company is now a media company.

Invest wisely.

Start creating content today.

SEO vs Content Marketing: What the Difference is and Which is Right For Your Business

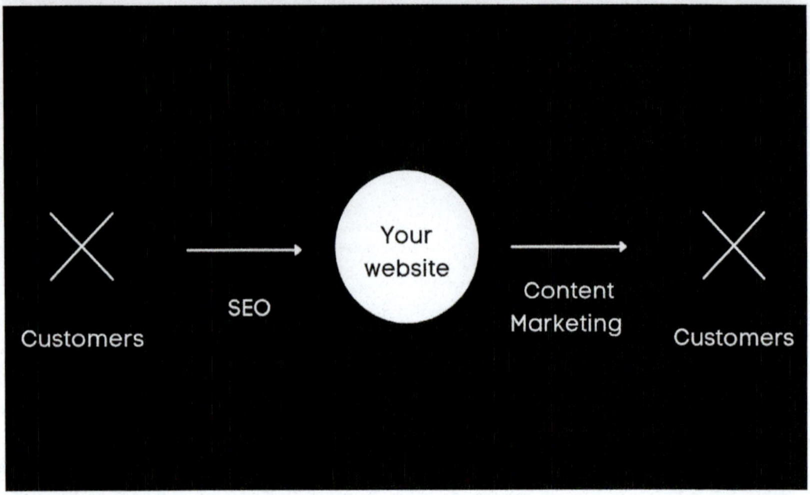

It's a subject that gets confused a lot.

So here's the simple version.

SEO causes your ideal customers to come to your site via discovery from search engines.

Content marketing is the process of you taking your website to your ideal customers.

This is very different from content promotion for SEO purposes.

Content promotion for SEO is the process of pushing your content to those that have the ability to link back to your site.

So which is right for your business?

The answer is neither.

It's an outdated model of marketing.

Here's what I mean.

The days of thinking of SEO and content marketing as separate activities are over.

Instead, we are entering the era of Evolved SEO.

What's that?

Evolved SEO is, in my opinion, the future.

It's the process of turning your website into its own search engine.

If your target audience has a question about your industry, the answers should live on your website.

But that's only part of the puzzle that Evolved SEO solves.

Because you need to create content that your target audience would never be able to find via search.

This is the content they never knew that they wanted to read.

It's the content that AI could never write.

Highly creative, out-of-the-box thinking that deserves to be read.

It's this content that you need to create and market to your audience.

You have to market this content and do so with courage.

Because it deserves to be shared.

And this is the process of Evolved SEO.

It's creating an online content universe around your business.

Yes, this is hard work.

Yes, this takes time.

And yes, this will take budget.

But become a digital builder.

Turn your website from something that people visit into a place that people stay.

That's Evolved SEO.

That's what happens when you combine content marketing with SEO.

Look For Patterns and You'll Find Your Road to Success Online

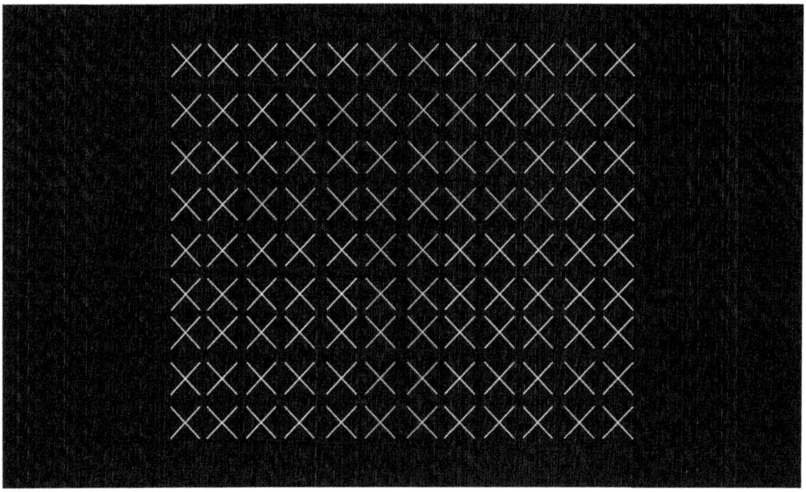

I get asked to create a lot of digital marketing and SEO strategies.

And one of the core parts of this process is to look for patterns.

Sometimes it's hard to find, but there is always a pattern of success.

Here's the secret.

Everyone is following the same pattern.

Post to social media.

Write content that matches search queries.

Make videos.

Create podcasts.

Use ads.

So, if it's easy, why isn't everyone a smash-hit success?

Why isn't everyone a YouTube star, a podcast legend, a 7-figure blogger?

And if it's so easy, why isn't every business drowning in clients and customers?

Well, that's because people give up.

We've been brainwashed into looking for short term outcomes.

"We spent £24,000 this year on SEO, what's our ROI been?"

"I created a YouTube video, it only had 100 views."

"My blog has only been read by 11 people, I spent hours on that."

The patterns I seek when I create marketing strategies are those patterns that can be observed over a long time.

And that's the key.

It takes a long time to make an impact.

It takes a lot of effort.

It takes consistency.

The reason I can analyse patterns of successful businesses online is because they DIDN'T play short term games.

They didn't look for short term results.

They didn't focus on hacks.

They made a decision.

"We are going to speak to the people we seek to serve, we hope they'll listen".

Amongst the patterns, you'll find the tactics and strategies they used if you know how to look, how to study them and break them down.

That's where I come in.

I break the patterns down.

The successful people and businesses online are the ones that didn't give up.

That's the pattern I look for in an industry.

Who didn't give up? Who's still creating content?

And who is serving their audience best?

If you are not having success online, it's almost always down to a lack of commitment.

Be that financial or physical.

And that's the first hurdle to cross.

How committed are you?

Be Searched For Rather Than Discovered Through Search

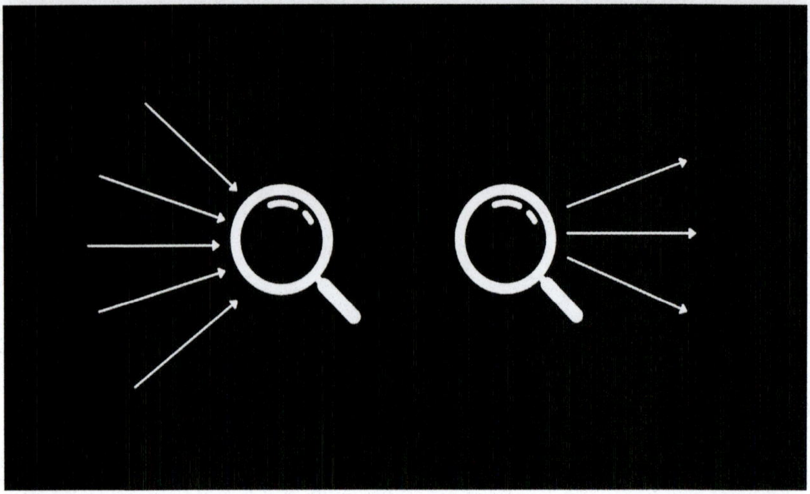

Aim for your business to be searched for more than it's discovered through search.

That's a game you can win.

When people talk about SEO, all they do is talk about more traffic and higher rankings.

And yes, that's important.

It's important to show up when customers need help and advice from a business like yours. But that's only half of the puzzle and potential of SEO.

The other half is that you must be aiming to be searched for more than you are discovered through search.

At first, many SEOs will gasp at such an idea.

But that is old school SEO where all people do is consider traffic and rankings.

Modern and evolved SEO is about thinking larger from the digital business perspective.

It's about actually thinking "what can we do to make people want to come back to our site?"

This will almost always involve variable reward content; something new that you offer each month, each week, each day or even each hour.

As an SEO specialist, you can stick your head in the sand and say that these things are the job of the content marketing team or the Marketing Manager.

And yes, that was right. But now, content marketing and SEO are merging into one larger field.

Add into this, digital PR, email marketing and variable reward content.

You soon open up more power to the SEO process.

Instead of being helpless to the ever-changing algorithm updates and scraping of SERPS where Google robs you of traffic you rightly deserve.

You are turning the tables.

You are empowering business owners.

You are reaching people and not relying on search engines.

Yes, this takes guts and yes you might fail.

You might create content that people don't want.

And that's ok.

You can go back to the drawing board and keep trying until you find an angle that people love.

If you are struggling to think about what this could be, ask yourself the question.

"What content could we offer to our target audience every Thursday that the people we seek to serve will love and go looking for, be that via search or their inbox?"

The day isn't really important, but naming it actually helps to focus your thinking.

Search marketing can be taken up several levels.

But yes, it takes creativity, and yes, it takes hard work.

And if your business is up for the challenge, the internet can be vastly more powerful for your business than you think.

Minimum Viable Link Building

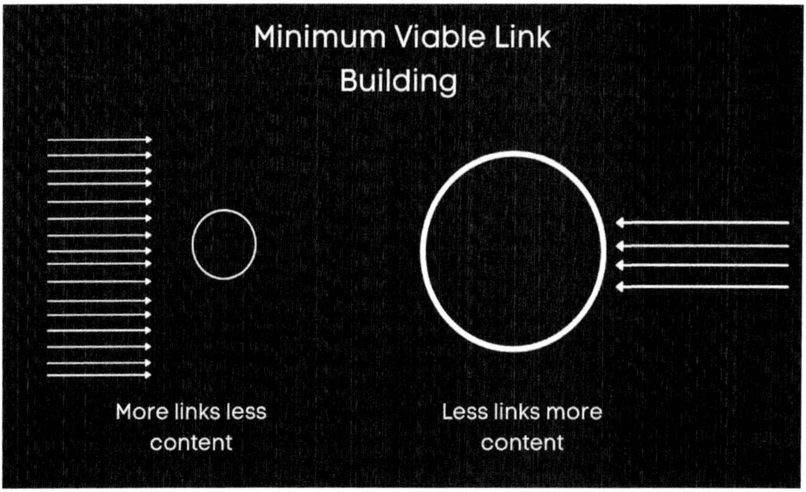

Very few SEOs or Marketing Managers get to work with the budget they truly desire.

As a result, they have to make choices.

Almost all will choose to gain more back-links over any other activity.

And for good reason.

The back-link business is HUGE.

It's a multi-billion pound industry where something that is essentially free, becomes traded for money.

The thing is, if you're a real business that is engaging in real marketing.

You probably have enough back-links.

But you probably don't have enough keyword-focused content that your audience will love.

That's the core place that almost all businesses should start when looking at their site.

Do we have enough links for what we want to do?

And if you're not sure, simply test.

Create several pieces of keyword-focused content and see what happens.

The obsession to see your authority rise in SEO tools can be an addictive game.

But in my experience, you'll have far better results doing two things.

1. Creating the best content for your audience.

2. Engaging in real and authentic marketing.

Both tend to be more rewarding for your business in terms of customer attraction and engagement AND back-link acquisition.

Nobody wants to get spammed via email asking for links with a terrible outreach template.

So why do it?

What does it say about your business?

The whole idea of back-links is that it allows your content to be discovered on the vast internet.

And that's exactly how you should view link building.

An approach that focuses on quality rather than quantity.

So before you press send on that outreach campaign, you need to consider whether the email will be the best that the person will receive that day?

If it's not, then why are you sending it?

There are far cheaper, more effective and less brand-damaging ways to generate traffic and back-links than sending out mass templated campaigns.

If you're a real business, market like a real business and not an affiliate website.

Be lean with your link building and generous with your content, and the results will come.

Aim For Solid Marketing Foundations

If you want your marketing to be successful in the long run, you'll need strong foundations.

Instead of trying to hack your way to the top, consider your marketing channels and, where you're weak, fix those weaknesses.

Having great SEO and bad PR isn't going to lead to long term success.

Doing a lot of link building and putting no new content out isn't going to lead to success either.

Great traffic levels and weak branding is not going to bring you a flood of leads.

Aim for solid marketing across the board and you'll win.

What People (and Customers) Really Want

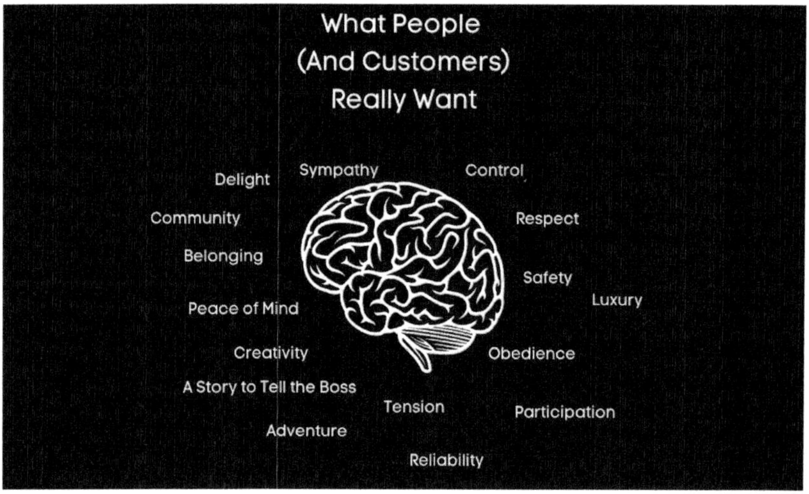

What customers really want.

Unless you sell lemonade to thirsty people on a hot day. Selling isn't as simple as people think.

People have needs. Such as food and shelter.

And for the people you do business with, these are already taken care of.

So we deal with wants.

The problem is that we don't tend to reveal our wants.

If you ask someone what they want, they'll likely give a vague answer.

Why? Because we are abysmal at articulating our wants and desires.

And we're naturally very guarded about them.

Our deepest wants say something about our personality if we tell others.

That's why the internet and SEO are so powerful for marketing.

If I search for 'holiday apartments in Cornwall.'

I don't just buy from the first website that comes up.

I compare the sites on the first page. I'm comparing the sites, apartments and suppliers based on my personal wants and desires.

And yes, I look at them all.

This is where honest and effective marketing wins the people you seek to serve.

So where does ranking higher come in?

Well, the search engine rankings tend to serve as an indicator of trust.

We know that ranking higher tends to equal a business that cares about being found.

It's a costly signalling mechanism that the business has put effort into their digital reputation.

We all know it, yet it goes unspoken in the background.

And that's why it's so important to invest in SEO.

Because it's one of the most powerful brand marketing methods around.

Being found online when your ideal audience searches for phrases around your business matters. Don't pretend it doesn't.

If You Market to Everyone, You Market to No One

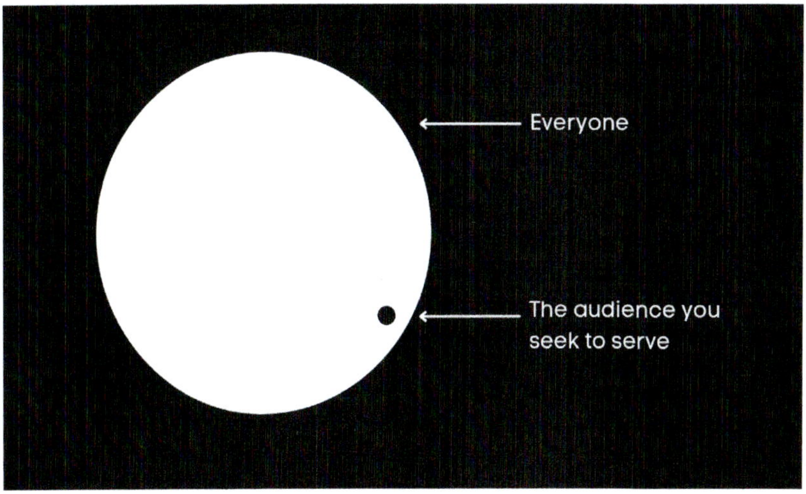

Not everyone is your customer, so stop trying to market like they are.

When I first started in marketing, I was asked "who are your target customers?"

My naive answer was "everyone with a business".

I later learned that not everyone can be my customer.

Here's how.

When I started I was trying to compete with the big local agencies for clients.

And I was losing.

What I was trying to do was to compete with the world-view of Marketing

Managers and business owners.

It's a battle I would never win.

People that went to this type of marketing business wanted to buy and believe in the big marketing illusion.

"People like us buy from people like that".

It was their reputation on the line with their boss or their partners.

And big agencies reduce the risk of failure.

No one ever got fired for hiring a big agency.

And it's fine to have that approach.

So I changed tactics.

I became a specialist who delivered results through depth of knowledge and experience.

And so the people who came to me and became my customers were those who understood the illusion of marketing agencies.

And they didn't want to be part of the magic show.

In fact, most of my clients have worked with over 15 different agencies over the years.

They've been there and bought the t-shirt.

And so today I find my customers are those that don't want to hire big agencies.

They are people looking for specialists.

They say "businesses like us, hire specialists".

Interestingly of note, today big agencies are reaching out to me.

They want to have my depth of knowledge injected into their teams.

And that's fine too. I can simply never win the types of customers they have.

Once you realise that not everyone can be your customer, you don't see everyone as the competition.

You are the best at being you.

Today I know of writers who specialise in LinkedIn bios.

Some write really long list posts.

Other agencies niche down.

Some agencies go big and work with huge chains.

The thing is, as you focus on a certain type of client and narrow this focus down, your marketing becomes far more powerful and your ability to gain customers becomes more effective.

And so, my number one marketing tip is this.

Figure out who you seek to serve.

Be specific.

If you market to everyone, you market to no one.

Write For People and For Search

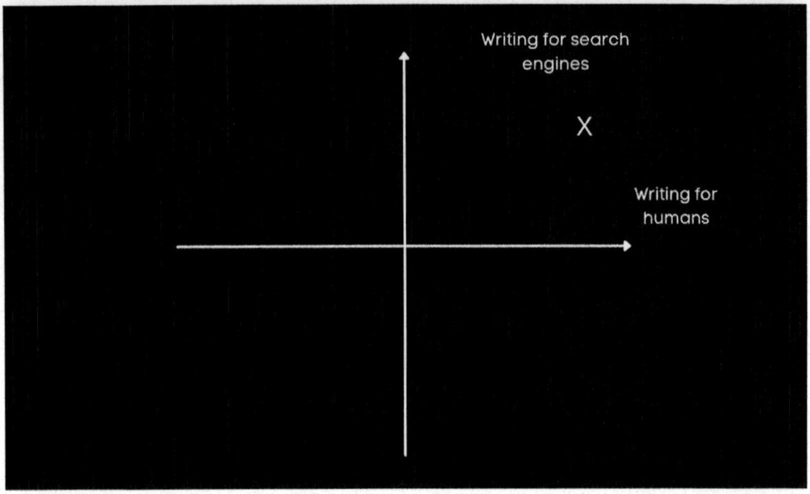

Almost everyone I know in SEO has thrown creative writing in the bin.

It's a big mistake.

I was invited to write for a huge site once.

The brief was so tight it was strangling.

But I fought back, created an intro that placed the reader exactly where I wanted them to be visually.

It got rejected as being against the tone of the brand.

The problem. It was an article in my name, my tone.

I'm still a customer of that business, yet I never read their content.

It's boring and robotic, all designed to rank online for searches.

If you're a writer like that, you'll be replaced by AI, sooner or later.

Robotic writing can indeed be written by a robot...and probably should be.

On the other hand, creative writing is what keeps people addicted to your brand.

They search for you, looking for any new content.

And some of the biggest websites in the world are based on this very approach.

Personally I feel you need both.

A 50/50 split.

Creativity and content written for search.

In the obsession to gain traffic, people have forgotten the importance of writing for humans.

And at the same time, so many creative writers go undiscovered and barely read because they never write to be found through search.

Do both.

Expected Content vs Unexpected Content

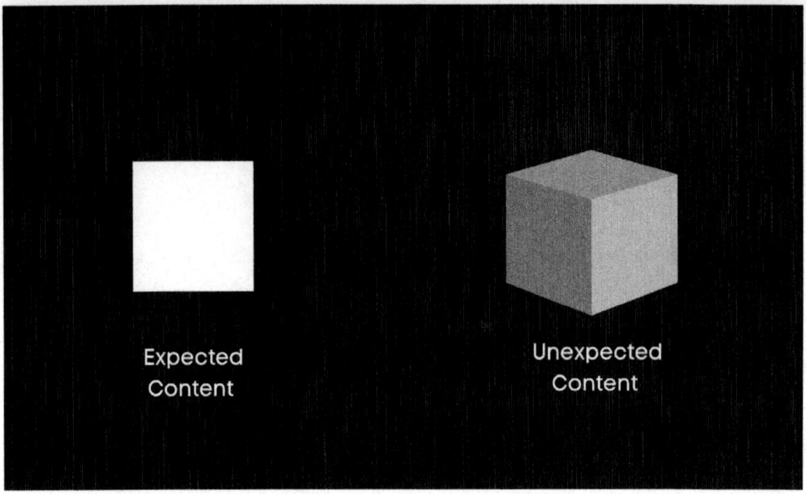

Expected content is just that; it's what you'd expect to see.

When you search for the best restaurants in London, you expect to find a list of the best restaurants.

And you'd expect the restaurants that want to be known as the best to have invested in SEO to show up on the first page of Google.

Unexpected content is different.

It's the content that you never saw coming.

It's a different angle, edgy, unique.

It's content designed to get people thinking differently.

It's content you never knew you needed or wanted.

If you want your business to truly succeed online, you need both.

Expected content gets you found.

Unexpected content keeps people coming back for more.

It excites people.

It makes people think.

It's creative writing.

The thing is, writing expected content is a specific skill.

One that understands search engines, SEO and also how people read expected content online.

Unexpected content requires creative thinking, good writing and a person who thinks out of the box.

Sometimes you'll find a writer that can produce excellent expected and unexpected content.

But often you're going to need to find writers for both types of content if you really want to get people to your site. And get them hooked on your business.

Remember, content written for search engines and people tends to look very different to content just written for humans.

Invest in both types.

How to Achieve SEO Results

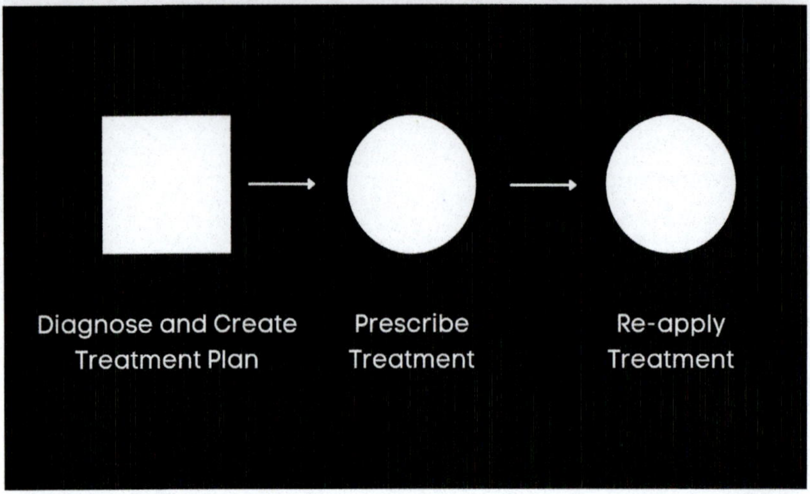

How SEO really works...and yes, almost everyone gets this wrong.

The problem with SEO is two-fold.

1. SEO agencies.
2. SEO clients.

The first issue with SEO is that most agencies oversell.

They imply a promise that SEO results can be delivered within a set timescale.

And this feeds the second issue.

That clients love to hear that results will come within a precise time frame.

The reality is this.

SEO is no different than medical treatment.

First, the agency needs to diagnose the issues that are preventing the site from dominating their industry or area.

Second, the agency prescribes a treatment.

And finally, the agency reapplies the same treatment until the desired results happen.

When SEO results don't happen, it is because of three reasons.

1. Incorrect diagnosis (the wrong strategy).

2. Insufficient budget.

3. Insufficient time.

This is why strategy is possibly THE most important part of SEO.

If you haven't got a documented SEO strategy, then I guarantee you are likely to be wasting money on SEO.

And having ranked well over 123,000 keywords on the first page of Google, driving millions of organic visitors and advising 7-figure businesses for the last six years.

I can help your business to thrive post covid.

Create Great Content Worth Linking To

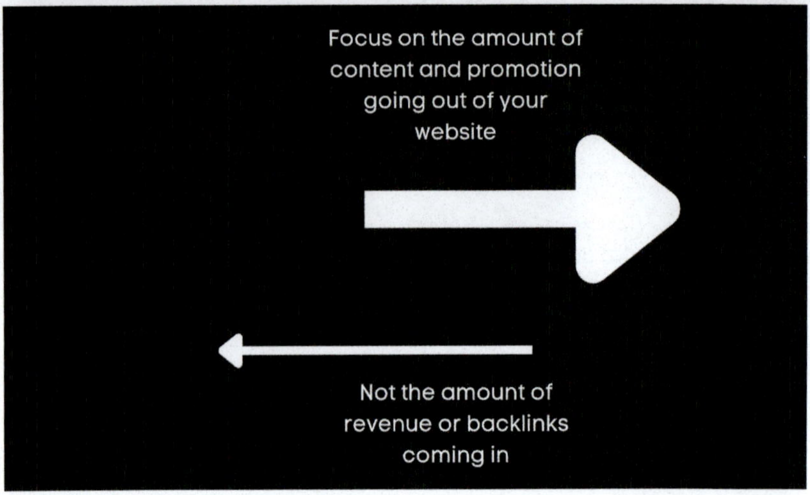

Focus on the amount of content and promotion going out of your website.

Not the amount of revenue or back-links coming in.

Mechanical marketers focus on numbers, such as back-links and revenue.

As an SEO specialist or content marketer, your job isn't to figure out what content generates the most back-links or revenue.

Your job is to help your business to be found by those you seek to serve.

Your job is to help those you seek to serve to connect with your business.

This is your primary focus.

If you want back-links, simply create content for those that have the power to link to your site and would want to.

But please note, rarely are these people the ones that will buy from you.

These are not your customers.

And while there might be an SEO case for creating content for those that will link to you.

There is a bigger business case to create content for your target audience.

And this is where the majority of your efforts should focus.

What content will delight, engage, inspire, educate, intrigue and be loved by those you seek to serve? And how can we get this content in front of their eyes?

The majority of real businesses will generate plenty of back-links through real marketing.

And for those that create great content, you'll reap the rewards of back-links naturally.

When it's time to focus on generating back-links, create content that is designed to generate back-links and not customers.

A good SEO specialist will know the difference.

Connecting your brand with real people through genuine marketing has never been more important.

Standing out from the crowd has never been more essential.

Doing SEO like a machine is over.

People hate outreach messages for links.

They rarely work.

The new approach is the old approach.

Create content worth linking to.

Create marketing that connects to your audience.

Stand out.

Create content.

Promote your content.

That's marketing.

It's Easy to Stand Out When the Competition is All Marketing Themselves the Same Way

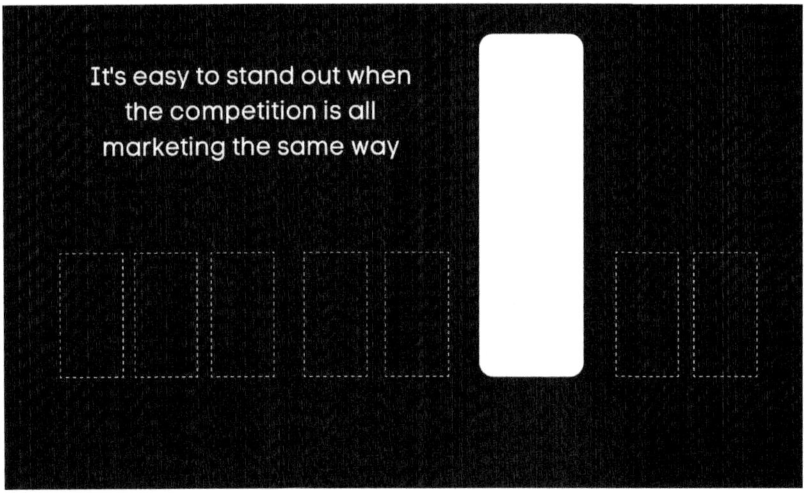

I get frustrated with businesses that don't try to stand out.

Especially in the B2B world where marketing is often treated as something you give to the interns.

Your market is there for the taking.

You just need to start taking your marketing as seriously as you take your business.

It's your business, don't expect others to talk about it if you aren't.

Make Sure Your Ideal Customers are Consuming Your Content, Not Your Competitors

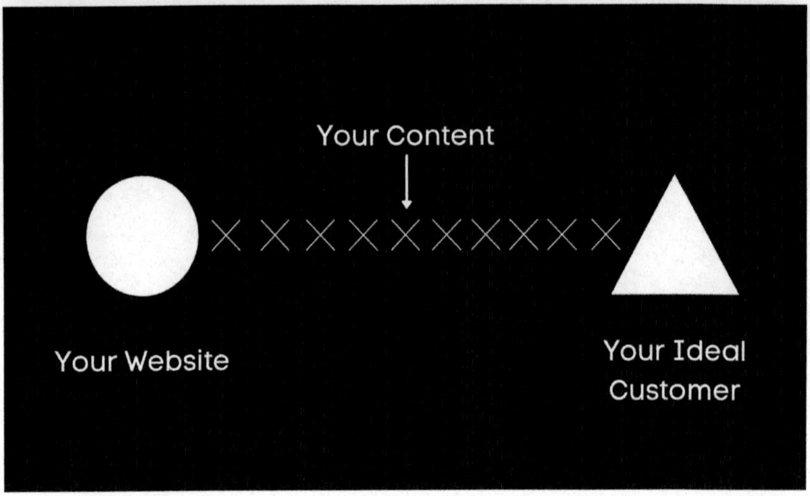

Your content is how you connect with your customer.

Less content = less connection.

Poor content = poor quality connection.

Great and frequent content = a great and frequent connection.

The gap between your business and your customers is minuscule thanks to the internet.

And so you really have no excuse not to engage, inspire, educate and entertain your customers.

What makes you so special as a business?

Why is what you do important?

What makes you unique?

What do you stand for?

What do the customers need to know about what you do?

What problem do you solve for people and why does this matter?

What change are you trying to make in the world?

Why should they care?

There are over a thousand subjects around your business and industry that you can create content around.

So why aren't you?

Budget? Really?

You can find the budget and if there really isn't any, find the time.

Content connects your business with your customer faster than any other form of marketing.

And if it is done the right way, they'll read the content and be changed by it.

Your ideal customers are consuming content.

Make sure they consume yours and not your competitors.

It's Only When You Truly Invest in Content That You'll See Success Online

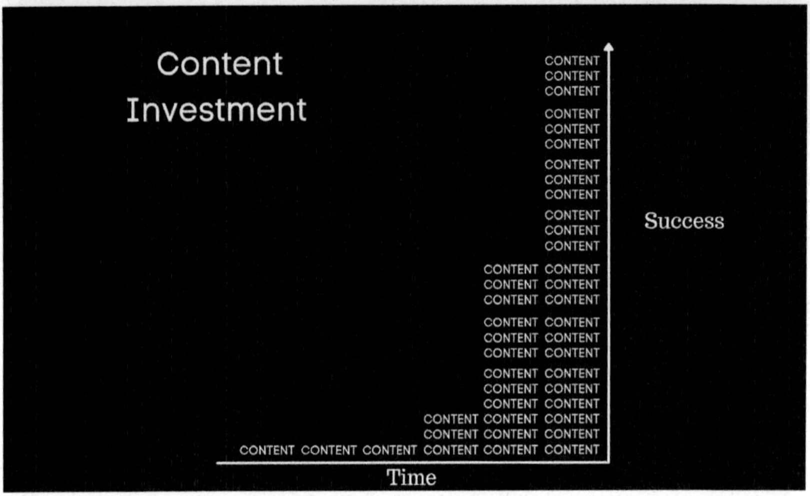

It doesn't matter what channel you choose.

Podcasts, videos, blog articles.

We are a planet of content consumers.

There simply isn't enough good content out there.

Your customers want content, they want to hear from you.

Some people dip their toes into the content water and never reach their potential.

Others try a bit but again, never get to where they want to be.

It's the businesses that truly scale their content that make an impact into the world of online marketing.

Eventually you'll figure it out on your own, over a long enough timeline, you'll see that content works and invest.

But why wait?

There is an abundance of examples where content scaling works.

What content should you use?

Expected content - content that people find by search.

Unexpected content - content that people didn't know they needed until you showed it to them.

Flip the graph, invest in content now, invest big and make landing on your website an experience that wows people.

"We Spent £24,000 on PPC and Haven't Had a Single Lead in 12 Months"

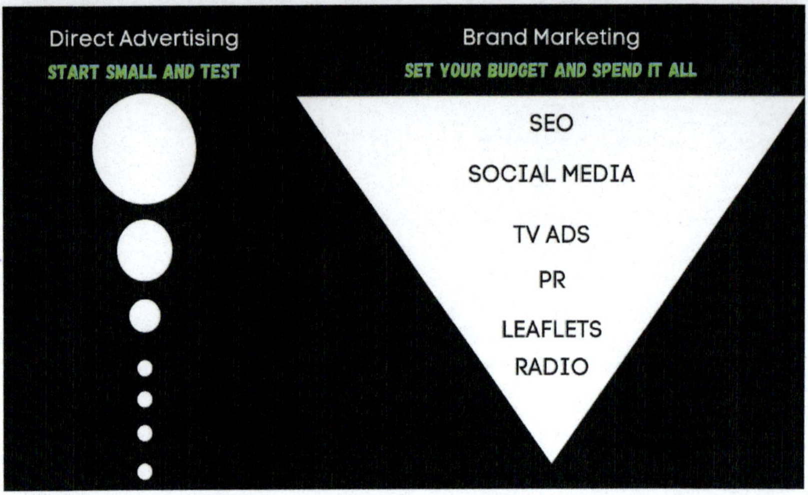

That's what a Marketing Manager told me who had inherited a terrible contract from her predecessor.

I have met, talked to and trained hundreds of Marketing Managers and business owners over the years.

And almost all of them find it difficult to maximise the results from their marketing money.

It's for good reason.

Often digital marketing is seen as machine-like, a race to the bottom.

"We need leads, lets spend on Google ads".

And so, the belief is that you just pay, send people to your site and the leads show up.

And for some that might happen.

The reality is that it leads to a waste of budget at untold scales.

Why? Because the ads haven't been tested by the PPC agency.

When it comes to direct advertising, you start small and test.

Once you find a winning ad, you scale until it no longer works.

Brand marketing is different.

You set your budget and spend it all.

And yes, SEO sits in this bucket.

A marketing budget is often criminally wasted because agencies use the wrong tactics for the wrong type of marketing.

And that's why I now operate a 100% strategy first approach.

Because if you don't pay upfront for marketing strategy.

You'll end up paying for it further down the line!

The Importance of Content Creation

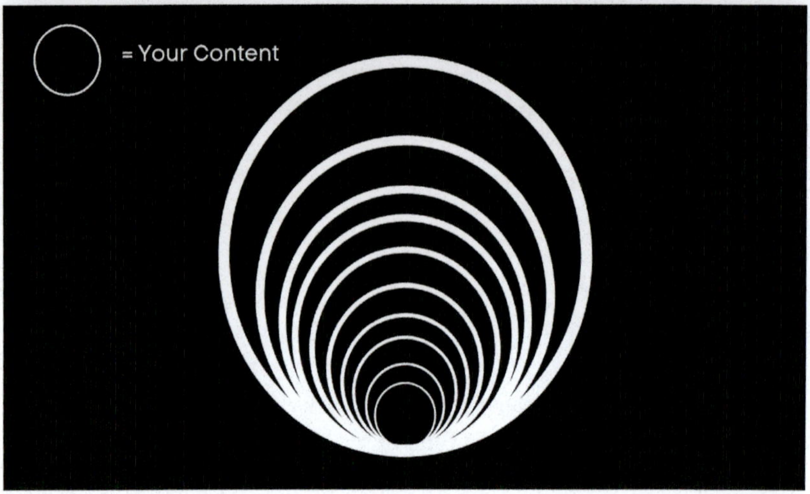

We are a planet of content consumers.

Last night I read books, blog posts, watched videos and listened to a podcast.

I do this daily.

I consume content 365 days a year.

I'm sure you do too.

This is why every business must create content.

Here are the two core types.

Expected content.

Unexpected content.

Expected content is something I expect to find.

When I google bathroom layout ideas, I expect to find content that gives me bathroom layout ideas.

Unexpected content is the content that I never realised I wanted in my life.

It's creative content that sadly gets ignored in the desperate demand to please the search engine gods.

The thing is, you need both.

A 50/ 50 content spread isn't only important, it must underpin your entire content strategy.

Today, there are blogs I no longer read.

Their content is boring. Tired and basic.

In the desire to grow their search traffic, to gain new customers, they stopped thinking about their current ones.

The relationship has gone stale. And so, if I ever leave them, they'll be unlikely to win me back.

Investing in content is creating layer after layer for your site, you make it bigger with each piece you create.

But you can't get lost in the salt mines of SEO.

Search engine content is almost always an answer to a question.

And the race is to create the most in-depth answers.

Unexpected creative content gives the reader options for thinking differently.

It makes the brain work in directions the reader never considered.

It's content that gets shared, talked about and rarely ranks for anything.

Invest in content.

Invest in SEO.

Invest in creativity.

And you'll see your site and your business grow as a result.

How SEO Value is Realised

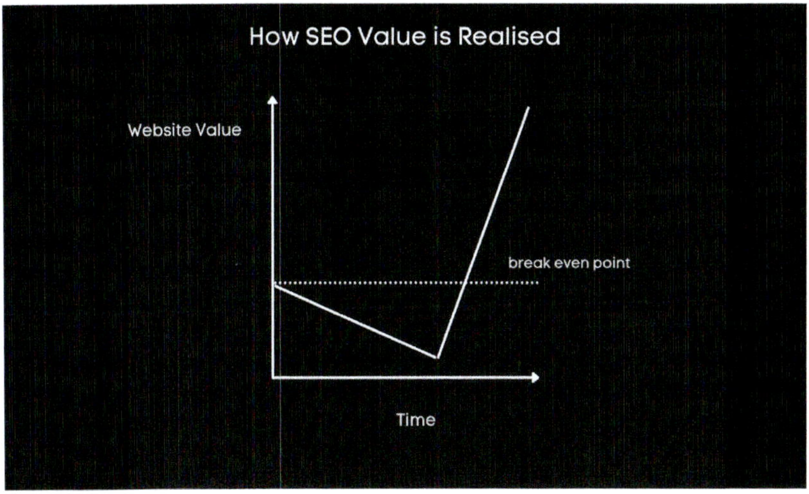

The second you invest in SEO it's a sunk cost.

You can't get the money back.

So if you want some kind of financial ROI early, you backed the wrong horse.

Modern SEO is all about building a digital asset for your business that has value.

It's not some kind of automatic cash machine.

If you think that, you're confusing business SEO with creating websites to earn money from AdSense and affiliate schemes.

Your house doesn't become of value until it's fully built.

Neither does your website.

And yet, there is an abundance of Marketing Managers who have cancelled SEO contracts over the years, long before the value is realised.

It's not all their fault, of course.

In a desperate bid to earn money and gain clients, SEO agencies have had to make big promises.

Often with lofty financial targets, vague analytical data to prove financial ROI and their fingers crossed that their clients know less than they do.

It doesn't have to be this way.

Buying into SEO isn't about immediate ROI, it's about buying into a vision that you are creating an asset for your business.

One that has you found by searchers via keywords.

One where the visitor is wowed by the scale and informational generosity of your site.

One that provides unique and variable content that they come back for.

One that finds your business searched for rather than found by search.

And one that leads to you being the number one brand in your industry.

Getting the client to buy into that vision is tough.

But that's the reality.

Judging SEO success by KPIs not ROI.

All of the largest sites planned to scale their growth.

They invested in SEO over the long term.

Aim to build your business a digital mansion and not a shed.

SEO is digital building.

Build a Website That is Searched For, Not Just Found

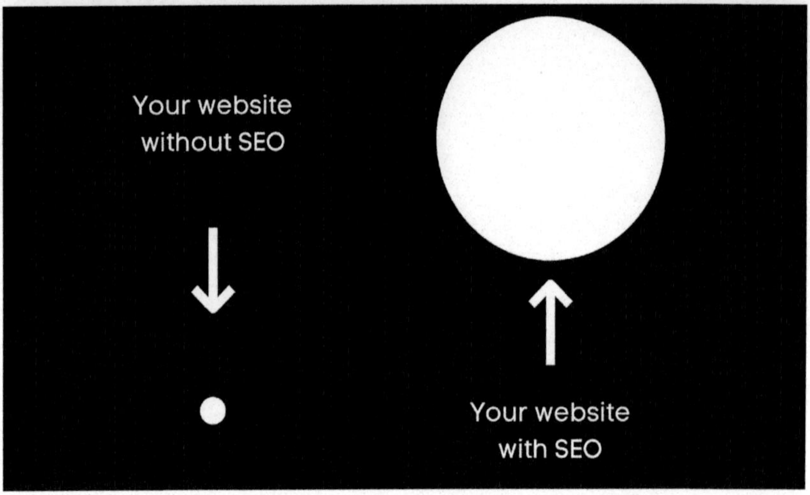

In the past, I would often say that SEO isn't for every business.

Well, the game has changed.

SEO is a must for every business.

But not how most people offer SEO.

Here's the old way of selling and doing SEO.

Find a bunch of keywords that have business relevance.

Write matching content, build links and ensure the site works well.

Today, that's just part of the puzzle.

Modern SEO is about building your business's most important digital asset.

One that builds over time with a range of content, expertise and industry information.

You want your ideal clients who have an issue, not heading to Google for the answer but heading to your site.

You want your customers to say 'wow, this is amazing and so useful' when they land on your site.

Yes, you'll create keyword-focused content.

But you'll need to create content that isn't based on search volume or the potential for leads.

This is content that your ideal customer base will love.

Without SEO, your site remains just four pages; home, about, contact, services/products.

With SEO, your site becomes an industry focus.

This isn't traditional SEO, this is evolved SEO.

Thinking of your site as an asset for your brand that you'll build over time, adding value to your business.

Evolved SEO is generous, it is a statement about your brand and that you no longer want to be at the mercy of the engineers at Google and their revenue model.

Yes, it takes guts. But Covid has shown us the importance and power of digital.

It's now time to start building a website that not only ranks but retains visitors.

A website that is searched for, not only found.

The 4 Key Elements of Great SEO

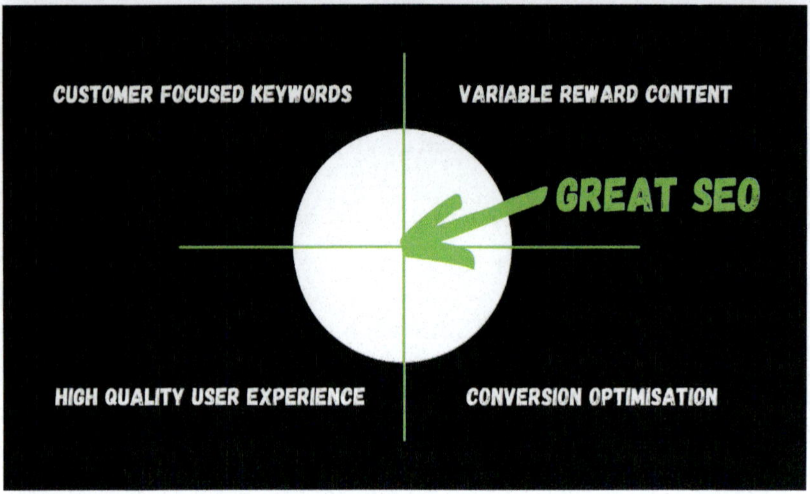

1. Customer-Focused Keywords

This is how you get discovered by the people you seek to serve.

For some, this might be 1000+ pages of content, others it might just be a homepage for a single keyphrase.

But the keywords are your hooks that grab the attention of your audience.

2. High-Quality User Experience

If your site is slow, sluggish, hard to read, confusing, doesn't state what you do or offer and is difficult to navigate.

Your visitors simply won't want to come back, no matter what you do.

3. Conversion Rate Optimisation

Most miss this, but you need a clear sales process that the visitor can stroll into.

This needs to be frictionless, easy, and ensure that the visitor knows what they need to do and what's happening next.

4. Variable Reward Content

This is what almost no one offers on purpose but is what allows YouTubers and Instagrammers to rise to fame.

What can you give on a regular basis to your audience that gets them coming back without you needing to pay?

It might be a round-up of the best deals, fresh content on your subject, interviews, stories, reviews, industry secrets, expert tips.

Regardless, this is content that people don't know they need in their lives, but when they find out you provide this, they'll be back of their own accord.

You'll notice that I never said back-links.

That's because back-links are a bi-product of great marketing.

Yes, you can build some in a focused and strategic approach.

But begging for back-links and spamming people with outreach emails is not the way.

People will happily link to your website if you help them prove their point, help them promote their content, you are an authority in your field and if you can help them raise their status.

Not because you begged for a link.

Great SEO happens on purpose.

Don't confuse this with bad SEO that has gained results.

The web is littered with high traffic websites that spammed their way to the top using the worst tactics.

Dare to be different.

Choose a bolder and better way to do SEO.

It will take longer to see results.

But the quality of those results will help your business and not harm your reputation.

Turn Your Website Into a Habit

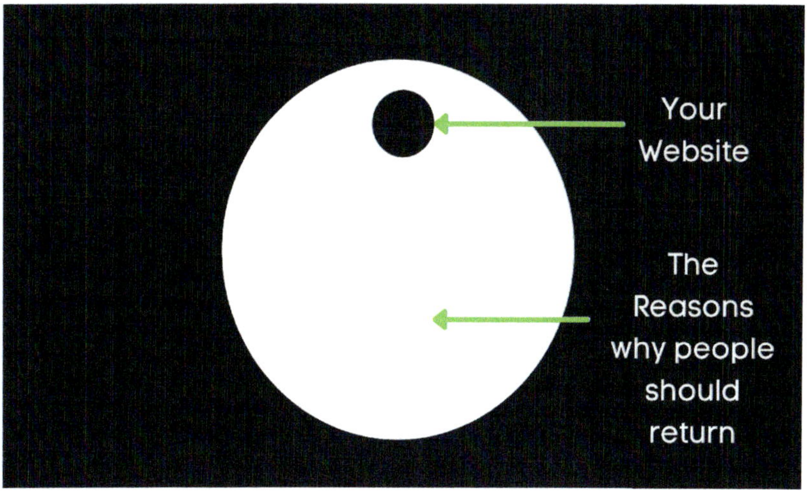

The reasons why a person would return to your site must always be bigger than the keywords that got them there in the first place.

As marketers, SEO specialists and PPC experts, we know how to get people to a website.

And yes, this costs money.

But when they leave, we need to have built a compelling reason why they should come back, without clients paying for it.

This almost always comes down to giving them something unique, regular and unexpected.

It's a variable reward.

Several websites I visit regularly don't even need to send an email to me,

I go looking for them.

This is, in my opinion, an example of SEO perfection.

I go looking because they don't only provide me with content, it's content I didn't know I needed.

If I search for hotels in London with amazing views, I'd hope to find a list post with a variety of hotels that have great views.

I'd click on a site and read the content.

But then, if I discovered that each week they create a list of discounts for London hotels, ranked by their personal reviews.

Well, that would easily get me to come back each week.

I'd probably sign up for their emails, just so I wouldn't miss out on a deal.

This is one of the reasons I get so frustrated with SEO being justified by financial ROI reporting.

Firstly, it's highly subjective and rarely is a CRO specialist hired by either the SEO company or the business (which could make everyone more money).

And secondly, because companies rarely fight to get people to come back to their site of their own accord.

It's seen as cheaper to cookie them across the internet in the hope that they turn into customers.

And yes, that can work, but we know it's difficult and with the rise of ad blockers, becoming more expensive.

Instead, the next level of SEO is not merely about getting people to your site.

It's about turning your website into a habit.

What can you offer, do or create that will encourage people to come back to you because they want to?

Can you curate the best content, deals, offers, interviews, news, data, ideas or even feel good content?

"We got them here, now how do we keep them coming back?"

Reason-based SEO, or call it retention-based SEO, if you will, is how you'll beat the search engines and the rising cost of ads.

And yes, it'll cost you to go down this route.

But it'll cost you if you don't.

The Right Way to Think About Link Building

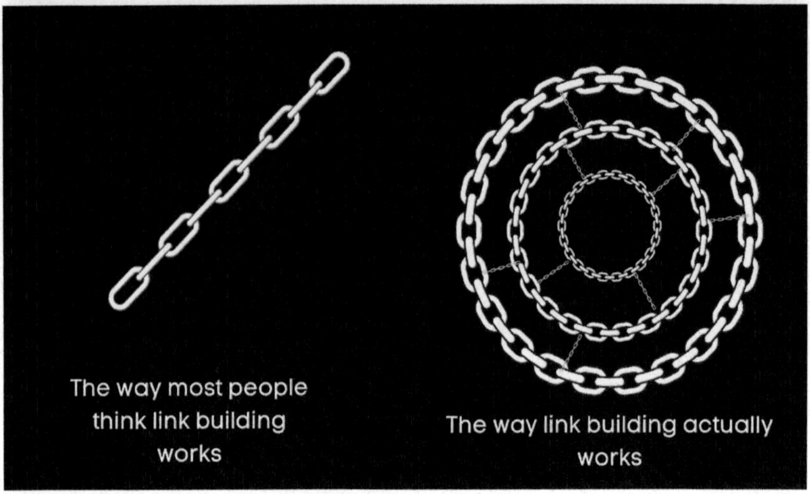

Most people think of link building as a line.

You build links from your site to others.

And yes, when you zoom in, that's what you see.

In truth, the whole internet is very different.

At the core is a central hub.

This is where most of the big sites and links live.

Off this are hemispheres, where B2B sites tend to sit because so few link back to the central hub.

I could go on. The main theme is that... it's vast.

People build links to sites they think are authorities because Google used to use a page rank algorithm. Relevance is rarely important.

Just the score the SEO tools give.

You'll never win this game.

Someone will always be building more links than you in this manner.

Instead, look to build links that get your business and site discovered.

In essence, what sites are the people you want to serve visiting?

And while they are there, they discover you via a link.

This is, of course, going to be subject and niche relevant.

It's a link that makes sense.

It's a link that adds business value.

It's a link that search engines will discover.

Moral of the story.

These are links you earn through marketing and relevant content creation and promotion.

Not ones you can buy.

How to Succeed in Marketing Today

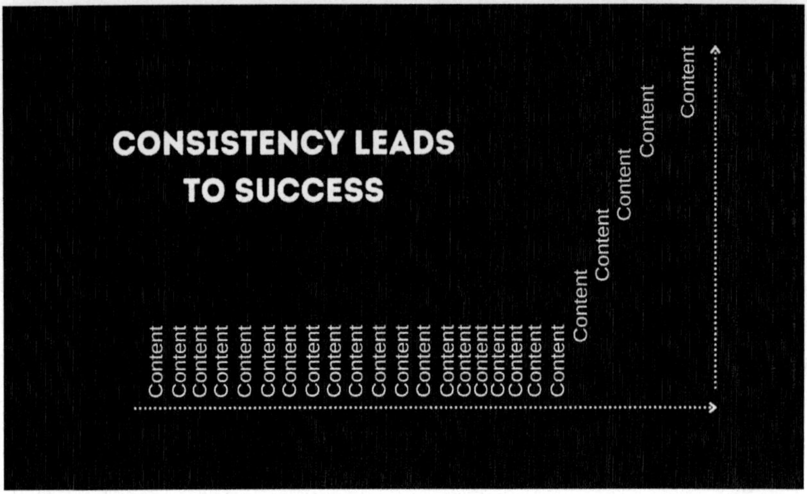

One word, consistency.

I entered marketing as a 36-year-old with no prior agency experience.

It took me just two days to create a profitable business (this was six years ago).

The reason this was possible was that I had written over 400 blog posts, thousands of social media posts and built numerous websites for my own enjoyment.

I have no traditional qualifications of any kind.

And yet, I've ranked thousands of keywords on the first page of Google over the years and analysed thousands of websites.

All through being consistent.

The magic is in the doing.

This is why I get frustrated with businesses that don't make any effort to reach out to their chosen audience.

SEO and content marketing is based on the idea you are building something of value for the people you want to have as customers and for people who are your customers.

It is your conversation with them.

Your business voice.

This is why SEO and content marketing rarely leads to instant success.

Because the frequency they hear your business voice matters.

We have our closest relationships with those we speak to often.

And so, as a business, you must show up.

You build a great web presence one brick at a time.

And then eventually you'll see a surge of success.

I know this because I've seen it hundreds of times.

The problem you have is simple.

Your competition is probably talking to your target customer base.

They are talking daily.

You probably think they aren't listening because they are your competition and you are doing as well as they are.

But eventually, more of your audience will be listening to them.

Until you are no longer a viable choice because, when they think of your industry, they think of your competition automatically.

This happened to Blockbuster when they ignored Netflix.

It happened to ToysRus when they ignored Amazon.

Don't let it happen to you.

Invest in your online presence.

Be consistent.

Don't worry about ROI.

And remember.

SEO isn't about fighting Google.

It's about building a web presence that people search for, not find.

You Don't Pay For an Hour of Time to Get a Job Done

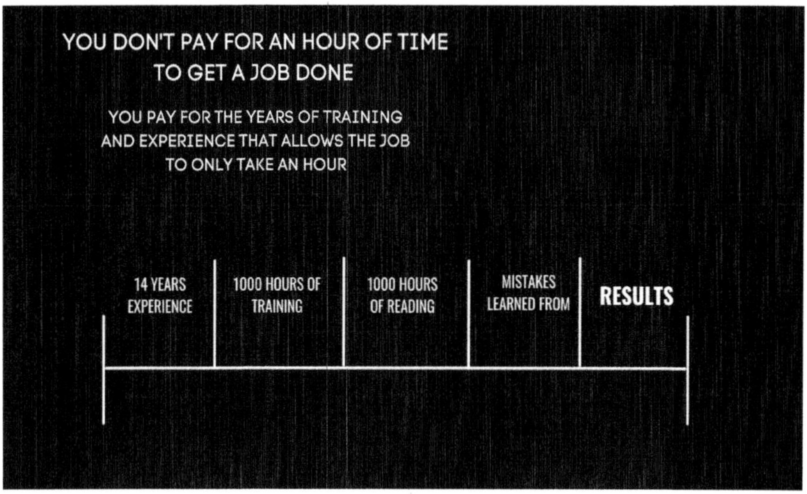

You are paying for years of experience and training that were undertaken so that job would only take an hour.

SEO is an industry where the experience of a specialist is key.

Here's why.

Every site an SEO examines, works on, builds, and creates links and content for, adds to their knowledge.

It's a network effect.

Each site and task adds to the value of their mental network.

And then you add every book, article and course they consume.

Followed by every test, success and failure.

It all adds up.

Please note.

It's an experience thing, not an age thing.

And that's why it's important to investigate the background of the person doing your SEO.

Because you can pay for experience or inexperience.

That's why I get hired by Marketing Managers and digital agencies to produce strategies for themselves and clients.

Because they often have junior SEO resources who are cost efficient.

They just need to be told what they need to do and follow this over time.

Build Reasons for People to Keep Coming Back to Your Site

In SEO and digital, we spend a lot of time talking about traffic acquisition.

But we spend very little time talking about where we want our traffic to go after they visit us.

You might say 'we don't care.'

But we should care.

Because if they leave our site straight away, it's because we didn't offer anything else for them.

We didn't offer them relevant content.

We didn't offer them an incentive so we could carry on the conversation via email.

We didn't give them a reason to share our site with others.

We didn't wow them or leave them with a feeling of awe.

We didn't give them a reward or offer a variable reward to entice them to come back to our site without any effort from us.

Most people believe that SEO is about generating content focused on keywords.

My view is that SEO is about developing a digital resource for your business that people search for, rather than simply find.

And so, on your website, it's not about just offering conversion.

It's about building interaction.

Ways to do this include:

Creating a world-beating blog that publishes often.

Offer a quiz.

Build a free training school.

Creating learning or knowledge centres.

Offer high-value content in exchange for email details.

Live chat.

Offer free strategy sessions, workshops.

Have a calculator on your site related to your business.

And there are many other ways.

If they're coming to your site and not coming back, you need to fix this.

Build reasons for people to keep coming back to your site.

And you can answer the question of where do they go next?

By saying "they go deeper into our site".

User-Focused SEO (and Why it Matters)

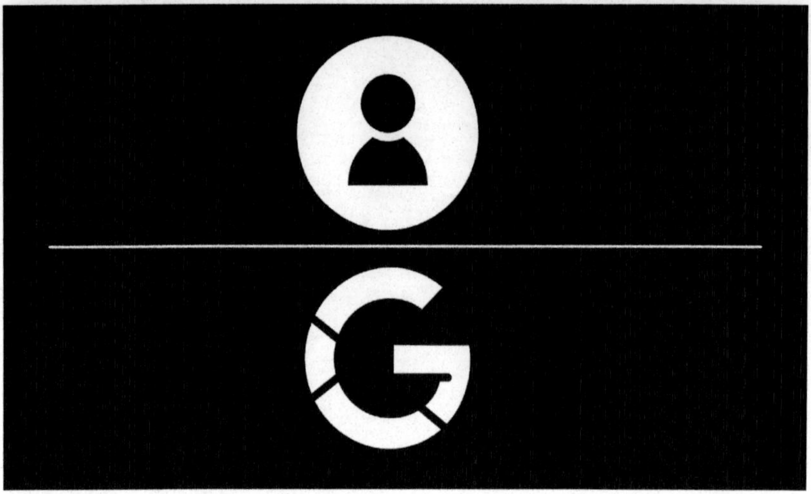

Users come before search engines.

That might sound obvious, but it is rarely the approach we see.

For too long the SEO industry has focused on the short click.

"Get a site on page one of Google for as many keywords as possible and hope they generate leads and sales" has been the implied mantra of SEO for years.

Why? Because that's what clients want.

A few years ago, I was working with a client and having great results.

The problem, their digital manager wanted to show directly attributable results from SEO.

"We need to see the ROI of the SEO".

That statement has killed more SEO contracts than the fire of London killed rats.

And it's led to an abundance of search engine first SEO.

"What do the search engines want us to do?"

The problem with that is that it treats the search engines like the Gods of ancient Greece.

Our sites are theirs to toy with, to steal from and send down to the depths of page two and beyond at their pleasure.

User-focused SEO is different.

It is the careful and focused approach of giving the user (your potential customers) what they want and need.

"But they need answers to queries" you shout.

Yes, they do, and you'll answer those because you'll be giving them what they need.

And that is a user-focused SEO approach.

But it's what happens after the first click that dictates the difference between search engine first and user first SEO.

Where do we want them to go next?

The business owner hopes and wants them to take the next step to conversion.

But in reality, we as the SEO know this is unlikely and so, the CROs and PPC people deploy an army of re-targeting ads.

And this works.

But it's expensive, clunky, and the cost is going up.

The alternative is to wow the searcher.

To give them something they didn't expect.

They came for ideas for their new bathroom and you ranked an article for this.

They stayed because you have created a step-by-step guide that guides the searcher through picking, purchasing and fitting the perfect bathroom.

And they come back, because every Friday, you showcase a real bathroom in someone's house.

User-focused SEO understands that keywords are just a hook to get people to your site.

User-focused SEO understands that we need something amazing for them to stay on the site.

And user-focused SEO understands that we need something incredible so that they choose to return to us.

And that's the cycle.

Search engines help you to be found when people need answers.

But they are best used to help people to search directly for you.

That's the truly difficult job of user-focused SEO.

A land where metrics such as increasing navigational searches and returning visitors are key indicators of success.

"How do we be a site that people search for, rather than just find?"

In today's age of ad blockers and rising cost per click.

This question has never been more important.

And that's user-focused SEO.

New SEO vs Old SEO

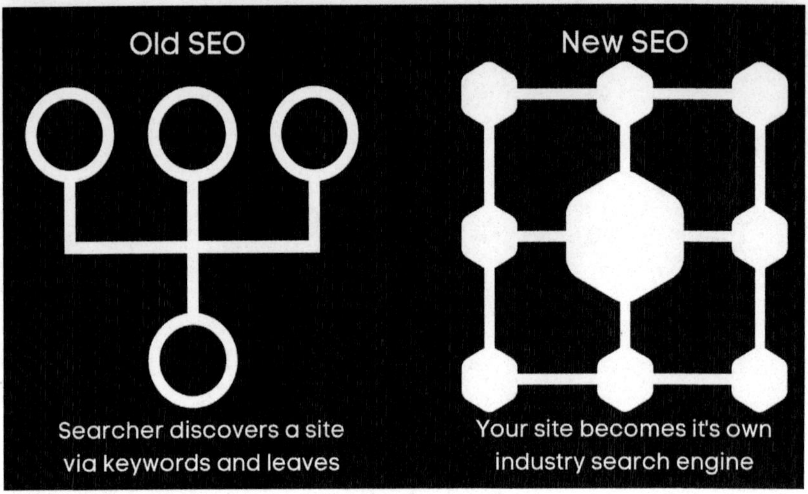

For as long as I can recall, SEO has always been treated as a replacement for PPC.

"What's the ROI of SEO?" is what clients have been taught to ask.

And this forced an approach to SEO that was focused on traffic and conversion.

Even now, we talk of 'buyer intent' when looking at keywords and top, middle and bottom of the funnel.

The problem is that this leads to massive SEO losses as Google changes its algorithm.

One day your traffic is up, the next it's gone.

The new approach isn't to even think of Google and ranking on that search engine (because other search engines will gain ground sooner or later).

No, the new approach to SEO is about building your own 'industry-specific search engine.'

Yes, this is your website.

But it ceases to become a website, it becomes a destination for your industry.

You go from being a website to your industry's ultimate solution.

A trusted resource packed with every question your customers could ever need to know about your industry.

This is actually what Google wants anyway.

It makes your site easier to define, crawl and of course, you answer searchers' queries, making its life far more simple.

But for your business, you go from being at the whim of search engines to actually being directly searched for.

Aiming to be a site a visitor can spend hours on at a time is the goal.

Aiming to be a site that people talk about offline with others is a must-do.

But to build an asset like this for your business requires commitment, effort and, of course, budget.

It also requires a change of mindset.

It's not about what you can get from searchers but what you can give them.

However, if you do this I assure you that you will GAIN as a business.

You'll future proof your business and create an asset worth a lot of money.

The old approach to SEO is to try and profit from search networks.

The new approach is to build your own search network.

How to Generate Amazing SEO Results (Easily)

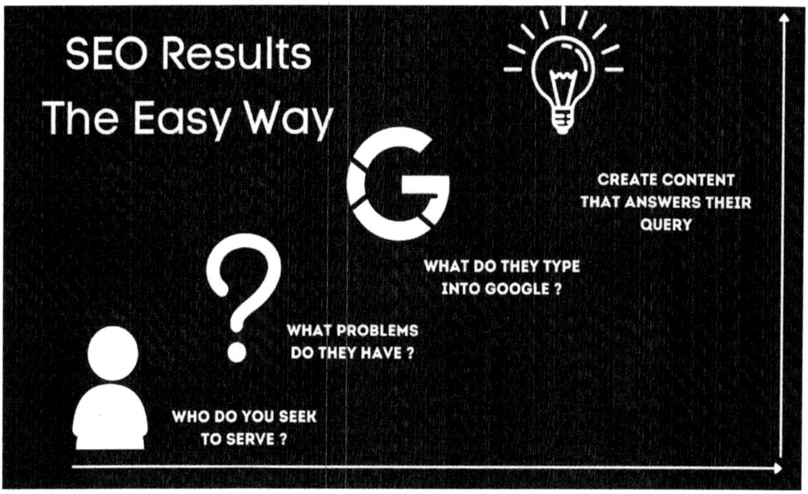

People overcomplicate SEO.

It's not about complex algorithms or outwitting Google's entire team of computer engineers.

It's about people.

And businesses being helpful.

In the past, a customer would find you in the Yellow Pages.

Call your business up and ask for advice.

"I have this problem, what's the best way to fix it?"

You wouldn't say "No, I'm not telling you".

You'd offer advice and be helpful regardless of whether they became a customer or not.

The internet simply replaced the need for a phone book and calling for advice.

And so, if you want great SEO success, follow this tried and tested plan.

Step 1. Identify who you seek to serve.

Eg. I'm a locksmith and I want to help people who are locked out of their homes late at night...audience = homeowners.

We're a training company and we want to provide qualified carers for use in care homes...audience = care home managers and people who want to work in care.

Step 2. Identify their problems.

Eg. Lost my keys and can't get in, relationship break up and need to change the locks quickly, etc.

I want to work in care but aren't sure how.

Step 3. Figure out what they search for in Google.

This is where a good SEO company can help.

Step 4. Create content that answers their search query.

The problem is, no one ever asked what the ROI of answering the phone was.

You just did it, because it made sense.

SEO also makes sense.

That's why every business should be creating content on their site that answers the questions their target audience has.

You won't rank online for all of them.

But that's not the point.

When they do find your site, through SEO and all of the other marketing channels you use, they'll see you as the company that bothered to answer their questions before they asked.

And so, when they do call you, they're calling to do business.

Not to ask questions.

That's the purpose of great SEO and a good website.

It creates customers, not only leads.

People who are sold before they contact you.

What's The Big Idea?

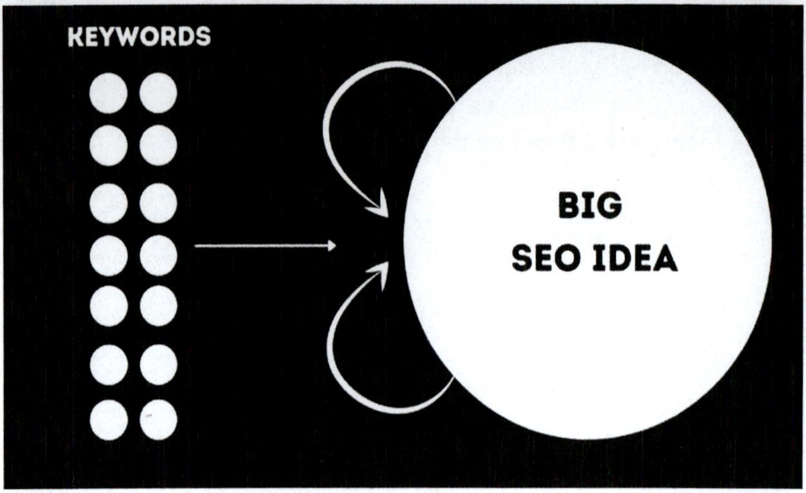

You MUST have a BIG SEO IDEA for your site, or you'll lose traffic at scale.

In the past, I've placed a lot of time and effort on keywords.

And yes, they are important.

But not nearly as important as your BIG SEO IDEA.

That's the reason why people will come back to your website.

If you don't have one, then you'll be a leaky bucket.

Traffic will come into your site, but it won't stick and will drop out of the bottom.

And you want people to keep coming back for more.

Without having to fight for them with money and more SEO.

So, how do you do this?

Well, you have to think big.

"Our website will be the ....in our industry".

The gap can be filled with.

The best resource.

The best comparison site.

The most informative blog.

The most entertaining site.

The largest marketplace.

Of course, there are many more variables to this.

But it's the big idea that goes far beyond traditional SEO.

Businesses view SEO as some kind of race for traffic that converts.

Yes, that is part of SEO.

But you need to identify what your big SEO idea is, so you can create a site people love to return to.

For example, what variable rewards will your site offer to entice people back each week?

Will you offer new content, interviews, best practices, shocking opinions, industry predictions, online calculators, product comparisons, new ideas, new products, new concepts?

You must be able to answer the question "why will people come back to our site?"

Otherwise, you'll spend serious money getting them there and hope that they purchase or sign up for your newsletter just so you can sell to them.

I'm sure you have websites that you just go to each week.

They don't have to spend a single penny to get your attention.

You search them out, you find them and you read their content.

When you create your big SEO idea, all of your other marketing costs will go down.

Because, if you show your site to people, they'll not only tell others but they'll keep coming back for more.

SEO Growth Cycle

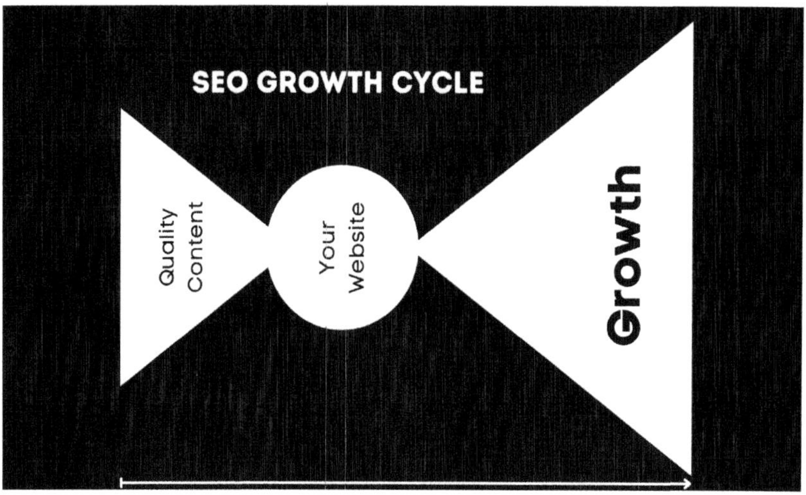

Put quality content into your website.

Growth comes out the other side.

You won't grow online unless you invest in content.

Businesses Have to Choose to Grow

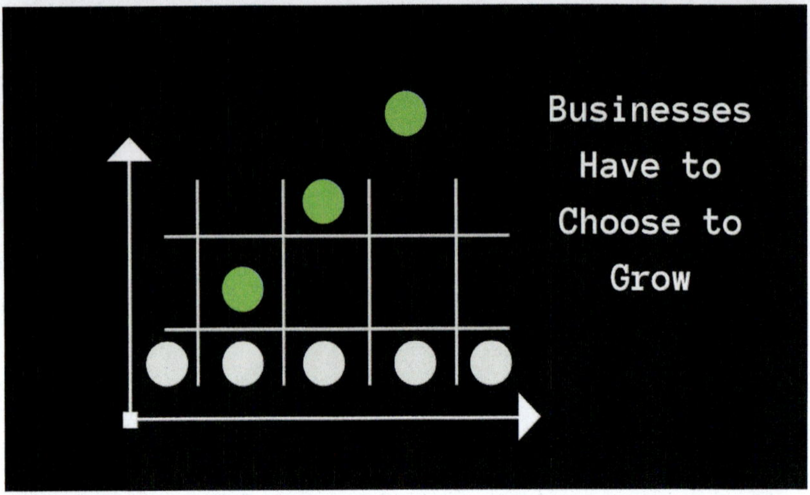

Growth comes through deliberate choices and budget.

If you go to an SEO agency and say "this is my budget, do SEO for me".

They'll do SEO for that budget.

And the results you'll get will be directly related to this budget.

In 2019, Backlinko conducted a survey of small businesses.

Only 30% would recommend their current SEO provider to a friend or colleague.

But also "Monthly Spend Is Tied To Client Satisfaction".

In other words, the more you spend, the more likely you'll be happy.

But let's face it, do you really think spending £24,000 a year on SEO is going to give you a brand worth £1 million?

Most SEO agencies I know struggle to get clients to move past the £24,000 to £30,000 annual spend.

It's because that kind of figure is anchored to the cost of an employee.

"We could pay a staff member to do that".

But you couldn't.

Right now, I know of agencies employing young SEO staff that have never ranked a website on Google for themselves.

They have never created content, done outreach and tasted success and failure in abundance.

It's because most agencies let the tail wag the dog. They bend to the client's budget, rather than the client finding the budget they need.

That's because they don't actually know how much it will cost.

They haven't done the research to know.

And so they give a figure based on hours.

And hours worked can always be increased.

The result is that the client spends £24,000 a year for three years and sees little to no results, rather than spending £72,000 in the first year and getting amazing results.

Growth is a choice.

Realistic growth requires a realistic budget.

A realistic budget will be determined by a data-driven strategy.

It's only after you have built a strategy will you know what it will cost to get where you want to be.

SEO works.

Growth will come.

But only if you choose to grow through direct and deliberate action.

And that needs the right budget.

You're Only as Good as the Team Around You

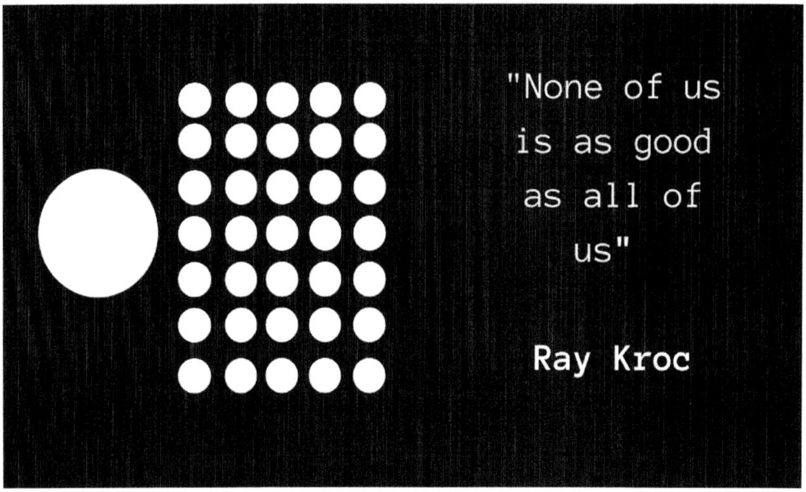

"None of us is as good as all of us"... Ray Kroc.

You're only as good as the team around you.

This doesn't only mean people you hire as full-time staff.

In today's world, it applies to your 'freelance' team, your outsource agencies and yes, even your software. Having the right team of 'digital robots' is key to success.

The internet has allowed you to hire the best talent on the planet, regardless of distance.

Since 2015 I've been using a team of people from all across the planet.

Some incredibly talented people that have helped my business to grow.

In addition, other teams have hired me.

I've been hired by digital agencies, Marketing Managers and business owners to help them to strategise and create content that drives traffic.

To reflect on a recent post I read by Carrie Rose.

"Build your personal brand, and you'll never have to apply for a job again"

This is true.

When you build your personal brand, people will seek you out to see what you can do for them.

You'll be asked to join teams and make them more powerful with your unique skill set.

The 'none of us is as good as all of us' mindset is helping people and businesses to thrive, stay lean and flexible.

Think like this and you'll see more opportunities open up.

If You Struggle to Create, Curate

Some of the best websites and articles online are simple curated lists.

The reason is that people are short on time, so we naturally look for 'collections' of information because it is the easiest way to advance our knowledge on a subject.

One of the early website successes I had was creating a website of Judo video instructionals.

They were already on YouTube. I just put the best ones in a single convenient place and in the process built an email list and social media following at speed.

Harry Dry built a 50,000 strong email list by curating the best marketing examples on the web.

Pat Walls built a $45,000 a month online business and an email list of over 120,000 people by collecting interviews with business founders.

Ryan Deiss built a huge survival site by curating the best information on survival and putting it into one place; Survival Life.

There are many ways to curate.

You can curate ideas, examples, information, how-to guides and even your own opinions.

Indeed, Google is just a curator of the internet. Serving up what it thinks is the best information you are looking for.

Being original is fantastic.

It's also very hard.

And to quote Austin Kleon in 'Steal like an artist.'

Good Theft = Honour, Study, Steal From Many, Credit, Transform, Remix.

This post is an example of curation.

The image idea came from the book 'Rework' by Jason and David Heinemeier Hansson.

I have honoured numerous people and given them credit.

And this post has taken concepts from two books and transformed them into a single LinkedIn post.

Curation is a powerful tool that leads to originality in a different form.

There are very few original ideas out there.

So if you want to be different.

Start by curating content and then as a by-product, you'll be CREATING content.

Reversing Imposter Syndrome

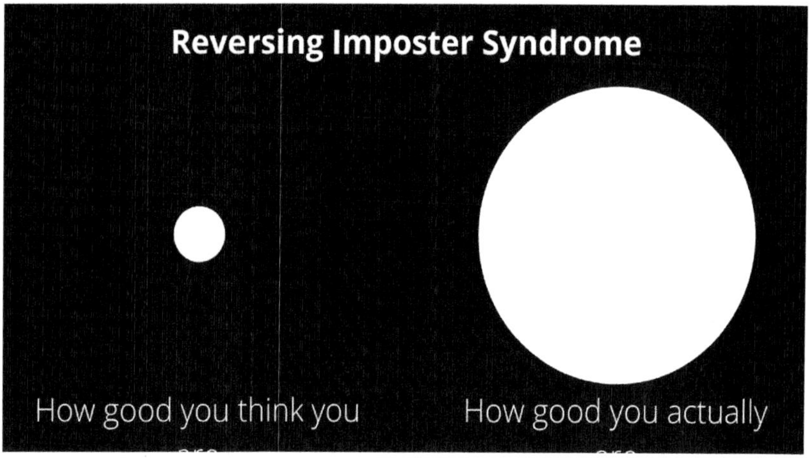

Like many, I have suffered from self-doubt...a lot.

We call it Imposter Syndrome.

To combat it, I keep a folder full of stats, rankings and content I have created.

When Imposter Syndrome sets in, I go back and look at it.

For the last two days, I've had a troll on LinkedIn.

He's now blocked.

He told me he was better than me at what I do.

He told me that I shouldn't have the title 'SEO specialist' because my views weren't the same as his.

He said he was better than anyone else at SEO.

Sadly, people like this exist.

They shout you down.

They try to put you down.

They try to make you feel bad to make themselves feel good.

And these types of people make you feel smaller than you are.

That's why it's essential that you keep a record of your wins.

Because you'll quickly forget them.

Build your own folder of success.

It doesn't matter how small you start.

Your latest blog post might have only got 10 views, but that's how we all start.

So, if you write a blog post, add it to your list of wins, regardless of the traffic.

As you improve you'll get better at whatever you do.

You'll create graphics and videos that go viral.

You'll rank articles online.

You'll create that amazing presentation that lands the big client.

The thing is, no one is as good as you at being you.

All of those wins compound.

People will pull you down.

Data will pull you back up.

Opinions of you may be negative.

The facts show your brilliance.

You're amazing.

Create systems that allow you to remind yourself of this.

Reverse Imposter Syndrome.

Write Once, Promote 20 Times

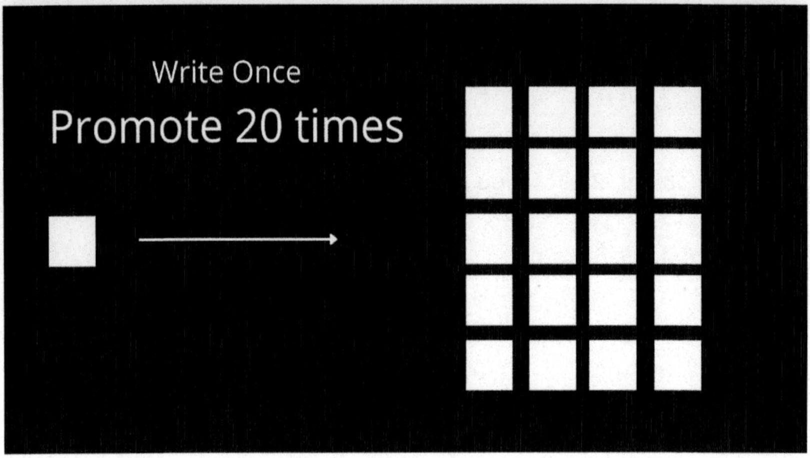

If there was one single thing I think content creators (myself included) could do better is content promotion.

Most content gets promoted at least once these days.

But unless it resonates with an audience quickly, we give up.

The problem is, this type of thinking is flawed.

We know that people are busy, life is busy and the web is flooded with content each day.

And sometimes, your amazing content didn't get read, shared or clicked on, because something else more important was going on in the reader's life, at that split second your content appeared.

In truth, we live in a world of distractions.

That's why I developed a system of 'write once, promote 20 times.'

For every piece of content you create, make it your objective to promote it at least 20 times.

And in 20 places.

You'll be surprised at just how powerful this can be.

So today, do this.

Step 1. Go to your content and do an audit of your best work.

Step 2. Promote it again as if you just wrote it.

Or even better, hire a member of staff to be your 'content promoter.'

Their only purpose is to promote your content.

Content costs time and/or money to create.

And in my experience, most businesses leave a lot of 'content money' lying on the floor going to waste.

Keep Going, Keep Growing

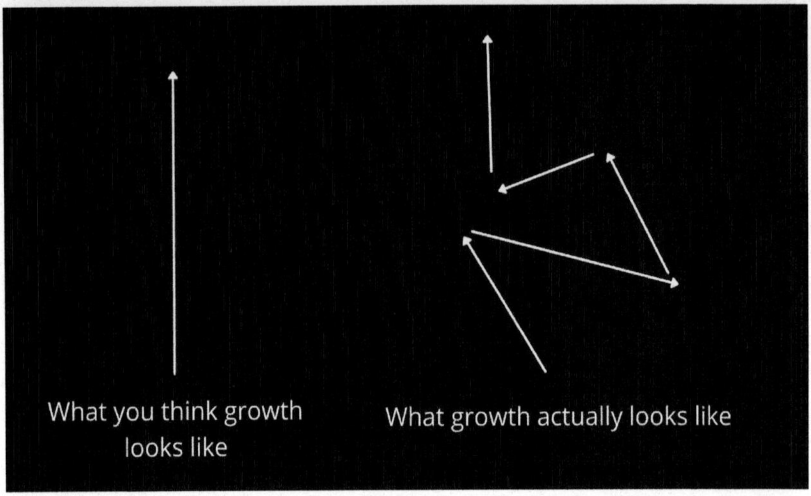

If you've done SEO for a single site long enough you'll know this is true.

It doesn't matter how good you are at SEO, you WILL have setbacks.

Google can change the algorithm in a second.

A competitor can acquire another site and merge it with theirs, forcing you down the rankings.

Other sites can be artificially boosting their rankings with black hat SEO and overtake you for a while.

The thing is.

It doesn't matter.

What matters is that you keep on growing.

You keep on showing up when your target audience searches for information related to your industry.

You keep on doing purposeful, targeted marketing that grows your brand and your back-links.

You keep creating content that is helpful and relevant to your audience.

Do this and you'll still grow online.

Do this and you'll grow beyond the setbacks.

The problem is, people abandon SEO because they don't see the long term growth over time.

Don't focus on results.

Focus on building a digital asset for your business and the results WILL come despite the setbacks.

"Great Content is Everywhere, Amazing Content is Harder to Find."

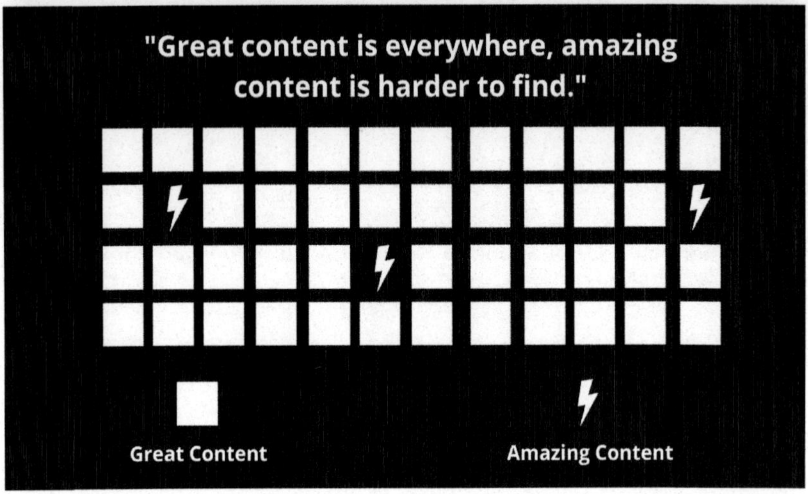

Yesterday, Brian Dean put out an amazing LinkedIn post about the need to create amazing content.

And it's true.

Great content is everywhere.

And that's why amazing content is harder to find.

But when you do find amazing content, it stands out.

It generates links, social shares, subscribers, followers, ranks online and helps to drive revenue.

Yet businesses tend to do everything they can to avoid the creation of amazing content.

"It costs too much."

"It takes too long."

"Where are the guarantees it will work?"

"What will be my ROI?"

Yes, creating amazing content is risky.

But the risk is very small when compared with the countless other marketing activities that people throw money at without a care in the world.

And if you use the right frameworks and strategies, the risk is reduced.

But that's part of marketing.

You must be willing to take risks so your brand stands out.

The Failure Path of SEO

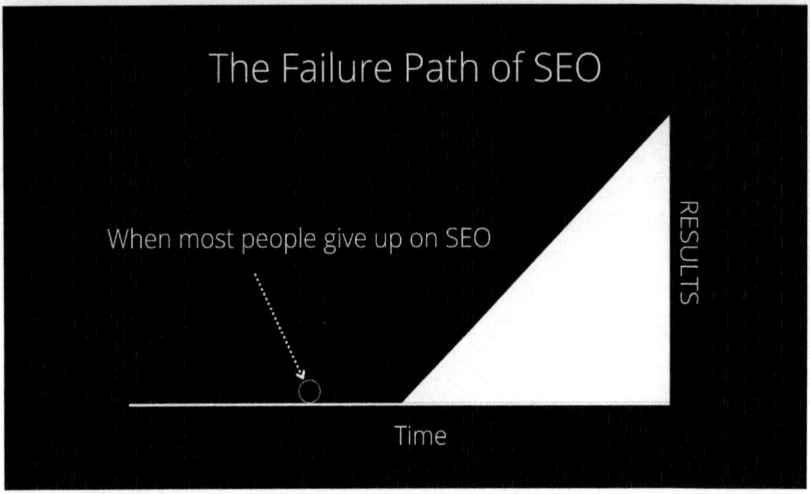

Part of the problem with SEO is that people give up too soon.

They swap agencies.

They have unrealistic budgets.

They give up because they can't see any ROI.

But that's because they are measuring success incorrectly.

Almost all of us know the importance of building a brand.

And most companies are happy to spend on brand marketing.

They'll spend on logos, PR, trade shows, radio ads, magazine ads, video creation, organic social media, TV ads and more.

And in almost all cases, no one ever asks for an ROI on these activities.

Yet mentally people always ask for an ROI of SEO because they don't understand where it fits in marketing.

The result is that thousands of Marketing Managers and business owners give up on SEO before they see the tangible benefits for their business.

SEO is the long path.

It takes time to build a brand.

It takes time to build your search presence.

Measure SEO results by KPI, not ROI.

Costly Signalling

"Quite simply, all powerful messages must contain an element of absurdity, illogicality, costliness, disproportion, inefficiency, scarcity, difficulty or extravagance". Rory Sutherland

(Quote from his book Alchemy: The surprising power of ideas that don't make sense)

Stop Measuring SEO Success as if it Were Direct Advertising

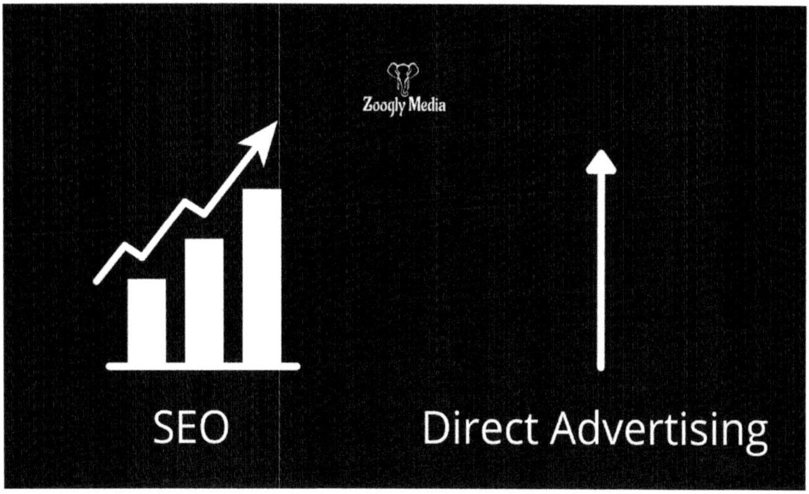

Direct advertising is simple.

You create an offer.

You then pay to place that offer in front of your target audience.

Success is measured by how many people take up that offer.

It's direct and it's difficult to get right.

SEO is indirect.

It lives in the messy middle of search, where your customers educate themselves and evaluate their purchasing options.

You show up when they need information.

Your brand wins customer loyalty by giving information freely.

They choose you because you were there for them, you showed up when others didn't, you answered their questions and informed them of things they didn't think of.

SEO is brand marketing.

You measure its success through KPI and not ROI.

SEO is not a replacement for direct advertising.

Smart businesses spend money on ads.

But smart businesses test direct ads.

They start small and test until they find one that works.

And when they do, they scale that ad.

Smart businesses have a different approach to SEO.

They set a budget and spend it all.

Never once thinking about sales.

Instead, it's all about showing up.

"How many people discovered our business?"

This statement is what SEO success should be judged on.

How you move those people from search to sales is what CRO is for.

If you're judging marketing success by the wrong metrics, I assure you. Your performance will never be as good as it could be.

And if your marketing isn't working.

Reach out.

It's probably not as hard to fix as you think.

Become Searched For

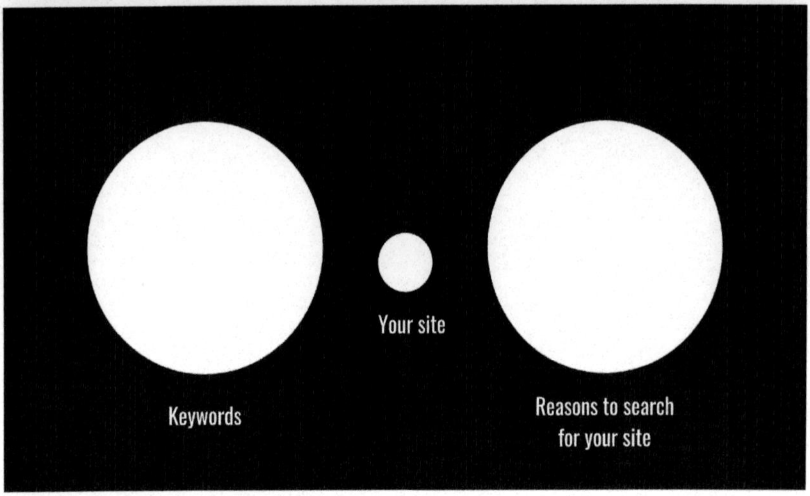

Keywords get your site discovered.

You must have a BIG reason for people to return.

That's how you win in SEO.

Make your site a habit to search for.

Expected content gets them there.

Unexpected content keeps them coming back.

Become searched for.

And not just found by search.

Low Leverage SEO Tactics v High Leverage SEO Tactics

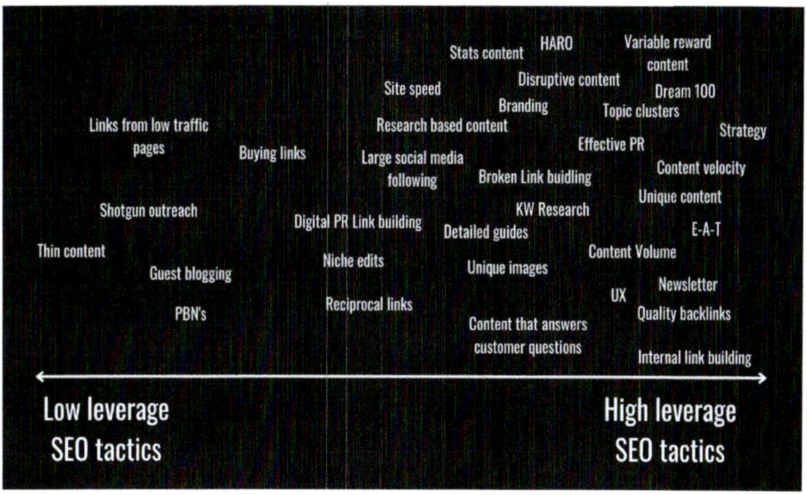

You only have so much budget and you only have so much time.

So choosing the right tactics is incredibly important.

Some of the things on this list you might know.

And I've probably missed a few.

But strategy is without doubt the best area to focus on.

Get that right and all the rest will fall into place, regardless of budget.

If I was to sum it up as to what to focus on to get the best results.

Be an expert.

Establish trust.

Create content in volume and at speed.

Build relationships first, not links.

Focus on the user.

Answer questions they have.

Create unique content that people can't find elsewhere.

Build your brand.

Build your list with a newsletter.

Link internally.

Focus on quality links and not quantity.

Aim to make a dent in the online universe.

Go for Content Depth, Not Length

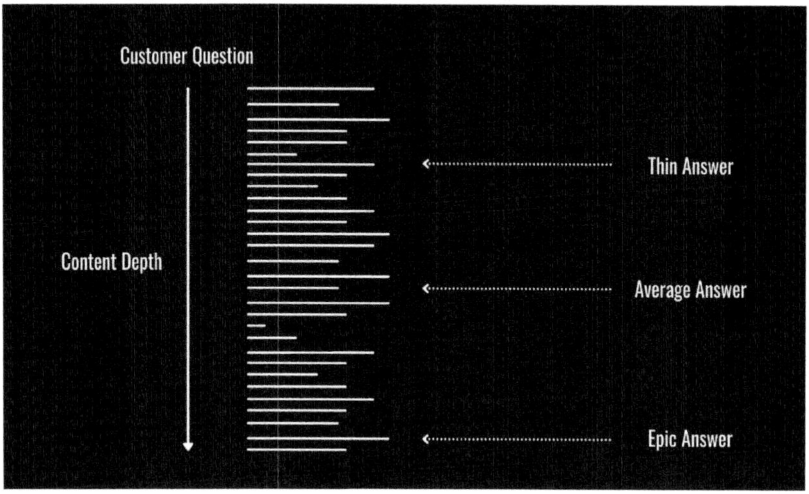

It's not about the length of your content, it's about the depth.

Word count is the worst metric used by writers and content buyers.

And yet, it's still an industry standard with regards to quality.

But that's not right.

I can fill any sentence with fluff and that's what most content on the internet is.

Fluff and waffle.

If you want to win in SEO, content marketing and indeed online conversion, you'll need content depth.

When users type a question into Google, consumers want detailed answers, not fluff and waffle.

And so, one of the hardest parts of creating quality online content is looking at each line and asking.

"Do we need this?"

Every word and sentence needs to earn its place in your content.

The thing is.

If you have this mindset, you'll win big.

You'll create better content.

You'll rank higher in Google because your content is read to the end, rather than the searcher leaving (because wading through waffle sucks).

And you'll create content faster.

Go for content depth and not length.

How SEO Actually Works

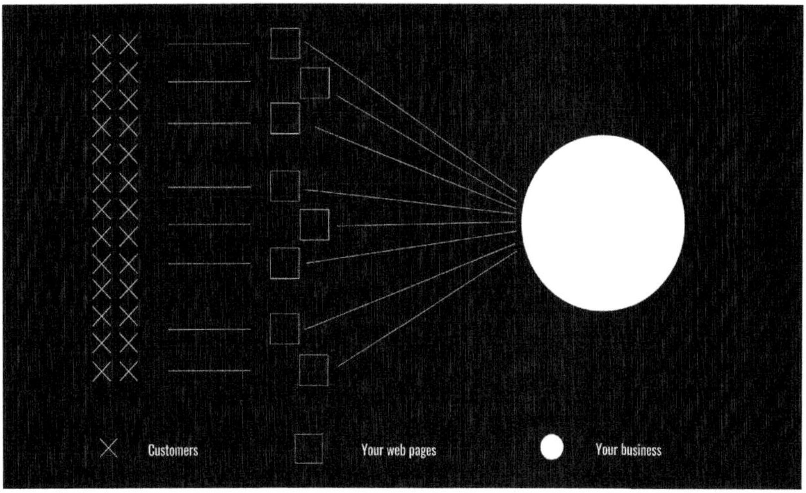

Your ideal audience is out there.

These are the people who are able to buy from you, will buy in the future or would be open to what you have to offer.

They are online, entering queries into search engine browsers.

And you create pages of content on your site that answer the queries they typed into the search engine.

They see your pages, they click on them.

And that's where they are exposed to your business.

You see, web pages are simply signposts.

They are signposts of expertise.

They are signposts of knowledge.

They are signposts that you care about your customers.

They are signposts that you're open for business.

More signposts = more potential customers.

Of course, not all signs are equal.

Some are bigger, some are seen by more people and some don't get seen by many at all.

But SEO is about building a digital presence for your business.

And if you aren't investing in SEO, it's probably because you're looking at it through the wrong lens.

SEO is a brand marketing tactic.

And a highly effective one at that.

Sure, you might make some money with SEO.

But that's not the goal.

The goal is to show your business to more potential customers.

And to do this, you set your SEO budget and you spend it all.

The problem comes when people see SEO as a short term game.

It's not...it's a forever game.

As long as there are search engines and people using them to find information, there'll always be SEO.

SEO is about focusing on the customer and giving them all the information they need to become customers.

And that's the basis of good SEO.

It's not trying to convert customers from a single page.

It's about trying to convert customers using your entire website.

Become the website that your customer doesn't want to leave.

Create web pages that your target customers will find really useful.

Show up.

That's how SEO works.

Great SEO is All About Spotting Patterns

You see, websites tell a story.

Some are old and carry a lot of bruising from years in the black hat era.

Some are young, fresh and are only just finding their feet.

Some sites are bloated, slow and overweight.

And some are near perfect.

The thing is, people who do SEO for long enough don't see websites.

They see patterns.

This is where true expertise lies.

They've worked with and studied an enormous amount of websites.

And this knowledge grows over time.

They see content types, link building methods, keyword focus, page and site structure.

Where the normal person just sees a website, SEOs pull both your site and your competitor's sites apart with their minds (and, of course, a few tools).

And so, armed with this information, experience and expertise.

They can plot a way to grow your site to benefit your business.

This is strategy.

SEO without strategy is hit and miss.

You wouldn't build a house without a plan and you shouldn't start SEO without one either.

And yes, strategy is what separates great SEO specialists from the mediocre.

Because SEO implementation can be commoditised.

It can be broken up into separate parts to reduce cost, improve results and maximise budgets.

But make no mistake, strategy is the brainwork of SEO.

It's the human element.

It's the expertise element.

And so, if you are using SEO right now, you need to know what your strategy is.

And if you are thinking about SEO as a tool to market your business.

You need to ask yourself:

"Who will build our SEO strategy?"

Because who you choose to implement your SEO might be different from the person who builds your strategy.

That's a business decision.

But make no mistake, strategy comes first with SEO.

Great SEO is Built Around What the User Wants, Not Traffic and Rankings

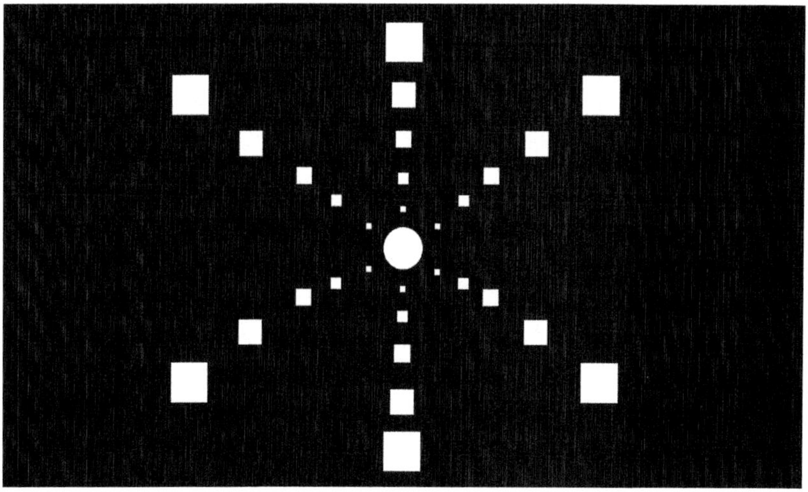

I've been in the SEO game for a long time.

And we all use the metric of traffic to gauge SEO success.

Why? Because in our industry...size matters.

The size of your graphs that is.

Nothing looks better than a great graph when it comes to SEO.

The problem comes in what the traffic is.

There are two ways to make great graphs.

Firstly, go after high volume keywords.

Secondly, publish a lot of pages for low volume keywords.

Both are perfectly reasonable ways to grow. If your target audience is there.

But often, SEO agencies and specialists look at this in terms of client satisfaction rather than user satisfaction.

"We grew your traffic by 75%".

Instead, a better way to look at SEO is this.

"We created these pages because your target audience is searching for this information".

It's not as glamorous but trust me, SEO tends to be more effective when you unplug from the metrics.

Of course, this takes bravery. Both as a client and as a service provider.

But it also removes the need for short term results.

Because let's be clear.

Your prospects don't care how much traffic you are getting.

They simply care whether the information they want is on your site.

Because if it's not, they'll go elsewhere.

Aiming to create a website experience that the consumer loves and puts your business front of mind is very different from graph chasing.

Sure, graph chasing is great.

The business owner is happy, the SEO agency is happy.

But is the customer?

So, when creating content, you need to look at this from a users perspective.

"How will my target customers use this information?"

If they won't...why are you creating it?

The reason might justify the decision.

But it also might not.

SEO is for users. Build around them and you won't go wrong.

You Can't Demand Attention, You Have to Attract It

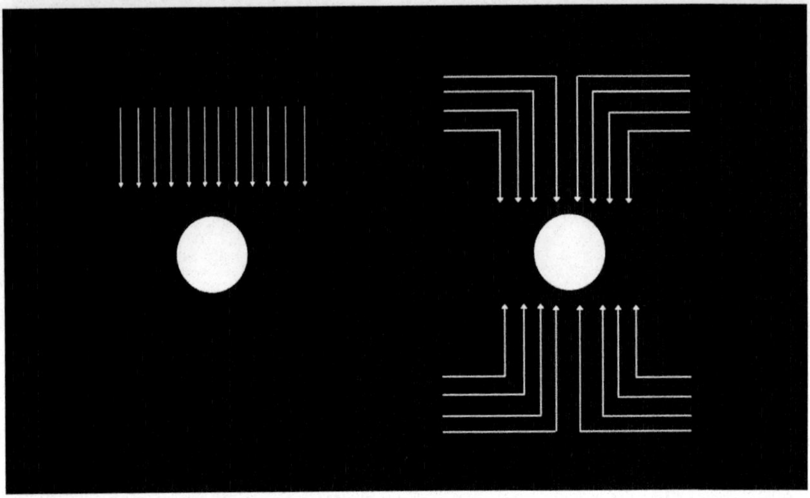

One of the key aspects of SEO, and indeed any type of marketing, is the 'how' you do something.

Toddlers are world-class at demanding attention.

They roll on the floor in a supermarket, stamp their feet and cry.

It works...they get attention.

But it's the wrong type of attention.

It stresses parents and other people out.

The noise from the cries can be screeching.

But it only works for a short period of time.

And eventually, parents and people ignore the toddler.

After all...it's just noise.

A lot of marketing today is based around the shock and awe tactics that are similar to the toddler's antics.

Spam email marketing.

Clever PR campaigns, and also the not-so-clever.

But they tend to be expensive.

If not the actual approach, but the fees for the consultants that come up with the idea.

And they carry risk.

The audience might not get or indeed like the joke.

The problem is, while there is a time and a place for this approach, the results are almost always limited.

They last a moment in time and then they are forgotten.

Secret bars lost their appeal when everyone knew about them.

Shock and awe becomes less shocking when everyone is doing it.

And indeed ads become less effective when people ignore them and eventually block them.

The solution is to play the long game in marketing.

And the long game is to attract your ideal audience.

You do this by showing up often with something for them.

"We made this for you".

Yes, this is hard work.

Yes, this requires a budget.

But building a body of content that attracts your ideal customer is essential.

Because digital buildings rarely collapse.

But campaigns that last a few days do.

They vanish, and they vanish quickly.

By far the most cost-effective method of marketing is SEO.

Why?

Because every item of content that you create for your ideal audience adds to the size of your site.

They enter through one piece of content and they stay for all of the other great content you have.

These doorways into your business compound over time.

And in the end, you'll have a site that people find by search.

But also a site that people search for.

Aim to make a dent in the internet universe.

Aim to make a website for your target audience and you'll attract your audience.

Don't be a marketing toddler.

In a World of Goliaths, it's OK to be a David

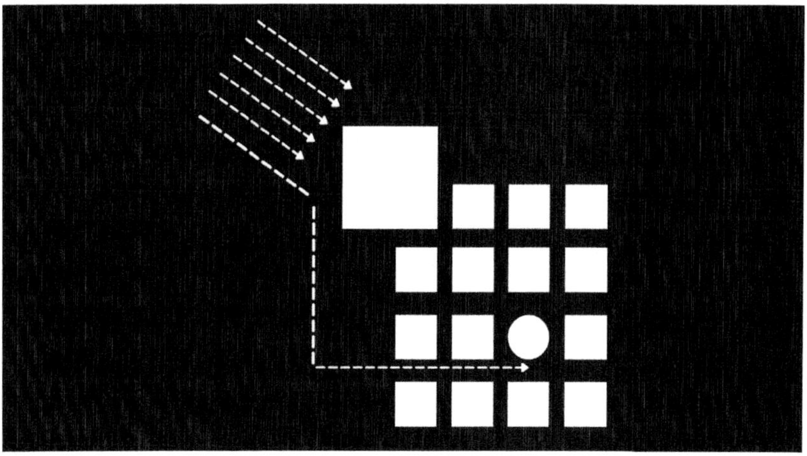

Customers who are initially attracted to size and confidence, eventually, search for and find expertise.

When I first started in marketing I was a risk.

People didn't know me.

And so, they chose the big agencies first.

It's easy to see why.

Confidence and size attract people because it inspires safety.

No marketing manager ever got fired for hiring a 20 person, award-winning agency.

But something started to change for me when I positioned myself as a specialist.

No longer was I seen as a freelancer.

I was treated differently.

I was seen as an expert.

The thing is, there are many experts who are freelancers.

But the word change made a difference.

When I changed that outlook, I attracted a new type of audience.

Those that had been burned by large agencies.

The good agencies keep their clients, but there is a huge number of bad agencies.

Factories that turn all marketing into a commodity but promise something else.

These types have mastered the art of confidence and client attraction.

But they haven't mastered the shipping of their creative work.

And truth be told, they aren't that bothered.

They aren't in the business of maintaining clients, they are in the business of winning clients.

And that's fine.

These companies are often seen first.

They are often the loudest, boldest and most confident.

You can't compete with this.

But you don't have to.

If you have put the hours in and acquired expertise in your field.

And you share that expertise with people.

You will be found.

Your breadcrumbs will attract the people you seek to serve.

The ones who were attracted to size and confidence will then seek out the expertise you have to offer.

In a world of Goliaths, it's OK to be a David.

And it's perfectly OK to be the person that people go to for specialist treatment after they've been burned.

And while others are focused on marketing their size.

You can market your expertise and still win.

Word Count vs Word Relevance

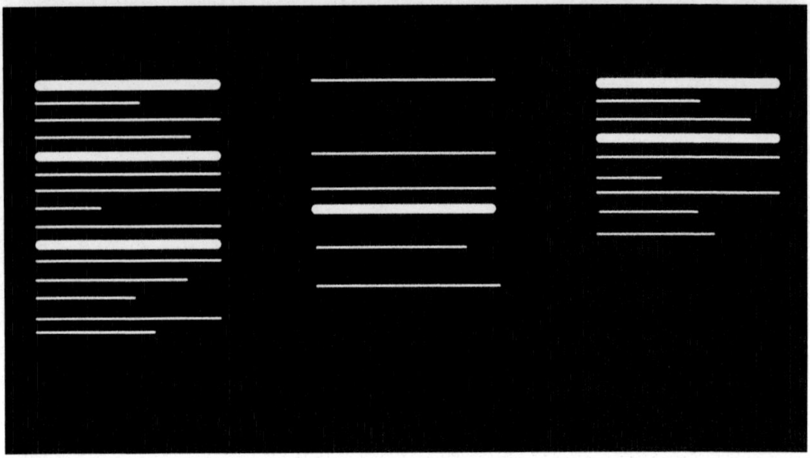

Often, it is not what you write in the first draft that matters.

What makes an article great is what you delete.

Every line in an article or lead magnet needs to earn its place.

This isn't something I really considered for a very long time.

Word count was my master.

2000 words at all cost, regardless of what that word was.

But guess what? Google now understands language.

It knows when you are writing about something.

An entity such as a person, place, organisation.

It also knows and understands grammar.

And it understands context.

Fluff or filler has no place in search engine rankings now.

Providing accurate information that has depth and not length does.

500 words of content can have far more subject depth than 1000 words of fluff.

And that's part of the new world of SEO.

Moving from word count to word relevance.

From content length to content quality.

Here's a tip.

Write your content quickly.

Edit heavily.

Kill anything that doesn't make the content either more engaging, more informational and a better quality read.

And then look at your content and ask yourself.

"Can I send this to someone and be proud?"

If the answer is no...don't press publish.

Be Strategic With Your Budget

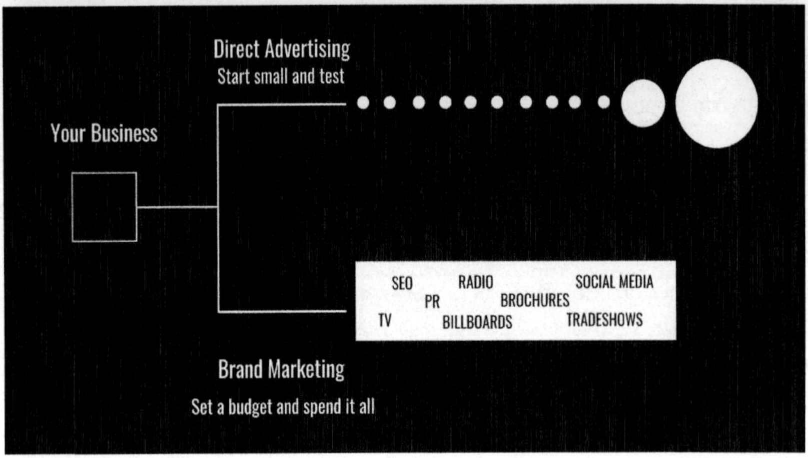

Top marketers get this wrong.

There are essentially only two types of marketing.

Brand marketing and direct advertising.

The purpose of direct advertising is to ask the recipient to take a specific action.

The purpose of brand marketing is to tell the story of your business.

But you can't assess the success of brand marketing as if it was direct advertising.

It just won't work and you'll be very disappointed.

Direct advertising is hard.

Most ads fail and so you should start small and test.

Once you have a winner, you scale until it no longer makes you money.

Brand marketing is different.

You set your budget and spend it all.

Yes, you set your SEO budget and spend it.

You set your PR budget and spend it.

You set your trade show budget and spend it.

Brand marketing is the cost of telling the story of your business to the people you seek to serve.

Direct advertising is about asking people to take action.

This doesn't mean you won't get data with your brand marketing.

It doesn't mean you don't assess the channels to see which provides more bang for your buck.

And it doesn't mean you won't make sales with your SEO.

You will.

But that's not the point.

It's a by-product of telling your story.

This week I purchased a Ninja Foodie Max Grill.

I love it.

But it's taken them countless ads, their website, their SEO, their YouTube videos, their influencer marketing, their TV ads, their Black Friday sale and their email marketing to get me to buy.

Who gets the credit?

Which marketing department can take credit for the sale?

It's too messy to know.

But here's the kicker.

Because I love mine, I told my parents to buy one and they did.

Who gets the credit for this?

Which marketing channel?

And this is what truly great marketers know.

Marketing is about making change happen.

It all works together.

But the key is this.

You should be watching the key performance metrics of every marketing channel.

And investing your budget in the channels that make sense.

Spending a fortune on radio ads might make sense for the local restaurant.

But it rarely makes sense for the online fashion retailer.

You only have so much budget...you have to be strategic.

Prospects Only Have to Find One of Your Answers Online to Find All of Your Answers

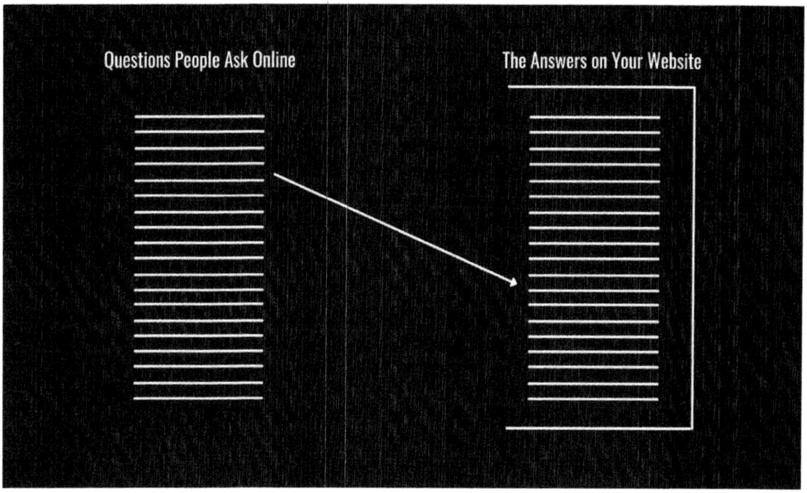

People type questions into Google every day.

But if you can only rank for one answer, your site is ranking for all answers.

Let me explain.

People get SEO all wrong.

They think of it as a traffic and rankings game.

It isn't.

It's a method for the effective marketing of your brand/business.

And that's it.

The problem, however, is that when you hire an SEO agency, it's a competitive process.

And so, SEOs are forced to try to show their worth and in doing so, they go after traffic and rankings.

But here's something that people rarely consider when looking at their marketing.

Each ranking page is a doorway into the online universe you created for your business.

So you don't have to rank for every question online.

But on your website, you need to provide answers to all of the relevant ones your customer has.

This is reverse SEO.

You create the website experience your ideal prospect would like.

You answer the questions they type into Google.

You create the content you know they'll want to read.

And you do so without giving a damn about trackable metrics.

Of course, I don't expect you to follow this approach.

Many would think of it as madness.

But building your site with the end in mind and not the journey is possibly the most powerful SEO and conversion method you can use.

Try it.

Rather than think "what's the ROI of SEO?"

Think "what website can we build for our customers that they'll really appreciate?"

And build it.

Remember.

They only have to find one of your answers online, to find all of your answers.

The Holy Grail of SEO... Visualised

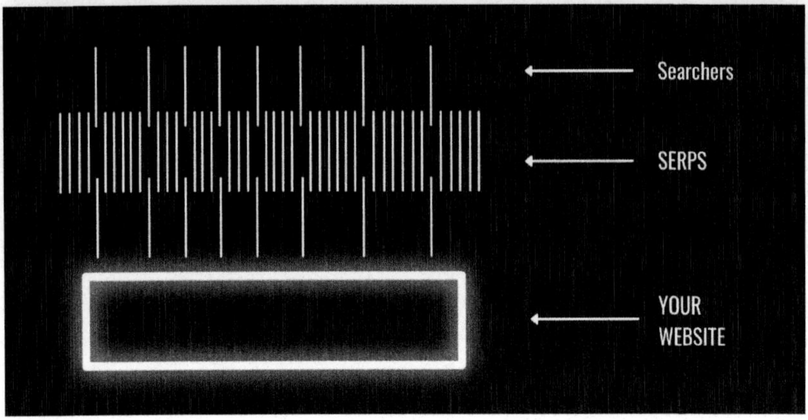

Your business website is a digital world.

This is the first way to look at SEO.

"What does our world look like?"

Is it a dry and desolate planet, uninviting with no life and grey skies?

Or is it a thriving metropolis of data, images and content? A Blade Runner/Tron-like world?

Yes, your website needs to be a place that people not only like to stay, but want to come back to of their own accord.

This is the ultimate goal of SEO.

To ensure you are not only found by search but are searched for.

You can't fake this.

Your website has to hook people in with not only content they find on search engines but content they can't find there.

This is what separates great marketing from the mediocre.

Once you start to build a great world, one that is growing and ready to welcome people in.

You need to build doorways.

This is your ads, your content, your social media, your brand marketing and direct advertising.

You only maximise these efforts if your digital world is worth their time.

But for our purposes.

Your ranking content acts as doorways into your business.

And that's the idea of SEO.

It's all about building doorways into your world.

The problem with SEO is two-fold.

SEO agencies and specialists are in a desperate and constant battle to act like night club promoters.

Bringing business into the 'club' by standing in the busiest streets and stopping people in their tracks.

This causes people to focus on high volume traffic and keywords as dictated by search engine tools.

But it shouldn't be this way. Somewhere, somehow, this is what clients have been taught to desire.

Traffic and rankings.

And it's probably our fault.

The fault of the SEO community and agency owners who desperately want to make money (don't we all).

We have educated the market with fat graphs and charts.

Because size and comparison is easily understood.

However, SEO specialists are digital builders.

They should be building something of value for your users.

Because that's how they win big for your business.

Not because they ranked a page for a certain keyword.

Google can click its fingers and wipe that ranking out with a few tiny algorithm changes.

But because your SEO built you a content and technical masterpiece.

A digital world that people talk about in your industry.

SEO is about users first and foremost.

It's about making them feel certain that you are the ONLY choice for them.

The ultimate way to measure SEO success isn't in traffic and rankings.

It's in a simple statement form your ideal customers.

"This website is exactly what I've been looking for".

Positioning is Everything

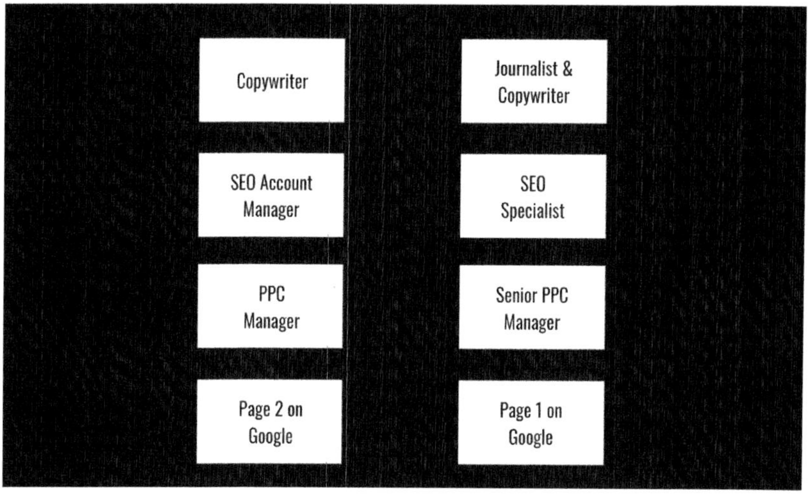

We act like it doesn't matter.

But we all know it does.

Sometimes the addition of a word changes everything.

A copywriter is very different from someone who is a journalist & copywriter.

This added skillset might appeal to some clients, and yet it might repel others.

It might be a signal of superiority to others, it might be a signal of generalisation to some.

An SEO account manager builds a different mental image than an SEO specialist.

One is running multiple accounts and the other is solving in-depth issues.

A PPC manager is one thing, yet a senior PPC manager denotes authority.

Even if the reality is different. They have placed themselves above anyone with the title of manager.

Their positioning is one of experience and parent-like status.

And yes, being on page 2 of Google is very different from being on page 1.

Job titles do matter.

Your business identity does matter.

Where people find you does matter.

How people discover your business matters.

And yet, we spend very little time thinking of our positioning.

Smashing ads and stalking people across the internet is very different from a recommendation from a friend.

Reading a long-form article that truly amazes you is very different from reading a keyword-stuffed long-form article that bores you.

The thing is.

You might actually be exactly where you are positioned.

It's OK to be the account manager.

It's OK to be a freelancer.

And it's OK to be the creative director.

The problem comes when we try to be something we aren't.

The digital agency that has 30 staff but in reality, it's six.

The full-service digital agency that only offers their clients PR.

The content writer who says they're a copywriter (but have never written an ad).

In today's world of marketing and indeed 'fake it until you make it' culture.

Position yourself with clarity and be proud of where your career or business is.

It actually makes choosing you or your business far easier.

The SEO Industry is Guilty of Mis-selling SEO

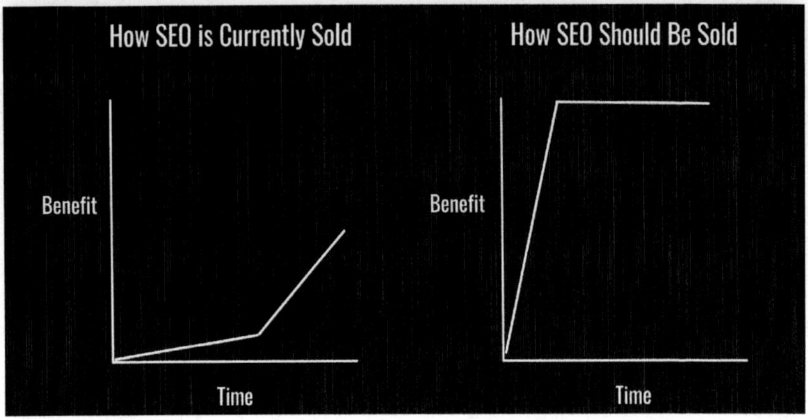

Here's how it's currently sold.

Hire an SEO agency.

You pay every month.

In 6-12 months, you rank online and maybe you'll generate sales.

No wonder it's a hard sell.

And no wonder people feel ripped off.

But this is NOT what SEO is, nor how it should be sold.

SEO delivers a multi-layered benefit to a business.

And those benefits happen very quickly.

Here's why.

SEO is about signalling.

You are signalling to humans and search engines through the creation of content.

And that signal says 'you can trust us.'

Your current traffic through all your other marketing sees the new content you are adding.

This builds your brand.

It builds trust and authority.

It gives your staff something to share on social media about your business.

It gives you a reason to email your past, present and future customers. "Here, we wrote this for you."

It signals expertise by outwardly showing your knowledge.

And perhaps most importantly, it shows your distinctiveness.

And this gives customers a reason to choose you from the crowd.

It gives you the advantage of not having to compete on price.

This is the immediate power of SEO.

It enhances your reputation from the first piece of content you publish.

Many people think the real value of SEO is in the traffic you get at a later date.

But ranking on search engines is a later potential additional benefit.

And it's something you can't control easily.

The same goes if you hire a technical SEO.

You get the benefits almost immediately as they make your site faster and more efficient.

"But we could just hire a writer, it's cheaper than an SEO agency?"

You could, but then you wouldn't get all the additional benefits of SEO that can come.

Because writers write content based on briefs.

Whereas good SEO specialists create content based on what your ideal customers want to consume.

And of course, they know this through their technical understanding of both your customers and their search engine use.

I find it sad that SEO has gone down the route of competing on long term benefits rather than immediate ones.

We've undersold SEO for far too long.

We've understated its benefits because we can't clearly articulate them.

We haven't clearly outlined the benefits of SEO.

And yet, billions in marketing budgets go wasted on vanity marketing that is too far away from businesses to benefit them.

Fleeting brand marketing projects that do nothing to grow the brand and are targeted at masses that don't care and aren't buyers.

SEO gives benefits immediately and then progressively.

Search Engine Optimisation is an awful word for what we deliver.

Online Business Optimisation is far more accurate.

"Noun: optimisation
The action of making the best or most effective use of a situation or resource".

As an industry, we can and must do better to state the value and benefits of SEO with greater clarity.

How SEO Should Be Sold... and Why It's Undersold

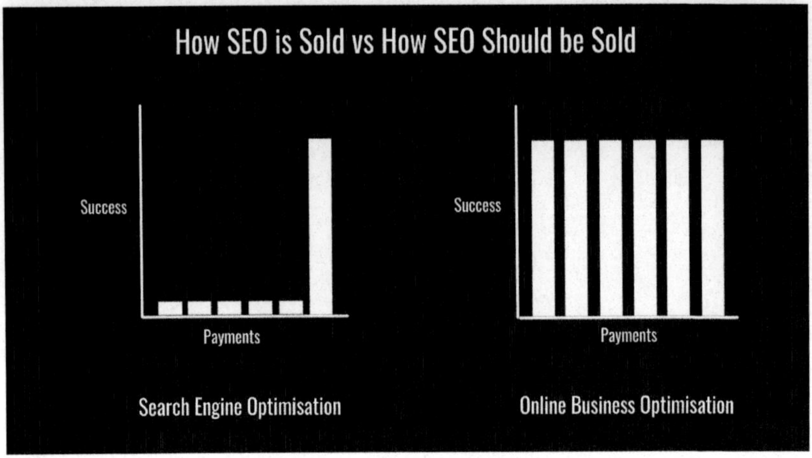

The number of people who don't understand the benefits of SEO is staggering.

And I'll explain why.

SEO is sold as a long term game that takes a long time to get results.

No wonder prospects walk away.

But here's a snippet of what SEO does for a business and why I'm so passionate about it.

Growth Strategy:

A business needs to be forward-looking, as such an SEO strategy will look at how to grow your business online, using data to drive budget and decisions.

No more shooting in the dark and hoping the future is rosy.

SEO strategy allows you to plan for the long road ahead.

Competitor analysis:

A good SEO will analyse your competitors, showing you the traffic they are getting and the content they are using.

This is how you will reduce their market share, by going to where customers find them and being an alternative choice (and your competitors will hate you for it).

Online Appearance:

You want to look your best online, ensure your company is easily found and displays the right data when your brand is searched for. Your SEO will take care of this for you.

This is massive and the value scales with your brand. The bigger your business, the more important it is that all search touchpoints are reflective of your offerings.

Strategic Content Development:

Anyone can order a few blog posts.

Your SEO will create content that your target audience wants to read.

They do this because they can analyse the best keywords and create content that buyers will love.

Network Effect:

Each piece of content you write adds to the value of the online experience you create for every new visitor.

So they find your business site via a business card and a web search, and they leave after consuming 15 pages of your content.

This is like a sales meeting where you put in zero effort and win them over.

Visible Expertise:

Strategic content is a signal of your expertise. You share a lot because you know a lot.

Reputation Signalling:

You show up on Google, you create a lot of content.

It's a heuristic technique that shows you care about your reputation and you're invested in it.

Traffic and Rankings:

And yes, eventually SEO delivers the progressive benefit of traffic and rankings.

This should help to bring in more sales.

Of course, there are more benefits of SEO.

Many that never get mentioned or get mentioned as an add-on.

SEO is undersold, undervalued and underused.
But that's because we are terrible at explaining the benefits.

It's not search engine optimisation.

It's online business optimisation.

Give Them a Reason to Return

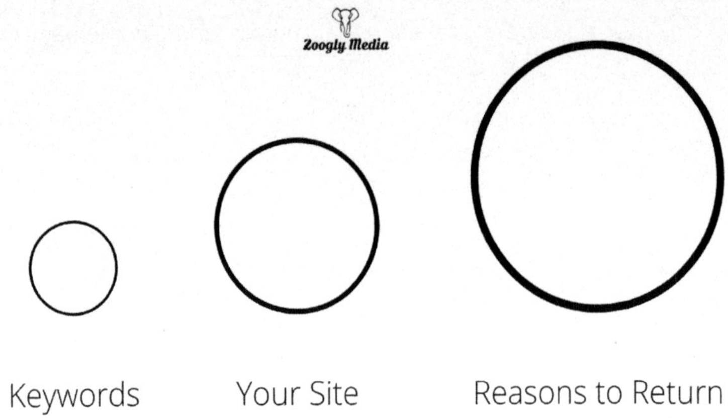

It doesn't matter how much traffic you attract.

If there isn't a compelling reason for them to return, they simply won't come back.

Reason-based SEO is all about giving people a reason to come back.

The thing is.

Figuring this out is tough.

Today, people are bombarded with content, ads and emails.

And so, you must stand out the minute they land on your site.

But how?

Well, it's not easy.

But here's a test.

Would people talk about your site off-line?

If not, why not?

Start here to develop your reason that visitors would come back without spending a penny on ads.

SEO is Dead

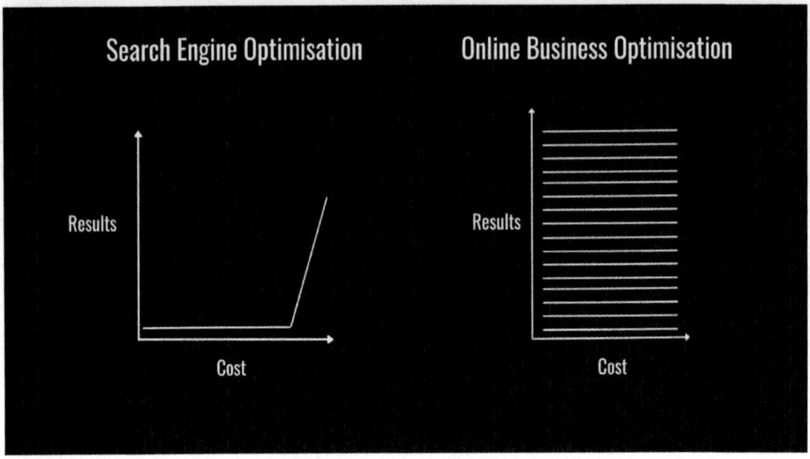

Not another 'SEO is dead' post...but SEO is actually dead, it really is.

Search engines don't like your business.

They like information.

They like ads.

They like search engine users.

They will steal your content, scrape your site and serve up your information via search and voice.

Google Lens is changing image search to such an extent that you can find out information without saying or typing a word.

SEO as you know it is DEAD.

The idea that your business can pay 12 monthly instalments and get results in a year is done and dusted.

If you are a marketing manager or business owner, and indeed if you sell SEO, you need to listen.

Pitching or even thinking of SEO in this old world-view is going to harm your business.

Because you are going to be the Blockbuster to your competitor's Netflix.

SEO is dead.

Long live OBO.

Online Business Optimisation.

The pandemic has shown the world the power of being online.

And yet, most businesses are not optimised for this world.

They aren't answering the customer's questions on their websites.

They aren't building an online experience that they'll return to without spending money on ads.

They aren't thinking of the digital world.

The result...there are epic gaps.

I know, because I spend a lot of time analysing the online presence of leading businesses (I release case studies each week)

And the big names are exposed.

The long-standing businesses are vulnerable.

Why?

Their marketing process is full of friction.

It's full of noise.

Smashing consumers with ads, poorly written emails and awful sales calls.

Don't believe me? Go and look at your email promotions tab.

I bet you only open emails for certain brands.

The 'who' of your email inbox is more important than what's inside.

So what should a business do?

Well, stop thinking of optimising your site for search.

Instead, optimise your business for your ideal customers online.

Become the online Disney of your industry.

Think experience and not traffic.

Think about what's useful and not what might drive clicks from search engines.

Think about what your prospects need, anticipate this and create it.

Make your website the ultimate salesperson that answers every question your prospects have.

Create unexpected content that can't be found by search engines but customers will love.

Make your site fast to load and great to use.

Make your site for your prospects and customers, and not some sleazy way to hope they buy from you because you ranked on page 1.

Create a web experience that people talk about offline.

But above all else.

Give prospects a reason to return of their own accord.

This is online business optimisation.

Building a site that is searched for and not only found through search.

Aim to be your own industry search engine.

Aim to be a destination.

Search engines are not the internet.

You have a huge unlimited playground to develop your own digital world.

Get building.

The Magic of SEO Happens Offline

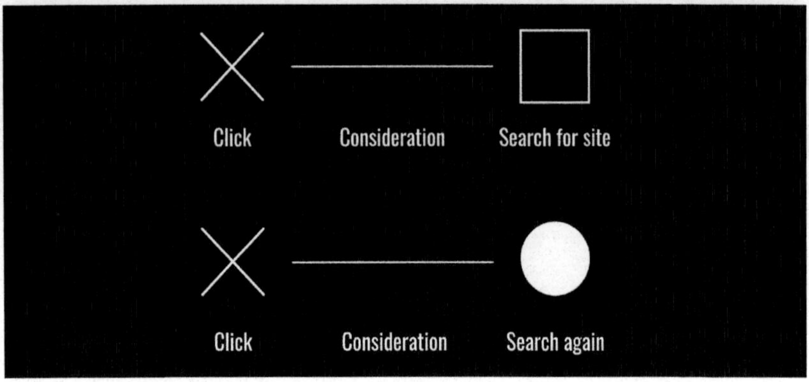

We might not like to admit it.

But the magic of SEO happens between the clicks.

In today's busy world, conversion from a single click is highly unlikely unless you exist in certain industries.

If you need an emergency plumber, when you search for one, land on the first page of Google, you'll probably choose one there and then.

But for the 99.9% of non-urgent queries, conversion doesn't happen on the first click.

No, the conversion decision happens away from the site.

It happens when the person is sitting at home, watching TV or reading a book.

It happens when your manager asks about the pros and cons of each service provider you researched.

It happens when the prospect is walking their dog.

If you're lucky, they'll search for you again.

And then convert, or perhaps the process will take 30 visits to your site.

But the opposite action can be harsh.

They search, find your site and never return.

They decide you aren't right for them, good enough for their business or there are better solutions.

This is why you must put in the effort online.

When a person lands on your site, it's like a person walking through a shop door.

They are browsing.

Your site is the shopkeeper.

They walk in and ask a question about a problem.

You answer and you educate the customer.

They go away, think about their options and maybe they return.

B2B or B2C, it doesn't matter. The mix is the same.

Services/products + information.

This is what both physical and online customers need.

And sure, other things come into play.

Such as the speed that information is delivered, the manner, the look of the store/business/website.

Yet, we know that to be considered after the click, you need to have made a great first impression.

And so, you have two options for SEO.

1. The trickle and flow approach.

2. The front-loading way.

The first is what most go for.

This is when a business has a budget and the SEO company tends to do what they can within this budget.

It's why hourly rates are so highly used and enjoyed by SEO companies and customers.

Front loading is what companies with big budgets and/or investment do.

They don't have time to waste, they go big, go fast and go heavy with content velocity and PR.

There isn't a right or wrong approach.

You have to do what you can with the budget you have.

And if it takes you three years to create the site experience you want, so be it.

But it's time the SEO industry focused on impact in the minds of the consumers.

Rather than short term hustle.

Because the magic of SEO happens off-line.

The End and Why It Isn't The End

If you made it this far, you should be unplugged from the Matrix and hopefully you'll see SEO in a very different way.

But this isn't the end of this book and indeed this story.

Because if the pages in this book have resonated with you, please connect with me on LinkedIn, here's my profile **https://www.linkedin.com/in/andrew-holland-seo/**

Yet, I want to leave you with this thought.

What can you build?

Because that is the heart of all SEO specialists. We are digital builders.

Build your blog, build an online store, create videos, write a book, create an app.

The 'what' doesn't matter.

But add something unique of your own to the online world. And I promise, you'll learn more about SEO and marketing than you ever would by being a passive observer.

And that's the real ending to this book. A beginning.

If you want to truly understand SEO, you have to do SEO.

You have to create something of your own, nurture it and watch it grow.

Get building. Get creating. That's truly how you discover the value of SEO.

Praise for Andrew Holland's Words on SEO and Content Marketing

James Welch
Chief Innovation Officer at Embryo
"I've been in SEO for just over 20 years, and it is very rare that I have come across someone with such a great mix of a strategic brain, and someone who is able to make the layman understand complex solutions. Add to this Andrew's enthusiasm, work rate, and his ability to inspire others, and you get a fiery, potent mix. Unlike 90% of those in the SEO industry, Andrew continues to learn and self-develop, so that his content and thoughts are always bleeding edge. He produces the opposite of the vast majority of SEO content out there, which is exactly what the world of SEO needs."

Dr Michael Oon
"Andrew Holland is the only person to explain to me clearly and succinctly how SEO is used in a website to make it productive."

Matthew Silverman, MBA
Digital Marketing Algorithm Wizard | Google Ads | SEO
"Andrew Holland explains complex SEO concepts so that a regular person can understand. I have been doing SEO for over 15 years, and his content is really well done."

Bojan Maric
0 to 1,500,000 Organics / Month in 24 Months | ContentDistribution.com
"What Andrew's words and illustrations have done for the SEO industry is something I want to strive for every day as a professional in Content Ops and SEO - be better and help others be better."

Alexander Kreule
(Digital Marketing Manager | E-Commerce | Technical SEO
"Explaining SEO so simple must mean you really know it and Andrew does. Buy the book, thank yourself later!"

Josh Willett
SEO Consultant
"Andrew's insights are a breath of fresh air and clarity in a sometimes confusing SEO space. The images have an uncanny knack to perfectly explain the underlying concepts of the SEO industry in such a simple and visually pleasing way. Well done!"

Saffron Sumner
Driving impact & generating leads with marketing and PR
"I try to save every single one of Andrews LinkedIn posts. I'm subscribed to his email send-out; I've read a lot of his content on his website."

Why?

Because it's some of the most insightful SEO knowledge out there. I have learned a lot and want to continue to do so. His content has inspired many of my actions and made me genuinely think about SEO.

The in-depth case studies are a must read too if you're looking to learn how to action SEO.

He positions SEO to be the future and how to use it in the future. He's an expert and continuously proves that."

Waseem Ansari
Assistant Director Of Operations at Globital
"To be honest loves Andrew's style of conveying the concept of SEO in illustrations. Therefore, there is no need for an explanation in brief. Always do follow and recommend to others his style of sharing content. You are a legend, Andrew."

Preeti Gupta

"I have read and watched hundreds of SEOs talking about different topics, but Andrew's approach to SEO is something different. The use of images, the writing style and the communication is second to none. I really love his writing style and his insightful posts."

Lynne Cullen

Freelance SEO / Local SEO and Content Marketing Specialist

"You are simply the most engaging person I know in SEO and on LinkedIn. You fight for SEO in the right way. It's inspiring and refreshing. We've been discussing within our own business how we change the perception of how SEO is seen, and most importantly measured! The job can be sole destroying at times. But it's addictive and we love it! Keep doing what you do. I personally crown you King of SEO."

Zain Khan

Digital Marketing Manager | Certified SEO Manager | Google Digital Garage Certified

"I can only say that your posts are the combination of wisdom, experiments and technical aspects of the field alongside the educational hub for a layman who doesn't know a single thing about the field. This mix allows customers to know what they need as a service and also the practitioner to deliver value."

Divij Sood

InGAME R&D Fellow: Technology Innovation | Co-founder at DyonisianWriting - Results-focused Content Marketing

"Out of all the marketing experts I follow, I've learned the most about the value and strength of SEO from your posts. Your understanding of SEO as a branding activity in addition to a traffic and lead generation strategy helped me get an important client a year or so ago."

Arman Mathur

Digital Marketer, Content Strategist & SEO Consultant

"Andrew's way of explaining complicated SEO concepts with the use of images and simple words makes it easy for a non-technical person to understand. Content created by him surely conveys his knowledge of

SEO and it's implementation in real world for business growth. People like him make the SEO industry a better place."

Mujahid Al-Majali
Chief Marketing Officer at Alpha Agency
"I enjoy Andrew's posts not only for the massive amounts of knowledge and learning I receive through them but also for the way he structures them as an exciting story. Hands down, the best SEO mentor I've ever come across."

Gabrielle Tan(She/Her)
SEO Manager at Heroes of Digital | Google Certified | Content Marketing
"Andrew Holland is a voice in the industry who took it upon himself to break down complicated concepts of SEO into bite size images, to not only showcase the goal of each concept, but ultimately reinforce what's truly important in SEO."

Umar Faizan
SEO Consultant | SEO Strategist | SEO Specialist
"Thanks for producing great content. I have been following you since long and saved a lot of your posts in my Notes so that whenever I need to answer quickly to new clients, I can just get the idea and answer them.

It really helps!

Being SEO, it's uber important how you brand yourself. Other than SEO, I learned how to actually create content, rather than curating it."

Nabeel Keblawi
Helping SaaS marketers increase revenue with SEO & Content
"SEO is often confusing to many, including even the most experienced marketers. Andrew Holland is the first, and perhaps the only one, who clearly and eloquently explains SEO through examples, storytelling, and simple illustrations in a way even a fifth grader can understand."

Divyanshi Juneja

WordPress Expert | UX Strategist | Digital Promoter

"Andrew Holland is exactly the right person to follow for SEO. His techniques & concepts are bang on. If I have to recommend someone for SEO, Andrew will definitely be on the 1st place."

Hammad Ali Khan

Search Engine Optimization Lead at Devrims

"One thing I am certain about Andrew is that he is highly capable in explaining the basics as well as complex SEO concepts using illustrations that are really helpful to the SEO community."

Printed in Great Britain
by Amazon

80605058R00159